TOPLESS

TOPLESS

D. Keith Mano

RANDOM HOUSE
NEW YORK

Library of Congress Cataloging-in-Publication Data
Mano, D. Keith.
    Topless/D. Keith Mano.
        p.   cm.
    ISBN 0-679-40275-6
    I. Title.
PS3563.A56T6   1991   813'.54—dc20   90-52890

Manufactured in the United States of America
98765432
First Edition

Designed by Oksana Kushnir

This book is for Laurie Kennedy—
My private dancer, my wife—
And the best actress anywhere.

. . . And if thine eye offend thee, pluck it out, and cast it from thee: it is better for thee to enter into life with one eye, rather than having two eyes to be cast into hell fire.

Matthew 18:9

ACKNOWLEDGMENTS

As far as I can determine, there has not yet been a thorough sociological study of the topless dance industry. Films and novels have touched on this world, a scene here, a chapter there, but no medium has yet given topless due credit as an important subculture, which employs thousands of men and women from all social classes coast to coast. It is, to say the least, an intriguing enterprise. Any field in which average-looking 19-year-old girls can earn $1500 per week *tax free* just for dancing seminude (I have *never* heard of a dancer-prostitute) is likely to hold some interest.

Topless is wholly fictional. And it certainly doesn't pretend to be an exhaustive academic review. But the mechanics of the industry, as presented here, are accurate—at least for New York. And I have tried to represent—in microcosm anyway—the enormous diversity of the women who have been attracted to topless. The addict and the working mother. The unstable girl-child who would be sleeping on a subway grate if it weren't for topless. The college grad, who paid her medical school tuition in three summers of dancing. They are all here: their stories are composites, of course, but they are composed of fact.

I would particularly like to thank John Rezek, my editor at *Playboy,* for suggesting that I research the topless game. The articles we planned in 1982, and later in 1984 and 1985, were never written—for reasons of timing, the magazine's and mine. But, during that period, I taped perhaps two hundred interviews in at least twenty-five bars—interviews with bouncers and owners and, of course, customers and girls. In 1988 the fictional plot line for *Topless* surfaced through that ocean of authentic detail.

I would like, naturally enough, to acknowledge and thank the women who told me their stories. But they prefer anonymity and would not, I suspect, appreciate a public expression of gratitude. They work under improbable aliases. When I refer to Apache and Shower and Taffeta and Blaze, I mean to mention them all in those names.

To one young lady, P.J., I am, however, especially indebted. She took me through the business end of topless step by step—from liquor invoice to liability insurance. P.J. is one of the few women I know with *chutzpah* enough to rise from topless dancer to topless owner. If you're on Queens Boulevard near 49th Street some night, stop in at Honey's, the friendliest, raunchiest topless joint in New York, and have a drink.

Finally, this book would never have been undertaken without the bright assistance of Erin C. Martz and Helen Broady, who construed my handwriting and brought me, albeit vicariously, into the computer age.

PART ONE

THURSDAY, JUNE 16

Tip of my shoe just snapped off. Cracked like an eggshell. I caught it on the step running up to my room. Comes of buying linoleum mail-order shoes. Now what do I do?

All I have is my scuzzy Adidases, which won't do for Sunday service.

Borrow, borrow, borrow. I owe cash to six different people—and the Rev., his righteousness, Schantz has caught on. Indebtedness is not becoming for a young assistant just ordained. But whadda they expect on $115 take-home?

You buy too many books. And dinners out.

What else happened? Or is this another day distinguished only by a broken shoe, poverty and Nebraskan sunstroke?

Had lunch with Kay at The Plough. Played tennis afterward so I wouldn't think of her carnally. Getting so that I've become a great physical specimen, just in an effort to circumvent lust. Did you ever notice how everything—except maybe a pizza oven—looks like a woman? There are hills here that remind me of buttocks—and the S-curve sign looks like BEWARE: CENTERFOLD AHEAD.

This diary, methinks, will not threaten George Bernanos much. Just bare jottings—never enough time.

Also—writing good is hard.

Tomorrow is, groan, the penny social. My assignment. The most important ceremonial act in the Episcopal Church is the folding and unfolding of folding chairs.

Damn air conditioner just iced over again. Lord Jesus, are you running with me? Or did you take a cab?

FRIDAY, JUNE 17

Getting just a touch claustrophobic around here. I never would've come to St. Mark's if I'd known the assistant had to live over the rectory. This morning, from my window, I saw Schantz picking through my garbage. Like an animal biologist, studying the feces of some disreputable species. Came up with eight beer cans, which he stacked. I've gotta be careful with what I drink. And write.

He's an OK guy, still believes in the Ptolemaic system. I think he had a low birth weight, something's not sparking up there. So serious—

yesterday, just kidding, I said what the Episcopal church needed was carbonated holy water. Pick up the image. Classic and diet. He says, "Well, I don't care how they do it in New York." I pray for his sense of humor. He's half patronizing around me, half insecure. He doesn't read much. Son of a farmer, gave it up to follow Jesus. Now, with the drought and all, he's doing a lot better than his congregation—and he feels guilty about it.

Also, the folks from McLane AFB tend to call on me, more than him—if they can get away with it. They're a redneck crew, like the farm folk, but they're rednecks who've been around. They tend to see the places they live in from 37,000 feet up, so to speak. Just passing through, Ma'am. Sergeant Clough was telling me about Bangkok the other day, wanted to see if I'd blush—I didn't. He could never've talked that way to Schantzy. Kay thinks I shouldn't take pride in being one of the boys. In having been around.

Truth is: I shouldn't have told her about Amanda. At lunch yesterday, Kay said she was afraid of being overwhelmed by my sexuality. Not a major chance of that. Two months have gone by since last we "made daisies," as Kay calls it. (I love that kind of dirty language.) And not just because we lack opportunity. I feel her edging away. Met her in the malt shop this afternoon (it is actually called The Malt Shop), and, believe it or not, Kay covered her marvelous knockers with a straw pocketbook. God forbid she should be accused of leading me on.

Little does Kay know this bashful innocence is titillating. Her eyes are so big and blue and wet—especially behind those thick glasses—that she resembles some kind of sacrificial animal. I think I scared her the two-and-a-half times we made it. And maybe hurt her. I was flaunting my male ardor. I roared so loud in the field that a cow answered. Moooo? It was stupid of me. I should've been gentle, but sometimes I can't pull it off that way. I need hard strokes.

Maybe I should tell Kay she's only the third woman I've had.
Nah.

If Schantz finds this book, I'll be folding and unfolding chairs for a congregation made up entirely of polar bears and caribou.

Lord, I miss New York.

Lekachman is burnt out. I stood on Main Street and there were water mirages all around. I was islanded by them. I don't understand growing things, but the fields seem to wail at night, when I drive by. The folk look punch-drunk, they won't even glance up at the sky any more. Been disappointed too often. Such dependence on nature seems absurd. Where I come from, when there's a drought, you open a fire hydrant.

My orbit is decaying here. Everyone guesses that, and they're watching me. Well, I won't crack. I know this is a test. Betty Schantz keeps asking if I'm homesick.

If I had a home, I might be.

Penny social grossed $566.57. Glad I've made my contribution to the triumphant progress of the Holy Spirit in Middle America.

SATURDAY, JUNE 18

The heat has made everyone in Lekachman just a tad swoony. This, of course, embarrasses them no end—they're all so proper otherwise.

Lois Baxter pinched my butt on the tennis court. Did it before she realized what she was doing. Then she stared around like a pickpocket, hoping no one had seen her. Then she glared at me and said,

"Don't get any funny ideas."

"About what?" I asked.

"I love Tim," she says.

"I'm glad."

"He'll be fifty-six tomorrow."

"He looks great."

"You think so? What do you weigh?"

"Hundred-fifty, fifty-five something."

"He had legs like yours once. All covered with dark hair. Like little bedsprings."

"Like bedsprings?"

"Coiled. Don't get any funny ideas."

Swoony, like all of a sudden living their cornball fantasy lives right on the surface. Just what I need, an affair with the junior warden's wife. Who holds my car loan. But she *is* sexy—brown like a moussaka, I mean her skin's so touchable, soft. Muscles in her calves, like apples in a Christmas stocking. And me, I'm in season. Everyone figures you can flirt with the young assistant—he's harmless. Baxter himself said kiddingly, "Hired you f'yer looks, makes a difference. Get more ladies in the congregation that way." Waal, yup. Bunch of hypocrites, selling sex appeal. His wife pinches my ass, and I better not get any funny ideas.

Kay threw herself into my arms this afternoon—like I was a storm cellar or something. Then she pulled away—snap, jerk—censoring herself again. Most of all Kay doesn't want me to think she's a cocktease. Believe me, I'd prefer a good, old-fashioned blue-ball cocktease to this formal, hand-holding relationship—especially since we've already made love. It's as if our relationship was going backwards, becoming more distant. If I get to know her much better we won't be talking at all.

"Give me time," she says. "You won't regret it. I'll get there."

She sure is taking the local train.

Kay loves me, she says. She'll always be there for me—just don't touch, not now. I believe her: the thought of her loyalty and strength is comforting. But she also resents the fact that I seduced her: the priest-me, he betrayed her. Took advantage of his office.

I just wanna get laid!!!

Well, it's not as simple as that, Miko. Not so simple.

We were taking the eucharist out to Mrs. Myrdahl on Omaha Road. The old lady is lying flat under a sheet. Let her horny feet protrude: these feet, there were big burls, the size of my briar pipe bowl, on each of her big toes. And the big toes themselves were bent UNDER the other four. How she walked a lifetime I'll never know.

But she wore lipstick—Magda, her sister, had slapped some on. The priest is a man, after all.

It was a beautiful service, though: the sun shone through a beaded curtain that made like a witch ball, scattering little pinpoints of light when the wind blew. And I was particularly concentrated—Kay helps me there, her faith is so clear. I didn't intone or try to sound like God, the way sometimes I do on the big stage. I just said the words. I know it was good, because I feel dizzy, tired now. It's like giving up coffee, a good communion is. All the poisons come out. And make me feel sick.

But there was a perturbing moment. When I said, "Take, eat," and leaned down, Bertha closed her mouth and shook her head. I get closer, and I hear her saying, "No. No. I'm on a diet."

Well, they don't teach you about moments like this at seminary. I thought, It's the heat. Also, she's got stomach cancer, which can kill your appetite. Or the morphine's got her. Or she's just plain crazy.

Meanwhile her mouth wasn't opening.

"It's just a wafer," I said. "Put it on your tongue and let it melt."

No. She's smiling at me, but no . . . And I want to get it in her, this might be her last conscious communion.

"I still have a nice figure," she says.

"I'm sure you do," I say. "But, Bertha, just between you and me, this has no calories. It's a symbol."

Aha. It's okay to eat a symbol, it isn't real. Bertha opens her mouth and I pop it in. So I lied. There may not be even a quarter calorie there, but it is food. Real food and real spirit. I don't like the wafer, practical as it might be. Makes the sacrament look like pre-packaged magic. Give me fresh-baked bread. Even if crumbs of God are lost.

When I leaned over to say goodbye, Bertha asked, "Is the carriage ready?" Someone from the early twentieth century, waiting to escort her home.

She was as dry and fretful as the fields of stunted corn around us. We all need moisture.

I kept my hand on Kay's knee all the way back to Lekachman. An assertion. And she accepted it.

Of course, the subject of our screenplays came up again—deadlock. We discuss plot and character, but she won't show me her first draft, and I won't show her mine. We're both afraid the other's will be better, I guess. Which better be the case. I mean, if we're both writing at the same level . . . well, it's hard to figure there'd be two geniuses in Lekachman, Nebraska. At the same moment in history. Two nicely matched mediocrities, more like.

As for Schantzy—this morning he decided I should teach a senior citizen Bible class—yes, on top of the young people's class (both of them), the teen class, the counseling program at the air base, the parish survey, penny socials and you name it.

This is too much. PRIEST GOES ON STRIKE.

On top of that, Schantzy had me mixing cement for his new patio— which, actually, I prefer to teaching Bible classes. He felt guilty about it, though, I could see that. The congregation didn't hire me as his personal handyman and indentured servant. Even brought me out a beer to show his big-heartedness.

And (this is how crazy things are), in the middle of it all, Schantzy says, "Let's arm wrestle." And I think, "Oh, no—here comes a big moral dilemma." Just as I figured, I'm much stronger than he (though he's bigger), and he's CHEATING, using his whole body for leverage. And I'm maintaining our balance—wondering whether to crush him (and make our relationship even more distant) or take a dive—when out pops Mrs. Schantz. Now this isn't your typical Christian scene—two macho clergymen grunting at each other. We're both sheepish—so we both quit pushing AT THE SAME TIME. And we both almost fall over, from the sudden lack of resistance. There we are, hand-in-hand like a couple of gay lovers. Gladys though we were nuts.

"So that's how they do it in New York," she says.

We're none of us wrapped too tight in this weather.

SUNDAY, JUNE 19

This morning I got me some Krazy Glue and stuck my shoe back together. Great idea—only I shouldn't have done it while my foot was inside. When I went to undress just now, my sock was Krazy Glued to the inside tip of my shoe. Had to cut myself loose with a pair of scissors.

Do I really want to live this way? Can I woo Kay, in all fairness, with prospects like these? Twenty-eight and earning a big four figures. Got a letter from Miles Holbrook, whom I haven't seen since we graduated from New Paltz. Regional sales manager for NYNEX, whatever that means. Means, Miko, that he can buy and sell you. Would the disciples have dropped everything and followed Jesus if they'd had to give up six-figure jobs with stock options and pension? After all, the fishing business was lousy—no future, no medical benefits.

It's a year today since Father Mac died—maybe that's why I'm so cranky. Foolish as I know it is, it gave me motivation, and great pleasure, to be a priest *for* him. To justify his faith in me. He was so good during my Time of Shame—carried me through it—when Dad (may he rest in peace) was more interested in seeing how many times he could *zetz* me in the head. And Mom was just grateful I'd given her another excuse to drink (may she rest there, too).

Never have I met a man with such joy in Christ. The Resurrection was a daily miracle to him. And he was fascinated by sin—not as a vulture might be, but because he thought it was an opportunity. He certainly turned it into *my* opportunity for grace. When I was near suicide. "Sin is a cry," he used to say, "listen to it."

I miss him. Not least because, with Father Mac at bat for me, I'd have a better shot at a parish back in Queens Diocese.

Jesus, Savior, buck my spirit up. This morning I heard a woman in the choir say, "I don't want to know the mystery of life. I just want to *live* for a change." She's about 40 years old, and her voice sounded dead. She was saying, "I need love, I need to be loved, I need a—

Lord. Lord.

Gladys just called me down to the phone. It was Ethel. She says Tony is missing. Missing. What does that mean? My brother is missing.

And she wants me back in New York.

MONDAY, JUNE 20

Tony, big bro.

It's not right, it's like *disreputable,* to be missing. Someone croaks you, you get hit by a Transit-Mix truck, okay, no problem. Our sympathies and those of our entire family are with you. But *missing?*

People don't like to waste their condolences—hey, listen, Tony could be in Hawaii with a redhead, far as they know. Missing is something that happens to Jimmy Hoffa. Something that happens to people who *deserve* to vanish.

I've decided not to go into details. Schantzy's reaction was enough to convince me of that. In Lekachman there's no place to hide. Folk drop dead in plain sight. No hanky-panky. I just say "a family emergency." Which it is—considering Tony is all the blood I've got left.

And I didn't realize just how much brotherhood mean to me until last night. I mean, it's not as if we spent much time together. Actually I haven't seen him but once since he and Ethel got married. Still, alone in my room last night, I felt afraid. The way I felt after Mom and Dad were killed in the crash.

I guess it was important to my sense of well-being to know my brother was there. Tony, he took my G.I. Joe doll. Tony, he poked me in the eye. Tony, tell Dad I need more allowance. I did a lot of that cry-babying. Tony was half my agent, half my personal enforcer.

And, face facts, he paid my tuition at New Paltz and Neshotah House. I wouldn't be a priest now if it weren't for Tony. Ethel is wiring cash so I can get a plane out of here Wednesday.

She wasn't any clearer about Tony this morning. Did she suspect foul play? Sure—but, I realize now, Ethel has a stake in foul play. No woman wants it known that her husband up and left. Doesn't reflect well on the housekeeping. But Ethel couldn't or wouldn't come up with a motive. Her tone seemed agitated—but I couldn't tell whether that was fear or anger or general despair. She's hard to read. But then, I hardly know her.

Well, with four kids to raise in New York, fear makes good sense. Ethel wants me to take over the restaurant full-time for a while. Said something about employees cheating. What I know about restaurants you could put in a cherrystone clamshell. But, God knows, it would be a welcome change.

In fact, let's be honest, it's a godsend. Not Tony being missing. I wish that weren't the reason. But a chance for me to hit the Apple and squeeze out from under supervision for a while. There's something about the Church that keeps you permanently at age 14. They call you Father, but they treat you like the Mongoloid child of a hired hand.

I'd like to sell my car—but I don't want Schantzy to think I'm not returning. In truth, I'm not sure whether I am or not. My contract comes up for review in October.

Later.

Kay is distraught. She wants to fly out with me—for moral support. ("Moral" as in "morality," I think.) But Kay can't really take a vacation from the library. And, of course, it'd be improper for her to follow me unchaperoned. People might get the wrong idea. New York, as all Nebraskans know, is Sodom by the Sound.

Then she said, "You're not coming back, are you?" I said, "Nonsense." She said, "But he could be missing forever—where will you look?" But I don't intend to look—where would I begin? I just want to help Ethel. In this case my moral position is unassailable.

I thought last night—Tony's the curator of my life, and I'm the curator of his. Who else can give evidence about Mom and Dad. Or about Uncle Ceece, who brought us up after they died. Or that dog we had, Maybe? What other family had a dog named Maybe? There are times when I hardly believe my own recollection. And then I think, But Tony was there, I'm not crazy.

Oh, Lord—I hope he's just missing, not gone. I truly love him: more than anyone else in my life. He was my foster parent, my mediator and advocate. And, you know, when I looked at him, I saw a variation of myself. A more successful variation. In Tony I saw my own possibilities.

But there's no use dodging the truth. Tony was never happy. He was reaching for something. And he was a lot braver than I am. Just brave enough to get himself into a piss-pot full of trouble.

Jesus, protect my brother. Don't let Tony end up in an empty lot somewhere. Let him not float to shore. Protect him and his little ones.

I never knew Tony. I was too busy asking him for things.

TUESDAY, JUNE 21

Catching a 2 p.m. flight out of Omaha tomorrow. Tim Baxter offered to drive me. Shantzy made strange, portentous faces all day. (He's been uncomfortable with me, come to think of it, since I caught him in the garage with his bridgework out.) Then, half an hour ago, he came upstairs. Which he hasn't done *once* until this moment. He has a strong sense of hierarchy: he doesn't stand when a woman enters the room.

"Are you sure you wanna do this?" he said. He considers my trip to New York a personal betrayal. All those classes he'll have to teach, and the patio only half poured.

I said, "Well, Tony is my only relative."

"Has this happened before?"

"What?"

"Has your brother gone missing before? New York is a big place."

"No, sir. This is his first time."

"Have you ever thought—maybe he doesn't want t'be found?"

Can you imagine? The gall. Then he said:

"I think this is a big mistake, Michael. You're at a delicate stage. You're champing at the bit. You need t'confront yourself, discipline yourself. You're just ripe for mischief. This isn't the time t'go."

I got a little short with him. I think I was polite enough, but the man has a nerve. Worse, I suppose, he's right. I am challenging God. To be my own man again for a couple of weeks. In a place where there is no end of temptation. My city. I'm running to it. Maybe I want to "go missing," too.

And in a few minutes, I've got to see Kay.

She wanted to know whether I was afraid. Not for Tony—she didn't mean that. For myself. Going to that place. I'm at fault there—I've been like Othello, telling her so many (slightly exaggerated) stories about New York. Street gangs and muggers and con men and the life of the senses. Kay must think it's Aladdin's Baghdad, but a lot more expensive. And then she said,

"I only look good in Nebraska. You wouldn't even have noticed me in New York."

Probably true. Then Kay said, "I'm going t'lose you. I never had you, and now I'm going t'lose you."

Is she right? I hope not: I hope I'm not that predictable. Kay is the woman for me. In time. But, now, yes, I wouldn't mind a little temptation.

Remember that last temptation, Miko? Cost you plenty.

Then she gave me a new Timex watch. Something to remember her by. A quarter to Kay, twenty minutes after Kay, Kay time.

Everyone else has been aces. Guess they want their money back someday. Gladys came up and told me about her brother who died in Vietnam. Mrs. LeFleur baked me brownies for the trip. And I had a fingerpainting from little Julia Serow: big airplane, me riding it like a horse—and a child's impressionist rendering of New York, which made it resemble a slag heap. In Lekachman that's how they imagine the Apple.

I'm scared and excited and already Nebraska is in another time zone. My past.

But, most of all, these 48 hours have taught me how little I know about my own brother. There was—I remember this—something precarious, rash about him. Something on the edge.

Tony was driving us home one night—in the station wagon, me seated way in back. I was thirteen at most. He must've been eighteen then. And there were three other guys. One of them bet Tony he couldn't get us home before some song on the radio ended.

I guess we were thirty blocks or so away. Tony hit 80 mph, going through those quiet suburban streets. No regard for STOP signs. I was frozen with fear. And one of the other kids started to scream. I watched Tony's face—utter, fearless concentration. He was—no, he *is*—some heck of an athlete. We got home before the last chorus started.

And that street fight, I'll never forget that. Tony had been talking to a Hispanic kid's woman. This José was 6'2", 200. Tony is 5'10" at most. And José—thud—sucker-punched Tony in the nose. Blood came dripping out. Tony didn't notice it. He just went after the kid. So José hit him again. He had fast hands. In the nose, again and again, at will. But Tony kept coming. It really scared José, because he was doing lots of damage, but Tony kept coming—and the kid is thinking, this guy is crazy, this guy I don't wanna deal with any more. He got so scared of Tony he started to run. His hands were faster, but not his feet. Tony chased him down. I can still remember José's screams. Tony picked him up and dropped him on a fire hydrant. Picked him up and dropped him. He broke ribs.

Then we walked home, and Tony bought me an ice cream on the way. All that nose blood, and still he bought me an ice cream.

I never asked him if he was happy.

WEDNESDAY, JUNE 22

Let me try to get all this down—in order. So many impressions have bounced off me today. The velocity of change from Lekachman to New York—even Queens, New York—is unbelievable. A constant acceleration. As I sit here on a bed five feet long, covered with Barbie dolls and their expensive, chic wardrobe.

The drive to Omaha was perplexing. I wanted to be alone with my thoughts—I was already out of the pastoral mode. Like, THE PRIEST isn't IN, thank you. And, at that moment, Tim Baxter chooses to make the confession of his life. Trapped.

Not that it wasn't interesting.

First he brown-rings me—what a breath of fresh air I've been. How he could never confide in Schantz, what a nervous wreck he's been—and how (pause for emphasis) Tim reckons he's queer.

Starts to cry at the wheel. Car is weaving through his teardrops.

No, I say. You're not queer.

Yes, he is.

No, I say. You're *gay.* Update your terminology at least.

Turns out Tim wants to join me in New York so he can come out of the closet. Just what I need. A novice gay.

Stay in the closet, I tell him. Being gay in New York is one thing. Being an unemployed hayseed in New York is another.

It was farcical on the one hand. (He's terrified of AIDS, publicity, Lois, Schantz and the Kiwanis.) Pathetic on the other (he was really reaching out—it was a brave moment, for all the farce). And you think—NEBRAS-KA—places like Nebraska exist so you don't have to think about being gay, having AIDS. They're supposed to be geographical parentheses—where serious problems cannot penetrate.

Then, as my plane leaves Omaha, we hit this big-shouldered thunderstorm. Lightning actually knocked a wing-light off. And we kept flopping into air shafts. Sudden elevator, whoops, going down. Stomachs turn inside/out. For me it's a thrill—after Lekachman, even near-death experiences are refreshing.

But the lady beside me is blitzed with fear. She asks if I'll send up a prayer for us all.

I say, "Don't worry, it'll be all right."

"Pray, damn it," she says.

"God is watching us. We're okay. If you want forgiveness, pray yourself."

"I don't believe in religion."

Whoomp, big drop. Someone screams.

"You don't believe, but you want me t'pray? That doesn't make sense."

"You believe, you pray."

"I believe—and I don't believe in bothering God with my problems. If he wants me t'die, there's a darned good reason."

"There may be a darned good reason for you t'die, but not for me."

"Lord," I said. "Forgive this woman her anger, and her mean-spiritedness—and if it be Your will t'take her to Thy bosom this day, be gentle and cleanse her narrow soul."

"Narrow soul" really got to her. She screamed.

"He's praying against me. He's praying against me."

How do I get into these things? I mean to be a humble, self-effacing servant of Him Who made me. Instead I turn into Scrooge McVicar. I'm tempted to say that no one is less worthy than I am to be a priest. I'm tempted. But I'd be committing a sin of pride.

Yes, I apologized, sort of. And anyway, the stewardess told me that she'd flown with this lady before and she was, "A real cunt, sorry, Father."

The stewardess was maybe 35 and she called me Father.

But then the plane made my favorite approach—up the full length of Manhattan Island at twilight, bank just over Baker Field, then circle around Queens for a landing at LaGuardia. The lights on the boulevards—Astoria and Queens and Northern—went on at the same time, as if bright necklaces had been draped on a beautiful woman.

Three years at Nashotah House and four up in New Paltz and now two almost in Lekachman. In nine years I've been back to New York maybe three weeks total. And it's as if I'd never been away. My pulse and the city's pulse are in wild harmony. I feel no fear: it's as if adrenaline had been shot into my veins. This is the center of the universe. Is that bad? As a Christian, am I expected to avoid the central, the active, and maroon myself in some contemplative boondock? Nonsense. Christianity was a religion of cities, and my apostleship is to people—and here, God knows, are people.

The women are gorgeous. The men challenge you at every crossroad. You're an adversary until proven otherwise. (In Nebraska it is presumed that you're a civil human being.) And it costs a Ford Foundation grant just to stock your refrigerator.

The cabbie at LaGuardia—noting my luggage tags—said, "From Nebraska, sir?" (He was from Beirut, I think.) I nodded and said I was headed for Malba in Queens. His face darkened (he wanted a fare to Manhattan, not to some nearby backwater where he'd have to deadhead back to the city).

"That'll be $35.00, plus what's on the meter," he said.

"Oh," I said. "Let's stop first at the 115th precinct on 92nd and Northern Blvd. They'll wanna hear that. How d'you spell your name? I want them t'get it right when they revoke your license at the Taxi and Limousine Commission."

He cursed all the way to Ethel's. It felt good to be home.

My first impression of Ethel. Reminds me of those Buddha statues: the kind that have little people crawling all over the Buddha's body. She answered the door with one child piggyback, an infant on her stomach and two others wrapped around her considerable thighs. The girls don't let each other out of sight these days—not since Tony dropped from circulation. "We don't want t'get vanished, too," said little Amy.

Ethel is robust. 5'10" and at least 160 pounds. She's put on weight since the wedding, when last I saw her. Fat, but taut fat. She wore shorts and sandals and moisture. She's a massive perspirer. And I think she's lactating, because her shirt front is always gooey. But good-looking in a Scandinavian sort of way. (Is she a Finn?) Big, broad facial planes, clear skin. Ethel's eyelashes and brows are very light and give a disturbing impression that she's blind.

Much to my shame, I hadn't thought to bring presents. The two older children (Amy and Wendy, age six and five, I think) served me peanut butter and jelly sandwiches with milk. Then they stood, hands behind back, waiting for me to reciprocate. Why didn't Kay tell me to pick something up for them?

"You can sit, kids," said Ethel. "He hasn't got anything."

"I was in a hurry. I'll get you something nice later."

"He looks like Daddy," said Amy or Wendy.

"He's your daddy's little brother." And she pointed—my ordination photo was on the Baldwin grand. For some reason I found that moving. They were proud of me (though Ethel had missed the ordination). Ethel got up and went to the piano: she played some jazz—she has a thunderous left hand—her arms around the drowsing, unimpressed baby.

I don't know what preconceptions I'd entertained of Ethel—vague ideas of the vulnerable, helpless young mother, if anything. But, hearing her play, the force of her playing, made me re-evaluate. Ethel isn't helpless by any means: I made a mental note not to underestimate her. (I do that with women, Kay has pointed it out.) She and the children make a cohesive, loyal female unit. I wonder if Tony was ever a member in good standing.

Amy (or Wendy) then took me up to her room—where I am now. I know she didn't like the idea of moving out—but all of Ethel's children are remarkably obedient (and neat and bright). She said, in the politest way, "Please don't move my dolls—they're having group therapy and they can't hear each other if you move them." I agreed not to. Then, quite suddenly, eyes closed, she hugged me. I think they're all rather disoriented by the Wilson male resemblance. I caught the others staring at me. Kind of a disappointed look.

After the kids went to bed, Ethel and I talked in the kitchen. In twilight, arriving by cab, I didn't appreciate the house. But Malba, as I now recall, is prime real estate. Tony has done well. There's a swimming pool. The grounds are too brilliantly landscaped to be my brother's work. Nothing ever grew for him. There are four bedrooms and a huge den. And there's a white 1990 Lincoln (rented, but still . . .) and an Olds Cutlass station wagon in the driveway. Apparently there's a summer house on Lake Something in the Poconos. I'm glad Schantzy didn't see this.

Ethel gave me a beer and took an iced tea for herself.

"Thank you for coming," she said. I made a don't-mention-it gesture.

"What do the police think?" I asked.

"The police are stupid."

"Do they think it's foul play?"

"Their attitude is—so she couldn't keep her husband. They smirk. Three days ago someone slashed the front tires on my Cutlass, right in the driveway. Random vandalism, they said."

"And you think—"

"I try not t'think. Tony didn't bring his problems home. I recall, looking back, that he seemed preoccupied. Maybe I'm imagining it. But that's not why I asked you t'come. You can't make him reappear."

"I suppose not."

"I rented you a new car—the white Lincoln outside. It's just like the one Tony was driving the night he . . . didn't come back."

"That's, uh, extravagant."

"Maybe I'm kidding myself, but it gives me comfort. Like things haven't changed. Anyway, the—the restaurant pays for it."

"If you say so."

"Is four-fifty a week okay?" I started.

"Four-what?"

"Four-fifty a week t'run the place. It's about all I can afford."

"Ethel—I'm Tony's brother. I didn't come here for the money."

"Don't be stupid. It's hard work and lousy hours. Don't unpack everything. I got you a sublet just off Northern Boulevard, maybe 15 blocks away. There really isn't room for you here."

"Well—how d'you know I'm right for the job?"

"You're blood. You're a priest. Good God, I should be able t'trust you—and that means a lot right there. I do the books and make out the checks anyway. But, since Tony went off, receipts are way down. I know everyone's got a hand in the till—a certain amount of special perks are expected in this business. But not that many. I just need someone there. You'll catch on soon enough. Just don't take any bullshit."

"But I know nothing about food. Unless you serve TV dinners. What's the cuisine, anyway?"

"It's more a nice neighborhood place t'meet. Nothing fancy. It's up on Northern Boulevard and 60th."

"Uh-huh. So how do I start?"

"They'll be waiting for you at noon tomorrow. The day and night managers, and the—ah, the rest of the staff. Listen carefully. But don't believe anything they say."

"A worker priest," I said. "They're very positive about worker priests in the Episcopal Church these days."

"Sure," she said. "But maybe we shouldn't tell them you're a priest."

"I'm not ashamed of it," I said. Ethel shrugged and got up.

"You sound like him. A younger him. Before he . . . before he learned so much."

Ethel got up and came across the kitchen. She stood behind me and massaged my shoulders for a while. It felt good. Then she kissed me, a very damp kiss, on the top of my head. Her chest leaked against my arm.

"Thanks for coming," she said.

THURSDAY, JUNE 23

I dreamed of my brother last night. He was angry with me, I didn't know why. And, for a certain while, he was wearing clerical black. (I don't remember what I had on—or was I naked?) He kept fighting it, ripping at the collar. But the material was binding: any time he'd rip a layer of black off, there'd be another layer underneath. And he kept saying, "If I don't get it off before they come, I'm dead."

And I was glad Tony couldn't get it off. And he sensed that and said, "Yeah, but it was you who got in trouble, not me. Let's play ball."

And, in the unrigorous way of dreams, we suddenly had gloves and a ball. And Tony was pitching to me like once he did at Memorial Park in Flushing. (I got a big charge out of catching my brother back then. But I was always a little scared. It hurt. My glove hand swelled up.)

But Tony was having trouble. When he went into his windup, in the middle of it, he'd have to cross himself, which sure took a lot off his fastball. And me . . . I had my jock cup in my hand (I woke up holding a child's makeup compact), but I couldn't use it, since I was naked. So I'd hold it in front of my genitals whenever Tony threw.

Then, somehow, the mound had become a pulpit, and Tony was taking his text from the Sadducees' question in *Luke:* "Master, Moses wrote, If any man's brother die, having a wife, that his brother should take his wife and raise up seed unto his brother."

And I started screaming—"Don't listen to him, he has children." (The kids were getting up at this point, so their voices probably infiltrated my subconscious.) In the dream there were now six children. And Tony came down from the pulpit and said, "You're so smart, which are mine and which are yours? Mine came from the left ovary."

And I woke up with a terrific erection.

I guess Tony was always ambivalent about my vocation—though he never said so. As a teenager he refused to attend church, I remember that. It drove Dad bonkers—Dad wanted to get on the vestry and Tony's atheism was an embarrassment. I used to tell Tony, "Make 'em happy, go." (Was that why I went—did I go to make them happy?) And he said, "You can't make people happy doing things that'll make *you* unhappy." Which was pretty sharp for a fifteen-year-old, or so.

Anyway, it's time I went to work. I confess to being a bit nervous. My first day. But I'm sure I'll be able to handle it.

I've just come back from The Smoking Car—and, shee-eet, do we have trouble.

I can't believe this. I just can't believe it. And Ethel shrugs it off . . .

Good God, what am I dealing with here?

Wait. From the beginning.

I take the Lincoln and head down to 60th Street and Northern Blvd. I'm wearing my monkey suit because my cords are filthy and my jeans have a hole in them. I'm full of anticipation. I mean, can I handle this?

Sure I can: a restaurant can't be harder to manage than a parish, probably easier. They don't hold you responsible for souls, just for appetites.

So I pull up. It's the weirdest-looking place. Façade like the side of a Long Island Railroad passenger car: a dozen tiny windows set into silver metal. The name is written out in flashy blue neon. It's at the west end of the block—there's an out-of-business dry cleaner at the corner and a hardware store to the right.

I figure they're just starting to serve lunch. So I take my little portfolio, with my just-bought three-ring notebook in it. And I set out across Northern, like I'm about to take a course in human digestion.

Naturally, it's so bright outside I can't see for a good few seconds after going through the front door. But I've got this big lasagna of a dumb smile on my face. Like, Hi, I'm the brother-in-law. Welcome to a new regime, my people.

And then I see—what?—a NAKED WOMAN. She's hanging down from a trapeze over a tiny stage. Je-sus Christ, *I am in a topless bar.* With my collar on. I turn around and blast into the sunshine, across the boulevard, into the Lincoln, where I proceed to eat my fingers.

I am, first off, furious at Ethel. She could've been a little more candid up front before hauling my ass away from Lekachman. So I get out and grab a pay phone and dial Ethel. Recorded message, *beep!* "Pick up, Ethel," I say, "pick up, we got problems." No answer. "Ethel, that address you gave me—it's a topless bar. I just walked into a topless bar with my collar on. Hello? Hello? Tell me there's a mistake, Ethel. People are walking around naked in there and I'm a priest. I did not come here all the way from Nebraska to be an apostle to the drunk and the semi-nude." But Ethel, if she was there, knew enough not to answer.

I'm scared. We are talking about a real career-buster here. PRIEST RUNS TOPLESS BAR. It isn't likely that anyone will recognize me and, Lord knows, Episcopal priests have probably done worse things, but . . .

I have to face the whole moral dilemma. Not nudity, not that by itself—but the seductive, subsexual transaction that goes on between customer and dancer. Doesn't that trivialize and cheapen our natures? It sure does. And am I not pridefully introducing myself to temptation? Putting overmuch trust in my own willpower? I sure am.

Well, for damn certain I can't go back in there dressed like a priest.

So, well . . . yes . . . I removed my collar. There was a Korean variety store up the corner. They were selling T-shirts: white lettering on red, a softball top of some sort. I bought it—and changed quickly in a back aisle, among the party favors. Only later did I realize that this shirt has BOSTON SUCKS printed over the shoulders.

And, after crossing myself, I went back into The Smoking Car.

It was a landmark moment: my first-ever drink in a topless bar. Skoal, Mike. I got so superconscious of temptation that I must've snapped my neck vertebrae six times looking away—the mirrors are ubiquitous (behind the bar even) and they constantly tossed nudity in my direction. At that hour—just after noon—there weren't many customers: just three elderly men, in fact. And, after my sun-blinded, skittish entrance, the gemütlich homeyness of the place calmed me down. On one wall I saw rather sophisticated free-hand sketches: dancers at work and at ease. On another wall there was a bulletin board that held a collage of business cards and local advertising. Some dusty Christmas decorations were still hanging here and there. And a leprechaun from St. Patrick's Day. And a jack-o'-lantern. A bar for all seasons.

But there was no touch of Tony Wilson. I didn't sense my brother's presence. I took out the scrap of note paper Ethel had handed me— 60-12 Northern Boulevard, it still said—and I began to laugh. Somehow, apparently, Ethel had misprinted the numbers. Then a well-crafted girl in a bikini passed me (the women wear bikinis or lingerie between dances) and my hand went to my throat. No collar—thank, yes, God. I began to laugh again. The entire incident was so absurd. I started rehearsing the story I would tell at our clergy conference when I got back to Lekachman: REV. WILSON AND THE TOPLESS BAR. Then a voice said,

"What can I do you for?"

At first I couldn't tell where the voice was coming from. Behind the bar I saw this Muppet rodent thing—which turned out to be a pink wig. The bartender, Pearl, is about four foot ten and at least 70 years old. Everything about her seems artificial. Fingernails: plastic. Eyebrows: painted on. Only the grindstone voice—a Forest Hills Jewish accent—is authentic. I went into laugh spasms again. This did not please her.

"You'd like a Fleet Enema on the rocks maybe? There something you find funny about my looks?"

"No. No. Not at all. It's me—my own idiocy. Just a Coke, thanks."

"Coke with Liquid Wrench in it. Coming up."

She went off. I was ashamed: my laughter had been less than considerate. I bent to look at Kay's watch, and, as I did so, a hand closed over the dial face.

"Guy as cute as you doesn't needta know the time."

She was half glamorous, half a caricature of glamour as we Americans have come to perceive it. Mae West, Jayne Mansfield—and Goldie Hawn's elfin smile, upper teeth raking over her lower lip. Young (18) and big. But more chubby than actually *built*, as they say. Bright red hair with a skunk's streak of platinum blond smack in the middle of it. And a beauty mark on her cheek that promptly popped off into my lap. I caught it between my knees.

"This is yours?"

"Thanks," she said. She took the beauty mark and ate it. "I'm Bubbles. Feel like buying me a drink since you didn't even tip me one cheesy dollar?"

"Oh? I'm sorry. I've never been in one of these places before. I didn't know that tipping was . . . I didn't mean any disrespect t'your performance."

"Listen, it's not that I need the money. Last week I made $1,500, tax free—working four nights."

"$1,500 a week? Doing this?"

"Well, you don't really *do* this." Bubbles was wearing a black shortie nightgown. Sheer. She kept positioning herself to engage my vision frontally. To avoid that I wound up looking over my own left shoulder. "I mean, you get on stage and it kinda happens—like puberty or a rash."

"I see—"

"Look, how's about I keep you? Huh? Your shoes're all falling apart. It knocks me over. I mean that grown-up men can be poor. It's kinda romantic. You could live off me—treat me like, oh, an end table—and I'd be happy."

"That's an attractive offer," I said. I got off my bar stool. "But—just so happens—I'm in the wrong place. Gotta get going."

"You sure?"

"Yeah. I thought this was a restaurant. Nice meeting you."

And I started to leave then. I did. It's important for my self-esteem to remember that—no matter what happens from here on in. I *was* on my way out. The Smoking Car held no particular attraction for me. I'm a male, with strong male urges, but I haven't much of the voyeur in my makeup. Bubbles didn't arouse me: her female—what would I call it?— female pressure, I guess—that pressure made me feel uncomfortable. Sad. I felt sad for her. And so I turned to leave The Smoking Car . . .

But, just then, this early Neanderthal specimen came trudging out of a room in back. His appearance diverted me: six foot five at least, maybe 270 pounds, unshaven and covered with the least artistic tattoos

I've ever seen. The kind of person who curses the way I say my prayers: for spiritual comfort. He was lugging a Steel Sack that clanked. And, as he made for the rear exit, one of the elderly customers hailed him.

"Hey, Leonard. Not so fast. Where's that forty bucks The Car owes me?"

"You'll get it, you'll get it."

"When, Leonard? Who d'you think you are, Tony Wilson all of a sudden?" My lungs inhaled for me—aaaah—I didn't order a breath. And the name, Tony Wilson, disquieted Leonard, too. He took a step backward. He clanked toward the man.

"Fuck Tony Wilson. At least I'm not all talk and no hard-on like him."

"He was hard enough for Rita. He had her doin' a maypole dance."

"Tony Wilson can rim me out. If he ever shows up again—"

"My friend," I said. It just came out of me.

"Tony Wilson can—"

"MY FRIEND," I said again.

"Yeah?" Leonard glanced over. "What's your problem?"

"My problem is Tony Wilson—I don't like hearing bad things said about him."

"Tough titty, asshole."

"Because I'm Tony Wilson's brother, dickhead. And Ethel sent me here t'run this place."

A clap of silence. It felt, well, satisfying. But suddenly, irrevocably— more out of macho than fraternal devotion—I had committed myself to The Car. Maybe Ethel hoped something like this would happen. If so, she has the nerve of a grave robber.

"Jesus," said Pearl. "Tony's long-lost brother. I shoulda figured—Ethel told me you were coming by, but I thought she meant later. Lookit that. A spitting image. The apple, as my mother says, doesn't fall far from the tree."

"What is this shit?" Leonard was pouting. Large men who pout are something less than winsome.

"Mike Wilson. I'm gonna be running this joint until Tony gets back."

"Run? You got experience in this line of work?"

"No. I'm hoping you'll break me in. I figure it's not like nuclear physics."

"Yeah? Ethel don't like the way things're being run now? It's summer—right Pearl?—people are away, things're always slow in summer. I can't make customers come in. We don't advertise on cable or nothin'."

"Ethel just wants me t'help out, that's all. She figured, with Tony gone, you must be overworked." I was being diplomatic.

"Yeah?" Leonard considered that. "Okay, sure, I am." He reached behind the bar and tossed me a large, page-loose black notebook. "Tony always hired the girls. Now it's your job. We're booked through June, but y'never know who's gonna come down with a bleeding ovary or an audition for the lead in *Phantom of the Opera.* Ha-ha. You handle their lives. I'm sick of it."

"Well, I'm not sure I'm the best qualified t'choose—"

"You're a guy, aren't you? If she strips on stage and doesn't fall down and you get horny, hire her. Pearl'll tell you which ones are on heroin or under 14."

"I'll help, don't worry, boychik."

Doris, one of the Silicone Sisters (so named because, well, guess . . .) yelled down from onstage, "You look like Tony—is your cock big as his?"

"I—I'm not sure—"

"You don't know how long your cock is?"

"I mean, I'm not sure I—"

"His was eight inches, with a dogleg to the left."

This will be the hardest part—the language (verbal and physical). I'm bound to come off looking like an uptight prig. And I can't meet eyes (or breasts). Offstage, the women saunter around in revealing gear—if there are two or three of them, I spend so much time averting my gaze that I get dizzy. I ended up staring at my broken shoe a lot.

This, unfortunately, makes me seem "shy." And shy—wouldn't you know—is going to make me attractive. If I draped myself all over these girls, if I groped them, they'd run away. Instead, as Bubbles hinted, I'm some sort of a challenge. They don't know I'm a priest, but—in this ambiance—I have the sensibility of one. They'll probably all want to seduce me. Or at least "bring me out."

Pearl introduced me to the regulars—one is a mattress salesman, one a retired homicide detective, one something else. Then I went behind the bar and drew myself a Coke. It was my first act of ownership. I reached into what looked like an ice drawer and out popped a tabby cat. This cheered me up: I'm a whiz with cats. I know just where to tap them behind the tail for maximum good feeling. Cats'll walk a mile to be tapped by me.

"His name is Lazarus," Pearl said. "He was locked in here when the old owner got shut down. He survived on tap beer and pretzels. How's Ethel doing?"

"Pretty good. Frankly, I don't know her all that well. Who's Rita?"

"A girl."

"Yes. I'd guessed that. Is she missing, too?"

"She's been out three shifts. But maybe she's back home in Puerto Rico. Or taking a trip t'Maine. On that stage, ladies and gentlemen, you'll find the least responsible women in the world."

"Were she and my brother—you know?"

"They call me Pearl because the clam kept his big mouth shut when he was making me. I'll keep quiet about your business, too."

"Okay."

"Now you're taking over—you got any changes in mind?"

"The ravioli has to go—it looks awful. Who makes it?"

"My mother. The guys love my mother's ravioli. I've trained them. Besides, what's a drunk know about taste? Lunch is poured around here."

"Your mother? How old is she?"

"Don't ask."

"The ravioli is fine, I guess."

"Well, frankly it tastes like toasted Modess. Maybe it'd have a little nip if you blessed it."

"Bless?"

"Tony said, you know—in Nebraska you were with some kinda church."

"Good God, does anyone else know?"

"I don't think. With me your secret is safe."

"Please. I'm dead if anyone from the diocese finds out. Dead."

"Start growing a mustache."

"Maybe I will."

I have.

I'm here with Amy's dolls at 2 a.m. Tomorrow I move to a furnished one bedroom apartment near The Car. I'm subletting from a friend of Pearl's who has gone to Colorado for the summer. I haven't resisted any of this very much, have I?

I tried. I had it out with Ethel as soon as I got back—which was a mistake. I should've let her put the kids in bed first. It's kinda hard to yell real loud at a nursing mother. According to Ethel, despite the cars and the swimming pool, matters do not proceed well. Tony is in hock to his eye sockets—there are two mortgages, plus some outstanding "loans" from backers that're overdue. Ethel showed me check stubs and agreements—most of which I didn't understand.

"Still, you should've told me," I said. It came out sounding petulant and not grown-up. "You shouldn't've let me walk into a topless bar unprepared."

"You're a man of the world, aren't you?"

"That's the whole point—I'm supposed t'be a man out of the world. Listen, I told my girlfriend, Kay, she could come have a meal in the restaurant I was managing. Now, what do I do? You're asking me t'risk my vocation and my love life."

"Yes? These children are your blood. This is all they have—I apologize for the sordidness of it. I wish I was asking you t'run, I don't know, a florist's shop maybe. But that's where it is. I'm a mother. I get ruthless when I haveta protect my children. And Tony's your brother. He put you through seminary. That topless bar you're so fastidious about made you a priest."

"Well, where is Tony?"

"I don't know." Ethel started to cry. I felt crummy. "Mike. They'll understand. And it's a business, that's all. We run it clean. Men come in t'have drinks and watch women dance. It's not a whorehouse. Tony never stood for any hanky-panky."

"All right. For a little while. Just till he gets back."

The kids marched in then—all those who were old enough to march. And they also started to cry: a kind of enthusiasm for tears set in. I rubbed my upper lip to hurry the mustache along. I needed a whole new wardrobe. Amy had already asked me what BOSTON SUCKS meant.

"Do you know a girl named Rita?" I said. Ethel looked up.

"I know two at least. Which one? Rita G or Rita the Hawk?"

"I'm not sure."

"Listen—take my advice. Don't get involved with any of them."

"I'm not getting involved. You can bet I'm not getting involved."

"They can be very attractive. They can be a lot of fun. But, take my word for it . . . there's always a little something wrong with a topless dancer."

FRIDAY, JUNE 24

Why am I here? What dark urge am I making room for? Or is this a chance to surprise and conquer grace? If there is a divinity that shapes our ends—and it is on that premise that I have charted my life—then my adventure with The Smoking Car is meant to prove something, I think. Certainly I'm jeopardizing, not only my insignificant career, but

my relationship to God. Not that He wouldn't forgive me. *I* wouldn't forgive *Him* for my own failure. I would run from Him out of shame.
Women.

I have unfinished business with women. And it is angry business. You walk down the street here, and they come along—one after another—beautiful, lascivious, with a YOU CAN'T HAVE ME sign on. It's my imagination, I know, I'm attributing motives to them out of standard male paranoia, but I feel it. So now, here. I'm going to withhold from them. YOU CAN'T HAVE ME.

They better want me. And God better endure my little game—because I gave up my promising career as a rogue male for Him and for Kay. So there.

I suppose this all has something to do with Mother. She lies, in my memory, framed by the door of her bedroom. Which threshold I was not permitted to cross. Her room contained, you know, "women's things." In my childhood I imagined those things to be delicate and sharp instruments. Femininity and convalescence are associated in my mind. The allergies Mother had, I know, were real enough. But they were also an excuse to avoid the men in her life. And to drink. "Let it go for now," she'd say, no matter what my need was. "Let it go for now—your mother isn't feeling well." They aren't sure—the crash ran my mother and father together, made them one—they aren't sure, but I guess Mom was driving the Chevy that night. You CAN'T HAVE ME. No matter what you do.

And then there was Amanda . . .

All this is a preface to My First Full Day Running a Topless Bar.

The Car is very low tech and comfy—sort of like a lower middle class paneled playroom. Directly opposite the bar is a stage that consists of a trapezoidal platform, about three feet high, covered with gritty, worn red indoor-outdoor carpet. The wall behind the stage is sheeted over with mirroring. To the left of the stage (as you look from the bar) there's a folding table with cold cuts and bread on it. (Lunch is free from noon to three o'clock.) Also the famous afterbirth-like ravioli. On the right is a jukebox, where, for free, the girls punch in dance music.

There are flashing colored lights and some modest strobe effects above the stage—and two poles, such as you'd see on a carousel. The trapeze hangs down between them.

Looking sharp left, to the rear of the joint, still sitting at the bar, you see a passage that leads back to the men's room (right) and to an office slash kitchen area (left). Beyond the kitchen is a back door that leads out to a small yard with one aged tree of paradise in it and some old Coke coolers. In that direction, behind the bar, there is a trap door and wooden staircase that lead down to the basement. The women's locker room is to the left of the stage, behind the ravioli table.

The bar has about twenty stools. Besides those, there are at least fifteen tables around the stage. I guess the place can seat sixty or seventy. Not much light enters. The railroad windows are heavily curtained. This makes The Car seem isolated in time and space. Photosynthesis does not take place.

It's surreal. The music roars and bangs, so loud it's impossible to communicate sense. Disco lights spark and flicker in the 24 hour darkness. Tonight, around 1 a.m., it was SRO. Maybe 100–120 men in The Car. Men who represent five million years of evolution. Men, most of them with families, staring up at these icons—because that's what the female figure is to them: a symbol, a device one might use in hypnosis. And they stare hour after hour: for each man, the dancer moves only in his honor. This, I have to remind myself, was my brother's line of work.

Leonard came in at noon (The Car is open from 11:45 a.m. to 4:00 a.m.). His formal hours are 8 p.m. to 4 a.m., but—this Leonard made a point of mentioning—he's often in mornings and afternoons, to help load inventory or handle special problems. He fixed a pipe under the sink in the girls' locker room last week. A plumber, Leonard says, would've run us a great deal more.

He introduced me to Jako, who comes in around 8 a.m. to clean the joint. Jako is an absolutely credulous black, about six foot tall and 120 lbs. *Thin.* His hair smoothed back with grease, like old photos of Sugar Ray Robinson. Obviously a drinker, if not something worse—but with a sunny disposition and a propensity for saying "That so? Ma-an!" on hearing the most trivial piece of information. Jako is fascinated by the resemblance between me and Tony. Keeps saying, "You lose weight, Boss?" He is convinced—Leonard says it's bullshit—that Tony offered him a raise just before he left. He's getting the minimum now—and when I look at the state of the bathrooms here I'm inclined to give him a boost. After 2 a.m. nobody hits the urinal.

Maybe I should clean it myself. Show a proper attitude, penance, something. And over the john, in what looks like lipstick, it says TONY AND RITA. I avoid examining the drift of that.

Leonard took me down to the basement storeroom and, on the way, I asked him about Rita. She's a real manipulator, he tells me. And a Puerto Rican. A *Puerto Rican*—if you knew how Tony and I were brought up—with a clear sense of whom we should associate with and whom not—you'd understand how crazy it sounded: Tony and a *Puerto Rican.* Mother left the Catholic Church and became an Episcopalian because it was a step up socially—and, of course, because she was marrying Dad. Marrying him, in part, I'm sure, because he had the barest remnant of a socially superior (though lower class) British accent. Dad had been brought up in the Church of England. Until his wedding, I don't think he'd been to mass in 20 years. I assume all that made Puerto Ricans and other exotic fauna interesting to Tony. I don't think it had the same effect on me.

The basement is much larger than I would've imagined, and dimly lit. Aside from the fast moving items—the beers, mainly—it's going to be damned difficult to find a case of this and a case of that without Leonard. There's a huge ice-making machine at the foot of the stairs. Then, to the left, a walk-in cooler that can keep a couple of pallet-loads of beer chilled. Snacks—pretzels, etc.—are kept upstairs in the kitchen pantry, where Leonard, they tell me, cooks for special occasions. Corned beef and cabbage on St. Patrick's Day. Turkey on Thanksgiving and Christmas. Just to show how difficult the job is, Leonard had me carry ten cases of beer up the wooden staircase which exits behind the bar. I think he was surprised when I didn't collapse.

But, uh-oh, there were two girls waiting for me when I came upstairs. Blaze and Cleopatra: the girls tend to take stage names—not with great imaginative reach. We actually have three Jezebels. Joe Solomon, the retired homicide detective, says that the customers, in self-defense, should assume names, too, like Stud or Hunk. Then we'd have a totally artificial atmosphere.

Blaze and Cleopatra, it turns out, are sophomores at SUNY–New Platz. They were both very nervous (which made me nervous) and New Age looking. Turquoise earrings and necklaces. Frizzy, wild hair—one brown head, one blond head—the sort of hair I associate with, well, liberalism. Cleopatra wears braces. Blaze has a nose ring. Not very seductive. Leonard watched with a flat smirk on his face. Pearl, too, was getting off on Mike's misery. My eyes were all over the place—and they hadn't even taken their clothes off. I made small talk—I almost said that I had gone to New Paltz, too . . . but thank God I didn't. They claim that ten or twelve girls every year commute from upstate during the school year to dance topless on weekends. (This is news to me. I'm always the last to hear.)

At this point Leonard got impatient and interrupted. I was fraternizing with the lower classes. "Eighty bucks up front," he said. "You work two afternoons before you get t'work one night. You flash, you're finished. You touch your tits or wear a see-through G-string, you're out. You're late, you're out. No drinks or smokes onstage. You spend time with the customers between gigs. How old are you?"

Blaze and Cleopatra were 19 and 20—which means they can only drink orange juice at The Car. Oh, beautiful for spacious skies—America the Ridiculous.

"The locker room is in there. Let's see what you got." The girls left: I was p.o.'d at Leonard.

"Who's supposed t'be in charge here?"

"Take my advice, don't get involved with none of them. Their whole life is one big trip to the intensive care unit. Move 'em along. Better call everyone in Tony's book and give 'em your phone number. Me, I'm going home t'crash, I should be getting overtime as it is."

He left, which was a big relief to me. Pearl and I started going through the list—I asked her to give each girl a grade from A to F.

"Sapphira."

"A-minus."

"Hedda."

"B, nice but drinks."

"Leslie."

"C-plus and stretching it. Has three periods a month."

"Noor. Is Noor a name?"

"B-plus, but flashes when she can."

"Changa. Tony has 'Brazilian' in parentheses."

"A-minus. All Brazilians get an A-minus. They always show up on time. They never flash or do floor shows. They love America—and they fuckin' well should, they're getting a seven million to one exchange rate on every buck they pull down. They all own at least a shopping center in Rio—and they've mooched their way into the topless business like roaches. The entire useless nation of Brazil is supported by tit. The country would go belly-up without boobs. Peons—they make me itch. And men can't understand a word they say. Even Spanish men can't."

The secret of Tony's success at The Smoking Car, she tells me, is his women. Most topless bars hire through an agency, which means they get chiefly Brazilians. But Tony scouted his own talent. Fresh young things. They're a lot more trouble, but they draw well. (I can't believe I'm writing this. I sound like the Merchant of Venus.)

At that point Blaze and Cleopatra came out, dressed in bikini bathing suits with men's dress shirts over them. Coupla kids is all. Blaze put her hand on my arm, innocently enough, to announce her presence.

Zang—my bicep balled up in a typical macho reaction. Be warned, Rev. Mike: you've still got a male's ego.

"Who's first?" said Pearl. Cleopatra volunteered. "You can take a break, Tanya."

I looked up at the stage then—it was the first time, I've been very scrupulous about it—and there was, well . . . a *vision*. Brunette hair, exquisite legs—every part of her body so slight, yet so articulated that it was sexless. Perfection, to me, is sexless. Cellulite and a swollen lip, now you're talking sexy. Perfection I just admire. And this was perfection with Vivien Leigh's face: a face so removed from the sordid circumstances around it that the contrast was mesmerizing. And Tanya could dance: not the usual packhorse gyration and crossover step. Pearl repeated her command. Tanya, not at all happy, threw on a white silk bathrobe and stomped down to sit beside me at the bar.

"What do I look for?" I asked Pearl.

"A pair of tits. Hire them, they look like friendly girls—they'll only last the summer."

"Stiffs, they are," Tanya said. "This is my earning time. This is costing me tips."

"Tanya does TV commercials," said Pearl, walking away. "She's better than the rest of us."

"You're the brother?" Tanya asked.

"Mike Wilson."

"Tanya Suslov. That's my real name. Listen we've gotta get things straight. Tony gave me $100 up front, not $80. That was our deal, when he brought me over from the Leopard Club."

"Well, now—"

"When I work night shifts, you—or someone from The Car—drives me home. I work one day shift for three night shifts. And two Saturday nights a month are mine."

"Look—I was told $80—"

"Are you the boss here, or is that knuckle-walker, Leonard? I've been putting up with his bullshit since Tony left. You can agree t'my terms— that is, you can honor your brother's terms—or I walk right now, in the middle of my set."

"I don't like to be bullied."

"Women are always bullied. I've learned t'be tough." At which point tears swamped her eyes and Tanya began to weep. This did not interrupt her conversation. It was as if her head were draining. "Look up there."

I did. I saw Cleopatra dancing for the first time. She had thick thighs and breasts so soft they puddled. Cleopatra licked tongue over lower lip in a corny show of sensuous élan. I smiled—to be supportive. I felt remorse: I had made a child take her clothes off.

"You're blushing," Tanya said. "You sure you're in the right business?"

"You're crying. Are you sure *you're* in the right business?"

"I need the money. I'm studying at Actors Studio and I need the money. What I meant t'say was—her, that one. Don't I rate twenty bucks more than she does?"

"I—"

"I know you hate t'judge." Tanya started crying again. "But look at this place—eleven, twelve—sixteen men. How often d'you get sixteen men on a summer's afternoon? I draw them. I'm as close to stardom as this place'll ever have. It's worth the money, believe me."

"Don't tell anyone," I said.

Not an auspicious beginning: Women 1, Mike 0. But I don't think Tanya was lying: I think she did have a special deal with Tony, a certain homage paid to glamour. And what else was paid, I wonder, on those nights that Tony drove her home? (I shouldn't allow myself to think about Tony like this: it's disloyal.) I did permit myself to watch Tanya dance after that. And I didn't lust for her. Perhaps because it seemed useless. She was on another plane—like great Majolica or a Whistler portrait. At one point, later in the day, some bozo handed her a five buck tip (the standard is a one) and then tried to slip it into her G-string. That is, tried to cop a feel. And Tanya took his bill and tore it into nickels and let them flutter around the stage. This is too much woman for me with clothes on. Naked, she's incomprehensible.

Instead, I was strict with Blaze and Cleopatra. They were children, not women. Hardly older than the kids in my Young People's Fellowship class back in Lekachman. Cleopatra was wearing a cross around her neck. I told her to remove it before she danced at The Car again. I couldn't use them until a week from Friday afternoon—unless they wanted to work separately, which they didn't—and this information was greeted with a groan and a certain amount of "pretty please" flirting from Blaze.

"Look," I said, "that may work with your English professor. But it doesn't work with me."

"Wow," said Blaze, backing off. "You must be great in bed."

"See you a week from Friday, 11:30 sharp," I said. They left. I looked up at the stage. And Tanya was laughing at me. What man could ever deal with her? A Black drug dealer, probably. Or a Nobel Prize–winning Oriental physicist. I doubt she has much respect for normal white men.

Tony? Could Tony have dealt with her? Not the Tony I used to know.

Soon after that I had to handle my first customer complaint. This bricklayer type—on his lunch hour, in painter's overalls and work boots—comes over. He's pretty ploughed (I'd love to see him try to lay a straight line of brick) and he has a beer glass in his hand.

"You the head honcho here?"

"Yes," I said. I had to think a moment. But I guess I am.

"Well," he says, "your cat just drank my beer."

"Cats don't drink beer." I figured he was pulling a shaggy cat routine on me.

"The one with stripes. Over there. He does. And I don't wanna catch some frikkin' mouse disease. Gimme a fresh one. On you."

"Here," said Pearl. She gave the yobbo a beer.

"Thank you. Lucky I don't call the health department."

"What was that, Pearl?" I said, after the bricklayer went back to his seat.

"Well. Lemme tellya. Truth is, Laz drinks beer. Usually I put down a dish with a head on it around five—I like t'wait until the sun goes under the yardarm. I don't want him becoming a total lush."

"I'm hearing things."

"But then he gets mad and goes for some guy's glass. Funny thing is, he'll only drink imported. Beck's is best."

"Doesn't he get—" I looked then. Lazarus was making his way to the backyard, where he suns himself in the afternoon. Sure enough, there was a dip and stutter in his walk. At one point he couldn't figure how to get around a barstool. The cat was plotzed. Cats in Nebraska almost never drink.

"I know," Pearl said. "A shame. The mice laugh at him now. It's from the time he got trapped in here and hadda chug out of the tap." She shook her head. "Anyhow, he has an addictive personality."

"AA. Have you thought about AA?"

"Nah. Those dogs talk all the time. They think they're the only ones who got a problem."

Then, and this is disconcerting, Pearl changed the subject. She said, "Why'd you become a priest?"

"Oh, complicated reasons. Not the kind I'd like t'reminisce about in this atmosphere."

"Was it because you knocked that girl up?"

I almost dropped my Coke glass. It's been so long since anyone mentioned Amanda and that miserable time of my life. I thought, foolishly, that I'd put the whole incident behind me. Not a chance. It's always there—to feel sorry for myself about, to get angry over, to recrucify myself on. And it's all my fault, I know that. I take responsibility like the consciousness people say you should, but still—yes, I became a priest because of it, probably. That, anyway, was the proximate cause of my decision.

Our child, now that I think of it, would be almost nine years old today. I have never felt as helpless as I did then. It ripped away my moral honor, my decentness, which had been my chief stock-in-trade. (I was always such a good boy.) I remember suggesting—in a roomful of adults who had met to discuss our shame—I remember suggesting that Amanda not have an abortion. And they literally hissed at me. Gets her pregnant, he does, and then he wants to saddle *us* with a child.

My Dad agreed with them, these Christians who proselytized for his grandchild's abortion. Dad had a greenhorn's insecurity—he never felt he was quite *American* enough. When I got Amanda pregnant, Dad thought maybe he'd have to forfeit his citizenship or something. It was irrational. He knew that. But emigration—from a poor post-war England—was his great achievement in life. It used up his courage. The Schlegels, Amanda's parents, had his number. Informally they retained George Lazen, the senior warden at St. Matthias and a ruthless divorce lawyer, to soften Dad up. It was all very cordial, that meeting. But Dad depended on church (and Masonic) connections. Without them his never very competent printing business would've gone under. That, and the threat of expensive legal action, buckled him. He hated me—for his own cowardice. From that afternoon onward Dad grew and kept a beard. He was incognito even at the dinner table . . .

Mother didn't interfere. Her contract with the world was roughly this: I won't bother you, if you don't tell me to stop drinking. And Amanda—she would've disemboweled herself with a coat hanger, I know that, had someone shown her how to do it. And yet Amanda had seduced me. (What a fretful, stealthy, unimaginative coupling it was.) We didn't need a condom, she said: this was her safe time. Still, they all blamed it on me.

All except Tony. I remember that now. He came home from college to give me moral support. Not that it did Tony any good with Mom and Dad—they were furious with him—but their fury deflected attention away from me a bit. And I was grateful for that.

When he heard about Amanda's abortion Father Mac forced George

Lazen to resign as senior warden. He made me first acolyte. The church went into convulsions: it seethed. Lazen despised me. It isn't easy for a sixteen-year-old boy to withstand the mature and elegant loathing of a powerful adult male. I spent my Sundays withering in front of him.

Now I'm a priest. That'll teach 'em.

Getting Amanda pregnant was such a suicidal mistake, not like me at all. I'm really a decent chap, an ethical drudge, in fact. A respecter of authority. A suicidal act it was—almost as bad as, well, running a topless bar. Do Episcopalians come in here often? I hope not—and they should be ashamed of themselves if they do.

At eight the shifts change. Two bartenders (both female) and a drink hostess (or two) replace Pearl. Leonard arrives, yawning. And, on weekends, a tall, skinny kid with long hair named Freddy works as assistant bouncer. The cash registers are turned over. Single dollar bills are crucial—they're the chief unit of exchange for those who tip. Singles circulate constantly. From customer to girl. From girl to bartender. From bartender back to customer again. It isn't unusual for a bartender to give a customer sixteen singles in change for a twenty dollar bill—after deducting $4.00 for the drink. On any given night there must be as many as 500 singles circulating around The Car. This makes it a hemorrhoidal pain to count up receipts at day's end. Quarters, too, must be available for the Joker Poker machine (though these don't have to be counted and rolled as often). Around six, people start coming in. A lot of people. I'm kind of astounded—there are usually twenty men standing against the walls from 8 p.m. until at least 2 a.m. Figure a transient attendance of nearly 100. Figure even one beer for each of these (and most drink a lot more than that)—The Smoking Car must be doing very well, indeed. I don't think anyone who knew Tony as an adolescent could've imagined—in the slightest—that he would own a place like this. He was Huck Finn. A good old kid with freckles.

Yet every other hour now I get a report about my brother that modulates my POV. Tanya was leaving around 8 p.m., and one of the Silicone Sisters said something uncomplimentary under her breath.

"You don't like her," I said.

"None of us do. Her shit don't smell. Just because she did a bank commercial. I mean she was an extra, just standing in line for a deposit."

"She dances pretty well."

"She dances lousy. This isn't, you know, the ballet. It looks stupid—a Swan Lake routine when your tits're going boing-boing."

"Well, now that you mention it—"

"And if you knew what she did t'Tony . . ."

"What?"

"Oh, I'm not supposed t'say. Forget it."

"Say."

"I shouldn't."

"Say or you're fired." I was surprised at myself. But it worked.

"Well, if you're *that* way about it. Tanya and him were getting it on. And I think, from what I hear, she hit him up for lotsa cash."

"Hear from where?"

"Around. It's all around. Everyone would tell you that. Tony was tough, but that one had his number."

"What about this other girl, Rita?"

"Oh, she hated it. He never lent her anything. She was jealous of Tanya."

"You wanna work here?"

"Sure. Hey, what's the strong arm stuff? You think you're Tony?"

"You wanna work here, you stop talking about my brother. And that goes for your clone on stage. Got it?"

She nodded. She really just nodded. And a surge of power—I'll do big penance for that one—rushed through me. I understand what Tony must've felt. It was something you could get addicted to.

Bubbles and a girl named Shane were dancing. Alternately, in a pair, Mayo and one Silicone Sister. I don't know how I'll ever keep their names and faces straight—especially as I tend to look away when I'm talking with any of them. I counted 150 names in Tony's notebook. (Seeing his handwriting there made my throat go thick.) Some names are active, some inactive—and two or three new ones come along each day. But there is a core group of ten or twelve that you could call regular. On Sunday (yes, this place is actually open on Sunday, from 8 p.m. to 3 a.m.) we use just two girls. Monday, Tuesday and Wednesday we use six: a pair alternating from 11:45 a.m. to 7:45 p.m., a pair from 5:30 p.m. to 12:30 a.m., and a pair from 7:30 p.m. to 4 a.m. This means that from 5:30 p.m. to 12:30 a.m., the busiest period, the shifts overlap, and we have two girls dancing at the same time. Thursday, Friday and Saturday we use eight: two extra from 7:30 p.m. to 4 a.m. So from 7:30 p.m. to 12:30 a.m. we have three girls on a very crowded stage. That means I'm responsible for booking 44 dancers a week. This is not going to be easy.

. . .

And is it ever, oh, boh-ring. All new to me and still I'm bored. I'd rather watch someone x-ray luggage at LaGuardia. If you're not here to get drunk or take a dancer home to bed (every john's dream), then the whole thing is just deafening dullness. (I must get earplugs.) There's a good pinball machine called Firehouse, but I don't score well (an emblem of my character—I can never bring myself to bang the sides of the machine, the way big league scorers do). Also—it doesn't look right, the boss playing pinball. Here I am already trying to find the proper, you know, *demeanor* for a topless bar king.

The electronic poker game has a large following. I don't quite understand the fascination—paying twenty-five cents to play an imaginary hand of five card draw. I mean, you could do the same thing with a deck of cards. We have a big sign that says FOR FUN ONLY, NO CASH PAY-OUTS WHATEVER, so it can't be the money, I think. I went over and played a couple of quarters desultorily—but my presence seemed to dampen everyone's fun. Most started to drift away, and Leonard seemed so passionately to be rooting against me that I gave it up.

Leonard has become a problem: I mean, yes, I have asked for instruction, but that doesn't mean Leonard has to climb inside my ear. Mostly what he talks about is people: customers, and what makes them go berserk. In fact, of course, he's trying to scare me off his turf with tales of violence. How he had to screw this guy's head off like a gas-tank cap or pry that man's eyes out. New York war stories.

The Smoking Car has been robbed twice at gunpoint: customers and dancers down flat on their stomachs, professional heists. One time Leonard wasn't on duty. Once it was just too crowded for him to do anything (humanitarian that he is). Leonard carries a gun—he's going to bring his license in and show it to me. He suggests I get one, too (especially since I plan on taking the receipts home every night). Leonard hasn't said so, but I assume Tony also carried a gun. (That's in keeping with my memories—Tony had an air pistol when he was twelve and he always appreciated a well-made weapon. I think he did some hunting, if I remember. That may be why Tony bought his place in the Poconos.) But me? The six-gun priest? Hopalong Clergyman? Somehow I don't picture it.

Meanwhile it's just hard enough finding a place to *stand.* Behind the bar is no good: people expect me to pour them drinks. For that, as I've said, we have two bartenderesses at night—and one or two cocktail hostesses to service the tables. Scanty dress is required: leotards and deep-cut necklines. The two regular behind-the-bar girls are Melissa, who stutters (y'want a B-bb-bud Light?) and Friend (her real name), who seems to be asleep on her feet.

When I stand at the rear end of the bar, near the kitchen, I'm stuck with Leonard. Still, this is probably the best place. From there you can watch the door and most of the tables. And you can see the stage, if you want to, reflected in the bar mirror. There seems to be a prejudice against anyone from the staff sitting down. Takes up a paying customer's seat. But I don't think I can put up with hearing about Lennie's adventures eight hours a day—on Topless Time.

(I say Topless Time because topless joints, figuratively and actually, are in a time warp. All topless clocks are set ten minutes fast—I'm still not used to it. The reason is utilitarian: it helps us clear everyone out before the 4 a.m. city curfew. But it means that dancers dance and things are done at The Car by *our* time. For someone like me who rushes in and out on various errands—I might as well be crossing a small International Time Line all day long. Add the night-day alternation and my biological clock is overwound. Add to this the fact that Kay's watch gains about ten minutes a day *anyhow,* as if trying to synchronize itself with Topless Time, and . . .)

And besides, who can hear? Every conversation is a double crostic puzzle: a word here, a word there. I've given up asking people to repeat their remarks—they aren't worth it, most times. Of course, what the Boss says is super-significant—so I have to chew my cud twice over. And most of what I say doesn't bear repetition—certainly not to me. So we learn to nod and laugh when the other guy is laboring through a joke. You can't call it a deepening experience.

My salvation (or my doom) may be Joe Solomon, the retired homicide detective. I like him. For all the violence he's seen (he's been decorated for heroism six times), Joe cultivates an almost feminine manner. Talks in an overprecise, slightly fey voice—under which there is a long habit of authority. He's gray and balding (there's a big scar on his scalp) and kind of sallow-skinned—I don't think his health can be all that good. Joe is a widower and sometimes goes to the track with Pearl: they come from the same part of Jackson Heights. But, best of all, Joe carries a miniature chess board everywhere. I haven't played in a while: still, we seem well matched. Around ten he and I went outside (the air conditioning is on OVERKILL, I'm bound to get a cold) and played a couple of speed games on the fender of my Lincoln.

Joe told me he played with (and most often lost to) my brother. So I tried a little exploratory surgery. I asked Joe what the police thought about Tony's disappearance—was it foul play? I regretted that. Asking.

"From what I gather—and I'm not in the office much any more—there seems t'be some cynicism in the department."

"Which means?"

"Tony was upta something—whether this was just adultery or something more profitable, I dunno."

"You think he's alive?"

"He struck me as a man who survives. Check."

"You liked him."

"A great deal. Not your average topless capo. A bright man, but sometimes, if you'll pardon me, not so *schmartdt*. Listen, Mike, I'm gonna tell you something. I'm gonna tell you just once. Because I like The Car and, I'd hate Pearl t'be out of a job. Just once and no names."

"Uh-oh. Yes?"

"Drugs are being dealt in there. A considerable amount of drugs. People are aware of this. And—unless it's cleaned up soon—action will come down."

"Christ. What should I do?"

"Stop it."

"Christ," I said again. "They'd close us down, I suppose. Right?" He shrugged. "Even if I knew nothing about it?"

"You're supposta know. You're management."

"Are you saying Tony knew?"

"I am of two minds about that."

"Maybe he tried t'stop them—and they got rid of him."

"It's a possibility." Joe forked my queen and my king. "You're a nudnik idiot t'get involved in this."

"You're telling me."

"One more thing. It's illegal t'pay off on the Joker Poker machine."

"We don't. There's a sign—"

"Holy Moses, where did they get you from, a monastery?" (Has Pearl told him anything?) " 'There's a sign,' he says."

"Hold on now. I may be new on the job but I'm not—"

"You're a babe in the woods. Though, give you—give anyone—a month in that place and—" He shrugged.

"You seem t'know enough t'get us shut down a half dozen times. So? Why hasn't it happened?"

"I'm retired."

"Isn't that complicity?"

"Maybe—but I like The Car. Tony and I had the same taste in women. I could reminisce t'myself about my lost manhood."

"Don't break my heart."

"Clean it up fast, Mike. You've got hours, not even days."

This depressed me no end. I can hardly ask Ethel for help—beyond a certain amount of moral support. I'm the male: she's hired me to straighten her business out. I have no doubt that Leonard Krause at least condones (if he hasn't instigated) whatever illegalities there may be at The Car. But, frankly, I'm afraid to make a move. Both physically afraid (yes, Leonard is an awesome pile of flesh) and afraid, also, that I'll find out my brother has been behind it all.

Worse, there was a guy waiting for me when I walked into The Car. He got up from his table and snatched at the back of my shirt. In so doing, his fingernails broke flesh. I saw Leonard and Freddy start lumbering toward me. But the guy was shorter than I am, and very soused, so he didn't seem to present a dramatic threat. He did, however, seem mightily annoyed.

"You Wilson?" he said.

"Yes."

"Well you or somebody owes me $7500 bucks. And I want it. I'm not gonna be jerked around, you get me?"

"I don't even know you," I said, and I walked on, but he caught at my shirt again. "Take your hand off."

"Not 'til I get some satisfaction." Leonard came over: he had the smile and saunter of a trained assassin. Freddy held something solid and leaden-looking in his fist—welded knuckles? A cosh?

"Get off him," Leonard said. The man got off.

"He owes me, $7500—you know that, Leonard. Tony was gonna get me the TV sets. You heard us talking."

"What is this?" I asked.

"This guy is a pain, Mike. He's always pretending t'do big deals—he does shit. Now he's getting out."

Leonard, upsy-daisy, just lifted the poor man by his skin—two nasty handholds under the armpit—and then carried him out to Northern Blvd. I should've followed: I should've tried to secure more information—but ignorance is bliss. In extenuation, there was no way to prove the guy's allegations: it was his word against Tony's—there are advantages to being missing. But *televisions.* There is something particularly sordid about televisions.

I was sitting at the bar around 3:30, when Bubbles came over to me. My brain had gone punchy with rock reverb and existential angst. Bubbles was dressed in an old poncho and, at best, she looked like a bag lady. It is amazing—the metamorphoses continue to shock me—

how a shlumpy, plain female can become—with makeup, glitter, lighting and her God-given bare flesh—a paralyzing vamp. Women are protean. They change so much more than men do. And Bubbles was an extreme case. All glitz and glamour on stage. Campy, overdone—broad as a gay's imitation of Bette Davis. And then—shazam!—a dowdy burlap sack on her way out into the street.

Anyhow, she sat beside me.

"Lemme buy *you* a drink," she said.

"That'd be a waste of money. Anyhow, I don't drink on the job."

"Yeah. But it's a gesture."

"Well, thanks."

"Here's another gesture." Bubbles took a key ring out and handed it to me. "My apartment's on the ground floor. Here's the address."

"Not tonight—" I handed the keys back. But why, I thought, did I say, "Not tonight?" I meant "never," didn't I? Or was I just being polite?

"Keep 'em."

"Nope. Hey, you don't even know me, I could sneak into your place and rape you."

"Please. Just don't rip off my VCR, I'm taping the Bon Jovi special tomorrow."

"You're cute," I said. I pushed the keys into her bag. "I like you. But I've got lots on my mind right now."

"How romantic. It's a big mistake—you playing hard t'get. Men who play hard t'get obsess me out. It'd be much better for you t'take me home tonight—then I'd get it all out of my system. It'd save you time in the long run."

"Very persuasive. But I'd be lousy company."

"Have it your way."

"Did you know Tony?"

"Sure. And I never got anywhere with him neither."

"I'm glad t'hear it. Have a good night."

"Those dark eyes, those dark brown, lost beagle eyes. Give me a tumble some day. You and me, we can make sheet lightning together. I'll raise your sperm count. I'll—"

"Good night, Bubbles."

"My real name is Cherry."

"Good night, Cherry."

So here I am at 5 a.m.—home amid the dolls and the money. As topless bar takes go, I have no idea if four thousand three hundred dollars is good box office—to me it's almost a year's salary after taxes. If money's the root of all evil, this, I think, may be the root cellar.

I'll speak to Ethel tomorrow: I don't look forward to it.

My brother is dead or dying: tonight I have an eerie premonition of that. There are just too many people who didn't like him. How or why he died, I don't know—but there are motives enough. I've learned that. He prospected in a dark territory. He crossed the border. And I think, for a little time at least, I'll have to follow him there.

I haven't prayed in two days. I must find a place to worship. My brother is dead.

Who was he?

Who am I?

SATURDAY, JUNE 25

Had an extremely unpleasant and even perplexing discussion with Ethel this a.m. When I got up she was already out at the pool with, eldest to youngest, Amy, Wendy, Lois and Little Ellen. But she rushed to make me breakfast. Tough and businesslike as she may be, Ethel seems dutiful around me—I'm sure she was that way around Tony. And the girls reflect this: they seem like little housewives.

Ethel was in a good mood: receipts, apparently, are up. The police got a report that someone answering Tony's description was seen in Seattle last week. I didn't share my gut feeling with Ethel—that Tony is gone. But, despite her buoyancy, Ethel can't be in a very good space. Either her husband is dead, probably rubbed out (for bootlegging, God, TV sets?). Or he's in another city—apparently willing to start a new life without his family. Not what you'd call a validation of her womanhood.

"Someday," said little Wendy, wearing her totally flat bikini bra, "I'm gonna work in my daddy's restaurant."

"Over my corpse," said Ethel. "Four girls—only a madwoman would try bringing up four girls at this particular moment in American history. That mustache is coming in just like Tony's. The resemblance is spooky."

"So people say.

"Women after your ass?"

"Nah. It's just perfunctory. Flirt with the boss. I haven't been tempted yet."

"You're doing a good job, I can tell that already. You're straightening things out."

"Yes. And they're gonna be straighter on Monday when I close down the Joker Poker machine. They've been paying off on it—and that's illegal." Ethel made a patronizing face.

"Is that wise? I think they only give a fine for first offenses." I hesitated: I put my fork down and stared at Ethel for a moment. I was willing her to shut up: but she couldn't. "If they catch on, we'll pay the fine. No big deal."

"It's against the law."

"Tony—"

"Mike. My name is Mike."

"I'm sorry."

"It's against the law. I'm gonna make a call and have them pick it up. It's the only way t'go—I can't supervise it every minute."

"Mike. The machine grosses two hundred bucks a day. That's six grand a month—that's our mortgage nut."

"Ethel—"

"I bet you've never seen a pay-out. Have you?"

"No. But I'm not stupid, Ethel. People don't donate six grand a month just t'watch little colored numbers blip on and off. Leonard or Pearl, they're paying out and you know it."

"No, I don't. Tony never said they were paying out. Why not give us the benefit of the doubt before you turn the machine off? You don't have evidence. You shouldn't ruin everything if you don't have evidence."

"I'm a priest. I'm not supposed t'condone even the appearance of evil."

"Listen." Ethel pulled two children into her lap. I realized they were all naked. Four sets of female genitals were staring at me. "If you catch them—close it down. I'll call the distributor myself. But innocent until proven guilty, right?"

"Right. But I'll catch them," I said.

"I can't get over how much like Tony you are."

I wanted to say, It's only on the surface. But I didn't.

4 a.m.

In my new apartment. So tired my eyes are crossed. And already, I know it, I've lost about 15% of my hearing acuity. My voice is as rough as a cheese grater. And my mind—my mind is like a nuclear pile. Bombarded by images.

Most of which, frankly, embarrass and disconcert me.

Out in Nebraska I was that wiseass kid from New York—the one with kinky ideas about sex. (That is: I refused to call gay men faggots or condemn their life-style out of hand.) Well, I *was* cool, I *am* from New York and I do know six hundred jokes about a rabbi and a priest on the golf course. But, in The Car, I'm life's eternal rookie up from Double A. Can't hit the curve.

And they know it. Especially the women. When Leonard says, "Motherfuck—fuck, mother, mothering fucking mother"—which is his way of wishing you a safe trip home—it doesn't bother me. When the 17th drunken Hispanic lifts his bottle of Miller and tells a dancer to sit on it, well . . . I cringe, but I understand. The man is drunk, he's earning $123 take-home, his wife is pregnant again, and *somebody* is gonna pay for it tonight. That's the main service—crude release—that we offer at The Car.

But, when I listen to the women . . . I just can't, you know, *place* them. Let me say, I think they're brighter—on average—than the men in The Car. But, I know, there are women of 24 on that stage with enough life experience credits to get a BA from NYU without taking a single course. They have *seen* so much. And they seem comfortable with it. It's like, I dunno, seeing hair in the armpits of a newborn infant. It doesn't belong.

I'm tired, but I've got to get this story down—it epitomizes what I mean. Thousand-volt culture shock.

One dancer tonight. Her stage name is Willow and she's older than most, maybe 32. Good figure, close friend of Pearl's apparently. Missing a couple of back teeth, and she drinks like a stevedore. But full of good spirit. Leonard says Willow flashes, but he hasn't caught her at it yet. Mind you—I *like* the woman. But this is the story Willow tells us in a voice that sounds like Our Lady of the Perpetual Bronx Cheer.

Let me try and imitate her—she's telling this to fifteen people at the bar, and pitching her voice so the boss—that simpleton—can hear. Me.

"Nick at Corleone's—you know, Corleone's, where once I got crabs from the rug doin' a floor show—Nick asks—he has his pecker on a string, so he can find it past his stomach—yeah, that Nick—he asks me t'do a stag party in his back room for about ten pre-yuppies, one of which is getting married and is a virgin still, Jesus help his bride. This guy isn't cleared for takeoff.

"So I say, Okay. It's the least I can do for the economy. And, before I start my dance, the host takes me aside, like he's a man of the world— me, t'me he's not someone I'd trust on the assembly line. So he says— big whisper—the groom-to-be still has his cherry. For an extra $200—an extra $200, The Wiz can't beat that price—for $200 would I take him t'my place, give him a big blue veiner, and let him, you know, *practice*—like he's learning t'ride a two-wheeler. Okay, I say. Hey, okay. 200 bucks—you're a prince. In advance, Mr. Prince.

"Okay.

"So okay.

"Okay.

"Comes three a.m. and Mr. Groom—who by this time would hit BONUS WHEN LIT on a breathalyzer—is all set up. Everyone is going hee-hee, and I'm having trouble even holdin' him up. But I am all over him, I am like his sweat. He thinks he has made a conquest. THERE ARE NO CONQUESTS FOR $200. Not in New York.

"Anyhow, I get him home and we're dry humping in the bedroom. 'Oh, oh, oh,' I say. 'Oh, oh, oh. Listen, let me get inta something more comfortable. You take your expensive suit off.' I mean, this is a child. I could feel maternal about him. BUT NOT FOR $200.

"So, listen, I strip off and go t'the kitchen. Then I take two hard-boiled eggs from the fridge and jam them up my twat. COLD. I think it sterilized me. Then, with my knees together, I go back into the bedroom, where Junior is now nude and wagging his tail.

" 'Oh, oh, oh,' I say. 'Take me, I'm ready.' Right? You got the picture? I'm lying there, legs spread, trying not t'laugh, and just when he's FINALLY got himself half-hard, just as he's about t'fall into me, I grunch and—ploop?—out pops an egg.

"There is silence. He's a little nearsighted and he's fumbling around.

" 'Hurry, hurry,' I say. 'I'm ready for you.'

" 'Uh,' he says." We all cracked up at this point. It was, I admit, pretty funny.

" 'Hurry, hurry.'

" 'Uh,' he says. 'I'm having some trouble down here.'

" 'What?' I say. 'You're driving me nuts.'

" 'Well,' he says. 'This. This just came out of you.'

"I sit bolt upright and I say, 'Jesus, I'm sorry—I must be having my period. How mortifying. I hope you'll forgive me.'

"And he has the egg in his hand and I'm trying not t'lose it and he says, 'I never realized—I never realized.' And I grunch down again and—ploop?—out comes egg number two and he says 'My God, another.'

" 'Jesus,' I said, 'thank God we didn't make love, it would've been twins.'

"And he—it was kind of sweet—he hands me the eggs and says, 'I'm not feeling too good. Can I go home now?'

"And I said, 'Sure. I've gotta do a lot of feminine things anyhow.' And I kissed him on the forehead. YOU DO NOT GET LAID FOR $200."

Well, y'hadda be there. It was funny. But—my God—what kind of woman can carry such a thing off? No woman I've ever known before. Shall we say I am dealing with a different sensibility here? I feel inept and stupid. And, frankly, a bit dull. Which is an unattractive feeling.

Then in comes a three-hundred-fifty-pound tube of Vaseline. Joe Linese, I am told, owner of Rabies, another topless joint maybe eight blocks up on Northern Boulevard. He has blood relations who kill people. At the moment, of course, I understand zip about all this. But, before I know it, Leonard and Freddy are out from behind the bar. Leonard is yelling "Get the fuck out, Joe. Just get the fuck out."

But Linese, who *lifts* his stomach with both hands when walking, Linese is not impressed by Leonard. He's barrel-up to the stage where Areola, or something, a snazzy Brazilian, and her sister are dancing. He yells, "You're both through, you work in this scum dump, you don't work for me. And I'll see you never get a green card."

Very pleasant, indeed. By this time Leonard has Linese by the collar. But Linese shrugs him off—"Eat my ass, Leonard, I've kicked your butt before, I'll kick it again. So where's the new boss—now they buried Tony with the Unknown Soldier in New Jersey?"

"I'm the new boss," I said. The place is SILENT for the first time. A break between records. I am standing at the O.K. Corral with a man who could kill me by sitting on me and I say, "I am the new boss." Incredible asshole, macho shit. I'm a priest, fer gosh's sake. And he says:

"You should die."

Meanwhile the Brazilian girls are crying and screaming in Portuguese. One has a shoe off.

"You take my girls, you should die."

"*Your* girls," I say. "These are people, not your personal property, first. Second, I did not until this minute know you owned a topless bar. And, third, it must be a shithouse if you own it."

Can you imagine, I said that. Okay, I was playacting and Leonard was behind me. But—my Lord—somehow I've developed a headlong crush on suicide.

At which point he—Linese—he hauls off, starts to torque his body. I think he's throwing a left, when—SPLAT—he gets hit in the face with a full glass of beer. I—Mike the Knife—I push him in a TOTALLY defensive gesture. Just to get out of his range—and Linese goes DOWN. Slipped in the beer, I think. He hits so hard, he busts a leg off the pinball machine. Leonard and Freddy start kicking him—their position having improved. And Linese sort of rolls out the front door like a 55 gallon drum.

And who threw the beer? Not Leonard. Not Freddy. Bubbles, who isn't even dancing, threw the beer.

I bought her another. And gave her a Saturday night booking. This firm, I want you to know, rewards loyalty.

P.S.—When I came out at 4 a.m., my car antenna was bent into a half-swastika. Linese strikes me as an unforgiving person.

I begin to understand why Tony changed. Just give me a few more nights like this.

SUNDAY, JUNE 26TH

An uneasy afternoon.

I dragged myself to church this morning—in disguise. The phantom worshipper. I don't want people in the Episcopal community to know I'm back home just yet. (Though I must make some contact with Bishop Plunk of Queens Diocese before long.) The mustache is coming in. But that wasn't enough—I parted my hair down the middle like a silent-film gigolo and wore Tony's camouflage jacket. Running The Car has made me fugitive and deceitful. I feel like I've infiltrated the world.

There was a supply priest at St. Anne's in Elmhurst—man of 60 or 70, probably retired. The Holy Ghost takes a vacation in July and August—it's an Episcopal tradition. No one recognized me (I spoke, at the door, with a southern accent—"Well now, jes visitin' the Apple from Moultrie, Georgia, y'all.")

I learned one thing this morning—the disconcerting power of naked-ness. Flesh signals to us. It engages the mind, the endocrine system—and, yes, even the spirit. All the resonance of Christian symbolism—cross and crucifixion, bread and wine—is gathered, it would seem, to counteract and answer the image of a single naked woman. Of course, guilt had supersensitized me. But my meditational life this morning was like an obstacle course. Breasts interposed them-selves everywhere—even breasts that didn't interest me. I had to turn away from the bare, sinewy thighs of Jesus in a stained glass window of the Crucifixion. They were, God save me, suggestive.

I understand what's happening, mind you. The animal is always there—hanging down like a python from some tree limb above. Christians aren't naive about this: we respect the body's power. Jesus sampled it. And in some senses—I think of John Donne—the one apt image for God's grace (powerful, ruthless, instinctive) is a mighty orgasm. Rape me, God, Donne said. Please.

And the greatest peril in sin is despair. The blasphemous fear that God isn't, can't be, loving enough to forgive. That BY OUR OWN ACTS of evil we can separate ourselves from Him. Only a loss of faith—a denial of His being—can accomplish that. But, she-eet, how painful it is, how poisonous, to encounter God when you are in a state of sin. My mind ran and hid all morning. And yet, in some ways, I was more alive to my faith than good-but-boring Father Mike Wilson ever was in the dry heat of Nebraska. More alive—because I'm playing chickie with damnation.

And, Lord knows, my diary is more interesting. What would Kay think, reading this? Kay would say, "Never mind John Donne and all the nice reasoning—you're an irresponsible male on the loose. And you're angry, young man, angry at your own priestly vocation." Never mind lustful, proud and cunning.

Kay would be right.

I have this melodramatic image of myself—St. John on Patmos, St. Anthony—tempted by lewd female demons. Maybe, you know, this is my chance to prove myself in the big arena of really athletic sainthood. Maybe, on the other hand, this is my last chance to get laid before the rigorous, inelastic life of my priesthood sets in for good. I begin to think I rushed—out of guilt, out of self-disgust—toward ordination. I should've lived some more.

Because these aren't female demons: these are coeds from New Paltz and aspiring dental assistants. If they have power, it is because I've given it to them. This isn't Patmos—this is a middle class topless bar in Queens. I could've walked right out last Thursday. I have led no one but myself into temptation. I haven't been compromised. Yet. But I can feel demoralization rising. I've eaten with the devil and my spoon isn't very long.

Twice this afternoon—as I lay writing in my room, afraid of my own nakedness—twice women have left messages on my Phone-Mate. Brazilians. I suppose I'm living the supreme male fantasy. Lust and power (and more money than I've ever earned in my life). Women are calling to ask if they may, please, undress in front of me. I am Paris, judging. I am the sultan in his harem. I am—

I am a priest.

Worse—my very solitude is sensual. It's been years since I was alone, unsupervised by the world. I walk naked from bathroom to bedroom. I have a sixpack of Amstel in my fridge—I haven't touched it, but I could. I could go out and buy a leather jacket with studs and chains. Such *opportunity*. Wouldn't I be a fool not to embrace it? Father Mac is dead. My collar is buried at the bottom of my rucksack. I am a plainclothesman of the spirit—looking for a bribe. On the take.

The apartment Ethel and Pearl arranged for me is pleasant—and rent free. One sunny bedroom above a florist's shop. Crushed flower scents come up through the floor. I have a bed, a TV and a bureau. One armchair and a throw rug in the living/dining room. The walls haven't been painted. I can tell where posters have hung. My predecessor must've had greasy hair. His skull is outlined on the wall above the head of my bed. But I won't imbue this place with my personality—no art reproductions or bric-a-brac. No cross, either. This is temporary.

Though, I suppose, I might at least unpack my bag.

Where is my brother? I'm afraid, most of all, that he disappeared years ago. That the boy who could fill me with confidence . . . the boy before whom I had no secrets . . . that kid who knew Mom and Dad and walked me across crowded intersections . . . Tony . . . Him . . . I'm afraid that he never was. Could I have been so mistaken about the person I loved most in the world? If so—if so, I am a blind man. If so, I can be mistaken about anything.

I've filled this entire notebook, just about.

I'm going to nap now. The mass this morning—the teeter-totter between flesh and spirit—has winded me. Then maybe I'll go to Manhattan and catch a PG movie.

Somehow I just don't feel like showing up at The Car on *Sunday* night. I dunno, call me finicky, it's an instinct I have. A matter of, well, taste. The Lord forgives sin. But tackiness is another matter.

Isn't it, Lord? Bring Tony back—the Tony I once knew. I'm in danger, I know it. Let me not hurt others in the fall—if it must be—of my kamikaze soul.

5 a.m.

It shames me to write this—but, yes, I went to The Car tonight. After all.

I'm having trouble relating to Ethel, that's what. I don't know who she is. Is Ethel just my sister-in-law? (But I hardly know her.) Is she my employer? (But I don't have to work here.) Who is she? The mother of my nieces, Tony's children—I guess Ethel is primarily that to me. (Damn, I forgot to send Amy a birthday card.) But Ethel has a tone

. . . an attitude . . . that makes me recite psalms in my head to keep from raising my voice. Like somehow I *owe* her this duty. Like—Tony being AWOL—I'm responsible for child support. As if I were a cosigner in the marriage.

Ethel called The Car. I wasn't there. Ethel called here in a snit. Freddy manages the place alone on Sunday night, and Ethel doesn't trust Freddy. It's my job. "I really think you should be there." So—with a bad grace—I agreed to go. "Say thank you to Uncle Mike, Amy." "Thank you, Uncle Mike." How can you have a discussion under these circumstances? When I find out where Tony is, I'm gonna run there and hide from Ethel with him.

But—as The Car goes—it was an acceptable evening. Only about a dozen customers. (Most people, Mike, are too decent to attend a topless bar on Sunday night.) I was able to tune the music down and the lights up so I could read a bit of *Seven Storey Mountain.* Freddy isn't Leonard—he gives me a wide berth. We had two girls dancing: Gudrun, from Germany, who has an iron cross tattooed between her breasts, and a black girl called—believe it—Plethora. Which name is justified by the enormity of her breasts. Total take $217. Freddy could've skimmed the whole thing, for all I care.

But I did meet Connie, who bartends on Sundays. It was slow and quiet enough for us to talk civilly. A very useful conversation. I now know a lot more about the topless game than I did this morning—and from a woman's POV.

First of all, Connie is beautiful: in the Raquel Welch mode—great Coca-Cola colored eyes. At least five foot ten. I was checking a liquor invoice and she totaled a six-figure column in her head. We are talking superior synapses here. Connie graduated summa cum laude from Cornell. (Me, I was busy pretending I hadn't gone to college. Partly because I need to disguise myself. More likely because I was embarrassed to mention New Paltz in that academic company.) She has been accepted at Cornell med school—but will be taking a year off.

How, I asked—as men must ask Connie two hundred times a night—how did a bright girl like you end up with an endless cleavage on Northern Blvd.?

Well, while in college, Connie got involved with some feminist group. Her chapter made a field trip, I guess you'd call it, to 42nd Street. They invaded a peep show, one of those places where you stick quarters in, a window slides up, and a naked woman does . . . whatever they do. The woman, Connie said, was black. And when Connie's companion, another female, told the black woman she was being exploited, the companion was spat upon. "I got three children t'feed. If I'm sploited, I just hope they sploit me more next week. And don't knock it when you don't know it, Sister."

Connie thought this was a legitimate argument. So she hired on as a topless dancer the next day.

Well, I said, do you feel exploited?

Sometimes. "Then again," she said, "I've saved twenty-two thousand dollars this year."

The figures, in fact, are staggering. I guess I knew that—but until tonight I hadn't done any hard arithmetic. A fairly attractive girl who works five nights can make over $1000 per week, *tax free*. A really attractive girl (with an ingratiating way) can count on at least $1500. Twice Connie has made more than $1,000 in a single *night*. Think about it—$75,000 a year, take-home. An executive at GM would have to gross $150,000 to pull that down. A twenty-year-old, with no education, will earn more in one year than her father can—and he has thirty years seniority.

Connie figures we could pay for the space program just by taxing topless dancers. At this moment, as Pearl suggested, the nation of Brazil is entirely funded by its breast export trade. (Public toplessness, after all, is accepted there.) A Brazilian girl earning $1000 a week American is automatically one of the richest people in Rio. The mind begins to bend.

A topless dancer is a private supplier of entertainment—we make all our girls sign a waiver that says "I am responsible for paying my own payroll taxes." But one woman in 20—Connie is that one here—will pay taxes at all. That's why Connie has been working behind the bar one day a week. She declares about $20,000 in bartender income—and launders the rest through her parents' savings account. They then give her the cash back, up to the annual IRS limit for gifts from Mom and Dad. I see why Connie graduated summa cum.

But, though the average topless girl is more than well off, she is also creditless: outside the system. She can't get a mortgage. She can't really invest. Even a savings account is suspect. So she tends to spend what she has—anyway, even the most immoral girl feels guilty about merchandising her body. The money is tainted. Incriminating. They piss it away. These are, mind you, kids. Kids who—six months ago, maybe—had just a $10 allowance to squeeze through the week with. Now dollar bills come OUT OF THE AIR. Grown men, like daddy, offer fur coats and trips to Bermuda. It could make your head rotate.

Anyhow, we're dealing with a terrific ambivalence here. "It's sexy," Connie said. "The power you have over men. I don't deny it. Half the time you feel like a slut—JESUS, I'M NAKED HERE—half the time you feel like a goddess. Hell, I'm a bookworm. I never thought in terms of my erotic power. But look, I'll be able t'pay at least my first year of med school without a loan. It can really distort your standards. Well, I'm a Leo. I like t'perform anyway. Listen, they say the two most powerful groups in America are men over 60 with at least $10,000,000. And beautiful women under 25. Which is why you see them together so often."

Ve-ery interesting. Connie also thinks that topless dancers, in general, have a low self-image. Many are children of alcoholic parents. "A lot of these girls're dancing for their fathers. Hoping Poppa will come in. See, Dad. I'm attractive, even if you didn't think so. See, the other middle-aged drunks care for me." The money and the attention are intoxicating.

I asked Connie if many girls were dancing to support a drug habit. Ten or fifteen percent at most, she thought. "Coke is part of the business. Probably four out of five girls will do coke if it's available. You'll see a guy tip with a folded up dollar bill—inside there'll be a line of coke. But they aren't hooked on it. It's the *money* that addicts you. It spoils you for 9 to 5 work. It's a trap. If you see me here next year at this time—remind me I told you that."

I think maybe I've made a friend here. Someone I can compare notes with. I wouldn't ask Connie to spy for me—but she can, you know, *interpret* things. Correct my impressions. I now understand what Joe Solomon meant when he said, "Next life, I wanna come back as a smart, beautiful bimbo."

MONDAY, JUNE 27TH

Afternoon
Bought Ear Stopples at Woolworth's.

Another weird day. My mind is as rootless as an air plant. The mad, paradoxical nature of this situation—man of God running a topless bar—exerts a kind of grotesque heft. Its own unwholesome gravity. Every ten minutes or so I fibrillate with nervous twitches. I touch where my clerical collar would be. Pearl, I know, looks at me like I was me-shuga, and she KNOWS my position. The others must simply presume that one of my cylinders has split.

Found out today The Car *always* throws Pearl a big birthday party. Twelve Dynamic Dancers. Free matzo-ball soup all night. (Made by Leonard, who probably squeezes an armpit into the pot. Ugh.) To this annual event, I am told, even Ethel will be drawn. The absentee owner. Interesting, that. How will she comport herself? As queen, as apprentice widow, as naive mother of four? As boss?

Meanwhile Pearl makes it VERY CLEAR that she would be HURT if the anniversary of her birth weren't accorded due respect. I think she'd like alternate side parking rules to be suspended. Pearl wants advertising. She wants invitations sent out. Free drinks for her friends. A BONUS maybe. These have been traditions at The Car. And she would like the new regime to honor them. Hey, like Leonard says, it's not my money. And—besides—I need to stay on Pearl's good side. She has the goods on me. First girl comes over and says, "Father, pray, is my G-string crooked?" and I'm gone.

If I'm not punted outta the priesthood before then.

Would that be a relief? You haven't the courage to quit, Mike, but maybe you're brave enough to get fired. Is that it?

I can see you working entry level at Bear, Stearns. And writing useless screenplays about St. Herman of Alaska on weekends. Picking up girls who might feel sorry for a defrocked man of the cloth. And may I remove your frock, too, dear?

Haven't thought about Kay once. Unless it's What-would-Kay-think-of-this-bimbo? So I'm building a case against Kay. Beats building a case against myself.

This afternoon—because my mind has been working like a plasma torch—I had a small revelation.

"Pearl," I said, "y'know what makes the obscene business we're in tolerable?"

"The fuckin' money," she says. "What else?"

"No, no," I said. "I mean tolerable to the *spirit*. Barely tolerable."

"I give up," she says. "What makes it barely whatever t'the fuckin' spirit?"

"The music," I said. I'd noticed that a vague embarrassment settles over the girls, over the entire place, between songs. "The music puts clothes on them, sort of. Movement, rhythmic movement, too. Nudity in movement isn't as vulgar. But between songs all you have up there is a naked housewife padding around her bedroom. They look at their fingernails. They bend down like, you know, people, not sex idols—and they try t'yank their jeans on, which no one can do seductively. Y'see what I mean? Without the music we're all just a bunch of cheap peeping Toms."

"You been eatin' bad mushrooms?" Pearl asked.

She then resumed her continuing monologue—it's called either "A Short Life of Pearl Metzger" or "Management Skills for the 1990's Topless CEO." Every day I learn a little more . . . For instance: one is supposed to monitor employee body weight. "Say you see a girl," says Pearl, "she's lost about 15 pounds in the last six weeks. What does it tell you?" Uh, she's on a diet, I say. "Maybe," says Pearl. "But go-go girls do not have—whatchacallit—discipline. And they eat *trayf* all day, not to mention the calories in a glass beer. They're full of gas. No, it's more likely she's on cocaine or uppers. So you make a mental memo to watch.

"*Gaining* weight—it could be they've gone off drugs. Or they're knocked up. Nipples can tell you a whole lot: they tend to get darker on a pregnant woman. By the way—a woman with dark brown nipples, who isn't pregnant, no matter how white she may be otherwise, she has schwartzer blood in her."

Bullshit, I thought. Incidentally, we have only two black girls working. This is a white middle-class neighborhood: call it racism, but white men in Queens do not integrate their sexual fantasies. Maybe ten percent of our clientele is black, and that got Pearl started on the black pimp, white prostitute relationship—certainly one of the more bizarre psychosexual phenomena in the human universe. Not that topless girls tend to turn tricks—apparently it's almost unheard of. (Why be a hooker when you can earn more—disease free—just going around without a bra?) But white prostitutes, according to Pearl, have no use for white men—because they *pay* for sex. Black men, on the other hand, almost NEVER pay: it's a macho thing. So, to a hooker, the black man represents another—and more alluring—species. Someone *she* has to pay. A real man, hard to get. Unlike the white customer for whom sex is a function of his economic power.

Then my (my?) second afternoon girl went up—a blond Brazilian with buck teeth named Magdalena, who has NO English whatever. And Pearl said, "Okay. Call her down. She doesn't know better, but she's breaking the rules."

"How?"

"Look."

I looked. G-string? No, it didn't reveal too much.

"I give up."

"She's wearing glitter." Yes, there were gold mica flecks in her hair. And a shiny yellow brick road between her breasts. Sexy, it looked. "So?"

"So she'll come down, she'll sit with a customer. He'll put an arm around her—his jacket'll pick up six million fuckin' glitter dots. Tonight he'll come home, kiss the kids and his wife will hit him with the Cuisinart. Your customers are seventy percent married men. You haveta protect them: it says NO GLITTER, NO PERFUME in the locker room, but she can't read English. Before every girl's first set, you should give her a sniff. You don't want The Car sued as corespondent in a divorce case, do you?"

I guess I don't. But the thought that I, Rev. Michael Wilson, should be *smelling* women—like some dog around a bitch in heat—is distasteful to say the least.

"Here she comes," Pearl groused. "Miss Tulip in her dark glasses. It's not black enough in here already—how she doesn't step on her own tits is beyond me. That's another one has the hots f'you."

And Pearl left me to Tulip's hots. A sexy thing, but she disturbs me no end. It's like there's the smell of something dead around Tulip. You don't want to look under the bed and find out. Tulip (her real name is Berry) stares at me: then she laughs. She poses—head on arm, arm on bar. Head back, breasts back. Then she does some complex number with her cigarette—like out of a Bogart-Bacall movie. She's either got some advanced form of cerebral palsy or she's trying to signal me.

Also, there is something in her tone, her accent, that brings my brother back. It's Proustian. Tulip/Berry is a Queens girl: I guess it's her speech rhythm. I could remember the kids, on a summer night, yelling up, "Toe-knee, Toe-knee. You goin' t'the Itch tonight?" Tony always carried a little canvas bag with him. His spikes in it, or his cleats— depending on the sport season. A towel. His glove. Vitalis hair oil. A comb. What else? Baseball cards. Some comic books. The thing was, wherever you saw him, on the street, in school—Tony looked like he was packed to go. On the move.

Anyhow, this afternoon, what Tulip/Berry said made me antsy. She might know something—she has the look that people get when they're holding a pat straight flush. What I mean, I guess: Tulip/Berry isn't afraid of me. Already I'm accustomed to a certain, uhm, deference here. Tulip doesn't defer. Why is this? She's tan, brown-eyed and—Jesus, I don't know what color her hair is, she uses so many wigs. Small breasted, long belly, sensual appendix scar—but not good looking enough to show *no* deference. To *me*.

"You know," Tulip/Berry said, "being cool is one thing. I like a cool guy. But, at a certain point, it becomes unpleasant. It becomes bad manners."

"I'm sorry, I don't get your drift."

"This is a sleazy business. I don't pretend I'm Isadora Duncan or anything. But you could look at me: I'm doing my job—it isn't an easy job—and I'm still a woman. Don't act like Mr. Superior just because you got your clothes on and I don't. You're part of this act."

"No, I'm not a part really. I'm doing this as a favor because there's been a tragedy in my family. Frankly, if I avert my eyes, you should feel honored. It means I don't like taking advantage of you."

"Hey, it's not only me. All the girls feel the way I do. It's like you're judging us. It's like you're a priest or something."

And I said, "I'm not a priest." It was late in the afternoon for cocks to crow—but . . . "And I'm not judging you—I'm giving you space."

"Mike," she said. She put her hand on my shoulder. "Mike, I'd rather you looked at me."

"Okay. I'll look at you. Ugh. So why don't you look at me in return? Why d'you wear those dumb glasses?"

"I've got a stye," Tulip/Berry said. "I'm going up now—this dance is dedicated t'you, baby."

Can't win for losing. Now it's unChristian for me to look away from sin. Ah, yes, the devil is a cunning sort. That reference to the priest-hood—it's one hell of a coincidence.

I hope . . .

Lord God—from whom, we say, nothing is hid—forgive me for making you look down upon my wonderful degradation.

I may plead madness.

Time for a nap, I thought.

Bubbles was sunning herself, elbows back against a car fender, when I came out. She is white as a ream of paper. I could see dark roots in her red-to-blond hair. (Bubbles actually dyes her pubic area, too. This she told me.) It is always disorienting, I suspect, to see a topless girl in daylight. Bubbles was wearing filthy sneakers, bicycle pants and a Whitesnake T-shirt. She is at least fifteen pounds overweight, but her fat is hard—it shines. And there is something about her ham-fisted idea of glamour—plus her silly charm—that tickles me. Also, I knew she'd been waiting for me.

"God, you look like Tom Cruise. Take me home."

"I couldn't handle you," I said.

"You like exotic women, huh?" She popped off her beauty mark and stuck it in the middle of her forehead like a tikka dot. "Goodness gracious, perhaps you would like sexual intercourses with me, yes?"

"Yes. But no. What's this?" I lifted her right arm up (she wears long gloves on stage). There were two initials—CJ—each at least three inches high on the inside of her forearm below the wrist.

"Oh, him. That's the last guy I loved as much as I love you. The prick. I used a bottle opener. He wasn't worth it."

"Bubbles—I want you t'know. That sort of thing doesn't encourage me, or anyone, t'have a relationship. I mean, self-mutilation. That's stupid."

"It was a stage. I'm growing up. Let me come home—make spaghetti for you."

"Did you like Tony?"

"Sure."

"You're being polite."

"No. But he scared me sometimes. With the mustache you look a lot like him. But your eyes are gentle. I'd like t'go skinny-dipping in your eyes."

"Thanks."

"The girls've started a pool. About twenty of us. First girl gets you in bed, she wins a leather G-string with BOSS LADY on it."

"Thanks."

"Thought you'd like t'know."

I am totally unattracted to Bubbles sexually—she is, in the nicest sense, garish. Not a pastor's wife exactly—even by New York Diocese standards. But, as sin goes, I could do a lot worse. Bubbles is unjudgmental and bright. She would regard my ineptitude in bed with kindness.

. . . And, frankly, it's been a long time since someone cared for me in that way.

5 a.m.

I'm tired. Bubbles left me two messages. Kay—be still my conscience—left me one. And, as usual, I sit here with a stash of more than $5,000 in small bills. There is a fire escape outside the bedroom that makes me nervous. It's barred pretty securely, I think, but lots of unprincipled people must know that I keep the night's take at home. I react to crepitations from the floor. I jumped when I saw my own reflection yesterday in the bathroom mirror. An intruder, yaah! I'm strung taut as the trip wire on a booby trap.

A lot of money. But maybe not enough.

Leonard showed me our liability insurance bill for the next six months. Just as an example. *Seven thousand, four hundred dollars.* Almost fifteen thousand a year. What deranged actuary came up with that figure? Good grief, someone who commutes to work daily by going over Niagara Falls in a barrel doesn't pay that much. Or are there risks I haven't yet been told about?

Tedium is a risk. And deafness. And flat feet. And indigestion. And Leonard.

Leonard *really* dislikes me. Me, Michael, and me, The Boss. Both of us. Leonard is especially unhappy when I talk with Joe Solomon, who dropped by to play chess tonight. Joe has never actually accused Leonard of malfeasance. But, up until now, you can be sure nothing has gone on at The Car without Leonard's blessing.

I was a little uncomfortable with Joe. I sensed his disapproval, though I couldn't locate it for a while. Finally he said, "The Joker Poker machine is doing well tonight."

"Joe, honest, I haven't seen a pay-out," I said. "There's nothing missing from the register."

"Look—it doesn't go through the register. Someone is bankrolling it himself."

"I don't understand."

"Okay. I'll tryta explain. The machine is geared t'pay out 20–30 percent of its take. That can be adjusted: but it's generally around 25 percent. Only someone who's been watching it regularly can sense when a pay-out is due. The guy in control lets other people kick in—win here and there—so later he can milk it. Because he doesn't pay to play. All he does, when he opens the change box on the machine to cash the take—he clicks up credits with his finger on the coin slot mechanism. He plays for free until the machine pays him its 25 percent. He can't lose because he isn't putting money in. It's very profitable."

"But you need the key t'do that."

"Bingo."

"You mean—"

"I mean nothing."

"I should take the key from Leonard?"

"Let me introduce you to Lars-Erik and Norm."

. . .

Before Joe does the introductions, let me make a few preliminary observations about my clientele. The Car's clientele. In many ways they're just as intriguing as the girls. And even more various. What Ethel said relative to dancers—that there's always a little something cock-eyed about them—probably goes for the customers, too. What that makes Tony . . . is something else again.

There are afternoon men and evening men. Usually they don't over-lap. Afternoon men are often retired and at loose ends, like Joe and Matt. They enjoy talk. (Music, in the afternoon, is kept at 4.3 on the Babel scale.) And, for someone on a fixed income, afternoons at The Car are a bargain. A beer is $3.50. You get all the ravioli you can eat with that, and a slight sexual *frisson* as well (depending on age). Add $3.00 in tips: it isn't a bad deal. I got a cheeseburger, large fries and a medium Coke at McDonald's for $4.75 yesterday. That means, for just an additional $1.75, you get fresh tit at The Car. Not bad, really. Tah-dee, you deserve a breast today—at McTopless.

There are also several salesmen who use The Car as a demonstration room. Jimbo Mize sells computers. "I useta come here when a deal fell through," he told me. "It cheered me up. Then this hundred-watt bulb went off over my head one day. If it cheers me up—maybe it'll cheer my customers up. So, next day I brought a purchasing agent to The Car for lunch. He went crazy: most married men have a problem going to topless bars. But if it's, you know, *business*—and I'm picking up the tab . . . that first day I sold a $25,000 mainframe."

How did his employer feel about it? "Their attitude is, whatever it takes. Pearl gives me a weekly receipt—and my boss treats it like a chit from Four Seasons. I mean, I don't talk about it. And, naturally, my customers don't talk about it. Which is good—let my competitors guess what I'm doing. I know all the girls. I tip them good. I make sure a foxy one sits with my mark. He thinks he's gonna get a blowjob, if I wink at the girl. Little does he know *I've* never had a topless blowjob. But, it is, believe me, much easier t'sell software when you've got a half-naked broad sitting beside you. I am—I think it's safe to say—the only com-puter salesman in Queens that purchasing agents look forward t'seeing. I just wish the ravioli was better."

Nights, by comparison, are harrowing. There's always an irrational element—usually made up of young, wiry, nervous types who can't hold their liquor. Get five or six post-adolescents together and Leonard starts fingering his gun. I start to finger my neck (this, I note, has become a habitual quirk with me—either I'm hoping my collar is there, or hoping it isn't).

Women are treated abominably by the wolf-pack types. It is, in a sense, predictable. These kids have been taught to respect certain women—mother, sister, nun. The girlfriend, she won't let José or Angelo cop a feel. All of a sudden José and Angelo are confronted with these nude, suggestive icons. It's liberating. But not quite as liberating as they'd like it to be. So if Angelo puts his hand on a girl's thigh—and the girl takes it off, however politely—you can expect tense misunderstandings.

The whole topless business is an exercise in ambivalence. The women seem available. In reality, NO WOMAN under the sun is harder to score. Think about it—any girl who has taken her clothes off eight times in one night will be somewhat rather reluctant to strip a ninth time for Angelo, who looks like he might barf all over her. You're much more likely to score a mother of four at Shop-Rite or a young student at Donnell Library. Moreover, though only 20 percent really *dance*, all topless girls have to at least MOVE for four hours out of eight. They sweat. They smell. Their feet scream. Cigarette smoke rises to lodge under their contact lenses. The libido is not pumped·up.

This contradiction is too subtle for Angelo. He sees a half-naked woman running her tongue over wet, puffy lips. WHY CAN'T HE GET LAID? He has money, but it isn't legal tender for "sexual intercourses," as Bubbles said. So friction builds along his fault line. He yells less-than-chivalrous remarks. (Listening, I want to resign all affiliation with manhood.) He makes unflattering comments about a breast, a thigh. Most dancers field these crazy hops pretty well—they can't afford not to. But what Angelo and his kind like to do best is take a dollar bill and fold it into the smallest possible wad. A balled up dollar (especially if it's newly printed money) is hard as an air-gun pellet. Dorinda, a Guatemalan, got four bits in the right buttock tonight. She almost jumped through the mirror and into her own reflection. It was funny. For about five seconds.

Dorinda couldn't figure which of the four Angelos—they were sitting together at a table—had bushwhacked her. So she came down, nude breasts swinging. (This is forbidden at The Car. You're at least "covered" offstage.) Leonard and I stepped forward. Dorinda bent down and removed one stiletto heel. I thought, Lordy, she's gonna de-eyeball them. But, instead, she took her pointy shoe—with its grungy sole—and dipped it, one, two, three, four, in their beer glasses. Then she climbed back up on stage. I cracked up. Four plotzed Angelos looking for floor lint in their beers.

I went over, before they could react, before Leonard could react, picked up the glasses as if I were handling the chalice and yelled, "Four Buds here!" While the bar maid, Julie, was fetching, I said—"It's on the house, my pleasure, gentlemen. And please don't throw money at the young lady again. There are four of you but they'll need eight stretchers t'cart your bodies out of here. I have family connections." I lit one Angelo's cigarette for him and went back to the bar.

Leonard was irked by this. He wanted a fight. Later, while I was talking to Berry (she tries to draw me out), Leonard made snide remarks about how much time I was spending with the women. Me, I said, I'll spend whatever time I feel like spending. "You're cutting inta yer own income," he said. "These cunts are paid t'make the customers buy drinks. Not t'jerk the boss off."

Otherwise The Smoking Car can have a kind of Left Bank tone to it (Left Bank of the East River). Morale seems high. Though the regular clientele may be blue collar, there is a college-educated, even arty element. Two or three writers. At least one professor (political science). A pianist. This is not to mention the 2,536 movie and TV producers—all of whom are casting next week—all of whom will give speaking parts to a topless dancer tomorrow, provided she'll sit on his face tonight. (That sort of language is becoming natural to me. Imagine what my first sermon after The Car will be like. "And Moses said to God, 'Listen Boss, cut the bullshit, parting the fuckin' Red Sea, we don't have the budget!' ")

For instance, there's Norm Hohol. Norm is an international backgammon champion with total recall. There were six of us standing around him. Norm asked us each for—what was it?—social security number, phone and one other thing . . . car licenses. Two hours and six straight shots of Wild Turkey later he repeated the information exactly. Norm gives a remarkable neck massage, which, he claims, has gotten him laid a lot. "Women cherish adept fingers in a man," he told me.

Norm dresses in a white suit out of Faulkner and affects a languorous way. He is also incredibly lanky. Long, lanky fingers. Lanky man's nose. His shoulders are rounded, as if he'd been ducking low ceilings. And his hand gestures seem to have one extra finger joint in them. This lankiness represents a marvelous performance—particularly when you realize that Norm is only four foot eleven. If that. He sits on telephone books at the bar. But the women really go for him—as they went for Toulouse-Lautrec, I guess.

Lars-Erik is an artist. A glib one. And art is also a good shtick. Lars-Erik wears a beard, which covers—not too successfully—a face gnawed on by acne long ago. Nature has turned this into a secondary sexual trait.

Somehow Lars-Erik's pits and pocks have the romantic clout of a Heidelberg scar. It looks like Lars-Erik has seen life. It ruined his skin, but it was worth it.

Lars-Erik sketches the women (he will ask their permission first—we don't allow cameras here either). His drawings are quick, accurate, subtle and ALWAYS flattering. You know how human nature is: farmers, as Father Mac used to say, love a farmer's joke. Everyone enjoys an image of him- or herself. Lars-Erik will do two sketches, give the girl one and keep one for himself. This is, I think, an economy. He's either poor or cheap—and it's less expensive than tipping. Lars-Erik can nurse a tequila sunrise all night. The bargirls get cranky around him.

Lars-Erik has done a drawing of me—at least that's what he says. He wouldn't show it to me: "I can't finish it yet," he said. "Your face hasn't settled. You haven't figured out what attitude you're taking yet." Uh-huh. It's probably my half-mustache.

I don't socialize that much—I wouldn't want Leonard to think I'm enjoying myself. And, anyhow, the sound level reduces conversation to a primate speed. But I see faces that interest me. Faces that are becoming familiar.

There's a gay couple—they come in to hold hands and comment on the lingerie. There's a 250-pound biker with agate-type tattoos and a T-shirt that says FREE LEONA HELMSLEY. (He is surprisingly generous.) And a condor of a man, very distinguished, with a floppy hat and cloak outfit that Svengali must have worn. He sits far from the stage, hat on. As if he were, I don't know, reviewing our show for the "Arts and Leisure" section.

And then there is the Gaucho. A man who exhales coldness through a well-designed facsimile of warmth and good fellowship. The Gaucho had his arm around me one minute after Leonard introduced him. And, throughout, I could feel this pressure in his fingers that said, "Dear friend, I'd kill you as soon as shake your hand. But right now I don't feel like killing you. So let's have a beer instead."

He's unbelievably handsome, the Gaucho. It's an old-fashioned look—Ramon Navarro or something. He wears a leather and silver outfit that's more Gucchio than gaucho. Boots, hat and a suntan so perfect it looks basted on. You could laugh at this Borscht-circuit ethnic kitsch. I didn't.

The Gaucho had a wad of hundreds so fat it was thicker than a rolled up Ace bandage. He gave each dancer two hundred bucks. There was one exception. The one—Gabriela, a Brazilian—wasn't indignant or hurt, as you'd expect. She looked panicky. As for Jako—to him the

Gaucho is a God. Jako got a C-note. He stood there with his broom, nodding, nodding. And not only because of the money (half his take-home), because he bought the whole costume bit. To Jako this was the Cisco Kid in Queens or something. Jako doesn't distinguish well between today and yesterday, real and unreal. He now calls me "Mr. Tony" with absolute conviction. And I've given up correcting him.

So the Gaucho put his arm around my shoulder (muscular as a fargin' bridge cable it is) and he said:

"Tony was a wonderful man. Bright, bright, bright. Tony had class, Tony was an educated man. Not like the *putas* you see in this business. It was a pleasure t'do business with him." All these past tense verbs unnerved me.

"I'm glad. Uh—what kind of business was that?"

"Little things. Maybe, now and then, we made a killing. I import from South America. Now and then, he'd see a bargain. Like I say, Tony was bright. Bright. So . . . What are the police saying now?"

"Not much. False alarms. He was seen in Seattle, of all places. Maybe. Who knows?"

The Gaucho then leans down and, with great sincerity, he says, "No matter what you hear, I did not kill him."

"Oh." I said. "I'm glad."

"Why should I kill Tony? Huh? I owed him money—he didn't owe me money. And, in case you think I'm gonna Welsh on my debt. Here."

He handed me $10,000 in hundreds.

"Give this to Ethel. Tell her my heart bleeds for her. Tell her I think Tony's brother is doing a wonderful thing—keeping the show open here. I know it must've disrupted your life."

"It's—it's interesting work. For a while."

"There you got it. For a while. After that, it starts gettin' to ya. Y'deal with creeps all day, you turn into a creep. Build it up and get out. My advice to you."

"Yes."

"Now I gotta tell that prick manager of yours I can't fix his parking ticket. Excuse me." He squeezed my rib cage like a python. "Anything I can do, just call. And, be careful, that money's gonna fall outa your pocket."

This place distorts everything. Naked women dance sensually, but they're unavailable. Ersatz good fellowship is spread and exaggerated and then turned into anger by alcohol. And there was $10,000 hanging out of my pocket. Where does this money come from? Does Ethel know? The import business, indeed. I feel like my feet are being set in cement. Tony. Did you want me t'know all this about you? Should I cut and run now before I learn any more?

And the women dance on. These sharp reminders of our sensual nature . . . They're all so strange. And young. Young. They live expressionist lives. Everything is hyperbole and heightened event. Like plants forced in a hothouse. They're so mature, so aware—that they've never had a chance to grow up. It's all movement, movement, movement. And no substance.

Lord, I wish them all some peace tonight.

TUESD—

TUESDAY, JUNE 28TH

It's not Tuesday, it's Wednesday.

It's not Tuesday . . .

Because I couldn't write this on Tuesday. I couldn't write at all. The horror of it gassed me—I kept smelling rot, human rot, inside my nose. The CORRUPTION of the body. And her stink was somehow, vulgarly, noxiously *sensual*. Fertilizer.

It was a terrible day in my life.

And there are moments now—God forgive me—when I *hope* my brother is dead.

Let me see . . .

Yesterday morning Jako came in late and drunk—at about 10:30, 10:40. (He should've been in around eight.) The john was a slit trench— I'd even begun to mop at it myself, while smoking a cigarette to mask the male stench. (It was a day for rich smells.)

So I was a little sharp with him. And, when Jako started talking nonsense—what I thought was nonsense—I didn't pay attention to it. After all, the man was drunk. Even when sober, Jako's brain isn't fully insulated.

It went like this.

"G'morning, Mr. Tony."

"You're two hours late. And you've been drinking again."

"It just went on and on, boss. Last night just went on and on. And, Lawdy, here's another day. But I sure was glad t'see your car this morning."

"I bet."

"It's been a long time." At this point I wasn't listening to Jako. I figured he'd gone off on one of his Pinteresque monologues. I was behind the bar. "It's been a long time in the shop—too long for a fine car like that white Lincoln."

"Mmm-hmm," I said.

"But it needs a wash. For fi' bucks I give it a wash."

"I don't feel like washing a rental car, thanks. And you've got plenty t'do right here."

"That's no rental car. I got the plates myself, Mr. Tony. That time you send me out t'the mo'vehicle bureau."

"Jako—"

"And it's got a ticket on it right now."

"What?" I said. "It can't." I looked at my watch. The meters outside are good for two hours on a buck. I still had forty-five minutes. I said that: "I still have forty-five minutes."

"No, sir, Mr. Tony. What you got is a ticket."

"God damn, that's crazy." But I headed for the front door anyway. Truth is, I'd gotten a $40 ticket on Friday and I was slightly paranoid. But there was nothing—just a paper handout from some carpet-shampooing place jammed beneath the wiper.

"Jako," I said—he had followed me out onto the sidewalk—"Jako, this is not a ticket, this is stupid advertisement. Now get inside and start doing some work for a change."

"That's not your car, Mr. Tony—" he said.

I really heard little metal objects jingling inside my head then—the man exasperated me. I said—loudly, I'm afraid—I said,

"I am *not* Tony Wilson. And this *is* my car. See, it has my *New York Post* in the front seat. See. Y'gotta stop drinking day and night, Jako. Y'gotta—"

"How come if it's your car it don't have your 'nitials on the door?"

"Because. Rented. Cars. Don't. Come. With. Initials. On. The. Door.

That's why, Jako." I was yelling at him in a brutal monotone. But it wasn't getting through. And then he said:

"Mebbe so. Mebbe so. But that white Lincoln up the *corner* got your 'nitials. Right there." He pointed east. "Got your lucky dice sittin' on the dashboard." I looked. I could see the rear left fin and half the trunk of another 1990 Lincoln. White. "It's got a ticket on it," Jako told me. "And the license plate say TOPLESS. Just like always."

It was Tony's car, of course. The one he'd been driving the day he disappeared. Initials on the door APW—Anthony Pierce Wilson. It was Tony's car and—to me, then—that meant Tony was around someplace. I even ran over to a Burger King across the Boulevard and looked for him. But then the ticket registered with me. It had 8 a.m. on it—when the 8–9 a.m. no parking restriction took effect. Tony (I only thought of Tony driving) Tony had parked it there during the night.

I ran back into The Car and called Ethel.

We made a mistake then. Ethel was so excited, so optimistic—and I could think of nothing beyond seeing my brother and getting free of The Car—that we didn't reflect. Ethel knew there was a spare set of keys for Tony's Lincoln on the big ring Leonard had. And Leonard came in at just that juncture. So I volunteered to drive the Lincoln to Malba. I could hear Amy yelling, "Daddy's car is back. Daddy's car is back."

It started right up. There was a quarter tank of gas left. I tried the lights and the windshield wipers: everything was in order. Aside from the lucky dice, Tony hadn't left much personality in the car. I began driving toward Malba. Now and again, at red lights, I rummaged through the glove compartment. Registration, insurance, Chrysler Corp. manuals, a pacifier, an ice scraper. No butts in the ashtray. And the radio was tuned to WKCR-FM, a college talk and jazz station.

I got to Bayside Avenue, driving down Murray Street, on the way to Whitestone and Malba when it hit me—I SHOULDN'T DO THIS. This, the car, might be evidence in some criminal proceeding. Auto theft at least. And now my fingerprints were all over everything. I tried to hold the steering wheel gingerly—I looked down to my hands.

And at that moment I almost hit a kid on a tricycle.

I swerved. Then, to avoid a double-parked car, I braked hard and swerved again.

And a thuddy sound came from the rear of the Lincoln.

It was an awful noise—though maybe, in retrospect, I give it too much credit. A thud in three parts: thud-thudd . . . d'thud. And a few seconds later I smelled it. The primal ooze had been stirred up.

I drove for another block or two. I did turn off the music—that was instinctive—but the denier in me drove on for a while. Then I stopped. I got out. I was in a middle-class heartland: hedges and rose bushes—the sort of place you see a million Christmas lights from, when your plane banks in to La Guardia. There were two women walking, each behind a baby carriage. And an old man painting a trellis. And sparrows rubbing themselves down in the dirt. And my heart beating its fist in my chest: punching me.

Because, I had guessed, you see, and I thought it was Tony. I thought my brother was dead.

And then I opened—God, God, God—I opened the trunk.

It was Rita.

And, I thought, Jesus, she's a black woman. Tony was with a black woman. But her skin wasn't black—it was putrefying. And, though most of her was wrapped in some kind of plastic, I could see—I will ALWAYS see—the face. She looked like a terrified horse, a bit in its mouth, the teeth so long, so horsey long, rearing back. And the wire around her dark blue-black throat had cut though, slicing as much as strangling— the tissue swollen and fatty where the metal had embedded itself.

And then I inhaled. The aroma of her rotting caught my vomit reflex perfectly. I didn't bend over and retch. Puke just blopped out of me and down my shirt front. I've attended the dying. But this was not death as I had ever known it. This was an artifact in the trunk of my car—an ancient leathery thing, dug from a peat bog perhaps. So different, so strange, as to be another species—but one that had known unforgiving human brutality. And maybe somewhere my brother lay black and still, too. I vomited again just as I reached the old man painting his trellis.

Of course, I didn't know it was Rita Madera then. I only learned her name today, Wednesday, this morning. Wretched, poor, throttled thing that she was. How anxious she must've been—to have screamed that way (or, worse, tried to scream and couldn't). Her face was screaming—lips pulled back over those long teeth. Had her gums rotted off? (She seemed to have no gums in my memory last night.) And she was only 20 years old.

The cops were (they still are) totally dicked off at me. They had this God-awful corpse and an irrelevant crime scene in the middle of suburbia. They went through the motions for a while, roping the area off—but after about 30 minutes they gave it up. Murray Street wasn't about to tell them anything. On top of that, I had covered just about every relevant surface with my fingerprints.

At first they weren't so bad: at first the cops thought I was their perpetrator—or at least an accomplice. But, as time passed, and it became apparent that I was innocent, that I'd probably been in Nebraska when Rita was killed, well, they got abusive. I wasn't a murderer, I was just an asshole.

One cop—in his thirties, thin-haired, lit-fused, Daniels his name is, looks like Peter Boyle, but smaller—Daniels kept saying,

"I don't believe it. He *drove* the car. He got into a car—missing four weeks, this car is—he got onto the car and *drove* it off. Like it was the most normal thing in the world—a stolen car delivering itself to his front door. Didn't you *think*? Didn't you think at all, There may be something wrong with this car?"

"Wait," I said. The taste of vomit on my mouth roof was like rancid Crisco. "Wait now. It's my brother's car. It's got a parking ticket already. I'm gonna take it home and call the police. What can you hope t'learn from the pavement on Northern Boulevard where it was parked?"

"The fingerprints—" Daniels said again.

"I know. I made a mistake."

"Stand back," his partner said, "he's throwing up again."

His partner was a man named Colavecchia: bronze skin, mustache, nose big enough to be a vacuum cleaner attachment. Older, maybe 50. The nice half of this manic-depressive pair. We drove out to Malba. Colavecchia was decent enough to let me go in alone and tell Ethel— over Daniels's protest. What I had found in the trunk did not suggest that Tony was headed home any time soon.

She was in the kitchen. As soon as she saw me, Ethel glanced out the window to her driveway. She put a dishtowel down, after folding it neatly. Then, as I guess she does when there is trouble, Ethel picked up Ellen and let her suckle.

"Ethel—"

"You took too long getting here. I thought, What's wrong? Tell me."

"I opened the trunk. On Tony's Lincoln. There was the corpse—the decomposed corpse—of a woman in it."

"Shit," she said.

"It was awful, I—"

"Who? Who was she?"

"No one knows yet."

"Shit," Ethel said again.

And she turned away from me. I thought she had done that to hide some powerful emotion, one she was too proud to show—fear for Tony, grief, something. So I, awkwardly enough, I embraced her from behind. Not a cool move. Not the right bedside manner. She *elbowed* me in the ribs—Ethel turned so suddenly and angrily. And she said,

"What're you huggin' me for? I don't need huggin'—"

"Ah," I said.

"Oh, I see. You think Tony's dead, you think maybe Tony's a murderer. But he isn't dead and he's not going t'do time. Your brother is a very special man. No one can touch him. And he doesn't involve himself with the kinda slut that ends up dead in the trunk of a car. Don't give me no look of pity, Mike. I know better than you. Tony's coming back."

At that moment Daniels knocked at the kitchen door. My five minutes were up.

"Uh," I said, going to the door, "These're two homicide detectives on the case. They'd like t'ask you some questions."

"Mrs. Wilson, I'm Detective Vince Cola—" And that was as far as he got.

"Oh," said Ethel. "Oh, I see. All of a sudden you're interested—now you think my husband killed someone, you're interested. When he was a missing person, leaving four kids with no father, all I got were winks and cheap innuendos. Now you maybe got a collar coming t'boost your pathetic careers, *now* you want to ask questions. Well, it's too late. Go talk t'the smart ass jerk-offs in the missing persons department. I told them everything I know." As Ethel left—Ellen hadn't missed a drop of milk through all of this—she said over one shoulder, "My husband didn't kill anyone."

I felt the need to be near water—because I thought (I still do) that my brother was dead. I took a bus to Flushing and then the number 7 train to Times Square, and from there I walked to the Circle Line pier. It was a beautiful day—but in all that blue sky, I saw only irony and misplaced effort. And underneath the summer afternoon lay a blackened skin and long teeth.

From a pay phone on the pier I called The Car. Leonard picked up. I know I'm sensitized—I'm looking for suspicious inflections and forced language—but his voice had, well, a studied sound. "Strangled?" he said. "Of all the fuckin' misery, now we'll have fuckin' cops coming out've our fuckin' ears." Leonard is profane. But just maybe I heard just one "fuck" too many. A "fuck" of phony insouciance. Like I say, I'm sensitized—still, I'd better keep an eye on Leonard.

So I went around Manhattan twice—into the night. Mostly I stared at the prow-thrown water. Flames and moving water settle me—they're images of the holy spirit because they can envelop. There is no shape, no matter how odd or recalcitrant, that they cannot lap around. I couldn't frame a proper prayer then: the formulas I've learned seemed trivial, and my spontaneous thoughts were fearful gibberish.

But I do pray now for one thing: to get the smell of Rita out of my head. The molecules of her death scent have burrowed into my nasal lining. Even on the water a whiff would come back and, with it, the entire event. It's our ambergris, that smell. It is the smell that includes all other smells. It is our damned, lingering essence.

Mostly, as I am now, I was afraid to sleep. I didn't want to be alone. I didn't want to be with people I knew. But that's the service New York best supplies—a kind of noncommittal companionship. A peopled loneliness. We are well connected here.

I walked until the morning joggers came out. Then I bought the papers. Thank God there was no mention of me by name in *Newsday*. And the *Post,* somehow, had misheard—they called me "Mark Wilson." "A relative of the missing owner, Mark Wilson, 28, discovered the body while . . ."

While trying to hide the fact that he's a priest who runs a topless bar.

Then I walked across the 59th Street Bridge and back to Queens.

WEDNESDAY, JUNE 29TH

Daniels and Colavecchia were waiting, with Jako, inside The Car.

They had bought coffee and two French crullers for me—a gesture, I guess, of conciliation that didn't sit comfortably on Daniels's stomach. But they were glad to see me—in part because I could send Jako away. Jako loves to volunteer information, but it tends to be the same information he volunteered yesterday. Jako lives in the present: he has no use for calendars. I set him to work in the men's room.

"He thinks you're Tony Wilson," Colavecchia said.

"Yes," I said. "He can be very convincing, too. But Tony Wilson is a better man than I am."

"You look like shit," said Daniels. "You didn't go home last night."

"I walked. You guys may be useta that kind of thing. Dead people in car trunks. I'm not. It shook me."

"It's shitty," said Colavecchia. "You never get accustomed to it. Listen, we checked with American Airlines—you did come in from Omaha on June 22nd. We haven't pinned down time of death yet—but it looks like you're in the clear. And, frankly, we need your help."

"Whatever I can do."

"A list, with phone and address, of the girls who've worked here. Anyone who might have known Rita Madera."

"Rita?" (The papers hadn't given her name.)

"Yes. You knew the woman?"

"Uh—no."

"According to Ms. Nancy Cortez, the deceased's roommate, Rita Madera was having an affair with your brother."

"Are you sure? Tony had four kids—"

"Stranger things've happened, Mr. Wilson," said Daniels. "Fatherhood doesn't make us saints. There are temptations in a place like this. You hire the girls here?" I nodded. "Beats being a detective."

"Tell us about your brother, Mr. Wilson," said Colavecchia. "You're close, you two?"

"Well, we were. Tony's been great to me. He was six years older. Our parents were killed when I was 8 and Tony was 14. Uncle Cecil—he died last year—moved in with us. We lived in Whitestone. Tony and I both went to Flushing High. Uncle Cecil was a drinker—not a bad guy—but Tony really brought me up. He put me through college."

"When'd you see him last?"

"I went to—to teach in Nebraska. And before that I was in college. I called. He called. We kept in touch. But it's four, five years since I've seen him." (I lied. Tony had come to my ordination.) "But before that—before that—it was at his wedding to Ethel I saw him last."

"So, in fact, you know nothing about your brother."

"No. I didn't even know he owned this place, but . . . let me tell you this, I know his heart. He could never've killed that girl."

"D'you know anyone who might've wanted Tony Wilson removed from the scene?"

"No."

"Were you aware that Rita Madera—" Daniels checked his notes, "—that Rita Madera had been the girlfriend of . . . Leonard Krause?"

I wasn't aware of it. And I had to wonder why Daniels had favored me with such a stimulating piece of gossip. As a provocation? The thought of Leonard Krause in bed with anyone—let alone a pretty, young anyone—was enough to lower my white blood cell count. It seemed to refute evolution. But I had known from Day One that Leonard did not hold Tony in reverence. And that irreverence had been passed on to me, as next-of-blood kin. In Rita I could locate a reason for it.

I guess Tony, my big bro, was screwing around. Part of me feels disloyal, thinking this. The other part of me, however, wants desperately to understand. A 20-year-old Puerto Rican, no less. Ethel refuses to accept it. I spoke to her at noon. (She finally granted C. and D. an interview.) Ethel has this enormous, almost mystic-like ability to block any information—no matter how persuasive—that might threaten her kinda slanted view of the world. If Ethel concentrated on their refutation, the principles of Euclidean geometry would cease to hold. The wheel wouldn't work. I know enough—even after this short time—not to contradict her.

But, on the way back from Xeroxing Tony's notebook for C. and D., I met Nancy Cortez. She had a fishbowl in her hand. It said RITA MADERA BERIAL FUND on it. She was a small, paunchy woman—not a dancer (or not a prosperous dancer anyhow)—with a long, graying braid thick as a ship's hawser. Nancy Cortez looked up at me without prejudice—a small courtesy which I have begun to appreciate. All night people were *staring* at me. I am suddenly a public figure, open to conjecture. Not to mention skepticism.

(And I feel the inevitability of it—someday soon an Episcopalian, out tom-catting, will recognize Rev. Mike Wilson. Lucky for me Episcopalians have a low sex drive.)

"Rita don't got no family here," Nancy Cortez said. "Her mother is in P.R. I send the body back, when the police let me. But this costs money. Can I put the fishbowl here tonight?"

"Sure," I said. "Let me start things off." I took $250 out of the cash register. "I never met her. I'm new here." I was distancing myself from the event.

"Thank you," she said. "Can I also ask for another thing? The telephones that I can call—of the dancers here. T'tell them where t'come help."

"You'll have t'use it here—but be my guest." I handed her Tony's notebook. "Can I ask you a question?"

"Yes."

"The police tell me you said . . . that Tony Wilson, my brother, that he was having an affair with Rita."

"He was good to her. She was sick—a stomach disease—she don't digest good. He paid for tests, a lot of money."

"So then maybe he was just helping her. Maybe they weren't, uh, making love." Nancy Cortez looked at me as if perhaps I had arrived from another culture, which, in some sense, I have.

"They made love." She rolled her eyes. "One night they broke my bed. Crash-bang. And they didn't stop." Nancy Cortez pantomimed love-making at a steep angle.

"And Leonard Krause," I said. "Did Rita go t'bed with Leonard as well?"

"Leonard?" Nancy Cortez shrugged. It seemed to me that she was being evasive. She didn't look up when she said, "Well . . . that was another kind of thing. You can't blame Rita for that. It was another kind of thing."

The night felt, I don't know, *Irish* to me. Savage. Sullen. Rain fell and thunder hit its gong outside. Inside . . . well, inside nude women danced at Rita's wake. It had the frantic energy of pre-Christian ritual. And in some senses, though certainly bizarre, it was appropriate. From that display of life—from bare, glistening breasts and jutted pudenda—the dancers meant to conjure up protection. You can't kill us, they said, they danced, We are THIS alive.

The fishbowl was on stage. Nancy Cortez leaned an 8×12 glossy of Rita against it. I would rather she hadn't done that. Rita turned out to be pretty and petite—so different from the grotesque image I had glimpsed in the car trunk that it made me feel unanchored, afloat. We forget what gross stuff flesh is. How frail and mysterious is the force that keeps us from disintegration. In her photo Rita was trying to ingratiate. Her smile, though bright, had insecurity in it. Women take such photos for men—casting directors and that sort. The photos say, "Please like me." But I, in my agitated state, heard Rita saying, "Please don't kill me, please."

Yet someone did.

And I remembered what Colavecchia had said, "So, in fact, you know nothing about your brother." Nothing. The person I had once been closest to in the world was now an enigma to me. And, given my ignorance, I was badly equipped to defend Tony against the universal assumption—it was everywhere tonight—that he had strangled Rita. People, mind you, were courteous enough. But I felt the difference. Those who used to say, "Boy, you sure do look like your brother," were silent. This evening it wasn't good to look like Tony Wilson.

Dancers dropped by throughout the night looking schlumpy and impatient—as dancers tend to look when they're not on duty. Many were Hispanic. All were generous: and they gave, so it seemed to me, in proportion to their beauty (and, hence, their earning power). Nancy Cortez took home over $2500. At midnight there was a formal moment of silence. Berry, who plays the guitar, sang an effective ballad about dancing topless. Afterward, she came over to me and said,

"You've had a terrible time, huh?"

"Oh, hell," I said. "this is nothing. I haven't been to t'sleep since I found her. I'm scared t'greet my dreams."

"Shit," she said. She used the word nicely. It didn't offend me. Berry put a hand on my arm—I think I saw brunette hair under a blond wig—and she squeezed. My bicep didn't ball up. I guess I'm comfortable around her.

"Thanks," I said.

"Your brother didn't kill Rita," Berry said. She seemed so certain that I had to assume she knew something. I said,

"Who did it?"

"I dunno," she said. "But it wasn't Tony Wilson."

I think Berry reminds me of someone. An authority figure maybe—maybe one of my teachers . . .

The dawn is well advanced outside. I'm overtired.

But I want to record this while it's fresh in my mind. It may have some relevance. (I see relevance in everything, when I'm not seeing absurdity there.)

As I was leaving The Car, as I was unlocking my rented Lincoln's front door, a red Cadillac pulled up even with me.

"Hey, Mike," a voice said. It was Linese. "Can y'gimme a minute?"

"I'm tired," I said. "I don't think we've got much t'talk about."

"That's not true—come sit with me a second. I'd get out, but with my gut, getting in and out is a major project." His car was blocking mine—he didn't seem in a hurry to move. And I didn't want to order him away. I didn't need a confrontation. "Hey—I'm not gonna put a hit on you. Come sit where we can talk."

I walked around the Lincoln, around the Cadillac and got in. It stank. Linese must have the only garlic-scented car freshener in existence. Throughout our little talk, Linese belched: a kind of punctuation mark, a comma of gas.

"Yes?" I said.

"First of all lemme apologize f'my unseemly behavior back a couple nights." Unseemly—he said the word with relish. There is a type of uneducated man who collects examples of elevated language—and then uses them, not incorrectly, but with such inordinate pride that they seem overemphatic and stupid. Linese had never done anything unseemly in his life. To be *un*seemly you must first be capable of seemliness.

"Yes?" I said.

"Well, you understand. We're in competition up and down this avenue. I get agitated sometimes." Agitated: agitation was a little too seemly for Linese. "I lost my temper, which I shunta done, because you, of all people, are not t'blame. If it's any satisfaction my bursitis is killing me from that night."

"Yes?" I said.

"Look, Tony and me did not get along. Everything was not copacetic between us. I will be the first t'admit Tony shook the boulevard up. He pays more, that means we gotta pay more. He gives free lunch, we gotta do the same. He gets a beautiful girl—we gotta bring free-lance chicks in, we can't take just what the agencies give us. I'm General Motors, he's Toyota. You capiche?"

"Yes?" I said.

"Now look, do not misconstrue . . ." He waited a moment, he liked that word. ". . . Do not misconstrue my purpose here. But I understand somewhat of your problem. Tony is gone—for however long we don't know. I hope everything turns out all right. I hope he's in Acapulco gettin' some rays. But, in the meantime, you have your own agenda. A life t'live, whatever your ambition is. Ethel has got four children. Leonard is a disaster. So . . ."

"Yes?" I said.

"Should push come t'shove some day—and you needta get out . . . I would be willing t'make a handsome, a handsome offer for The Smoking Car. I know its worth. I would be proud to own it."

"You're talking to the wrong person." I opened the Cadillac's front door. "I'm just passing through."

"Do not underestimate yourself. You are a player. A major player. Now, just between us and the lamppost, well, Ethel and me are not on speaking terms. Some hard feelings in the heat of battle. I may call on you t'be a go-between."

"Good night," I said. "We're not thinking of selling The Car."

"Have it your way, Mike. But after a month with Leonard you may change your tune."

. . .

And all the way back to my apartment I thought, Was that an offer or a threat? Linese has a motive for wanting Tony dead and gone.

In fact Linese has a motive for wanting *me* dead and gone.

Good Lord, what've I gotten myself into? I'm nervous as a squirrel.

Fortunately, Pearl gave me some valium. She's been kind to me since yesterday—by that I mean she's used about half her normal allotment of four-letter words. And she hasn't teased about my collar. But once this afternoon, unconsciously, I think, Pearl said something that really stung me. She said:

"You gave her a blessing, huh? You said words over Rita, didn't you?"

But I hadn't. I was too HORRIFIED to stay beside that mutilated, stinking corpse. And, yes, I was probably scared to betray my identity. So I short-changed a human soul. I've lost my instincts as a priest already. Next go my instincts as a human being.

De profundis, Lord. *De profundis*.

THURSDAY, JUNE 30TH

I dreamed of fetuses last night. The Smoking Car was a—what was it?—a frightful delivery room, I guess. But there were no births—only miscarriages that pounded womb-contracting rhythms out. And men tipped—as fetuses did or did not please them.

I'm no good at dream interpretation.

Then there was Ethel—wearing a hoop skirt—and the four naked little girls around her. They each had a fetus cuddled close. Barbie fetuses. Little knee-to-chest, unshaped Barbie dolls. And I blessed them—even though I was in pain. There was a swelling pressure in my belly. "Indigestion," I said. Everyone laughed as if they knew better. And Linese put his wide palm on my stomach very gently.

What does this mean? By their fruits ye shall know them?

The Gaucho was naked and I found him attractive. My nieces, one by one, slipped under Ethel's hoop skirt—they didn't appear again and Ethel was wearing leotards soon after. Pearl was on stage. "She's too old, she's too old," the men chanted. And her vagina opened—as if it were a trunk—and the fetal, tiny corpse of Rita strangled lay there. "For Mike," someone yelled. "It's for Mike. Get him a plate."

I pushed away from the bar. I intended to run. Then I stumbled—I couldn't walk. I was wearing baggy pants like those black rap singers affect. And something heavy and wet had dropped inside the seat of my pants. "I've befouled myself," I thought. But the Gaucho came over to me. He had a baboon-red erection. He wouldn't let me pass. "It's mine," he said. But he spoke with kindness.

I nodded yes when the Gaucho opened my fly.

The phone rang then. It was the Silicone Sisters and the impatient World of Real Things. S. and S. want an extra Saturday in August because they got stuck with July 4th and—next to Good Friday—that's the worst tip day, and, after all, they're around when I need them (they talk alternately on the same phone), besides, they're a specialty act, more an exotic act, and they can make $16 an hour in New Jersey without taking their clothes off and—

And I said, "No! Goodbye. No!" And hung up.

Whereupon the phone rang back and I—without listening—I said, "I don't care if y'have four tits—you don't get an extra Saturday."

And it was Kay.

Not the Silicone Sisters.

It was Kay.

"Oh, hi," I said. "Listen I've been up to my neck—"

"Four . . . tits?" she said.

"Kids. Four kids. I thought you were my busboy, Jako. He's got four kids—but they're like 35, 36, 37, and 45 years old. I feel no responsibility t'feed them."

"I heard four *tits*."

"Kay. It's kids. You misheard. Who has four tits, fer gosh sake?"

"Two women," she said. Oh, I won't need to worry about fidelity if I marry this one. This one is Hawk-Lady. "Two women," she said. What an ESP performance that was. I'd've been impressed, if I wasn't so busy improvising away.

"Well," I said. "Good thinking. Two women. I was talking t'two women at the same time."

"Michael," she says. Kay will use my full name when I've been bad. Otherwise, it's Mikey. "Michael. Listen. I can't put a straitjacket on you. I don't wanna act as a policeman. I love you. Even if I lose you to—to New York—I'll always love you. You're a grown man and a priest of God"—Yaaagh—"you're old enough t'work out your own destiny. It isn't *that*—"

She let her meaning dangle so I'd have to say, "What is it?"

"It's the anger in your voice. It's ugly. I know that's not you. If you're angry, then something terrible is bothering you. You only get mad when you're confused."

Me? Confused? Nah.

Kay was, as usual, perfect. All good instincts and forbearance. And—woe is me—love. I return it. I need Kay now. I need her to be far away, but there. Yet she senses, I sense, that there is something I've got to work out first. And that something may be dangerous to our love.

MEANWHILE, I live in unreality. Sur-reality. Kay says she'll visit me some time in late July. I can't wait. I'll show her the Empire State Building, Rockefeller Center and the inside of Tanya Suslov's thighs. The complete tour.

I don't want to lose Kay.

Evening

For the first time, I'm actually writing this at The Car. I get home so late it's hard to concentrate—I thought I'd use my time here in an improving manner. Place topless in some sociological context. (Anything to take my mind off what happened on Tuesday.)

The Smoking Car has more traditions than a Princeton frat house. All of them expensive.

It's a tradition—Leonard tells me—to tip Mr. Hinkel $200. Mr. Hinkel is the health inspector. He came in this afternoon and said to Leonard, "The prick didn't even offer me a free belt. What's going on, Leonard? I'm carrying you guys—and I don't even get no appreciation." That's what he said. Leonard gave him $200. We all deserve appreciation.

Then there is Sister Calvin of the Salvation Army. Bubbles introduced me. Major Barbara this is not. Sister Calvin is 72 and sly. Gray hair pulled back into a door knob. The Smoking Car is Sister Calvin's turf (so designated by Tony). She comes in twice a week—Monday, Thursday—and a half-naked girl (Bubbles this time) takes her around to the customers. It's a splendid gig. Here she has four dozen guilty, secretive men with dollar bills spread around them. Not much of a sales pitch required. Sister Calvin left with about $45, Bubbles said.

Not that we are a charitable institution. Yesterday this deaf-mute came in and dropped a sign-language card on Leonard's knee. Wrong knee. Leonard grabbed him by the ear until he yelled something very much like "Owww." A miracle. Tell them that the blind see and the dumb have their speech restored to them.

Bad idea, writing this. Everyone has gone self-conscious on me. Leonard thinks I'm writing a report for Ethel. One of the customers left—his drink unfinished—because Friend behind the bar told him I was doing an exposé on topless for the *New York Post*. And the girls: everything

I do is interesting to the girls. I told Bubbles I was writing a screenplay. Now everyone wants to be in it. Or not in it. I'm afraid to leave this anywhere.

I'll go play chess with Joe Solomon.

5 a.m.

Got a machine gun headache that goes *pain-pain-pain* in rhythm with my pulse. I know it's just stress and shock from Tuesday. The music is so loud, and I'm so preoccupied with my shield of nonchalance—I get startled five times each hour. A voice (howled) in my ear. A hand on my arm. Soldiers in the great Huertgen Forest artillery barrage were driven to nervous collapse by the relentless bursts of sound. It's just white noise to me: I don't hear the music. The conversation isn't worth listening to anyway. But the constant roar erodes nuance and grace. I stand outside whenever I can.

Joe and I played two games of chess on the fender of my rented Lincoln. I asked him about Tony.

Joe shrugged. Didn't have any inside information. Pawn to QB four: let's change the subject. But I pressed him.

"What's your instinct? You were a cop for a long time."

"Mike—let it alone."

"He's dead. Right?"

"I don't know. He might be alive. But I don't think you'll ever see him again."

"Why d'you say that?"

"Because he loved this place. He was the tit maven. The maker of two-bit stars. He circulated, he glad-handed, he could give his undivided attention t'six people at once. And he brought the best-looking girls in New York t'The Car. If he could be here, he would be here."

"Did you know Rita?"

"A little."

"D'you think Tony killed her?"

"She was very dependent on him. It was a real teacher-pupil relationship. I don't know. I don't see Rita pushing Tony t'the point of no return. She didn't have the spine for it. She accepted Ethel, everything."

"I—it's awful to say this—but I haven't been real close t'Tony . . . Could he have done it, killed her?"

"What am I supposta say, Mike?"

"Just give me reading. A feel."

"He was human."

"By that you mean . . . ?"

"Of course he could've killed her."

I moved a piece and lost it. I stared at The Smoking Car. The blue neon is fashioned to represent movement, like the cartoon dashes behind Bugs Bunny as he outzooms Elmer Fudd. Movement westward along Northern Boulevard toward Manhattan. (Thwarted by that derelict dry-cleaning establishment in front of it.) And I wondered if, you know, it stood for Tony. His aspirations. The sum of his hope. The color of his soul. Tony didn't have the advantages I had. He wasn't humiliated and broken at an early age, as I was. He thought he could rise, vault past the commonplace, without paying a price.

"Take that move back," Joe said. "You were distracted."

I did. It was a good positional game. Worth playing out.

"You're in the wrong line of work, kid. They're too much for you."

"I met the Gaucho."

"Listen—when I said there were drugs going down in The Car . . . I didn't mean f'you t'run up against the Gaucho. I didn't mean that."

"I wasn't confronting him, believe me. I know power when I see it."

"No, you don't. You think money is power. You think organization and hardware are power. No."

"What is it: what's power?"

"Power—criminal power—lies in the ability t'break a moral code when those around you can't or won't. You can't kill. He can. You might as well be different species. He has a license t'act that'll always be denied you. The law might break him—some day. Meanwhile he has privileges that only a high priest in the temple can have. He can approach the high altar. Believe me, it gives him a hard-on. He enjoys it."

"The Gaucho says he didn't kill Tony."

"That could mean anything. Or nothing. Be sure—if he didn't kill Tony it's because Tony was useful to him."

"Does Leonard have the killing power?"

"That's yet t'be seen. Your move. Must be hot in Nebraska this time of year."

At which point the front door opened and out—out in bikini bra and G-string—came Glenda, screaming. Just as a homeless panhandler went past. He held out an empty coffee carton, as if to borrow some of her monumental nakedness. And she said,

"You think I got pockets in this outfit, asshole?"

Then, to me,

"I've been robbed, Mike. Some bitch took my watch."

Glenda is, you understand, another tradition at The Car. She's had five children, and right now her bra is wet with milk. In Tony's schedule book, on June 15th, it said GLENDA DUE AGAIN. Her fecundity is amazing to me. You'd think she'd have stretch marks—or at least be overweight. She isn't. She's big and blond, with legs that Praxiteles might have carved. And breasts like hard kegs. I'm a little uneasy with her. A nude woman is one thing. A nude mother is another.

So I followed Glenda back into the girls locker room (which smelled of marijuana, I think). "Locker room" is a euphemism. It's a john, like the men's room—only bigger. Two stalls, space for a soggy mattress. There is lot of pilferage. (A dance-quality bra can cost $100.) Most women take their valuables on stage with them. Because the locker room is just across from the kitchen (and ahead of the men's room) almost everyone has access. Leonard or I check the women's room at night, but during the performance I can't bring myself to go near it. I see these girls naked, but there are things more intimate than nakedness. The equipment of womanhood can be both prosaic and sad. And the place has a high stink of intimate liquids.

In fact, as Jako has reminded me, the men's room is a test kitchen for cleanliness in comparison to the dancers' locker room. Brazilian girls, for instance, NEVER flush the toilet. Pearl thinks this is because they're unfamiliar with modern facilities—a reasonable assumption, I suppose. (They're certainly not worried about a New York drought emergency.) So slovenly, indeed, are their habits that you tend to consider them part of a different cultural sensibility—rather than lazy. I watched a Brazilian do her makeup. She put her Big Mac on the *floor* between bites. No napkin, no waxpaper, she just put it on the filthy, wet bathroom floor.

Not that any of the women—of whatever race, creed or nationality— are scrupulous about my/our property. The mirrors are plexiglass: full of warps and bulges. You look at that reflection: it's like putting mascara on a Picasso from his cubist period. But, Leonard told me, dancers, when dissatisfied with management (when you fire them, say) have a habit of shattering mirrors. There is anger in the ladies locker room. Yesterday I read a graffito that said MEN ARE LIKE KITTENS—THEY SHOULD ALL BE CASTRATED. I have not escaped, despite my charm, good looks and pastoral touch. Willow, I suspect, wrote MIKE IS TONY WITHOUT A DICK. Very perceptive, I thought. Needless to say, I hear on good report that the topless profession is conducive to lesbian reveries. I don't blame them, frankly. They see us, men, at our worst, day after day—raunchy, gross, pissed off, cheap, drunken, slurring, and whatever—I don't wonder a gentle, sweet, vulnerable young female breast might console.

Glenda felt that Aleesha, a Brazilian girl, had copped her watch. She wanted me to search Aleesha's bag. Aleesha's very young, with a large posterior and stunning, surprisingly shapely legs. The birth certificate she showed me had a fabricated look. (As all things in Portuguese do. To me.) She's young and wild and charming—but her outfits are seldom washed. And her hair, stuck up like a rooster comb with mousse, is *never* washed. Glenda may be right.

But I couldn't search Aleesha. And Glenda knew better than to leave her watch unattended. And I told her so.

"Thanks," she said. "I've been dancing for your family since 1985 and this is the gratitude I get."

"We appreciate it," I told her. "But what evidence have you got? You can't prove it."

"That's what Tony said."

"About what?"

"Never mind," said Glenda. And she stripped off her wet bra in front of me. I could see gluey milk droplets on the right nipple. I stared. And Glenda noted my fascination. She laughed out loud. Then she leaned over and tousled my hair.

"A kid," she said. "I should nurse you."

I blushed. Hot, my cheeks were hot.

FRIDAY, JULY 1ST

I am stoned.

See the pile of stones

See ✔ Broke my pencil point.

Willow, tit Willow, tit Willow gave me a cookie.

• • •

Now she claims, what does she claim? Well . . . Willow claims she *told* me it was a pot cookie. Given in compassion because I'm so upset over Rita. Willow claimed this—at great length—soon after I fired her. Goodbye Willow. You do not make an ass of the boss, when he is the boss of your ass. Nicely lathed phrase.

All night I'm thinking to myself, Hey, everyone's staring at me. Do I have an open fly? I am not THAT charismatic.

Where was I?

Yeah, right, she musta told everyone, Watch Mike. I just gave him a magic cookie. Watch Mike stare at his shoe like it needed supervision. Watch Mike dip his glass in the hot, soapy water. Watch Mike sit at the bar with a glass of hot, soapy water in one hand until LEONARD, *Leonard*, takes pity on me and says, "You don't wanna drink that."

And I said to Leonard—No, I didn't say to Leonard. I put my finger in the corner of his mouth—where is collected all the crumbs and scum of his breakfast, lunch, dinner—and I wipe it clean.

Aaggh.

"There was something on your mouth," I said. At which point he brushes off my shoulder. "Little dandruff," he says. And for three minutes at least Leonard and I are like two chimpanzees grooming each other. Very moving experience.

"I told you it was a *special* cookie," Willow said.

"Special—to me," I say. Remarkably articulate for someone whose horizontal hold is going flip, flip, flip. "Special to me meant good tasting, not like sucking on a nine-volt battery." (I used to do that as a kid— funny flavor—to see if the battery was good. Zap the taste buds.) "You're fired. Fold your tits up, say goodnight, Gracie. You have collected your last dollar bill at The Car."

"Come on, Mike. I didn't mean no harm." Willow has tears in her eyes. (She is also wearing a Republican Convention straw hat from 1964: it says GOLDWATER on it. Willow is older than I thought.) "Lighten up, huh? You never smile."

"I never smile," I said, "because I run a topless bar and I'm surrounded by evil people." And then—Good grief, I forgot—then I made the sign of the Cross. Yes, I did. To bless her? To protect myself?

"I'll give you a blow job," she said. In a whisper.

"I'd rather have a catheter in my head," I said.

Actually—now I'm home—feels pretty good. Haven't done boo since seminary. With Ernest, who had a crush on me—who was worried about dirt when he had white vestments on. And lint when he had black vestments on. Watch some TV: on pot you can always tell when the commercials are lying to you.

Will I forgive Willow? No, I willow not. Why? You ask why? Because, when I got into the car I . . .

FROZE

No way I could drive those two tons of metal home—my hands and feet were getting nothing but static from the control tower. (I put my ignition key in the *glove compartment* lock.) I was blastissimo. Bonk-thud? That wasn't a pothole, that was a pregnant woman.

So I hadda walk home. And now I haveta get up again at 8 t'move the car so I don't get an alternate side of the street violation. G'bye Willow. Nobody, but *nobody*, makes me get up at 8 a.m.

But maybe, with the dope, I won't dream of Rita now.

SATURDAY, JULY 2ND

Afternoon

For a nasty moment this a.m., I could not find last night's take. Large panic—no laxatives needed. Last night, full of pot paranoia, I dumped it all in the freezer. Had to wait half an hour until the bills thawed.

Kay left a message: great news. Mrs. Wong will take over three weeks early so Kay can come to New York in mid-July. Great news.

What will I do? Maybe I should call and tell her the truth now. Running a topless bar, found a corpse in my car trunk—otherwise it's been quiet. At least save her the airfare, which she cannot afford. The message had a forced kind of lilt to it. This is Kay-being-sexy. She intends to show Sailor Mike a good time when she gets here. A good time with Kay means she bought a pink bra or something. Could break my heart.

In fact—a little modesty for a change would be welcome. Right now I feel like a, well . . .

A mammographer.

Slow afternoon—it's beautiful weather, and even those with satyriasis are at the beach. Fourth of July weekend, Pearl said, The Car might as well be a bible camp. Thank God for the Brazilians—for them the Fourth isn't a holiday. Even so, the two I got to work the early shift look like they came out of an aging vat. One had an ass—behind, derrière—like a land tortoise.

Watched the Yanks lose. Shopped for my week's food. Read some of *The Seven Storey Mountain* (I'll never get through it). Worried about Tony. Worried about Kay. Worried about Tony again. Worried about my vocation. Not used to eating with a mustache and REALLY hurt myself biting into a hero that included some of my lip hair.

Colavecchia and Daniels came in looking peevish and stupefied. Topless dancers are an itinerant lot: they sublet and share and bunk down wherever. Of the 150 or so active names in Tony's notebook, at least 60 had changed their addresses since May. Moreover, to question the Brazilian contingent, a Portuguese lady cop named Gomes has been attached to the investigation. She apparently cramps their style—won't let Colavecchia and Daniels use threats of deportation, etc. They bitched a lot. But they weren't exactly forthcoming. As Tony's brother, I'm not trusted.

"We like questioning you," said Daniels. "Gives us a chance t'see some prime cooze."

"Don't mind him," said Colavecchia. "He's jealous."

"You get laid a lot here, Mike?"

"No," I said. "Not once."

"C'mon. Good-looking kid like you. Really?" I shook my head. "But your brother got his rig lifted plenty, huh?"

"Have you found something out?"

"We thought you might tell us," said Daniels.

"I've been out of touch."

"Well," said Colavecchia, "as a kid, was your brother wild?"

"Were you?" I said. "I don't mean that as an evasion. But teenagers drive cars fast and, you know, Tony was red-blooded."

"D'you think he liked women?"

"Look. I wish you wouldn't use me t'build a case against my own brother."

"Okay. Fair enough. We're just frustrated, is all."

Lars-Erik stopped by—to take a leak—on his way to Jones Beach. He said, "Know how I can tell this is a classy joint?" How? I said. "Ice in the urinals," he said. "And the best graffiti in Queens."

I knew there was a certain *Je ne sais quoi*.

5 a.m.

To continue the French theme: *La merde va se presenter au ventilateur.* I am up a certain creek. My ass is grass. If, dear reader, this is the last entry in my journal, please tell Joe Solomon that Leonard did it.

PRIEST FOUND IN DUMPSTER.

Tonight I closed the Joker Poker machine down.

We were playing to about half a house—and that only because Tanya and Connie (our big stars) were both dancing—so I guess it was quieter and less crowded. I was noticing things (maybe it's the pot residue) and Leonard, well, Leonard got careless.

A big spender named Valerio (a Cuban in the garment business) came away from the machine, then sat at the bar. He was winning, I had seen that when I passed walking back from the john. I didn't think much about it. But there was something in his demeanor, his swagger (even worse than the usual Cuban macho bullshit) that said BIG WINNER to me. You know, his body was wide open, arms spread, expansive. It was saying,

"Look at me, I am a stud and lucky, too."

So I watched, while pretending to read Leonard's *Sport* magazine.

Valerio ordered a tequila sunrise, and Leonard (who hates to get his hands wet) made it for him. Then Valerio pays the tab with a single bill, I didn't see what denomination (tequila sunrises cost $4.25). Leonard makes change, but he doesn't just slap it on the bar—he tucks it under Valerio's napkin.

So I flex on over, and I sit beside Valerio. How's the bra and pantie business . . . oops, cough, something in my throat, let me borrow your napkin, thanks, gag.

And, plus $5.75, there were three twenty-dollar bills under the napkin. Unless we are charging $40 per sunrise and Valerio gave Leonard a $100 bill, well, there has been a payoff.

I can't get a handle on myself these days. Maybe guilt, maybe fear of exposure, maybe Rita's death are nudging me towards suicide. Believe me, I am scared gasless of Leonard. The man can kick someone in the ribs and look like, oh, a carpenter, some kind of disinterested *craftsman* while doing it. He outweighs me by maybe 70 pounds. But Joe Solomon was in the bar—probably we both knew that. Joe still carries his gun. So . . .

About two a.m., there's a fair crowd around the JP machine—when I hear an "aooh" go up. Leonard is playing and he has just hit a straight flush, worth 500 points. At two bits a point, we've got $125 up there. Leonard is bowing to his audience. And I—I just slipped in and started playing off his points, betting 50 at a time.

"Hey," says Leonard, "those're my points. Get off there." Leonard wants to push me away, but I'm still his boss.

"Relax, Leonard," I say. "It's just a game—no payoffs. Right?" I lose 50 and bet another 50.

"But I won them, I paid quarters t'play."

"So, hell. Just open the machine, stick your finger in that doohickus behind the coin slot and click up 200 or so. I give you permission." I lose and I bet another 50—I'm costing Leonard $12.50 a shot and he says,

"Fuck you," he says.

And, with a kind of pneumatic whoosh, Leonard shoves me aside. This is a big man (he broke his own toilet seat in half just by sitting on it last week). I was kind of swept away like seaweed. Meanwhile, everyone has left the JP machine—in a hurry. It's just me and Leonard—who is now playing at 25 cents each hand, to keep his big win on the board.

And the priest—like Jesus in the temple (you have made this den of thieves into a *bigger* den of thieves)—the priest leans down and pulls the plug. Darkness. Leonard's winnings fly off into the electronic hereafter. And Leonard pins me by my denim jacket to the wall.

"Hands off, Leonard," I said.

"You little fuck."

"I caught you paying Valerio off. I want this machine out by Monday, Tuesday. Meanwhile the screen stays dark."

"You little fuck." Louder.

"Leonard." I said. (Can you believe this?) "Leonard, you're messing with the wrong person. I was middleweight boxing champ in college." (At New Paltz boxing is what you do with a Christmas gift.) Then I pulled free—mostly because Leonard's mind was doing rapid arithmetic. If he kills me, he'll lose his job. He might do time. Joe Solomon is here. And, anyway, as Leonard said:

"Ethel's gonna hear about this."

"Um?" I said. "Is she? Well then she might fire me—which would suit me just fine. But she won't fire me, because then she'd be left with *you* and you've been robbing her walleyed since before most of these girls had tits."

"Jerk-off—listen t'me, jerk-off. You see that? Five big spenders just left. They'll go up the block to Linese's if they can't play here." He was right. So much for Valerio. And everyone in The Car was subdued—the way kids get when their parents argue.

I better cut church and see Ethel tomorrow.

Worse—I'm sitting at the bar about an hour later and I hear this general male guffaw. Guffaw again. I look up and see Tanya dancing. What can I tell you?—the girl is beautiful. Disney dust flashes around her. And Tanya's dancing—she works *hard* at it, so serious—her dancing is complex, graceful, and, well, imaginative.

Still, men—about ten of them—are laughing at her. Tanya executes an athletic leg kick, they laugh. She performs an acrobatic plié, they laugh. Tanya is distressed. She can tell something is wrong, but doesn't know just what. I don't know either. She stares at herself in the mirror: nothing. (I think she's myopic, I've seen her with glasses.) More laughter.

Tanya is about a sweat's thickness away from tears.

At which point Leonard arrives above my left shoulder.

"Better go tell your girlfriend her tampon string is hanging out. I think it's a health violation—you care so much about the law." And he walks away.

More laughter. Sure enough, the string is hanging and it's—oh, Lord—pink. Whaddem I gonna to do? I can't humiliate Tanya by pointing it out. But she's being humiliated anyhow.

I go over to Connie—bright, humane, mature Connie. The sensible person I can count on. I whisper:

"Tanya's—"

"Got her period, yeah. We all noticed. I'm surprised she's got any blood in her. I thought she already had formaldehyde in her veins."

"Would you tell her, I—"

"No, I wouldn't tell her. Not if her nipples were on inside-out. And no other girl in this room would either. You been onstage with her? She'll put her stiletto heel in your eye if you cross into her 'territory,' which is three quarters of the stage and all the men."

"Connie—for me—"

"Mike, you're banging her, you go tell her."

"I am not banging Tanya."

"That's not the way I hear it."

"You hear wrong."

"I don't care who you fuck, anyway. But your taste comes off a movie theater floor."

"Thanks, Connie. You've been my rod and my staff."

So *I* had to tell Tanya. It was gruesome. She leaned down to me, hands on kneecaps, eyes wide. So young. So flawless. So light-as-a-kitten's-eyeblink.

And then she ran off the stage. And didn't come back. Which pleased the Brazilian girl who was dancing with her. Until then the Brazilian had been upstaged, out-danced and made to look like a gravid tapir by contrast.

Tanya came out of the women's room at about 3:45, having missed one-and-a-half sets. She had made up her face twice, but I could still see tear paths. They all seem so little, so helpless, off the stage, off their high-high heels.

"Please take me home," she said.

"Sure," I said. I left Leonard with the cash—but I know roughly how much should be there. And, from the stage, Connie said, "Good night, you two."

We drove in silence over the 59th Street bridge, down Second Avenue. She lives on 8th Street—with what Tanya earns I'd expect better. When we had pulled up outside the door, I handed Tanya her pay, and said:

"I didn't dock you for the sets you missed. Don't tell anyone."

"Thanks."

"Why don't you get out of this insane business? Look what happened t'Rita. You'll crack. You're too sensitive. You have real talent—I mean, I think you do. I enjoy watching you dance. Go be a secretary, waitress—something. Model—aren't you beautiful enough t'be a model, f'God's sake?"

"This is New York, Mike. It's hard. Everyone is beautiful. In The Car I'm beautiful—at Elite or Ford I'm just another face. And I'm only five-foot-six. A model hasta be at least five-nine."

"Tanya—"

"Besides. I've got someone t'take care of." And—bingo—Tanya started to cry again. I touched her arm and it was as if I had pulled—I don't know—the rip cord of a parachute. Her emotions, I mean.

She fell into my arms. Her lips kissed up my cheek, up my neck. And I was knocked hazy by a cloud of lilac perfume. Tanya had just a T-shirt on under a light jacket, no bra. And my hand—inadvertently, I mean it—brushed her left breast. Just enough to feel that marvelous, young, feline, springy resilience.

Then she was out of the car and gone.

I'm *not* in love with Tanya. I do not have a crush on her. I'm sure she just likes me, just likes. That's all. I am not going to bed with her.

But, frankly, I don't mind if people think I am.

SUNDAY, JULY 3RD

Morning

Woke myself twice last night with vicious leg cramps. I must be tensing in fear as I dream (don't remember what about, thank God). And yet . . . and yet there was a damp, slippery area on the sheet. It seems crazy, I haven't had a wet dream in ten years, but . . . could it be? Could it be that my nightmares—my terrors—arouse me sexually? That sort of nightmare REALLY frightens me. Is there a lovely, evil incubus hovering in the air?

Sleep also not helped by endless cherry bomb explosions—I'd forgotten how noisy New York can get on the 2nd, 3rd, 4th and 5th of July.

Late afternoon

I am EXASPERATED with Ethel. I cannot figure the woman out. Okay, it is understood that I won't bring Rita up. Too "negative." Tony is alive and he didn't kill anyone. (Certainly he didn't kill his mistress—Ethel is heavily into denial when it comes to Tony's relationship with Rita.) Ethel sits there talking about The Car like she was Don Corleone, all the while diapering an infant. She is—I will say this—she is the Total Mother. She's always attending to those kids. And they respond to her: they're beautiful, very open, confident, bright. Amy, for one, reads better than I do. This afternoon she said to me, "No, you aren't Daddy." Slapped her thighs in a petulant way. It was cute and heart-clutching. Whenever I come over, for the first ten minutes, they all hover around me. As if they expected me to metamorphose into Daddy. As if I were a Tony in training. Which maybe I am.

Leonard—

No, before I go into that—one hilarious scene I must set down.

We're sitting near the pool, Ethel and I. I'm sucking on a Coke (I have no intention of drinking around Ethel). I'm sucking away, a little preoccupied, and I look over to the pool—about, say, ten yards away from where I'm sitting.

And there is an *arm* coming out of the pool. It's fumbling around on the pool edge, obviously trying to find something. Which kid? I thought. But then I did a quick count, and all four girls are there. Who is in the pool? The arm is now very agitated. It rejects a rubber duck, it rejects a beachball. It's a pissed-off arm.

And so I say to Ethel, "Uh, I do believe there's someone in your pool."

"Yes," says Ethel.

"Uh—I think the someone is having difficulty."

"Yo," yells Ethel. "You all right?"

"My wig! My wig, dammit! He's here and I can't find my wig."

Sure enough, about four feet away from the arm, I see a bright pink hairy *thing* . . . I thought it was a Nerf ball or something. And right beside the wig is a pair of glasses.

"Com-ing," says Ethel, as if this were another of her children. "Vanity, vanity, vanity."

From the pool. "Don't gimme that bullshit. I got a right t'my dignity—don't go snotty just because your ovaries are still working—"

Meanwhile Ethel has picked up the wig and glasses. By now she is kneeling poolside. Ethel jams the wig on someone's head as if it were an army helmet. Then she grabs with one arm (she is powerful) and—alley-oop—up comes PEARL out of the pool (like she was a pot roast Ethel had left on the stove too long). In a string bikini.

"Time you got out," says Ethel. "You're turning blue."

"That's my regular color without makeup, you schmuck," says Pearl.

"I'm not looking," I said.

"Why not, prick?"

"Do you want me to?"

"No."

Indeed I got glimpse enough. Imagine a Perdue chicken in a G-string.

Another thing I don't understand is the Pearl/Ethel relationship. They've known each other a long time, so there is much history I haven't shared. Sometimes Pearl is rude to Ethel. And Ethel doesn't mind, or seem to—except for bad language in front of the girls. Other times Pearl is almost maternal. They're close, I must remember that.

Right off, Pearl (in Ethel's bathrobe, which fits her like the Atlantic Ocean fits a porpoise) Pearl, to gain back the face she's lost, says:

"So if the church cops find out you're running a tit-joint—so whatya think they'll do?"

"No one'll find out," says Ethel. "You certainly won't tell them."

"Would they excommunalize you?"

"Excommunicate," says Ethel. Then, to me, she says, "Hold this." And hands me a full diaper. You cannot put a full diaper down anywhere.

"Would they make you wear an iron collar? Would they burn you as a steak?"

"At the stake," says Ethel.

"I can speak English—you didn't go to Harvard, miss. All you are is a human incubator."

"You wanna get dumped back in the water?"

"No. You almost broke my back last time."

"Just girls playing." Ethel said to me: her smile was kind of comical. I smiled back, and then Ethel said, "Leonard tells me you shut down the Joker Poker machine last night."

"Leonard gets up early—"

"You did?" says Pearl. "You shut the machine down?"

"He did. Just after Leonard rang up a straight flush. He's just like Tony—headstrong."

"Leonard must've been irked," says Pearl.

"He had some choice expressions."

"Mike," says Ethel, "I'm gonna ask you t'turn the machine back on tonight."

"Ethel, I caught him paying out. That was our deal. I see a payoff and I close it down."

"Now, wait. Hear me out."

"What?"

"Leonard agrees he made a mistake. Put the machine back on—no payments, but at least we get the small customers."

"No, no, no. I don't believe Leonard. He'll start paying off outside or something. You hired me because you didn't trust him—now you listen to his bullshit."

"Just like Tony," said Ethel. "Mike—the problem is, you see a lot of money at The Car. You see it coming in, but you don't see it going out. We're working on a tight margin here. Tony left me debts—"

"The answer is no. You hired a priest because you thought he'd be honest. Now you're stuck with me."

"I hired you, Mike, because you were my only man's brother. And your blood is in these kids' veins."

"Ethel. I promise you: I'm making the right decision. I don't want the cops coming in. I hear things—in the long run it's better."

"Okay," said Ethel. "But it'll be harder—"

"No, it won't be. We don't need that illegal stuff. We'll make just as much money if I haveta walk up and down Northern Boulevard with a sandwich sign on."

"The church will love that," Pearl said.

"What d'you think?" Ethel asked Pearl.

"He's doing a good job. He's fair. The girls like him. Joe Solomon loves him. I think, if Mike says sales will go up, you should give him rope enough t'hang himself."

"Watch out for those women, Mike," said Ethel. "That's the start of trouble."

"I have a woman already, and that's another thing—Kay said she'll be here in two weeks or so. What do I do then?"

"No problem. I've thought about that. Lou Maso, who owns Tony's Trattoria—even the same name—says he'll let you come in and pretend t'be the owner. So you can show your girlfriend. It's a big place. You'll sit at Lou's table and he'll give you respect. On me."

"Don't ever underestimate your sister-in-law," said Pearl.

I don't. Oh, I don't. I went out there meaning to be firm. I was firm. I stood up for my principles. And Ethel turned it all back on me. Now I've got to work like a Stakhanovite to beef up our gate receipts.

This is quicksand, I do believe.

Evening

Slowest night yet. But, of course, when you deal with topless dancers, NOTHING is easy. Even the boredom—it reaches such an intense level it seems, well, thrilling. Like passing a kidney stone.

First of all, someone yelled "Fuck you" and threw a string of fire-crackers in through the front door. I suspect two pre-teen black kids who are ALWAYS trying to sneak a look. There is a diamond-shape glass window set in the front door. You can't see anything through it—as long as the girls stay on stage. But last week I opened the door and there's Kareem and Ali—or, rather, Kareem is on Ali's shoulders. They both gave me an "Ain't me, boss" smile. Then Ali ran away—forgetting that Kareem was on his back. Kareem got deposited on his coccyx.

"Don't rush it," I said. "What's your hurry?"

"Man, I got time t'make up for," said Ali, giving me the finger. Apparently he considers his infancy and childhood to be one long sexual opportunity lost.

"It isn't worth all the fuss," I yelled after them, remembering Amanda. I don't think they have pubic hair yet.

At one point—about 9:30—there were *no* customers in the bar. I read. Connie studied. (We weren't talking after last night—so much for enduring friendships.) Freddie slept. Bubbles, topless and tipless, was gearing up to toss a fit. Not an angry fit: in this girl there are those adolescent forces, huge power surges of passion, that, psychics say, can make poltergeists appear. Set mysterious fires. Cause sofas to move. She overwhelms me—she always wants SOMETHING TO HAPPEN.

After a while Jako walked past with the garbage, and Bubbles invited him up on stage. At first I said, No—then, hell, what did it matter? And, much to my astonishment, Jako can dance. He was an old tap hoofer in the 1950's. (Bubbles knew this—it's typical of her. I've seen her *listen* to toothless men and idiots.)

It was fun to see. This skinny old black dancing arm-in-arm with a huge (I didn't realize how huge) adolescent child. First he taught Bubbles a shuffle-off-to-Buffalo. Then she showed him her famous shuffle-to-the-bedroom. They took each other off. Then they did a rather complex *pas de deux* which had—I don't know—a rehearsed look to it. Fetching, it was.

I gave Jako a five dollar bill. He nodded, picked up a Steel Sack full of old ravioli and left.

· · ·

How long, I ask myself, can I get away with this? Fortunately, both tabloids seem to have lost interest in Rita's death. For the time being. Someone from *Newsday* called requesting an interview. And Lars-Erik has a girlfriend who freelances for *New York*. But I put them both off. I don't need publicity just now. I'm supposed to check in at the diocesan office. I've put that off: now I'll need a good excuse for my procrastination. I hate lying to bishops. I don't know why: they're just men, they deserve the same disrespect we give everyone else.

Tuesday, no—Wednesday. Wednesday I'll go out to the Cathedral.

In many ways—think about it—my occupation hasn't changed. I'm still a pastor, still an authority figure. I still have a congregation that comes to me for advice. In fact, it's the same stupid confessions, hassles, pretty much. "My boyfriend is seeing another woman." "My landlord is harassing me." "My parents don't understand me." I try to avoid fly-paper involvements at The Car. After all, my position is, shall we say, equivocal. The Christian advice I should give is compromised somewhat by my present occupation. Here I speak as mediator and surrogate for Ethel Wilson, sitting beside her swimming pool. Which is not an enormous moral franchise.

And, of course, The Car is no different from St. Mary Mouldering in Hackensack—women fall in love with the rector.

Must be the uniform.

Bubbles is a NUISANCE. And, God, a sweet, lonely, yearning child from—of all places—Jackson Hole, Wyoming.

She has decided to fall in love with me. Fall, as in avalanche. But Bubbles's passion is so volatile that the whole thing might be a parody, for all I know. Can she possibly have contracted such a case in two weeks? Is she making fun of me?

And, on top of it, she's pregnant. Three women—since I got here— have told me, in passing, as a casual remark, that they were pregnant. Abortions, apparently, are just as casual. I HATE that. I never have liked it. But after the adults-that-be made Amanda abort, made her kill my child . . . Okay, I know we were young. I know it would've ruined my life—deprived me of a chance to ruin it again. But NO ONE ever *asked* me. I was a kid, I was a schmuck, I did a bad thing, but I was the FATHER. In America they only treat you as a father when they want child support. Otherwise, the female machine grindeth or grindeth not.

I wish, at least, that Amanda had brought my child to term and put it up for adoption.

Worse, Bubbles asked me to lend her $250 for the clinic. I don't believe in abortion, I said. This intrigued her. Everything about me intrigues her. I'm an intriguing man.

"You don't believe in abortion?"

"Yes. I don't. And I run a topless bar. I know. It's inconsistent. I'm just made that way. Sorry."

"But, like, what about a women's right over her body?"

"A woman should exercise that right when she gets in bed with a man. Women forget about that other right. The right not t'get laid."

"But I'd make a terrible mother."

"I suppose you would. Who's the father?"

"Like most things today, you know, it was done by committee. Please, please, please lend me the money. You gave me a lousy booking, and still I came in. I'm gonna make eighteen dollars in tips. And I gave $300 for Rita's fund. And I'll need some time off after the D and C. Don't lend me the money for an abortion. Lend it because I'm me." She smiled and caught her beauty mark before it hit the floor.

"Because you're you is the problem."

"Then gimme a mercy fuck, huh? Huh?"

"I don't like committee work."

"I'll fire the committee."

"No, Bubbles."

"Drive me home at least. A cab'll cost me eleven dollars and with my hair style I'm a target for trouble."

"I—" She caught my hesitation.

"You do it for Tanya."

"All right, I'll drive you home. But no fooling around."

"Not me," she said. "You know what you remind me of?"

"What?"

"A married man. An unhappily married man. Who doesn't have the guts t'let go."

The unhappily married man line got to me—the Church was my child bride. How does the Song of Solomon go? "Thy navel is like a round goblet, which wanteth not liquor: thy belly is like a heap of wheat set about with lilies. Thy two breasts are like two young roes that are twins."

The car ride was worse than a tag-team match. I swear, I almost dumped Bubbles on the verge of the Brooklyn-Queens Expressway. First she sat in the back.

"Why are you doing that?" I asked.

"Because you said 'no fooling around.' "

"You take everything to extremes."

"I'm a kid, whaddya expect?"

"I feel like a chauffeur. You can come up front."

Wham. 135 pounds of pre-bimbo jackknifes over the seat back. From sitting demurely in the rear, Bubbles is now prone with her face in my crotch. I pull her up (all this while doing 55 mph over the Kosciuszko Bridge.) She has a hand on my cock, she has a hand up/under my shirt, she is kissing my neck. Nothing will stop her—it's so extreme, it's sexless. But ve-ery distracting.

Finally, I throw her aside and in so doing, break the rearview mirror off. Smacked it with the back of my hand and—oh—I had a July Fourth of pain. This sobers Bubbles up at last.

"I'm sorry," she says.

"Don't. Just don't."

"I'm hurting my chances with you."

"Not really. You never had a chance."

"Oh," she said.

Silence.

"What're you thinking?" I ask.

"Gee, these Lincolns sure are made cheap."

Then, from annoyance, my mind flipped into amazement and fear. This child lives in one of the worst parts of Brooklyn. All black. Empty lots. Gutted buildings. Half the windows in her tenement were boarded over. And, on the stoop, there sat seven or eight black men smoking dope.

"You live here?"

"It's cheap. I have, you know, expenses."

"Cheap? Aren't you afraid of getting raped?"

"I was raped the first day I moved in. Long as you don't hurt my face, I said. I made them laugh. Two of them. It was good sex. Now they protect me from the others. I have a way with people."

"I'll walk you in," I said.

"Okay," she said. But she didn't need my protection. Her great, cordial, open, foolish, feminine manner is a shield. "Hi, boys," she said. I nodded (I was scared green—I don't have a great, cordial, foolish manner.)

"Hi, Cherry [her real name]—want a hit?"

"Not now. This is my pimp," she said.

"White pimp don't give you no benefits," someone said. But it was good-natured. (Though I didn't like the way they mentally undressed my car.)

. . .

Bubbles's room—her one, 10×12 room (toilet down the hall)—could make you cry. Wall and ceiling, it's papered with rock star posters. Maybe a hundred of them. She has a mattress, she has a chair. She has six or seven items of clothing. The telephone lay torn out of the wall. She has a tiny, old-fashioned record player that must have come from the room of her adolescence—if ever Bubbles had such a common-place thing as an adolescence. She has a TV and VCR. She has a box of cookies. She has cat food for her kitten, Roadie. She has a sink with two dishes, one knife, one fork, one spoon.

She has nothing much.

Lord Jesus Christ—I don't know these people. They are wild strangers in my sight. I would pray for their needs, but I have no idea what they want.

MONDAY, JULY 4TH

Went to a doubleheader at the Stadium—and screw Ethel. Had to get my mind off Tony, Rita and The Car. (Pearl said, Go ahead, you deserve it, I won't tell *her*.) Yanks lost 6–3, 6–1 . . . dreary. But what a pleasure to get out in the sun. And to see, again, that cavernous blue place.

How I wanted to be a ballplayer: drifting back under a deep fly against high clouds on a summer day. Makes me want to sing the national anthem. How uncomplicated a life, compared to the profession I have chosen. (Yeah, yeah, until you're 38 and you can't get around on a 90-mile-an-hour fastball, and the crowd boos, and you start free-basing. The grass is always greener in center field.)

But the evening was hell. One argument, one confrontation after another. And it hasn't been easy booking 12 dancers for Pearl's party. Bubbles, for sure, gets a slot. (And, after what I saw last night, a regular Friday or Saturday.) But a lot of my regular dancers don't care for the odds. That is: 11 to 1. They know I can't triple the crowd without breaking fire laws. Maybe I can double it. But I'm tripling my supply of women—which means tipping will probably be off a third. I may have to offer bonuses. Or prime bookings. This has become a point of honor for Pearl: she considers herself an institution on Northern Blvd. And, God knows, she is useful: the afternoon crowd, old stage door Johnny types, are loyal to her. It's rather Old Worldish and romantic, with "Fuck you!" thrown in. Of course, she also pours one free shot for every three her regulars pay for, which custom generates very large tips. Everyone's got a scam.

At 8 p.m. this accountant-looking guy bolts in. Wire-rim glasses, bald. And—well, we print up these match pads. Our address is on them. A slogan, TOPS IN TOPLESS. And our LOGO—a railroad car with smoke coming out of it. Also, on the reverse, a photo of an attractive nude model. Our accountant friend screams that SHE! (pointing to Raven, a young and cynical barmaid, who would dance if she weren't flat-chested as Gumby), that SHE! put match pads in all his pockets because SHE! was rude and he didn't tip her—which was his right, dammit—and now his wife's threatening to leave him. Because, worse, Raven wrote fake numbers and names inside (he produces his evidence—CRYSTAL 555-6190 and so forth) and now Mrs. Accountant thinks he's having an affair.

Raven says, "Bullshit."

He goes for her. Leonard and I restrain him. It might be comical, but this guy is distraught and we don't (I don't) want to hurt him. His marriage is in severe snafu. He'd like to blame us—but we are, ah, just a palace of cheap dreams and never liable for the damage we cause. This is where-love-has-gone.

I said to Raven, after we got the accountant outside and called the precinct cops (who talked to him firmly about taking responsibility for his life—Leonard's free drinks do pay off), I said to Raven, "Try that again and you're fired."

"You take his word over mine?"

"He's a customer. He pays. Or he *did*. Please don't cost me money. You aren't worth it."

"You're a cold son of a bitch, aren't you?" she said. "Seeing Rita like that didn't even faze you, did it? It just bounced right off."

Come join me in my dreams, you little whore.

But that was just the beginning. Lars-Erik comes in with a "friend," who is considering topless as a moonlight job to go with her regular gig as a perfume lady at Bloomingdale's. "She wants an audition. Isn't that right, Daphne?" says Lars. "Yes, it is," says Daphne, the way you do at a wedding, when you've committed yourself and it's too late to back out. And—LIGHTBULB—I catch on. This is how the famous artist El Cheapo gets by. He finds himself a susceptible broad and turns her to topless. Sort of safe-sex pimping for the Nineties.

Daphne is *dense*. Thicker than a wall of Hitler's bunker. Her attention span cannot be measured by any technology known to science. Quarks are longer. While Lars-Erik is in the john, this conversation takes place.

"I just got a phone."

"Great."

"My first."

"Congratulations."

"I mean, my first in an apartment."

"Uh-huh."

"Of mine. My parents had a telephone."

"How advanced of them."

"And tomorrow I'm gonna go t'the store and buy my telephone books."

I just stared at her, but she was serious. Daphne was going to a store—which one did I think was the nearest?—to buy her telephone books. Daphne comes from Arkansas. After Daphne I'm afraid to fly *over* that state.

L-E comes back. Can Daphne go up and have an audition? Gee, she only has cotton underpants on, and they're black, and would it be okay, but she's never undressed in front of—Go up, I said.

I had four Brazilians on. Two up and two in the locker room: Chinga, Chunga, Changa and Roxanne their names are. Approximately. I tell Changa to take five. She heads for the locker room. Daphne goes up: very brave, very disoriented. I look at L-E, and he says to me:

"I find great stupidity in women arousing. But, at my age, it has to be *great* stupidity. Mere dumbness doesn't do it for me, anymore."

What we haven't considered (which is an oversight of mine), what we haven't considered is Daphne's tight blue jeans. I should've told her to strip down in the locker room. There is NO WAY to remove her tight blue jeans sensually. In fact there is NO WAY to remove Daphne's blue jeans at all. The blouse, okay. The bra, okay (though, frankly, she had trouble with that). But the blue jeans, NADA. She gets them down like someone chased from a public john by a police raid. Not, at any rate, *sexy*. L-E has to pull her pants off, one foot up against the stage. And she is pissed at him. Everyone (all 16 of everyone) is whooping with laughter.

At this juncture I hear "Eeeahhhh!" in Portuguese. It's the only word I understand in that language. "Eeeahhhh!" again—coming from the locker room. I get there before Leonard: to find Changa standing over the prone and, respectively, supine nude bodies of Chunga and Roxanne. In passionate friction. Changa's taking five took them by surprise.

And Changa has a knife. A very big knife. It is a major tool. I can't tell whom she intends to use it on.

Apparently Roxanne was her fiancée, Chunga is her sister and, well, Sophocles would've drawn a veil over it all. Changa keeps making really distasteful cunnilingual motions with her tongue. My appearance doesn't distract her at all. Leonard, because of me, can't get into the tiny room. I do not want to be stabbed. It is a gruesome mess.

Finally Changa decides that stabbing is too merciful a punishment. She starts to kick rib with metal toe-tap shoes. Chunga grabs her ankle. Chinga, whose stake in this is too deep for me to contemplate, begins screaming behind Leonard outside. Chunga and Changa wrestle to the floor. I dive and start working on Changa's wrist to dislodge the knife. Roxanne, this dove, this love-tossed flower, decides I am out to injure a fellow countrywoman. She punches me in the left eye. Now I have the knife and *I* want to kill *her*.

Then, all of a sudden, Roxanne's face goes white.

Leonard, with his vast experience as a cat-fight referee, has reached his hand between Roxanne's nude legs from behind. And grabbed her by the lush pubic hair. I don't approve. I really don't approve. But it was effective. And I needed help. Roxanne kinda curtsies, says bye-bye and tiptoes out, peaceful as a Quaker.

That leaves me with Chunga and Changa. Good grief, these women are like pythons. I'm not weak, but I've never taken on lesbian jealousy before. I just don't have the passion. At which point Changa unloads a spray can of Adorn—splat—in my face. I'm half blind. I almost topple into a toilet stall.

"You're fired," I say to Changa, while splashing sink water in my face. "Open your mouth and I'll call the police. *Po-li-zi-a*."

"She fired, too."

"No. You started it."

"She fired, too. She got no green card. Roxanne got no green card. Only I got green card. I tell im-mi-gray-shon."

So I have got to fire Chunga and Roxanne. This is another Brazilian problem. Mind you, they had both shown me green cards and ID to go with the cards—you employ an illegal, it's a monstrous fine—but all were borrowed or phony. I said to Leonard, we should go through agents and let them screen everything. I'm tired of personnel problems. But even an agent can get fooled. Changa has a card. Agent gives her ten bookings: Changa sells them to Chunga and Chunga arrives at your joint claiming to be Changa. And she has Changa's card. And they can't quite speak enough English—ever.

Still there is something, oh, distancing about the Brazilians. I prefer to work with them (though they aren't that good for business: talk is an important aspect of topless). Same way you hire a foreign maid. It is harder—for me, anyhow—to discipline an American girl. Brazilians are anonymous, different. And they don't require the personal attention, the prodding and validation that a dancer from Brooklyn will demand. I mean, I guess, that Brazilians don't insist on being treated like human beings. Which is an immense relief.

This fracas left me with Chinga and, yes, Daphne alternating for the entire night. Lars-Erik was ecstatic. And we had to watch Daphne de-pants herself three more times. It is not an act that bears repeating. L-E, the snake, didn't tip her once.

But, Lord, we know that the law is good, if a man uses it lawfully. Knowing that the law is not made for righteous man, but for the lawless and disobedient, for the ungodly and for sinners, for unholy and pro-fane, for murderers of fathers and murderers of mothers, for manslay-ers, for whoremongers, for them that defile themselves with mankind, for menstealers, for liars, for perjured persons and for those who fre-quent The Smoking Car on Northern Blvd. in an evil time.

TUESDAY, JULY 5TH

5 a.m.
My hand is shaking. I have a case of panic-induced diarrhea—it's taken me sixteen minutes to start this paragraph.

I've been found out.

Maybe I brought it on myself. Maybe I shouldn't've fired Glenda. But, you see, that happens when you take one morality and then juxtapose it against another—esp. when that other is totally antithetical. Strains are likely to occur. I've been operating in the DMZ between two ethical systems. I've been trying not to judge (compassionate liberal that I am). But every once in a while something so grotesque, so inhuman occurs that it awakens the sleeping priest in me. (The priest I've put to sleep, rather.) Because, with him looking over my shoulder, I could not func-tion here. I would close the place down tomorrow—nieces, Ethel and all.

But tonight what Glenda did sent voltage through my Christian nerve ends. And the priest came alive, in an epileptic fit of indignation.

You see, too many guys were ordering Kahlua. A little thing, but even the amateur me registered it. Men just don't drink Kahlua in front of

other men. It isn't, shall we say, the macho thing to do. And a Kahlua
hangover is like the final Yoo-Hoo.

But there they were: two cabbies with Kahlua. Two UPS men with
Kahlua. This went on for about three hours. I had to send Freddy down
for a couple more bottles. Actually, I guess that's what alerted me. Until
now we've had the same half-empty Kahlua bottle in the rack since I got
here. But, you see . . .

Glenda was selling her breast milk at $10 a shot.

Yes.

I caught Glenda just as she was coming out for her 1:15 a.m. set. She
passed from table to table—she's been dancing for a decade, everyone
knows her—and I saw her pour something white into each Kahlua glass.

I confronted her. She admitted it readily enough.

Glenda is one of those women who try to be super-ballsy. (Willow is
another.) Because they're wild (and women) you're meant to forgive
them for being outrageous. It's supposed to be eccentric or cute. Glenda
said something about Grade A, homogenized. Something about being
a universal mother. I didn't hear her, I just blew. All my impacted guilt
and anger and fear broke through.

"Get out, you disgusting slut," I said. "You're fired and you'll never
work here again."

"Hey." Glenda went to anger. "Listen, snot-nose—I've done this after
every kid I had. It's a tradition."

"It's a fucking abomination," I said. And I took her bag—she had put
it on the stage lip—I took her bag and threw it toward the locker room.
"Get out," I said. "Get out now." Then I grabbed Jako's pail and I went
from table to table. I dumped every Kahlua I could find. I offered drinks
on the house: no one took me up on it. And most left. Leonard gave me
an eye-rolling look, like "Your days are numbered in this business, kid."

That left Berry on stage. Berry of the wig, dark glasses and 1940's film
mannerisms. Berry who isn't intimidated by me. I sat at the bar—empty
stools on either side of me. (No one felt like small talk with the boss.)
After a while Glenda rushed past, her face sheeted and pasty with tears.
I looked up—to avert my glance—and saw Berry. And suddenly I was
swept by an incredible surge of lust. I started getting an erection right
there—the first I've had at The Car. My God, I thought, I enjoy hurting
women. But it wasn't that. Or not entirely that. It was Berry's flesh.

Her breasts are soft, they don't have great tone, but they're sloped
like the tip of a Dutch girl's wooden shoe. With the big pink nipples
poking up. Her waist is slim, but her belly—in it—is distinct and round.
A Botticelli. And her legs are coltish—without adult definition—but full

of prancing fun. I looked up. Berry took her breasts in her hands and offered them to me. I looked away. Not because I was offended. Because she could see I was turned on.

And when her set was over, Berry came down. She sat beside me.

"Michael," she said—and in that "Michael" I heard, should have heard, another time, another place. She sounded like Kay. "Michael," she said, "I think you're being hard on Glenda."

"I don't," I said. "You can't tell me there's no health department violation in what she did. If there isn't, there should be. Exchange of bodily fluids—"

"But that's not why you fired her."

"No, you're right, it's not."

"Give her a suspension. She needs this gig. She's a great mother."

"She's a caricature of a mother. And, anyway"—this just jumped out of me—"I'm sick of great mothers."

"You're wrong. Her husband's on disability. She's supporting the whole bunch with topless."

"Not my problem."

"Well," Berry said. "I thought priests were supposta forgive."

I slapped my legs together like a little girl whose skirt has hiked up. I wanted to deny it. But I saw that would be impossible. Berry *knew*. And I knew why she had never been afraid of me.

"Who told you?" I said. "Pearl?"

"Does Pearl know? I guess she would. No, Pearl didn't tell me—I'm Theresa Ottomanelli's little sister. Berry. Bernadette. You remember Theresa—she was Amanda's best friend. You wouldn't recognize me. I was thirteen and fat when you knocked Amanda up. And, son-of-a-bitch, you never paid me the slightest attention. I was in love with you once. We all were. We younger sisters."

"Berry—"

"Drive me home tonight," she said. "And give Glenda another shot."

Angie. Amanda. Luke the Duke. Mouse Calich. Gina. Lois Manheim. McAlevey. Ellis Lodge. And our Junior Auxiliary: younger sisters, younger brothers. Berry wore braces then. She had a chubby, androgynous body. And, Lord, I was too preoccupied to notice, anyway. I was just another kid who attended Young People's Fellowship meetings at St. Matthias because it was the only place you could meet a girl. Father Mac knew we had not gathered to make His path straight—yet he tried, anyway, to use the opportunity as best he could. While we went from crush to crush—and dreamed of dark purple hickeys.

Berry. *That* Berry. I tried to extract—from the lush stuff of this sensual woman—the child core. But all I could remember was a little troll-girl who covered her mouth when she giggled. If I'm 28, she must be 25 now.

"Where d'you live?" I asked, when she got into the Lincoln. But Berry took her time. She felt the upholstery. She examined my dashboard. She lit a Marlboro.

"On Twentieth Avenue," she said. "With my parents, where I've always lived."

"I'd rather not drive through that neighborhood just now."

"Nothing has changed, Mike. They go t'bed at 10 p.m. We'll pass through like ghosts." And Berry put her hand on my knee.

So we drove: and I enjoyed it. Past Shea Stadium, along Northern Boulevard, left on 154th Street. Through Flushing, into Whitestone. Past the house I spent my life in. (The new tenants have added a second story, made it a two-family.) Through the quiet, tree-thick streets, where a black man would feel out of place, as I felt out of place in Bubbles's neighborhood.

My ball field is gone. The rude wooden bleachers behind Our Lady have been knocked down. People park where once I went deep for fly balls. There is a shopping mall where Mr. Zinkle's azalea farm stood. But, otherwise—Berry was right—it hasn't changed. I asked about Amanda.

"She's in Georgia someplace. Two kids. Married to an air force pilot. She came back to St. Mat's last Christmas. Ugly kids—she's put on thirty pounds. You got out while the getting was good."

"I didn't want to. I had no say in the matter. I was the wild oat sower—in another time they would've castrated me."

"D'you know how much we loved you? All of us—Diane, Sue Welles and Sue Harbort. Kitty Spelling. Me. You were a star: it's not that we begrudged, you know, Amanda. We were rooting for both of you. But any of us would have given up, oh, American Bandstand, t'have that baby in us." She laughed. "And I hadn't got my first period yet."

"I was preoccupied back then."

"You were beautiful. Shy, with your hair wild, and your biceps shining. And we all looked for your cock when you had tight shorts on. You threw me over your shoulder and tossed me into a pickup truck that last church field day we had before you left. You touched me. You, who never smiled. Who had the world on his shoulders."

"Can that be true?"

"Hey, it was a pretty boring neighborhood. Little girls haveta fanta-size."

"You're not a little girl now."

"No. I'm not."

"Berry—"

"Are you still a priest?"

"Yes—"

"And no one but Pearl knows?"

"No one must know. I'm doing this for Ethel and Tony and my nieces. I don't want t'ruin my career. Believe me, I don't."

"I won't tell. My parents think I work at an all-night diner. So—"

"So—"

"We're both on the lam, you might say. And we know each other. And, you know, you can talk to me."

"I'm glad."

"There's just a couple of things—"

"Yes—"

"I need some Saturday bookings. And I want you t'kiss me."

"Berry—"

"Mike, I know you're a priest. I know why you became a priest. I knew your brother when he was a kid. You can be yourself with me. I've watched your face in The Smoking Car. You hate lying, you hate being someone you're not. I hate it, too. God, I'm no sex merchant, I'm just a music student who needs money. We're both in hiding. Let's hide together. Please, please, please. Kiss me."

And I did. I kissed Berry often. Our mouths fit one inside the other, perfectly, as nature engineers things when it wants a species to survive. I touched her: I touched her breasts. And tears, like children on sleds, rushed down her cheeks. She was grateful to me. And I was grateful to her.

God, the release, the release. It was exquisite.

WEDNESDAY, JULY 6TH

Can't write, too tired.

Thought of Berry the entire day.

. . .

Ethel called, furious. Police all over the house. Colavecchia and Daniels got a warrant to search Tony's things. It is a murder, after all. But, as of ten p.m., they had found nothing. I could've saved them their time—Tony didn't kill Rita. But who did?

The Gaucho? He came in tonight and scared us all. I didn't think Leonard was capable of deference. But he is deferential to the Gaucho. So, for that matter, am I. Leonard and the Gaucho "talked" in the kitchen. And, from time to time, others—even little Norm Hohol—went back to . . . pay respects, I guess.

Berry Ottomanelli. Does that mean Little Turk in Italian?

Kay called. I was so nice to her, so effusive about our future, that I made her suspicious. I think.

Lazarus has a huge abscess near the base of his tail.

Berry's breasts. Soft as soap bubbles.
Better buy some condoms. In New York, Brooklyn, somewhere.

Can't anyone hear me? I'm yelling "Catch me! Catch me!" as loud as I can. Catch me at it, Kay. Catch me, Queens Diocese. Catch me, please.
Before I get away with it.

Berry. I tell myself this can't be just a coincidence. That some circle—from my previous sin to my present sin—is closing. That this is fate. That this was meant to be. That it is all, you know, a learning experience.
But it isn't.
It's just a weak soul giving way to temptation.
And, deep inside—at center—I'm truly worried about just one thing. I worry about how I'll perform in bed.

THURSDAY, JULY 7TH

Afternoon
Just got back from the vet.

Cats are eerie. Pearl brought a cardboard animal carrier in and—zow—Lazarus disappeared. He's never been to a vet. He's never seen a cat carrier. Nonetheless, some instinct said, Splitsville, I'm on my way, you won't have this cat to kick around any more. He dove into the basement and simply vanished. It's a big place, but neat, and there were four of us saying "Kitty, Kitty." No sign. Gone.

Animal instincts interest me of late.

So we sat for three hours saying things aloud like, "I hope we don't see a cat around here. The one thing I really can't stand is a cat. Nice day, lucky there aren't any cats t'spoil it." This conversation was orchestrated by Bubbles. (She was dancing with Rochelle, my token Black, who has a Cockney accent.) Cats are perverse, Bubbles said. They can't help it. If you want a cat to eat nutritious food, hide it. Human, in other words.

Sure enough, Lazarus appeared. Wary but interested. "Oh, no," said Bubbles. "If that cat jumps up here it'll ruin my set." (Lazarus has been known to sleep on stage, paws up, through an hour's worth of dancers.) Then Bubbles lay down—with a long peacock feather. She made irresistible feather movements: she was a shrew, she was a garter snake, she was autumn leaves falling.

Got him.

And the vet says to me, "Jesus, this cat has beer on his breath."

"I'll give him a Cloret," I said.

5 a.m. or so

Now, of all things, I'm worried about money. Having promised Ethel that I'd increase our take at The Car, I feel like a yuppie computer salesman trying to make his July nut. And everyone is watching me. In the midst of raunch, sleaze and brutal murder, an even gamier stench of bourgeois materialism pongs my olfactory nerve.

No question, pulling the plug on our Joker Poker machine has hurt the house—and the higher-spending part of it, as well. Jako and Leonard and I humped the J P into a distributor's truck, like we were bumsrushing a drunk.

To compensate—even in lust there are marketing strategies—I have instituted the audition hour. (Good idea, if I do say so.) From five to seven on weekdays—a slow time for us—we hold open try-outs. Customers, like Romans in the Colosseum, get to thumb up or thumb down after a five minute set. That way we all sample free flesh, the clientele and me. (Word has only been out since the weekend, and already seven girls have gone up. Some good ones, too—three will make their debuts at Pearl's shindig). With us the girls don't have to pay an agency fee. So we are at least 10% more attractive than Linese's joint.

Tony evidently felt that the quality of his product mattered: sexier girls, bigger crowds. I snuck up to Rabies and scouted Linese's roster:

some of his women have about as much sensual élan as a molded plastic suitcase. (I'm looking at my suitcase now, hence the image. Maybe I should just pack and leave.) My girls are fresher: college kids who want one or two gigs and don't have time enough to get involved with a booking agency. It's more work for me, but the customers respond.

There's one customer I can do without—Mr. Floppy Hat. Jako told me this. Jako has trouble expressing a personal opinion—at least in front of white men. He kept nodding and excusing himself, until I put my palms on his shoulders and drew him outside. Since my sad afternoon with Rita, I pay more attention to Jako.

"What's wrong, Jako?" I asked.

"I don't keer for that doctor."

"Which doctor?"

"One what weah the funny hat."

"And the cloak? He's a doctor? What's he a doctor of?" But those distinctions are lost on Jako—to him there are doctors, period.

It seems that the doctor poured a neat shot of Stolichnaya on Lazarus—which roused him about as effectively as Jesus's "Come forth." The cat was still woozy from anesthetic, but I had brought him back around six—I hated leaving what is, after all, a feral cat in some vet's cage. His tail area was furless—the stitches were obvious. The vodka must've stung like shorted wires. Jako was very upset. I calmed him, but I was perturbed, too. Humans deserve whatever they get. But cats are free of original sin.

Joe Solomon was doing one of the dancers' summer school homework—Cleopatra, the girl from New Paltz. Advanced calculus, it was. We have such bright people at The Car.

"Well," I said. "How'm I doing?"

"You might make a pretty decent topless bar owner some day."

"What a prospect."

"Mike, the department is feeling embarrassed right now about Rita's murder. No leads. Cops are insecure enough, we don't feel loved. We get petulant. We take our bad feelings out on other people."

"What're you telling me?"

"Getting rid of the poker machine was good. But it wasn't enough. The Car will be made an example of."

"Drugs?"

"Sure."

"Where?"

"You know."

"Christ."

Booked Berry for next Saturday night—in Glenda's open spot. I left a business-like message on her machine. But my heart was banging.

FRIDAY, JULY 8TH

Afternoon

No one, but no one—NO ONE—would believe what I've been through this morning. No one. I've got to get out of this business—missionary work, yes, that's it. I'd rather do missionary work up the Amazon with headhunters. Solid, dependable citizens. Not—topless—dancers.

I'm asleep at about 11 a.m., half-asleep. Aware enough to watch hypnopompic colors in paisley and neon blue race around the inside of my eyelids. I'm asleep and I hear a rap, rap, rap of metal (a quarter) on glass. I awaken, looking like someone had to sign an exhumation order before I could get up, and there is . . .

Ta-dah. Bubbles.

On the fire escape, behind the grate, in short-shorts, halter top and sandals. Waving at me. With a large stuffed elephant under her arm.

Of course, I've got NOTHING on under the sheet—God knows how long she'd been watching out there. I cannot maneuver. I wave her off and turn over, pretending to sleep.

"Let me in, huh? I've got a present for you."

No response. I do not need a stuffed elephant. Or that other thing she has for me.

"Come on. I'll make you breakfast. I'll do my Jackie Mason routine."

No response. Though, now, yes, I'm feeling cruel and, worse for an Episcopalian, I'm feeling uncivil.

"Oh, gee. Oh, gee. Mike, I got an urge. I got an urge t'take my clothes off out here."

Jesus. The fire escape, you understand, is on the street side. Where six old Jewish women sit in beach chairs at 11 a.m. Tanning themselves to parchment. I do not want scandal. NUDE ON PRIEST'S FIRE ESCAPE.

"I'm topless."

So I swing around—is Bubbles bluffing maybe? No, she is not bluffing.

Her big, hard breasts are pressed (one in each glass pane) so flat they look like buttocks. And the fly of her short-shorts is coming unzipped.

And from the street I hear, "Oh, a flasher. Look, Estelle, a flasher. Look, Estelle, a flasher."

I leap out of the bed, trying to make a toga, a loincloth, a *something* out of my sheet. Naturally I step on my own drapery and—wang—now I'm naked, too. Worse, I don't have any idea how to open the metal grate.

Hey, no problem. The damn, rusted, orange-cruddy thing *falls* inward the minute I jerk it. Corroded to rice paper. There I am, nude, wrestling with 8 feet of double-gauge metal, which is pinching my fingers and turning my chest into an orange waffle, when Bubbles, never one to be Reticence Afoot, hoicks the window frame up, dashes, breasts dribbling, across the room, picks up the sheet, burrows into my bed and says,

"Oh, I'm home."

"Perverted goings-on up there!" yells a Jewish voice. "Next time it's 911 on you."

I zang the steelwork down, grab my blue jeans and go into the kitchen to make coffee. Maybe it's best to ignore the whole thing.

The whole thing is still in my bed, however, when I get back. "Hug me," it says from a fetal position.

"Why d'you do this, Bubbles?"

"Because I don't feel whole until a man has his arms around me. I feel like I'm falling apart. It's a very scary sensation. I love you."

"You don't. You just decided t'fixate on me this week."

"If I could have a month with you—just a month."

"You can't."

"A week. This afternoon. Just, FOR GOD'S SAKE, hug me."

I did. I sat on the edge of the mattress and hugged her. She tried to pull me prone (she's a strong girl), but I wouldn't go down. She kissed me. I didn't return her kiss. She put her hand on my groin area—but blue jeans are the best contraceptive.

"Did you get that abortion?"

"No."

"Why not?"

"Because it's something that cares for me. Why can't I have it a little longer?"

"The longer you wait, the more it becomes a sentient being."

"A sentient being?" Bubbles let me go and fell backward onto the mattress. Her breasts followed like an aftershock. She had to push them away from her chin. "A sentient being? God, you're so matter-of-fact."

"I'm just trying t'do the honorable thing. I don't want t'take advantage of you."

"Please. Couldja be a little less, you know, with the scruples and *take* advantage? Please."

"I don't love you, Bubbles."

"Yeah, well tell me something. Didja give Tulip a Saturday night booking?"

"What if I did?"

"I can't stand this. You gave that rodent a Saturday night booking. Her tits are, like, printed on. I mean, it looks like her push-up bra *missed*. You're seeing her?"

"Who says?"

"I know. She doesn't belong on Saturday night—you wouldn't give her Saturday, 'less she was giving you something back."

"She's a nice girl. Not everyone can be as voluptuous as you are."

"Gimme a cigarette from my bag."

I opened her carryall—this is part of the topless dancer's uniform, a big duffle. Full of G-strings and bras, a pungent body odor mixed with fragrances of another week. I dug, with some distaste, through the lingerie and saw—

One million pills. Okay, one million is an exaggeration. Green and red and yellow pills. Loose pills and pills in bottles. Time-release capsules released. Pills glued to each other like jujubes. One *thousand* pills. At least.

"You're carrying a drug store. No wonder you can't afford a better apartment."

"You want some? You wanna do some Percoset with me? I got uppers and downers and things, wow, that make one half of your body go stiff like a stroke victim. Here's a placidyl. Here's a nice, nice quaalude."

"These look deadly." I had two big pink tablets in my hand.

"Those are beads from my G-string. It's falling apart. It has VD." She popped something.

"Where d'you get all these?"

"From those friendsa mine you met."

"Not from The Car?"

"No."

"D'you know what's going down in The Car?"

"Everyone knows."

"What?"

"Leonard deals cocaine."

"You're sure?"

"Mike—huh? Don't be like you're from Mars."

I was going to say, I'm not from Mars, I'm from another galaxy, when there was a rap on the door. Pearl. Returning the keys to my Lincoln, which she had borrowed yesterday so she could take her mother to the chiropractor this morning. Pearl, outside.

"You up yet?"

"Yes, yes. Coming." I turn to Bubbles and put a finger over my lips, but Bubbles is already out of the bed, still topless, bag and bra in hand, at the door, before I can stop her.

"It's all right, Pearl," she says, opening the door. "We just finished, you have perfect timing," as she flounces, with her naked breasts echoing the flounce, onto the landing, past Pearl, down the first flight of stairs, singing "Feelings, ta-de-dah, feelings . . ."

"You had the pick of all those bimbos—and you go and prong that little meshug."

"It's not what you think—"

"Who am I t'judge this generation? Do. Do. Whatever you want, *do*." Aaaaaaaaaaaaaarghh!

And now I have a stuffed elephant.

5:32 a.m.

Nothing is as it seems, ladies and gentlemen—we see through a glass darkly and no one wants to grow up. They strut and they slide, they lick lips lightly in imitation of lust. They flaunt and they taunt and their favorite audience is not you and me, sorry fellas, their favorite audience is that image in the mirror.

How often I've watched them, these naked children, absorbed almost to unconsciousness by a reflected self. Upsweep the hair or let it pour down, braid it, lap it over a shoulder, drape it—how mysterious and beautiful I am. Stomach in, lose weight, raise the G-string crotchline to give me more leg, cover that spot on my buttock. Always with a thoughtful smile. In another world, swept off their feet with self-longing—in front of a hundred irrelevant men.

The narcissism here is overpowering: like funeral flowers. This part of the dance they love—the self-seduction of it. The mental masturbation. They could swoon. Come here, you in the mirror—you-who-alone-understand-me. My secret lover. Twine around my body, let's be feminine together.

Even, yes, Pearl. Poking and plumping her dusty wig, as sedulously as a grower of orchids might. Made up so severely an African witch doctor would step aside and give her preference. A dear old egotist . . .

Who, I now realize, has such a following on Northern Blvd. because she is witty, large-hearted and, yes, a bookie. Matt, the ex-mattress man, is her runner. We are, in fact, providing a secret OTB outlet in the afternoon.

Everyone is someone else. Everyone has something on someone else. Everyone has agreed to follow the eleventh commandment, to wit: I will not blow your cover if you don't blow mine.

And the boss is a priest.

Am I officiating at a black mass? Some corrupt, foul inversion of the sacred meal? Was The Smoking Car built over an ancient pagan temple site? Do we draw fertility to the land by paying the earth goddess to expose her breasts here? Was Glenda's milk set apart for worship?

I'm going nuts.

Began the day with Bubbles and ended it with Tanya. And the end was worse than the beginning.

It was a four-thousand-dollar night—some beer league softball team was celebrating. Tanya had made at least six hundred dollars. The sulkier she got, the more men paid. Tanya is just emotion, surrounded, held in, by the thinnest membrane. I admit it, I was thinking—after our last car ride together—that maybe it was me, the reason for her dance of sadness. I couldn't quite convince myself. Tanya is, of course, surpassingly beautiful—surpassing, certainly, me. But I was up for intrigue.

Enough to be patient with her—Tanya takes FOREVER to change. It's as if she molts her Car persona, scratches the shell of it off, rubbing against the wall. She never wears makeup on the street. (I have never seen her do so, anyhow.) Tanya is always last to leave, and Joe, sitting with me on the Lincoln's fender, as he folded the chess board up, said:

"Tony useta wait for her, too."

And—the thought crossed my mind (insane, narcissistic thought)—I thought, I never want to lie where Tony has lain. Nor fish in the same warm stream. So I said,

"Was he having an affair with Tanya?"

Joe laughed. "Your brother sometimes misjudged his options. But he wasn't stupid."

"She's beautiful," I said.

"She's beautiful," he said. "Such beauty is disfiguring, such beauty is a curse. It's like being a celebrity without accomplishments. That girl cannot find herself. She gets nothing but misinformation from the world. How would you like it—havingta live up t'that face? I feel for her."

"Let's go," said Tanya, coming out. As if *I* had been keeping *her*. I locked The Car up. Tanya kissed Joe goodnight and, I swear, his knees bent in obeisance.

Tanya was silent across the 59th Street Bridge. I made little openings: she didn't seem to hear me. But, as we reached 14th Street, Tanya said,

"There's usually parking this time of night. Why don't you come up for a drink?"

Chung, chung, chung went my pulse.

"I—" I said, "I don't think that would be wise."

"Please," she said.

Shall I, I thought, run my lips up along that cheek to where the ear lives eaved in brown hair? Shall I really? Will I remember anything else as long as I live? Not because I love her, but because it is to participate in a heightening of things. The exaggerative world that beauty lives in.

"Just a drink."

"That's what I said."

Her brownstone apartment building is, as I've noted, third rate. There was unbagged garbage in the foyer. I watched the back of Tanya's neck as she peered into her pocketbook for a key. I wanted to kiss that neck. Thank God I didn't. Because, after we proceeded along a dark hall (she lives in the first floor "garden" apartment, a euphemism for "airshaft"), as we proceeded, suddenly the hall was flooded by reddish light and there—in the doorway of Tanya's apartment—stood . . .

An enormous bull dyke.

"Get in here, you bitch," it said. "Get in here before I make you ugly."

"We have company, Costanza," Tanya said. "This is my boss at The Car—he does all the booking—Mike Wilson. Costanza, Mike."

I put my hand out. There are Jewish sects that consider the touch of a woman unclean: with such passion, a deep religious pride, did Costanza ignore my hand. But she stepped back. Tanya had become small. A pirate's prize, taken in battle, and far from her native land. She urged me with her eyes. And I went in. Because I sensed that I was her buffer state. A device. A buying-of-time for Tanya. My best dancer, who would never let me run lips up/along her cheek.

Costanza is from Puerto Rico. She has an enormous behind: anger and complexity are locked in her hips. Costanza is pretty enough, but whatever charm she may possess has been blunted by aggression. I have seen her male counterparts: she has modeled herself on them. Men who will not be crossed. Men who stake out territories by lifting a leg and urinating. Men who know that jagged, unexpected movements can destroy the confidence and rhythm of those around them.

We had drinks. And I understood why Tanya—earning maybe the equivalent of $200,000 a year—was, nonetheless, poor. Constanza sat beside Tanya. I was placed in an isolated chair. Costanza, who accepted my significance—the employer of her employee—made her power known.

"She have a good night?"

"She always does."

"Men go crazy for her, don't they?"

"Well. They're respectful. Tanya commands respect."

"I taught her that."

"Oh," I said.

"But she's lazy. You can't believe how lazy she is."

"She works very hard at The Car."

"She better. We had a little argument about that this afternoon."

"I'm tired," Tanya said. And she nestled against Costanza's arm.

"Her stepfather beat her. The prick useta beat her with an old fan belt. She hates men."

"I do not," said Tanya, but lightly—not with much conviction.

"But she likes you," said Costanza. And this sucking up was more distasteful than the aggression. She drank from a beer neck. "She says you're a gentleman."

"And what d'you do for a living?" I asked.

"I do Tanya. I'm Tanya's agent."

"She's a remarkable dancer."

"But she's lazy. She wouldn't even get t'her gigs, if I didn't keep on her ass."

"I sleep a lot," Tanya said. And I thought: so would I.

"She could go far—she has star quality."

"No. We could go far. We."

"Whatever. Pleased to meet you. It's late—I better be moving on."

"Thank you, Mike," Tanya said.

And I thought as I left—remembering what Joe had said—that beauty had driven Tanya to the grotesque. After all, how boring we men must be to a Tanya: servile, lustful, so easily manipulated. So insecure before beauty that we force dreadful power on the Tanyas of the world. Power they have no interest in exercising. Decisions they're too tired to make.

Because, underneath, they're just children locked in a golden monstrance and on display.

I'll never be in awe of Tanya again. I feel like I've lost a part of my innocence.

SATURDAY, JULY 9TH

8 a.m.
Berry danced for me tonight, amidst one hundred men. It was her mating display. She got me so aroused that, well, my ears clicked, as if I had risen above a certain critical altitude. Everyone could feel it—even those who had no idea where all those sexual ions in the air were coming from.

She was, you understand, super-nude to me.

Not only bare breasted: breasts shiny as wet seals. Not only bare buttocked: buttocks long, part of the yet longer leg, so that her muscular thigh reaches to her coccyx. And all brown, between medium and well-done. But wigless for once, dark glasses–less. Out of disguise. Not Tulip. Someone I had known, naked. So that—to my normal male randiness—there was added a titillating curiosity. This, once, was a childhood playmate of mine. Remembering that, I remembered St. Matthias again—and my own Will-this-girl-let-me-kiss-her? juvenile sexual hopes. It was all, in a very special way, improper. Underaged. We got young together: we shared a past, secrets, and the peculiar raunchy innocence of adolescent love again. It was—I say this in extenuation—irresistible. And I had no intention of resisting anyway.

I have a hard-on now, just writing about it.

Most of all, I knew that somehow—despite guilt, preoccupation, insecurity—I would be potent with her. Berry knew my history, she had me at her mercy. And I, her. We could be ourselves. It was an enormous relief, after so many days of pretense. Berry wanted me-the-priest. I wanted her-my-childhood. And I sensed, younger though she might be, that Berry was a craftsman of sexuality. She wanted to prove herself to me (I am better than Amanda). And—if it pleased me—I had only to lie back and receive.

The lust jumping from anode to cathode in my body could've made iron filings sit up. Everyone felt it: we created a barometric high in the room. People groused. The music sounded atonal. Leonard almost killed a construction worker who climbed up on stage. I had to pull him off—no simple matter. Leonard is irritable: Colavecchia and Daniels have questioned him three times.

Berry lies asleep and naked on my bed as I write this now. I will lean forward and draw my hand down/along the inside of her thigh. I can do that. It is permitted. I haven't gotten over the novelty of it yet. This body I am allowed to touch.

Let me do it again.

We came together so violently in my apartment hallway that our mouths hurt with the impact. Berry was stripping before I had gotten the door open. And I prematurely shucked myself nude, too. We fell on the mattress, side against side, kicking the spread angrily down with our feet. Her breasts, flat, roll with a lolling motion. Her pubic hair has been shaved—making her, even now, little jailbait Berry. I wanted to please her. She wanted to please me. We got in each other's way. There was so much, you know, to do.

But, of course, I couldn't manage an erection. I pulled at myself when Berry wasn't looking. I brought up rich fantasies. Nothing. I felt male performance fear—and most of all, I didn't want to *insult* Berry. My flaccid member was being, as it were, discourteous. I had been invited to a feast, but I wasn't eating. I loathe bad manners.

Yet, as expected, I was in the hands of a master. She touched me there. Then—it was quite a surprise—she said.

"Go put some pants on, Father. Those cotton jogging shorts. You got undressed too quickly. You can't feel yourself. Let's bundle, you need some friction. You need t'know where you are."

How simple, how brilliant. It worked almost at once. I did wonder, for an unchivalrous moment, just how many men in jogging shorts had lain between her legs. And again, later, when she applied the condom with her mouth in one easy unfurling swoop. But I knew Berry was—is this blasphemy to say?—God-given. She threw herself backward: her hands, on the edge of the mattress, seemed in spread-eagle binding. She made herself helpless and unthreatening—she groaned for mercy. She was in bondage to me. The rhythms of our love, I knew, were mine to control.

And I came on her, as once I saw the side of a rotted brick building collapse. I was a landslide. I was as inexorable as gravity. It was the best orgasm of my life. Such pleasure scares me.

"Thank you," she said. "You're wide and long. I've fantasized that orgasm for almost ten years. It knocks the breath out of me to think that he—you—*he* is really in me."

"I'm horny as a lifer."

"I love you," she said.

"I'm—crazy about you, too." There was a distinction being made. We both ignored it. I don't love Berry (I don't *know* her), but such passion strips my male reserve away. Would you believe, getting up to bring a post-coital Coke, would you believe *I danced for her.* I put her G-string on and did parodies of women at The Car: Glenda and Aleesha, and Tanya refusing a dollar bill because it was crumpled, and Connie swinging her legs around. I was immensely foolish. In the presence of those who love us, we are released from shyness and propriety.

And, just before we made it a second time, Berry said, "Leonard hasta go."

"Why?"

"He's dealing and he's getting greedy. He'll take the whole place down with him. I love dancing at The Car—but I don't want t'go outa there some night with my hands cuffed behind my back. We'll all be under suspicion. And Rita's death makes it worse. Leonard's stupid. Anyone else would lay low for a while."

"What should I do? Wait until the Gaucho goes back there—"

"Oh, no," she said. "Never surprise the Gaucho. If I'm around, I'll signal when it's safe."

"Okay," I said. "But now I wanna fuck you again."

I have a way with words.

And so I've been unfaithful to Kay. Unfaithful to my vows. I played the two-backed beast with Berry so fiercely that I brought her period down. I dug within her and I roared. Spit came out of my mouth. Orgasm is the devil's dance: and I partnered it.

And, in a few minutes, I'm leave for an eight o'clock mass. Satan won't have an easy time with me. One thing I've learned is stubbornness—I won't despair of God's ability to save me. I'm a Philadelphia lawyer of the spirit.

Just looked in Berry's duffle for a pad of matches. I found a G-string that says BOSS LADY on it.

SUNDAY, JULY 10TH

3 a.m.

Slow Sunday night: terrible rain since church. Girls danced with hard nipples. No one could seem to get drunk. Lalique hung down from the trapeze like a three-toed sloth and refused to dance. There's a roof leak just beside the lunch table—we had a pail under it all evening. Connie said, "Feels like a trapper's cabin in here."

She and I, Freddy and Jako spent the night putting up decorations for Pearl's party. I'd already made one tactical error—I asked Pearl's mother to cater for us. Which made her happy. Which made Pearl furious. "We're not having that ass-wipe ravioli at my party," she said. So I had to hire the Greek to cater hors d'oeuvres, and pay old Mrs. M. something extra for her services, anyhow. Leonard will prepare three turkeys. And matzo ball soup. I'm assured he's a cordon bleu chef. Tony, why did you leave me with all these *people*—these unraveled strings of relationships? This entire sordid world.

Connie and I have made up. Pearl caught Friend stealing—so I gave Connie two bar nights a week. (A bartender makes about one fifth what a dancer makes.) This pissed Leonard off. Leonard senses that Connie is really just passing through. Connie doesn't need The Car: therefore, she may be less obedient. Also, her allegiance is to me, not Leonard. I'm just afraid we'll find out that Connie's been cheating, too.

She said, "Have you looked at yourself in the mirror?"

"No," I said, handing her a string of colored lights. "I'm surrounded with mirrors. Of course I look at myself."

"You haven't really. You did, you'd see you've lost at least ten pounds since I first met you. Gaunter and handsomer."

"Could use t'lose weight." Connie came down the ladder and embraced me.

"Get out of here, Mike," she said. "Run. Ethel can take care of herself. Run. You won't survive this if you stay."

"And you?"

"I'm tougher than you are," Connie said. "And even I'm in trouble."

Great.

. . .

Everything's ready for the party. I've got a dozen girls lined up after 7 p.m. And a $150 opal brooch for Pearl. Ethel will be there to imbue me with her authority. I'm The King of The Car, watch out.

Let's see what happens to screw things up.

MONDAY, JULY 11TH

7 a.m.

I'm crying here, alone. This has been a dreadful night. I can still feel her soft, slack lips on mine.

And Leonard will pay for it. I'll take my guilt—I swear, Lord—I'll take my guilt and my sadness and I'll forge them into the tools of my revenge. Don't mess with me, Leonard—you fat motherfucker. I'm not scared any more. I'm gonna put a match to you, the way they burn leeches off. I'll make you squirm.

I'M GOING NUTS.

Let me
carefully,
chronologically,
write things
down.
As I remember
them.

Pearl's party.

It was a bacchanalia. From eight o'clock onward, Pearl sat enthroned—in a chair on the bar. And there received homage. Like a Fury surrounded by naked maidens—all twelve of whom gave her presents. (No girl would've dared not to.) And, to me, it was like Goya or Hogarth. Beauty in its sexual prime paying court to shrunken death. Every girl there must've seen her destiny in Pearl's bony decolletage. In that besotted (Pearl drank tonight), narcissistic, blind—yes, lustful—mummification of womanhood.

And the men came: gentleman callers in straw boater and white vest. With arthritis and liver spots and dentures and wistful impotence. Once good-looking men of substance. (The rumor was going around that Pearl had been a noted Park Avenue madam once.) They gave her jewelry and perfume and the benefit of their nostalgia. At one time three limos waited outside. My little gift was put in the discard pile. The place got crazed—for hours we were way over our fire-law limit. And Pearl made a point of introducing me to Morty Stern, big stockbroker, to Walden Mintz, big real estate man, to Nubar Katchenian, just big. Big-big, old-old men. Who were joined like wires to the hundred-way plug that has been Pearl's life.

And the Gaucho handed her a thick envelope.

The girls danced—three at a time, twelve an hour, in special fifteen-minute sets. Our stage is small—they elbowed each other and fought to make eye contact with the antiquated rich. Bubbles, I remember now, simply gave up after a while. She leaned against the mirror—and her wet body left a steamed outline there when she shoved it up to dance again.

Then Ethel came. I hadn't seen her wearing heels until last night: with heels on she must be almost six foot tall. And immediately Ethel became the enabling spirit, the mother goddess. Leonard, Christ, kissed her hand. Jako swept his broom in front of her feet. Ethel is quite a striking female. And all the girls, those who knew her and those who just knew of her, began to strut. They ignored me: and, yes, I felt left out. These people, they know where the power resides.

Ethel, like Queen Elizabeth at an orphans' hospital, made a grand tour of inspection. She knows The Car inside out. Behind the bar (Ethel told me the hot, soapy water wasn't hot enough—and, yes, we had run out of sanitizing tablets). Into the kitchen, into the locker room, even into the MEN'S head. (One guy was taking a leak and pissed down his pants when Ethel came in.) On to the basement, where her eyes looked like mini-calculators, doing inventory. I'm NEVER to pile cases up against the beer cooler. Then, to the tables we had set aside for staff and family, where Ethel ate a trencherwoman's helping of matzo ball and turkey.

Inevitably, I guess, the conversation turned toward Tony. Men and women came to Ethel, the presumed widow, and—to flash their credentials as friend-of-the-family—they told how Tony had said this and done that. For the first time, if occasionally, the verb "to be" and Tony were used in the past tense: Tony was, Tony has been. The name Rita was never spoken. I became immensely distressed. (Especially when Berry arrived: I waved her away, I didn't want Ethel to suspect anything. Berry, to her credit, understood and left.) I was distressed and yet, let me be honest, *angry* with my brother. Ethel, seeing me withdraw into myself, tousled my hair. Women do that to me. And some girl laughed—to see the bossman made a child.

Norm and Lars-Erik told an adventure story: both of them and Tony, the three Musketeers. Tony betting $50 that he could drive from here to Norm's house in twelve minutes—some enormous distance. Norm lives near Douglaston. (And I, of course, remembered *my* wild drive with him.) How a cop sat on their tail for the length of the Van Wyck Expressway and how Tony had jumped the divider, made a U and then re-U-ed back across the divider while the cop was trying to hump over the first U. We all laughed.

And no one was surprised, on second thought, that he was missing. But they were all "sure" that Tony would return. Richer. With stories to tell. He was a survivor, you know. Couldn't get the best of old Tony. He's probably outside now: timing a dramatic entrance.

You might've thought Tony was Pat O'Brien. (And you might've thought The Car was Girls' Town.) Tony had advanced money for Cheryl's abortion. He had pulled an angry customer off Susannah. Jill and Sadah, pointedly, told how Tony had respected their lesbian life-style. Tributes that only the dead are accorded. But Ethel took it all in. She looked young, listening. As if she missed that dangerous energy in her life.

Lars-Erik presented a drawing of Ethel and Tony—done from memory, he was drunk enough to say. Then it was time to honor Pearl again. Leonard brought in an immense cock-shaped birthday cake. And Pearl, yes, circumcised it. Then she got on the stage and danced—tottered around the floor really, while we all went stiff with fear. There were cries of, "Take it off!" Then louder cries of, "Put it back on!" Ethel had to go up and lead Pearl down.

It was noisier than a "Night on Bald Mountain." Everyone was trying to make a good impression. Even, it seemed to me, the poor customers—who gave out senseless rebel yells and shouted for seconds before they had finished firsts. My head ached (I had some champagne against my best instincts). And then—at midnight—Ethel stood up.

She signaled to Connie. Connie hit a button behind the bar and our jukebox shut off. Everything stopped. The silence echoed in our heads—like it will when you have a fever. Ethel cleared her voice. I thought, perhaps, that she would be shy in front of so many men. But no.

"Time f'me to go," she said. "I thank everyone here for being faithful t'The Car. Leonard?" Leonard came out with a big cardboard box. It was full of souvenir T-shirts that said I SURVIVED PEARL'S BIRTHDAY AT THE SMOKING CAR. "I thank Pearl for making senior citizen sex fashionable again in Queens. I thank Leonard for being so mean and unpleasant-looking that everyone pays for his drink. I want t'thank Jako, who tells me not one of you, not one, has flushed the john tonight. Most of all," Ethel came over and pulled me toward her. "Most of all, I thank Tony . . ." Her face went blank for a second. "You see where my mind is. I thank *Mike* for jumping into the breach and fucking up his own life in the process. This is my man here." She hugged me. "This is my man. You all listen t'him." I turned red, I could feel it. "Get drunk everyone. This round's on the house." And she left. Carrying Pearl, more or less, under one arm.

A stopper came out of the evening then. Though the crowd slowly decreased, a manic energy picked up and began chasing its tail around the room. By 3 a.m. we had two fights—and a *Niagaran* incident of vomiting. One foot away from me. Splashing all over my new Pumas.

It was a kid—no more than fifteen years old. Leonard and I were aghast. Neither of us, in all that milling around, had seen him come through the front door. He was virtually unconscious, with our liquor license riding on his continued good health. This kid had taken a seat behind the cigarette machine, a blind spot. Someone had been slipping him drinks, but no one owned him now. He hung from Leonard's arms like Christ crucified—smelling of digestive fluid and Sambuca. It was a predicament.

We fished his wallet out—he lived somewhere in Little Neck (an expensive wallet, it was). Leonard drove the kid home in my Lincoln. (He refused to use *his* pickup for obvious reasons.) Lars-Erik understood the possible consequences of our inattention. He went along to hold the kid upright. I turned and went back into The Car—

About ten minutes later it happened.

Bubbles was dancing—by now there were only two girls on stage—and she smiled at me. Bubbles, given an opportunity, always smiled at me, so I waved or nodded and I turned my back on her. You see, I didn't want to encourage her infatuation. She had been reasonable since the fire-escape incident. I thought she was over it.

And—I'll never know now—perhaps she was.

Maybe once after that I glanced back at the stage. Bubbles was squatting, hunkered down like a bushman, that same, vacant smile on her face. I thought it seemed phony then. It was stiff—the way, when you ask a child to smile for your camera, this synthetic, tooth-bared rictus takes over.

The next thing I know, Connie is yelling, "Hey, no floor shows! No floor shows!"

Bubbles was lying on her stomach, her big, shiny behind in the air. And this old geezer was swaying over her, shoving bills in her G-string—where it hid between her buttocks. I wrenched around on my barstool and went over to the stage.

"I'm tipping her," he said.

"Get up, Bubbles," I said. And then I saw her eye. It was frozen. It looked like an artificial thing—such as you might pluck from the head of a Teddy bear. "Get up," I said. And this guy is still sticking dollar bills up her ass. I pushed him. He almost fell. I said, "Stop tipping her, dammit, she's dead."

But Bubbles wasn't—not yet. Her body convulsed. Her legs kicked out so abruptly both her shoes came off. There was a tick of pulse in her neck. "Out of here!" I yelled. "Everyone out of here now! Connie, call 911!"

I flipped Bubbles over and her large breasts wobbled. Then I put my mouth to hers—oh, how she had wanted that, my kiss—and I started doing CPR. She convulsed once again, her head came up and her teeth bit the inside of my lip. But, when she fell back this time it was with a certain finality. I banged at her chest, knocking to find the source of her life and waken it. But there was nothing. It must've been a massive overdose.

When I looked up again the joint was empty. Just Connie and Jako. I sent Connie to get Bubbles's coat. And then, with Jako beside me, stealthily, quickly, I gave Bubbles the last rites of my church. Who knows what her soul made of them as it wandered free. The EMS men interrupted me, in any case. I didn't tell them I was a priest.

Lord God, a child with a great and open spirit has come to you tonight. Book her into a better place than this. Let her get a crush on you. She'll make you smile.

I don't know if Leonard gave her the drug—I don't care, in fact—but he's finished at The Car.

TUESDAY, JULY 12TH

About 6 p.m.
Full of sadness and regret this afternoon. Her heart was as big as Long Island Sound. And I disdained her love.

Then—around 3:30—I got a visit from two narcotics cops. And I handled it—I don't know—clumsily. I was taken off balance. I sounded defensive and guilty. All they wanted from me was a witness deposition covering the circumstances of Bubbles's death. But I talked too much, I'm sure of it.

Most of what they asked was routine enough. Then, the taller one—I forget his name, he hadn't spoken much—said: "How long've you been aware of drug use in The Car?"

I kind of jumped. I said: "I've seen no evidence of drug use. I've only been here two weeks."

"Cherry Watson's bag contained several hundred pills—most of them controlled substances."

"But she wasn't dealing," I said. "Those were her own pills. She got them out in Brooklyn. She lived in a ghetto neighborhood."

"Mr. Wilson," said the tall cop. "You just told us there was no evidence of drug use here. Now you say you were aware that Cherry Watson used narcotics."

I got confused. For one shaky half second I almost said, "I mean, I didn't know until Bubbles O.D.'d." But then I realized—aha—I'd already said Bubbles had told me where the pills came from. Which Bubbles couldn't have done after she O.D.'d. I was GUILTY and defensive under scrutiny. Why was I guilty?—because of Leonard. Because I knew (and I think they knew) what Leonard has been doing at The Car. But it looked like I, the boss, was covering up for myself.

I finally fudged it by saying, "When you mentioned drugs I thought you were referring to cocaine or heroin. I didn't make an immediate connection with, you know, pills and that sort of thing. And I never saw Bubbles—Ms. Watson—use them."

"You thought she was a dealer, not a user."

"I didn't say that—" This cop is good. He had me on the defensive— and then he just smiled and shook my hand.

"Joe Solomon says you're a good guy," he told me. I felt so relieved I almost squealed on Leonard. I must never commit a crime: I'm no good at it. "But," he said, "I think you'll be seeing us again."

She-eet.

Otherwise, a donkey-work afternoon. Jako and I had to pull down all the decorations (and *store* them neatly for next year—Pearl, we are instructed, is superstitious about her birthday paraphernalia). Not that Pearl herself was on duty this afternoon—no, she came down with a convenient indisposition. (Jako told me that, in fact, it wasn't an illness at all: Pearl apparently got so squiffed last night she, um, lost her wig.

And was doing a Garbo until she could find it. Fine with me.) But it meant I had to bartend and act as the curator of Pearl's memorabilia at the same time.

Worse: in sweeping under the cigarette machine we found (Jako found) a veritable lake of vomit. Congealed like week-old New England clam chowder. And just beginning to smell like *Eau de Wino.* So we had to move the machine. And while we're doing this I hear "Earrrg-hhaaaowww," the unmistakable sound of a puking cat. RIGHT ON STAGE. This did not please the Brazilian dancer—Graciela—who hates whatever the word for cat is in Portuguese.

She won't dance on the "feelthy stage." I run over with my all-purpose vomit rag, sweet-talking and being reasonable, saying, "Hey, it's not vomit, it's just a hairball." (Which is much, much nicer than vomit, as we all know.) And what do I see—I SEE WORMS. White, spaghetti things stretching and coiling on the dance floor. Lazarus has a case of worms. And I gotta scoop them up before Graciela catches on and screams until she has a varicose face.

Ugggh. I like cats. I really do. But this is not MY cat. Do I really have to chase him around the bar twice a day and give him Hartz instant wormer? Is this what the topless business is about? Where is the magic, where is the romance . . . ?

Berry just called. She's agreed to be an extra dancer from 7 to 12. Berry also agreed to signal if she thinks Leonard is dealing coke in the kitchen.

This may be my last entry.

6 a.m.

It's done. I fired Leonard and I'm still alive. So far. And, baby, I will not need a laxative tonight.

Our plan was . . . I mean, Berry's plan was . . . (She's street sharp, she impresses me. I wouldn't have thought it out as clearly. And she loves me, I can see it in her eyes: what a pleasure, when usually all I see in women now is defiance or fear or mockery or just a big VACANCY sign.) What Berry said was:

"You wanna catch Leonard dealing, but you don't wanna catch him dealing with a regular customer. Or a girl." She had someone in mind. This guy, she spent a set with him at another topless joint, The Purple Plum. Apparently he offered her coke for a blowjob. Told her he copped from Leonard at The Car. On Tuesdays. Berry said she would signal when the guy went back to our kitchen. By putting her policeman's hat on. (Berry often uses a cop's uniform in her dance: fake shoulder holster over one naked breast. Sexy.)

So I waited. And I waited. Ten o'clock, eleven o'clock. I can't go up to her because we make a point of showing no affection, not even eye contact, in The Car. (Still, everyone seems to know—Berry might as well sit in my lap.) So I waited, and sweated and rehearsed all sorts of confrontation scenes.

Finally the hat went on. I had been in the john. Without reflection, I was so keyed up, I took off for the kitchen. And, sure enough, there was Leonard with an enormous *mason jar* full of cocaine. A young, very small Latino kid was with him, leaning over the table with a straw in his nose. (I hadn't seen him go back. And I was grateful to Berry—what I needed right then was a very small adversary.)

"You," I said to the kid, "get out or I'm calling the cops." He didn't even finish his snort. He was all sneaker juice and gone.

"What the fuck is this?" said Leonard.

"This is your last day here, this is your last minute here. You're fired, Leonard." I almost went for the jar—but the stuff is expensive, and I didn't want Leonard to go berserk on me.

"Hey, Mike," he said. "Take it easy. I know you're upset. I liked Bubbles, too. But I didn't sell her nothin'. Cocaine wasn't her thing. You know that, you were banging her. Jesus. She was a pill freak. I don't front pills here."

"Leonard," I said. "Let us not engage in small talk. Take that jar of shit and get out. You aren't welcome here any more—not as an employee, not as a customer."

"There are things you don't know, Mike. Take my word for it. There. Are. Things. You. Don't. Know."

"Not interested in knowing, either. Get out, Leonard, before I call the narc cops who visited me this afternoon."

"Them? Don't worry about them, Mike. I got that covered. They're not the ones you haveta be worried about. You saw what happened to Rita, didn't you?"

"You scare me, Leonard. You scare me a lot. But you're still out. *Now,* damn it."

"Mike—you don't know. I own 10% of this place. Tony sold me 10%— ask Ethel. You can't kick me out."

"You may be telling the truth—if so, you are now an absentee owner. Good-bye, Leonard. Walk through that door and keep on walking."

"You are the biggest asshole in the world, Mike. You just signed your own death warrant."

"Good. I'd rather be dead than smell your stinking breath again."

"Come on," Leonard said. "You want it. Come on. You want me t'kick the shit out of you, right? Right? You like it, don't you?"

"Get out, Leonard."

"You think y'can take me, Mike?" It was getting nowhere, so I went toward the pay phone—yes, I pulled a quarter out, showed it to Leonard and headed for the phone.

And, as my father used to say, Leonard went bonkers. He barreled out of the kitchen and along the bar, knocking bottles off as he went. (He had the cocaine jar inside a paper bag in his left hand—this restrained the mayhem a bit.) Down to the end of the bar. Then back, this time while swatting at each customer's drink. He flicked a full Tom Collins into Matt's lap.

Then back toward me like a rhino. And (thank God) past me. And toward the door. But before his exit—which, believe me, had everyone's attention—he stopped. Then Leonard pointed up at Berry, who looked extra-nude on stage, and yelled:

"You'll wake up some morning with a tire iron for a tampon, cunt."

And he was gone.

I give Berry enormous credit. She didn't flinch. She just picked up her dance where she had left off. Connie, on the other hand, had gone white as feta cheese. She came over to me. My eye was averted—I was trying to clean up the mess and give everyone a refill—as Connie leaned down and asked,

"You fired him?"

"Yes," I said.

"My God," she said. "Don't leave here alone tonight. Promise me you won't leave here alone."

So I took Connie and Berry and Norm over to the Empire Diner for breakfast. For some reason or other Berry and Connie don't get along—a woman thing. I tried to eat, but I was swallowing more air than food. As a result I became painfully flatulent—nerves—and spent most of the meal trying to relieve myself discreetly. Norm and Connie kept a skeptical eye on me: maybe they expected a bullet hole to appear in the middle of my forehead. Berry, by contrast, finished her French toast and half of mine. With her hand on the inside of my thigh. I love that. I love a woman who puts her hand on the inside of my thigh.

"We did it," she said, as I pulled up in front of her door. "Leonard was a low-life. He was gonna get us all in trouble." Then she kissed me—and I couldn't respond, I felt like a straw thing. My mind was in its spin cycle.

"You're tired," Berry said. "You've got the world on your shoulders and you're tired." It was sweet. If fucking Leonard dares to touch Berry . . .

God, did he touch Rita? And Tony? Is he a psychotic killer?

And, great, I just noticed my Phone-Mate is flashing.

Ethel wants to see me tomorrow—as soon as I get up. This will not be fun.

And who will I hire to replace Leonard?

I'd rather have a parish in Iraq.

WEDNESDAY, JULY 13TH

2 p.m.

Well, I'm surprised, it didn't go all that badly. I think Ethel respects me for what I did. On the other hand, maybe I'm kidding myself. Ethel's a pragmatist. And quick on her feet. "Naturally, Mike . . . without Leonard . . ." Well, *naturally* she's more dependent on me than ever. So I've made things harder for myself. No way can I leave now without training a replacement first. (Pearl has nominated her cousin's nephew, Bert Weiner. I'm to meet him this evening.) I feel cornered. Then I try to empathize with what's going on inside Ethel, inside those kids. Any minute they expect to identify Tony in some morgue body-drawer. There is a feeling of grim anticipation around. And Leonard, I fear, is capable of anything.

I told Ethel I'd be taking tomorrow afternoon off: I've FINALLY made an appointment at Diocese House to see old Bishop Plunk—no doubt the Christian reference startled her. I've been here, let's see, almost three weeks. What Ethel doesn't want is for Jesus to call me now. So, at that point—she's a sly one—she said:

"I hear you were banging that poor kid, Bubbles." Just to remind Father Mike of his general unworthiness.

"No, Ethel," I said. "You hear wrong. Even if Pearl told you she saw Bubbles naked in my apartment—"

"Naked? Was she?" said Ethel. "Pearl didn't tell me anything." Was Ethel lying? "Actually the girl herself said something t'me on Monday night—she was a little unstable, wasn't she?"

"To put it mildly. Likeable, really good. But, yes, strange—and desperate."

"A topless dancer."

"A topless dancer."

"But sexy, from what I saw. And you resisted that. You're a strong man, Tony. You amaze me."

"Try not t'call me Tony, Ethel. The kids get mixed up as it is."

"Damn. Did I?"

"And I'm not strong. It just so happens I wasn't attracted t'Bubbles. Thank God. She was pregnant when she died."

"Oh, damn." And Ethel burst into tears. "I hate this business—all the time you see people who have, you know, no roots. No self-esteem. And, you know, you watch them kill themselves. And they have all this money, but no common sense. And they're just, you know, female children." She got very emotional then: she started drumming fists on her thighs. It was the first time Ethel's let her guard down. So I jumped in with:

"Maybe you should sell The Car, Ethel."

"Oh, I've thought about it. Believe me, I have. But it would mean, you know, I was giving up on any hope of seeing Tony again. We need time t'build The Car up. Profits are way off. Leonard is gone now. And where d'you find a buyer, Mike? The liquor license is in both our names, thank God, Tony and mine, but you can't sell a liquor license—if I push the panic bar and sell now, providing I could even dredge up someone with a license—it's too much. I'd have to sell the house. I'm trapped."

"Uh," I said. "Linese spoke t'me a coupla nights ago. He said he'd be interested in The Car, if you—"

"Fuck Linese," Ethel said.

"He's not a savory character—"

"Fuck him again," Ethel said. "You think he hasn't wanted this? To see us down. So his greasy joints can pick up the slack."

"I—"

"Daniels and that other stupid cop, they won't listen t'me. Why? Because Linese has family connections and the whole fuckin' precinct's on the take, that's why."

"You think Linese—

Later.

I broke off writing because Berry knocked. She stood there in cutoff jeans and a midriff blouse with no bra. Boy, the male mechanism is a terrific reflex. See. Drool. Want. I had been tired and distracted and depressed and then, ding-dong. I was Mr. Deep-Voice Smoothy. Berry sees this and finds it amusing. Her visit, shall we say, was mischievous.

I protested too much: I really had to get back to The Car, interview Bert, blah-blah.

"I know," she says. "You've got too much on your mind. That's why I came."

So for the first time in my life, I had a quickie.

Berry just leaned over the edge of my mattress and slipped her shorts down. (Oi. Gotta get a lockbox for this journal.) Berry has beautiful, slim-long, hard buttocks, brown with the outline of her VERY brief bikini bathing suit bottom. Makes me think I'm having sex *through* the clothes or something.

And WHAT WAS I GOING TO DO? Huh? Say no? Why? I've already made love to Berry. Jesus said you're cooked if you even lust after a woman in your heart. So why not baste the roast? Oh, it was good. Because it was offered so innocently, lovingly.

Oh, shit, shut up you hypocrite. You fucked her. Neither of you was innocent. And, in the middle of it,

Kay called.

Yes Kay, with her remote-sensing device, which detects whenever I'm having pleasure—Kay, that solvent of hard-ons—Kay spoke on the Phone-Mate. Which interested Berry not a little. Kay said,

"Hi. Just being a nuisance again. Just wanted to say I missed you. Mike? I do miss you. And, guess what, my geraniums won best in show. Exciting, huh? Well, give a call whenever. Can't wait to see you again. Bye . . ."

All at once I was Silly Putty inside Berry. Not for long, mind you, but long enough. Berry was gracious about it. She didn't begrudge me my pleasure, but afterward she said, "Geraniums?"

"They're flowers."

"I know, Mike. I'm a topless dancer but I've heard of geraniums. This is your girl back home? She sounds pretty."

"*Sounds* pretty?"

"Not a knockout, but pretty. And very nice."

"Uh, look," I said. I am really a scumbag. I really am. "Uh, look—being a priest is a little like running a topless bar. People get crushes on you for the wrong reasons."

"And she's got a crush on you, like Bubbles, like me?"

"Not like you."

"I'm different, huh?"

"Yes."

"Say you care for me, Mike. I know priests don't marry topless dancers. But say you care for me."

That was easy. So I did. Then I put my tongue inside her navel and saw the light brown hairs against the browner skin, across the taut drum of her stomach. And for a moment it was the whole wide world.

5 a.m.

A stupid, perplexing night. I hired Bert and probably I shouldn't have hired Bert—who knows? But Freddy quit on me—said he was too scared to work at The Car anymore—and Leonard, apparently, is telling every bouncer in the Tri-State area to steer clear of me because something is "coming down" on that fuck, Mike Wilson. Great news. DISMEMBERED MAN WAS EPISCOPAL PRIEST. Head found in Plaza Fountain.

Joe Solomon perked me up. Joe Solomon is a mensch—he went out of his way to congratulate me for sacking L. He also told me—much to my relief—that the narcotics men believed my story. Something to the effect that, oh, I was too stupid to be telling a lie. I take praise where I can get it these days.

Then in came Bert. There was a big crowd, and it was a crowd made up of groups, which is always the primal ooze of violence. Six Italians. Three Greek waiters from Astoria. The inevitable four or five Latinos. And all of these ethnic groups appear to hate Brazilians. I have Chinga on one shift and Arugula (can that be her real name?) on the other shift. Both Brazilians, both are earning more than any Wop-Greek-Latino in the room. Both of whom want what's in your pants, i.e. your wallet and nothing else. (Both Virgos, too. Pearl has this theory that most topless dancers and whores are Virgos. Virgos apparently are women who like to use their sexuality for power and money, but don't really like sex. I must say in our informal poll five out of 12 dancers were Virgos. You see what I'm reduced to: four years of college, and I'm asking people what their sign is. And I'm nervous about seeing Plunk tomorrow.)

Anyway, back to Bert. The Italians and Greeks and Latinos are calling Chinga and Arugula wetback and whore and piece of fried placenta. I've already once asked for a little gentlemanly restraint. Raven has just shortchanged a Greek. By accident *maybe*. In other words, I'm expecting a riot and need help.

So, first off, Bert looks good to me. He's big and he's worked in security somewhere. Also, Leonard hasn't gotten to him. And, of course, he's Pearl's cousin's nephew.

But I realize in no time that Bert is ineffably clumsy: TWICE in our first half hour together he steps on my foot. And I mean he *clomps*. Not only does he clomp—Bert doesn't even *notice* he's standing on your instep. You have to tell him. And you better do this quickly because Bert weighs many stone. Most of this weight is in his upper arms, which hang down like giant dewlaps. He is not attractive. He looks like a Minus-Zero Mostel, without the comic timing.

I soon realize what half the problem is—half the problem is that Bert can't see. Beyond, oh, three feet, Bert is just estimating the world—in the most general terms. Maybe that's you out there, maybe it isn't. Ooops, it was a wall. Bert is strong and willing—but to be of any use I'll have to launch him in the right direction like a torpedo. Still, presence is important. Bert's presence quieted things down. A topless bar is not a topless bar without at least one big fat man. Squatting there like a household god.

I was glad to have him. All night long I watched the door, expecting Leonard or a Molotov cocktail to come bouncing in.

Berry is here with me tonight. Taking a shower as I write. I've given her one drawer of my bureau. They say that's very significant in a relationship.

I must call Kay.

THURSDAY, JULY 14TH

5:30 p.m.
I'll write this down, but I really don't believe it. Maybe it wasn't me—maybe it was some dream, maybe an astral projection of Mike Wilson—that flew out to Diocese House. And flew—oh, flew—back. I sit here half terrified, half convulsed by giggles—which is probably a short-form definition of madness.

Don't worry, Mike. It'll be over soon. They're closing in on you.

So, I took the LIRR out to Diocese House. (Somehow I didn't think driving up in a 1990 Lincoln that still smells of vomit was, well, canonical.) And I wore my monkey suit for the first time in weeks. It gave me an odd sensation. Singled out again. One man—he probably thought I was Catholic, Episcopalians just don't inspire anger, we're too harmless—one man walked up and spat on my shined shoe.

"Would you care t'try again?" I said. Turn the other shoe.

"Free the Irish," he said. And walked off. But then, while I was waiting to change trains on the Jamaica platform, this Rastafarian—drunk on male hormones or something more expensive—started shouting and then yelling A-men! to his own shouts. Such high energy comes to Nebraska only in tornado season. And, suddenly, nervous women on the platform started gathering around me. Around my collar, that is. I had an instant congregation. They were taking sanctuary in my presence. Most of them looked Jewish. And I remembered my favorite saying of Jesus's: "Oh, Jerusalem, Jerusalem, which killest the prophets, and stonest them that are sent unto thee: how often would I have gathered thy children together, as a hen doth gather her brood under her wings, and ye would not!"

Which made me susceptible to tears. Since I was early, I strolled the grounds of Diocese House for fifteen minutes or so. The landscaping is exquisite. Say what you will about our dying sect, we have good taste.

The roses were in their prime. And the topiary work—which must cost a tycoon's tithe to maintain—was magnificent. So Anglican. Not much had changed since I was last there (as a convention delegate) seven or eight years ago. They've added one unfortunate modern sculpture called "Jesus Bearing the Cross"—which, to be frank, makes Jesus-plus-cross look like a helicopter gunship. But otherwise, beautiful. And silent enough to hear a sparrow's fall. In so many ways the priest's vocation is still attractive.

But I couldn't fully relish it—because I've chosen to become an outcast. (I kept ducking behind bushes, lest I bump into someone I know.) And in time—displacing my guilt—I got into the anger and pride place. What-right-do-they-have-to-judge-me? Who-says-what-I'm-doing-is-wrong? Jesus-ate-with-sinners. And so forth. Because I was all pumped up for a big wad of lying.

Old Plunk, of course, is a sweetheart. Bit of a nance, as my father used to say. But good-hearted and trusting and easy to con. Easy, but you feel like Judas doing it. Worse, he remembered me.

"You're MacFeeley's project, aren't you?"

Nice way to put it—I guess that's what I was. A project. The sinner turned into a man of God. The young boy who went from lust to piety. We talked about Father Mac for a while. (Mac, if he were alive, would be a contemporary of Plunk's.) And then I told Plunk this seamless garment of half-truth and high invention: Yes, my brother was missing. Nieces to support. My only family. Learning to make ravioli and fettucine Alfredo in the kitchen. A full-time job.

"Well," said Plunk, combing his eyebrows—great gypsy-moth things they are—"You know how I feel about worker priests. I think they're a good thing. We need priests who are grounded in reality. And we've got too many damn priests and too few churches anyhow. But you must miss the eucharist."

No, no—not me. I told him I was worshipping here and there. Altar-shopping.

"Of course," he said. "I mean, you must miss celebrating the eucharist. Like an athlete, you get out of shape."

Yes, I said. Oh, yes. Totally unprepared for what was coming.

"Now, let's see." He opened his pocket calendar. "Hmm. Oh, yes—that'll do nicely. Sunday the 24th. Week from this coming Sunday. I'm making an episcopal visit at St. Lebbeus's in Bayside—nice, liberal congregation. And the rector, Larry Lapham, will be in Aspen. We'll concelebrate, you and me, would that be nice?"

Oh, nice.

"You do the sermon—I'll do a homily. That'll save me digging through the trunk for something t'say." He leaned forward and whispered, "Took an old sermon out of the file yesterday—and it slipped from my hand. Fell on the floor and broke into six pieces." He laughed. I laughed. He has charmed this diocese into bewildered submission for twenty-two years. "That's how old my sermons are."

He got up and walked to the French doors that overlook the cathedral and the Scissorhands circus out there. I was befuddled. Concelebrate—with Saturday night's topless receipts under my vestments. I'll knock the chalice over, sure as anything. And they'll all know I'm a sinner.

"What's Nebraska like?" he asked.

"It's like a long, enforced meditation," I said. He laughed.

"You're a bright kid," Plunk said. "Mac knew what he was doing. Must be culture shock t'come back here. Why not talk about that? And the drought, we hear about the drought a lot. Whatever you want, naturally. But the Nebraska, New York thing might be interesting."

Oh, yes. I'd been thinking about that. Uh-huh. Just what I need now—to write a sermon. Keep the old rhetorical sinews in shape.

"It's a date then?" I nodded. "I'll drop Bishop Watts a note t'say you're not chain snatching or smoking crack back here." He shook my hand. "Just stop by that big office down the hall—give Gus Manning your phone and address so he can put it in the sacred computer."

And I thanked him. And—in a total daze (I'd gotten away with it!)—in a total daze I walked down the hall. In a total daze I came to the office door. REV. AUGUSTUS MANNING, the sign said.

And in a total daze I saw that Augustus Manning was—is—The Man in the Floppy Hat.

He didn't see me. He was in profile, bent over a computer keyboard. I backed out like a disembodied spirit—pure ectoplasm. And ran until I got halfway across the cathedral grounds. From Jamaica I called in my (Ethel's) phone number and address—using a fake midwestern accent. Manning didn't seem to make any connection. I'm safe for now. But, if he sees me, if he goes to St. Lebbeus's on the 24th, say . . . I'm dead meat.

Or maybe not. My mind is whirling. It cuts both ways after all. Manning can't want the Bishop to know he's a topless bar devotee. I've got him, he's got me. But, most of all, I remember what Jako told me—how Manning dropped that shot of vodka on Lazarus's open wound. Good God, what kind of man is this? I may be a pander and a satyr, but I don't torture cats. This is a sick man.

Sick . . . Judge not that ye be not judged.

My time is running out. Mike Wilson is a common name, but Manning or someone will make the connection before long. This is my last chance. I could quit tomorrow, and yet I'm—

That was Bert. He lost his set of keys. Gnnnnnnnnng . . . Gotta get back to my new vocation.

5 a.m.
My God.

Colavecchia and Daniels came in tonight. While I was playing chess with Joe. And I thought, Uh-oh, this is it, they've found Tony. My brother is dead. Their attitude toward me had changed, I was no longer just a useful civilian—I was something else.

But it had nothing to do with Tony or Rita.

They think Bubbles was MURDERED. She didn't die of a narcotic overdose. They found *strychnine* in her system.

Who, who would commit such a heinous crime? My God, can it be? One of those damn Brazilian girls . . . OK, truth is, Bubbles was a bit pushy-cute. She could get on your nerves . . . but enough for murder? And hideous murder, too. That last excruciating convulsion, where she bit my mouth, that was brought on by the poison.

Remember when Bubbles threw beer in Linese's face?

The cops grilled me about Pearl's party. You might've thought we'd never met before. Who had access to the women's locker room? Well, of course, *everyone* had access. The place was bedlam that night. Anybody could've slipped in. So we settled for cataloguing women—dancers and bar girls. (And I could only remember 9 of the onstage women—gotta check my records and call tomorrow.) But then I asked—smart ass me—who says the poison was given to Bubbles in The Car? Someone in Brooklyn, where she lived, might've had access to her bag. And Daniels said,

"You had access to her bag."

"Me?"—I'm a suspect. I suppose it's just a formality, but now I'm a murder suspect. Great. "I guess," I said.

"You guess? That's what you told narcotics."

"I had access to her bag—as much as anyone."

"More than some." I got peevish then.

"Should I use my one phone call and retain a lawyer?"

"Mike," said Joe. "They're doing their job. They watch old *Dragnet* re-runs, they can't help themselves. No one thinks you killed her—if she was killed. It could be an accident, it could be suicide—"

"You know I was super-fond of Bubbles. Everyone was—she was like our mascot here."

"But, in fact," said Daniels, "in fact you were having a sexual relationship with her."

"In fact, I wasn't. I've run into this rumor over and over. And I guess nothing I say will correct it. I never went t'bed with her. I never even made-out with her."

"Bubbles," said Joe, "had a terrific crush on Mike. We all knew it. She wanted people t'think Mike and her were getting it on. Listen, for that matter, *I* had access to her stuff. Bubbles left her bag around everywhere."

"Stop acting like Mike's lawyer, Joe," said Colavecchia. "He can answer for himself."

"Fuck you, Cola."

"Fuck you, Joe."

Which interchange, thank Joe, gave me time to regroup. Daniels then said, "Can you think of anyone who might've had a motive?"

"No. No one."

"You mean this topless dancer was perfect? Nobody had a hard-on for her?"

"No one that I know of. Maybe her good spirits were a little forced, a little irritating. But you ask Jako, our custodian, he's been crying ever since Monday."

"Did you know she was pregnant?"

"Yes."

"Who's the father?"

"She gave me the impression it was done—so t'speak—by commit-tee."

"Gave you the impression—"

"All right. She told me there were several candidates. She didn't give names."

"You weren't one of them?"

"Joe," I said, "aren't they supposed t'read me my rights or something? I mean, would you tell them I've only been in New York three weeks. When Bubbles conceived I was 2,000 miles away in Nebraska."

"We're just jealous," Colavecchia said. "We'd like your job. Daniels is the only cunt I get t'work with. But you can be sure we'll stop by t'question you a whole lot."

"Well," I said, "at least one good thing. At least you know Tony didn't do it."

"Do we?" said Daniels. "Do we really? That's interesting."

I showed them around after that. Men's room, women's room, kitchen, etc. It was a slow night and the presence of two homicide men did not lend it a finer aspect. Word soon got out—*policia!*—and one of my Brazilian girls, Aleesha, panicked. (She thought they were from Immigration.) Aleesha simply walked out onto Northern Boulevard in her bra and G-string. I found her hiding around the corner, where the side entrance to Big Marty's, the dead dry cleaning place, is, surrounded by ten-year-old boys who were quite impressed by her proportions. Aleesha wouldn't come in. Finally I went back to pick up her clothing and duffle bag. I felt sorry for her—it isn't Aleesha's fault she was born in that giant moth closet, Brazil.

Well, Bubbles has gotten my attention at last—that muscular waif, that sexy clown. There was a dangerous energy around her—and she was a lightning rod for it. "I'm accident prone," she once told me, "but never prone by accident." Bright and lost. She said a lot of amusing things that took me by surprise. I shoulda treated her better. But that's me—even when I'm being "moral," I hurt people.

I can't get Manning out of my mind—that image of him pouring vodka on Lazarus. Of course, I can't even remember if Manning was around on Pearl's birthday. But my suspicion is nothing more than my fear projected. I'm afraid of Manning—and I want him (a priest) to be more corrupt than I am. The more corrupt he is, the smaller the threat he is to my cover.

But, after all, why should it surprise anyone—I mean, that there is a murderer amongst us? The Car exists in a twilight land—just on the thinnest edge of human civility. A border crossing. People come and go from here to their depravity. And in the crossing and recrossing Bubbles got snuffed out.

Maybe they're right—maybe I did do it. I dream terrible things. I'm going to hide this journal from now on.

Bert sat on a barstool and broke it. But he is the only one among us presumed innocent.

Lord God, I am steeped in my sinfulness. I can't remember when last my heart was comfortable. I have no assurance in me now.

Lord God, I'm afraid to consider You—because now You are the God of judgment to me, not the God of grace and forgiveness. I'm in a dusky place and unrepentant. I'm stepping over. Protect me. Teach me.

Yes.

My prayers are too glib, I know it.

FRIDAY, JULY 15TH

Afternoon

Eight-line item about Bubbles in the *Post*: my name—praise Him—not mentioned. Pearl, on the other hand, is miffed. The article said only, "an employee's birthday party." Ah, the vicissitudes of N.Y. celebrity.

In fact, Pearl has been, shall we say, *unforthcoming* with me of late. I get quizzical, even hostile glances from her. These I attribute to Pearl's own sense of guilt. I just KNOW she couldn't resist telling the cops that Bubbles was seminude in my apartment. Some sense of decency kept her from blowing the whistle about my vocation—but, if the right moment arrives, Pearl will barter my soul for a paragraph on Page Six. Ethel, of course, would squeeze Pearl's head as though it were a loofah. And that may keep her quiet.

Rita and Bubbles—and Tony. Everyone except Ethel (and me) seems to think there is some connection. But how could that be? Rita and Tony were intimate—Bubbles hardly knew him. The methods of execution have been totally different. The first was angry, male, physical—strangulation. It required great strength. The second was clever, female, secretive. An ambush, not a confrontation.

Yet Daniels wouldn't exempt Tony from consideration. What are we supposed to think? That Tony murdered Rita, went into hiding, then emerged on Monday—to enter The Car, disguised maybe as a drunken teamster, and slip strychnine into Bubbles's orange juice?

Uh-huh.

Moreover, unless Daniels thinks Tony is a psychopathic serial killer, there was no motive. Well, for killing Rita, maybe. Maybe Rita had something on Tony. Maybe Rita was going to tell Ethel. There are reasons, I suppose. But none of those reasons would apply to Bubbles as well. (Unless Bubbles knew something about Rita's murder—No, Mike. Your wheels are spinning. That doesn't make sense. Start again.)

What do these murders—and Tony's disappearance—have in common? They hurt The Car. Girls won't dance for us if they're afraid of being poisoned. Tony made The Car numero uno on Northern Boulevard. So who profits? Linese and his shareholders profit if Tony is out of the picture.

And Bubbles, Connie tells me, used to dance for Linese at Rabies.

Furthermore (this I also learned from Connie), Linese has a piece of Spotlight—which is the first or second largest topless-dancer agency in New York. It operates out of one seedy office—couch and telephone— on 22nd Street near Sixth Avenue. But, Connie says, appearances deceive. Like everything else in this business.

Figure each girl gets an average nut of $70 per night (not counting tips). Ten percent ($7) of that nut goes to Spotlight. Doesn't sound like much. But figure Spotlight provides dancers for 80 bars (out of 300 or so)—in New York, Westchester, especially Jersey. (In Jersey girls make a bigger nut, AND they dance with their tops *on*—you figure it.) So . . . do the math. $7 per girl, times 50 girls a week, times 80 bars, times 52 weeks a year—calculator. About $1,456,000. Not counting stag parties and strip-a-grams. Good money. All of which is well deserved by anyone who deals with topless screwballs 365 days a year.

We, however, are the equivalent of a non-union house. Our women are scabs, so to say—and good-looking ones at that. If Linese were to take over The Car—well, not only would he get rid of competition on the boulevard, but Spotlight would take our bookings. Which are worth about $20,000 a year in commissions. And salaries would be driven down from Queens Plaza to Flushing.

It makes sense.

But so, I have to admit, does the drug angle. I remember, that night when Chinga and Changa went berserk, how Leonard grabbed Roxanne brutally by the pubic hair. He has rage enough to strangle a woman. And now it comes to me what Nancy Cortez meant: Rita had a sexual relationship with Leonard, but "that was another kind of thing." Maybe a sexual relationship based on drug dependency. It makes sense. So Leonard is supplying drugs to Rita and Bubbles, and maybe they fall behind in their dues and so Leonard . . .

But what about Tony? Was he involved in the cocaine traffic, too? Jesus, Mike, don't go blind, deaf and dumb on me—what's the answer? Could Leonard turn The Car into a junkie's Quik-Stop without Tony's knowledge? Be serious. *I* knew Leonard was dealing after two weeks. But maybe Leonard didn't start dealing until Tony disappeared. Is that *why* my brother was made to vanish?

No matter what the circumstances, no matter who the killer—Leonard, Linese, the Gaucho, Freddy, Joe Solomon, Lars-Erik, some TV set hijacker, ME—my brother and benefactor, my surrogate father, Tony is dead. I can't keep lying to myself. And I realize—no matter how cool or callous he may have made himself—at the moment of extinction Tony must've been terrified. Did he die angry, bitter, full of ripened evil, unrepentant? Yes—most likely he did. I know now that my brother had enemies. That people, in turn, were frightened of him. That something illegal was probably going on. And that my brother, my big brother, was a desperate man.

God damn.

There's another motive, one I avoid thinking about, though it's ubiquitous here: the sex thing, I mean. Leonard was having some kind of affair with Rita. And then Tony seduced her. (Maybe *she* seduced *him.*) Sex makes men ugly. I see it in Daniels's eye—he envies me my position at The Car. He has made it hard on me because of that. The truth is: sex can never be underestimated. I heard one girl say to another this afternoon, "Well, I'm only attracted to him physically." Only? Only? Only the primal chemistry driving an entire genus of apes along.

Like Norm Hohol said night before last. (Norm is a strange, decadent little man.) There was this foxy chick on stage: not curvaceous, not big-breasted, but deer-like, awkward and shy in a purposeful way, like she could be a prep school cheerleader. Janice. Actually I think she's 24. But Janice wears loafers and a plaid skirt with a big safety pin. Very effective. In fact, the sexiest outfits are those which most nearly approximate normal underclothing. Feathers and G-strings with little neon lights in them (there are such things) may be cute, but they say, This Is An Act. I'm Wearing A Costume. With Janice you feel like a 15-year-old peeping Tom.

So Norm is sitting next to me at the bar when, all at once, he breaks into a lyrical reverie. "Lookit those breasts," he says. "Every time her torso moves, they're so soft, they take a different shape—like blown glass in a breeze. And her ass: the jut of it. If they padded dashboards with what her ass is made from no one would get hurt in accidents." And so forth and so on. When you're very short, you have to talk a good line.

"Unnnh?" I said.

"Mike, I want her," said Norm. "I'm sweating inside me, I want her so much. I want to sculpt those breasts—aaah."

"Calm down," I said. "It's normal."

"No—it isn't. I'm desperate to know how those breasts feel—desperate. And yet . . ."

"And yet, Norm—?"

"And yet I spent last night with her. I fucked her three times and ate her out like a Barricini box. I've touched every part of her body—"

"Gentlemen shouldn't tell tales."

"It's wrong, I know. Treat it as privileged information—but I'm trying t'make a point. The monotony of male desire. IT NEVER STOPS. My ex-wife would undress and I'd start t'drool on my lapels—after fifteen years of marriage. IT NEVER STOPS. Even when you've had it, you haven't had it. We're the only species whose females are always in season. I lie ontopa some lovely piece of strudel and I know, I know— NO PROGRESS is being made. I wish maybe when you fucked a woman she'd deflate and disappear. Like one of those rubber Judy dolls. Just, you know, pop and be gone."

Norm is short-man pompous. He was bragging and pontificating at the same time. (Plenty of truth in what he said. I had Berry just two days ago and her body is terra incognita again—I throb for it.) But, bragging aside, I couldn't help registering what Norm said about wanting to kill women. Even in metaphor. And he noted it, because five minutes later he said,

"Not that I'd ever kill a woman."

"Of course not," I said.

"I love women," he said.

He's too small to have strangled Rita. I think.

7 a.m.—a dawn I never expected to see. Horny, deceitful, disloyal, angry—all those things—and add *coward* as well. I was scared to second childishness tonight. Sheee-it.

You're playing with the big boys now, Mike. The guys who aren't afraid to kill.

.   .   .

First of all, it rained spittoons of water from about 8 p.m. until this morning. Great white gusts that streamed up Northern Boulevard like a giant choir in a giant recessional. Thunder, too. The old wood floor at The Car takes a licking in heavy rain. People drip in—water just seeps through the wood. (This block of buildings dates from 1923. The Car was a speakeasy even then.) After three days the wood still isn't dry. And all that time you can resmell the acrid bouquet from every spilled drink since April.

Small crowd. I had Nana—blond, blue-eyed—and Florian—a redhead with freckles—dancing the last shift for three people. (Who were they? I can't remember their faces.) Believe it or not Nana and Florian are from Brazil. Nana told me there are a lot of Germans (which she is) and Italians in Southern Brazil. What an ethnic stew that country must be.

I ran out and hailed them a cab, while brandishing a tiny pink umbrella. The wind turned it up like a brandy snifter. So I was drenched and crotchety and impatient to see Berry—who was waiting at the apartment. (I've given her a key. Another significant moment in our relationship.) Since the Bubbles thing and all the unfounded rumors, I don't want Berry meeting me at The Car.

Of course, there's Bert. Bert takes a bus down Northern Boulevard to catch the R train at Queens Plaza. I can't make Bert wait for a bus in this weather. So I offer him a ride to Queens Plaza.

Oh, no, says Bert, I couldn't. Oh, yes, you could, I say. Oh, no. Oh, yes. The man drives me crazy. On the other hand he is (or was?) totally loyal to me—and that's a new experience, very welcome. But is he a good bouncer? Who can tell? This afternoon I heard him talking in the men's room. "Okay. That's it. I'm counting t'three and you're outa there, you little *goniff*." I push through the john door to help him and no one's there. Just a lot of Bert. He apparently practices these intimidations to see if he can scare himself.

So out we go to the Lincoln. Bert runs the way the San Diego Chicken runs: his belly about sixteen inches behind him, trying to catch up. And, naturally, the seat belt does not fit around him—we are short at least six inches of strap. And Bert is soaking the passenger seat, and he already smells of mildew and . . .

A screeek.

I look up—through the beaded, pocked, steaming windshield, I see that a car has angled into the parking space ahead of me. I'm furious. I can't pull forward. I'm about to open my window, but it won't go down without power, and this figure gets out of the car in front. SLOWLY.

I can't see him, maybe he's thin and Latino, maybe not—but I know

I'm in trouble. He got out SLOWLY. In that teeming rain he got out SLOWLY.

And also, he had a rifle in his hand.

I waited. Bert is still trying to buckle up when—BLAT!—this guy blows my right front tire out and—BLAT!—he blows my left front tire out, and you can feel the car settle forward, and Bert is holding my arm and keening like it was Yom Kippur—*oiiiiiiii.*

BLAT! Now the guy has taken my left rear tire out. And we knew it would come—this was a thorough man—we waited, staring straight ahead like truants caught. We waited and—*oiiiiii*—BLAT!

No more tires. Bert has froth on his upper lip. Do we duck? Does it make any sense to duck? Yes, says Bert and he dives—aiiiiii—across me like a surge of molasses. I am stuck: upright and vulnerable. And very still. Now I lay me down to sleep.

BLAT!—*keerash.* The back window is shot away. I feel pinpricks of glass on my nape, and I say—oh, what a pathetic sound—"Ple-asssse."

And the figure is now in front of me—rifle up and aimed at my head. My pulse is in my cheekbones: it's pounding there. He waits. I can't stand it any longer—and I avert my face.

And the next thing I hear is the car engine. He's gone. Bert had befouled himself. Smelled like burnt galoshes. I kicked him upright with my knees.

"He's gone, you big coward," I had the nerve to say.

"I quit," Bert said.

"I'll tell you whenta quit," I said. "I'm not quitting."

"They're your enemies, that's why. You can't quit. They're not my enemies, they're—"

"Oh, shut up!" I said.

I stepped out of the Lincoln and both my legs gave way. Just whoosh and down like a kneeling bus. On the soaking sidewalk. And I'd bitten my tongue half off.

Ethel took it very seriously. She told me to rent myself a nice new Lincoln. And to be careful. Be CAREFUL?

"Ethel," I said. "When a man wants t'kill you—he can kill you."

"But he didn't," she said. "That's the point. He could have and he didn't. It's just Leonard. Leonard is still pissed off. But he's not a killer."

"You're sure of that?"

"Yes. I know him. He just wanted t'frighten you."

"But what about other people—it could be the Gaucho. It could be Linese."

"The Gaucho, Linese, they would've killed you."

"Oh."

"So, you see it's all right. Listen, Mike, we can't let them ride us out on a rail."

"No."

"I'm behind you 100%. And, you'll see—Rita and Bubbles, maybe they were murdered, but it had nothing t'do with The Car. It had nothing t'do with Tony."

"Ethel," I said, "I'm scared. My life is coming apart. I don't know who I am."

"You're our knight in shining armor," she said.

SATURDAY, JULY 16TH

5 p.m.

Bert is back. Don Quixote (me) has discovered his Sancho Panza.

I walk in at 11:45, and there he is—Bert, in a raincoat, mopping out the girls' locker room. (I'll say this: If you point to it, Bert will do it. If, that is, he can find it first.)

"I thought you quit," I said.

"I couldn't do that," says Bert. "An impossibility. Neh."

"Because you like me?"

"I like you all right—but then I've worked for some real turds in my day, you don't mind my say so. The truth is, listen, I owe Cousin Pearl six months rent and, frankly, she said she'd evict me if I quit here. I'm a Trekkie. I've got 4,000 pieces of Star Trek memorabilia in my apartment—worth a fortune before you know it."

"So you couldn't move?"

"Neh. A momser hassle."

"Cousin Pearl owns a house?"

"Cousin Pearl, let me tell you, owns two square blocks. Cousin Pearl could buy you and give change. She scares the shit out of me."

"Me, too. So you're still here?"

"Yeh."

"Bert, since we're being frank—let me ask you something—"

"Yuh."

"Are you any good in a fight?"

"If I can use my weight—if I can roll over on a guy, pretty good. Yeh."

"I'm reassured. Where did you work in security?"

"Eh. A school out by Rockaway."

"A school. Oh."

"They were pretty big kids—ten to thirteen. Pricks."

"You rolled on them?"

"Eh—sometimes you haveta."

"Bert, why don't you get glasses?"

"People wouldn't be scareda me in glasses. I'd look like a Talmudic scholar."

"Good thinking."

"I get pinkeye a lot, so I can't wear contacts. But, if I remember correctly, this isn't a china shop here. I can see someone good enough t'roll on them."

"Right. I didn't mean t'be critical. In fact, I'm very glad t'have you aboard." And then, old tactile me, I lean forward and give Bert a friendly poke in the stomach.

The stomach goes BOINK and I almost break a knuckle.

In this heat Bert is wearing a bulletproof vest *under* his raincoat. No wonder he's sweating. But this isn't your ordinary bulletproof vest—this must be the *original* bulletproof vest. Solid steel. Worn first by scabs during the Boston Police strike of 1919 or something. No lightweight alloys for Bert. This thing was made over an anvil. He looks like a backwards Galapagos tortoise.

"Bert—uh, isn't that a little extreme?"

"I'd personally prefer it if you didn't make snide remarks," he said with dignified reserve. "I need this. I feel better when I have it on. I was scared so bad last night I got hemorrhoids."

"I can relate," I said. "I can relate."

Then, around 2 p.m., Colavecchia and Daniels leaned on me again. They had examined the Lincoln. (I called 911 at 5:20 a.m. It was a quarter to eight before a patrol car got there. Okay, it was raining, but . . .) I took a told-you-so attitude. I'm the innocent bystander, that sort of thing. But somehow, getting shot at doesn't impress them— maybe it even, you know, cheapens my image.

Colavecchia and Daniels don't have much to go on—only that the weapon involved was an Uzi. That word makes my scalp crawl. Uzi, in my mind, is associated with desperate terrorists and great Israeli competence. This was a professional job.

"You saw nothing?"

"A silhouette—maybe a dark complexion. The rain was really coming down. It certainly wasn't Leonard."

"You were on bad terms with drug people?"

"Well," I said self-righteously. "I won't tolerate drug use at The Car."

"Very noble."

"D'you think there's a connection between this and Bubbles's death?"

"No."

"Why not?"

"Well, between you and us, Bubbles—Cherry Watson—it looks like she was a suicide. We've found a note: several notes, in fact. Also she had a history—she cut her wrists once."

"What did the note say?"

Daniels cleared his throat. "She had the hots for you, cocksucker. And you wouldn't give her the time of day. Must be fun diddling 18-year-old girls."

"Did you call me 'cocksucker'?" I said—it was a question, not defiance. I couldn't believe he had said that.

"Yes, cocksucker."

"Hal," said Colavecchia, "go easy."

"I have a teenaged daughter. Forgive me."

"Listen," I said. "Yesterday you were all over me, telling me I'd fucked her. Now you're on my case because I didn't. Make up your mind."

"My mind is made up," said Daniels. "You're too good-looking, and I'm sorry that guy didn't kill you. In fact it's kinda funny he didn't, kinda funny. You sure you didn't arrange the whole thing?"

And they walked out—leaving me with this monstrous imputation, that I had caused Bubbles's death (not to mention a murder attempt on my own life). But I won't buy it. I've got a fine apparatus for locating and measuring guilt—it's my other profession—and, sorry, that just doesn't compute. Besides, Bubbles wasn't ready to die—no. If she had really wanted suicide Bubbles would've done it more dramatically. She would've killed herself in front of me, when we were alone. Not out there in front of old men in raincoats. She loved me, didn't she?

No. I still think she was murdered.

6:30—

Ghastly, flat phone conversation with Kay. This furtive mode doesn't become me. I'm so used to gossiping with her—it's the thing we do best together. Speculate on the day and people's motives. Examine relationships. Kay has a marvelous instinct when it comes to character study— if she had any aptitude for plot and structure, she might be a better screen writer than I am. (But she isn't. I know it. And, God forgive me, I've found a *subject* here.)

Naturally she wants to hear about the people I've been meeting. I can describe Ethel and the kids. (Yet even there I'm cautious. If I ever vocalized my anger about Ethel, said I felt she was using me—which Ethel is—Kay would say, "Get out." And she'd be right. But I'm not ready to get out.) As for the other people, I make composites up. I put Pearl together with Bert and turn them both into a "next door neighbor" of Ethel's. Since, of course, my memory stinks, these ersatz characters are neither believable nor even consistent. And I know *bupkis* about Italian food. I stole a menu from Angelo's last week, keep it by my phone and say things like "The scungill was overcooked tonight."

Lying, lying, lying.

And, naturally, I can't tell her that some hitman just gave me four flat tires and a glass bath.

More than that, Kay has a good ear. She knows me. She may not realize I've been lying . . . yet. But Kay certainly feels my impatience with her. I'm snappish and hurried—no matter how I try to discipline myself. I plead the kitchen workload, but it doesn't hold much water. And Kay inevitably, says:

"You don't want me t'come."

"Of course I want you t'come."

"I won't know any of your new friends, I'll be out of place—"

"I'll introduce you." (Hi, Berry—this is Kay.) "You'll take t'New York like a duck t'water. You wanna write, don't you? This is where the action is."

"New York. Imagine, New York. I miss you—"

And so on. With such pretty, sweet endearments that I feel like Megaheel. I return her sentiments—"Love you. Can't wait."—as if I were reading the text of an eye chart.

Right now Kay intends to land at LaGuardia on Thursday, July 28th. In large part I have blocked this bit of reality. I just pretend it will never happen. The rational, conniving part of me hopes that Ethel can perform a miracle. Or that I'll somehow manage to train Bert in little over a week so he can stand by for me while I sightsee with Kay. A far-fetched assumption, which I have not yet talked over with Ethel.

But Kay will be here until August 12th—two weeks. How can I sustain such a complex charade for that long?

Shouldn't I confess over the phone and save the poor woman a trip?

Still, part of me wants to see Kay. Like Berry said, "Priests do not marry topless dancers." And I want to marry someday, but not yet.

On the other hand, I may not be a priest for much longer.

5 a.m.

Just now, God help me, I found a Ziploc bag full of cocaine under the front seat of my new rental car. I dropped some change and was fingering down for it between my feet when I felt a soft thing. I only picked this car up at noon yesterday. Who could've put it there? Avis may try harder—but somehow I don't think they're trying *that* hard.

What to do? Right now I've got the bag stuffed under my sink with the Ajax and Boric Acid Roach Control. Pretty obvious. I expect a court-ordered search momentarily. I could throw the stuff out, but I suspect there's more where that came from. All someone has to do is plant a half-ounce or so at The Car and we're out of business. And it doesn't take much imagination to figure who's behind this spider's stratagem.

Fucking Leonard.

OK, what I'll do, I'll give the coke to Joe Solomon tomorrow. If I'm up front about it, maybe the narc people will think I'm innocent. (THINK?—I *am* innocent. But I've forgotten what being innocent feels like.) Also, I better take Berry into my confidence when she gets here. I trust her judgment. In ways, oddly enough, Berry's like Kay. She knows how people think.

Oh, and I forgot, Manning was in tonight—a touchy moment. I broke into three layers of sweat when I saw him. Raskolnikov and the whole of *Crime and Punishment* flashed before my eyes. Between the cops and Kay and Ethel and drug plants and Uzis and the church I'm begin-ning to lose the coordinates of sanity.

So—what else?—I decided to bite the bullet and confront Manning. I went to his table and said, "I'm the manager. Can I get you anything?"

Manning looked right at me and a really freakish smirk flared in one mouth corner. His face is fleshy as a bloodhound's, but he has many tiny teeth. And he's bigger than I thought, at least six two. Manning said, this priest said,

"What you can do, you can put some decent cunt up there on stage. I'm sick of all the Brazilian twat." (Tanya was my one U.S. citizen.)

The way Manning pronounced those rancid four-letter words for the female portion made me sick—they had a schoolboy prurience to them. I felt he was getting some kind of release by talking filth to me. (Of course, if I hadn't known who Manning was, "cunt" and "twat" would've struck me as standard lift-the-leg male tastelessness.)

But Manning certainly doesn't recognize me.

Yet.

. . .

Took Tanya home—the only bright moment in my day. (It makes Berry jealous and, mea culpa, I enjoy that.)

Tanya was in a positive mood, having pulled down no less than $850 dollars. I commented on her drawing power. Men, I said, seemed to know when she was dancing—even if it wasn't one of her regular Saturday gigs.

"Oh," she said, "that's because I call them."

"You *call* them?"

"Well Costanza does it mostly. I have a Rolodex with forty-five names on it. Men appreciate that: a personal call makes them feel special. I thought you knew about it."

"Knew?"

"That's why I get paid extra, silly. It's for my expenses. Tony and I agreed on that a long time ago. I work hard, Mike, I'm going t'make it as an actress, because I'm motivated. And I know howta use my resources." Tanya started to cry—one of her more available resources.

"Are things better at home?"

"Better? They're fine."

"Aaah. Well—last time I drove you home, well, I thought there was some tension."

"Tension?" She seemed surprised. "That was excitement you felt. Costanza is a very exciting woman."

"Yes." I thought that one over. Then I said, "Have you always been gay?"

"Mike. Don't tell anyone about me and Costanza. It turns men off. Men live in hope."

"You're, uh, sick of men, is that it? Because they all fawn on you and act stupid?"

"Men are OK. I like men. I had a normal childhood. And it's important t'my aspirations that men care for me. I'm really a down-home girl. I want kids and a fireplace. But right now men are, well, kind of predictable. The men I meet aren't, you know, *stars*. A star will put me in my place some day. The way Costanza does now. I need t'be put in my place."

"I see."

"But—and I'm not just saying this—if it wasn't for Costanza, I'd be turned on by you. You treat me pretty cool. That's a pleasure."

"The strong, silent type."

"You're a mystery person," she said. "There are very few mystery people in the world."

So now, of course, I'm thinking lewd thoughts about Tanya, too. She got to me. She put me on her Rolodex.

SUNDAY, JULY 17TH

5 p.m.
It's quite domestic here. I sit in my underwear—the radio said 94 degrees—and write this journal. Berry is across the room, on my bed, sewing a G-string. (I booked her as a replacement for Graciela tonight.) On TV, the Yanks are losing to Detroit late in the second game of a doubleheader. Berry made burgers and a very imaginative salad for late lunch. Then she played her guitar. (She's taking a course in music composition at The New School.) Her fingering is quite accomplished. And her voice, though small, is accurate and graceful. Witty, too. Her ballad "Topless Girl," sung with a mock country/western twang, goes:

> *Her tits ain't all homegrown*
> *Mostly stuffed with silicone*
> *Yet they're worth fifty cents apiece*
> *So stick a dollar to her thigh*
> *She'll manufacture a sweet sigh,*
> *Aaah, yes, baby, harder, mmmm—*
> *And send you running, running, running*
> *To your wife.*
> *(Refrain)*
> *She's topless once again,*
> *The bosom buddy to all men,*
> *Standing there—fleshing out the night.*

And, since we got up at noon or so, Berry and I have screwed three times. I roar so loudly when I come that I'm hoarse now: there is pained despair in it. And such pleasure. Such shocking pleasure.

Berry woke me twice—I was, she said, arguing in my sleep. I don't remember an argument. I remember a terrifying moment—though it sounds funny—when I was confronted by all the chickens I had eaten in my lifetime. And an angry bunch they were. I presume they represent my sins. Or the people that I've hurt. But it was quite distressing. You can put away a lot of chicken in 28 years. Imagine them all fluffed up and indignant, with sharp TEETH.

We almost went to church. I wanted to. (I've gotta start that sermon.) But it seemed to tempt fate—showing up where I might be recognized. And then there was the coke. I didn't want to leave it under the sink unsupervised. And the thought of kneeling at an altar rail with (Berry says) at least four ounces of cocaine in my pocket struck me as, I don't know, blasphemy perhaps. So we fucked instead. I like easy answers.

Ber has remained an Episcopalian and still attends St. Mat's with her mother and father. Or so she tells me. It may be unfair, but I suspect she's just trying to impress me. My guess is: Berry's spiritual life is rather pedestrian. (On second thought, I wish mine were *more* pedestrian.) But, oh, the look of love in her bright brown eyes.

Orgasm is a pretty revealing thing. No wonder John Donne compared it to God's ravishing grace. Men and women spend so much time maneuvering (personeuvering?) for control. He's cool. She's disdainful. But no woman can disdain you when she's coming. (*If* she comes, and Ber COMES.) It is the nakedness-of-nakedness. The vulnerable, shameless, grateful moment. No greater gift is there for a man—when a woman presents him with the pleasure of her helpless pleasure. God's love comes that way, without reservation . . . have I found a sermon text?

Do I love Berry? I wonder. I certainly can't keep my mitts off her. It's a magic moment—we live with so many voluptuous images that say DON'T TOUCH—magic when a man first realizes he has permission to be familiar with a woman's private zones. Without getting slapped, reprimanded or, horrors, laughed at. I keep exercising my new license: and, better yet, Ber does the same. (Kay would NEVER touch my cock.) Ber went down on me this morning while I was still asleep. "Just to watch it grow," she said.

Best of all, we kiss. And kiss. Our mouths are the same size—NOTHING in a sensual dynamic is more important than mouth-to-mouth ratio. I once dated a bright, sweet girl with a huge mouth. She ate half my face when we kissed. Couldn't get her to pucker. Finally it became so distasteful, I picked a fight and lit out. But Ber is imaginative and gentle. No tonsil swabber. It's lovely. Restful. We dock like space capsules and orbit, just orbit.

Ber is now in charge of booking—tho' no one realizes it yet. I let her make up the schedule, since Ber knows the women better than I do. I may give her some nights behind the bar as well—that way I'll have at least two employees that I can trust.

And, of course, I'll be able to sidle down the bar every once in a while and put my hand on her ass.

. . .

As for my prayer life, I would pray for it, if I had any.

5:30 a.m.
It wasn't cocaine. It was, Joe told me, some kind of French laxative—I forget the name—that dealers use to cut cocaine with. What should we make of this? They just wanted to scare me? They wanted me to stick frog Ex-Lax up my nose? They're too cheap to waste good cocaine on me? What? And who are they? (And yet—between you and me—I tried the stuff. It made my head buzz. I got high. Am I going crazy?) *I wish people would stop jerking me around.*

But I did the right thing, going to Joe. He'll tell the narc people. Leonard, apparently, is working at Belle's in College Point, a topless dive owned—GET THIS—by Linese. Have our enemies gone into league? Or . . . Or was Leonard on Linese's payroll while he was working here? There is a certain logic to that. It would give Linese access to sabotage. Who knows? I'm on my way to the weirdo ward.

And, at around ten p.m., I had a really unpleasant confrontation.

I was seated at the bar watching other men watch Berry (it's more of a turn-on for me than watching Ber directly). In fact, now that I have an emotional stake in her, it's hard for me to watch Berry dance at all. I mean, her sub-sexual transactions up there—tongue wetting lip, making eye contact, separating her buttocks ever so slightly with her hands—I mean they're very persuasive. It's hard to distinguish them from the gestures that I'm honored with when we're in bed together. I don't say Berry's insincere with me. I KNOW she isn't. But THEY, the men, are so completely taken in. They suspend disbelief and—for a moment, at least—think they have been chosen.

By MY woman. Eatcha heart out, Charlie.

And, of course, Norm is right. I'd been to bed with Ber, on and off, all day—and still she was separate, a mystery. A spectral land of soft curves and interesting nooks. There is no let-up. Repression of the male sex urge is a matter of constant vigilance. And not worth it.

I don't mean that.

Anyway—throughout my sexual reverie (it was a slow night) there was this ruddy-faced, short, white-haired man sitting maybe six barstools away. About fifty-five years old. Could be sixty. He was keeping us in the black—knocking shots of Wild Turkey down with beer. A practiced drinker. Broken veins all over the nose. After his eighth shot in two hours, Connie put me on notce that there might be trouble. (We get sad, methodical drinkers on Sunday night.) I wasn't worried—though something about the guy struck me as familiar.

Finally he calls Connie over. Tells her he'd like to buy me a drink. Connie reports this, and I wave to him and say, "Don't drink on duty, thanks anyhow." And the guy comes toward me, off his stool. He's pretty steady. But there's an energy around him that I'm not pleased by.

"Not even a drink with *me*? Special occasion." He touches my knee. I don't care for this intimacy.

"Pardon," I say. "Have we met?"

"No," he says, "but somehow I feel like I know you. Prick."

"Ah—" I said. "I think you've had one too many. Connie—this gentleman won't be drinking any more tonight. Not here at least."

"No more drinks? Not even for John Watson—whose daughter you killed? Prick."

"You're Bub—Cherry's father?"

"Yah, I am. Come t'take her poor carcass home. But I hadda drop by here and pay my respects—to the place, to the man who drove my child t'what she did."

"Look. I can understand—"

"You have no kids. You can't understand shit. And this"—he pointed at the stage—"this sucks. This is an unholy corruption. Not even as honest as being a whore. I curse you for dragging my daughter into this—"

"Wait—hold on. Cherry was a dancer long before I met her."

"Bullshit. I've read her letters. Detective Daniels showed them t'me. They can't get you on a murder rap—but it was murder, nonetheless. You seduced her 'til she was crazed. They should castrate you."

"I didn't touch your daughter—"

"That's not what her letters say. Her letters say you had t'do with her. Prick."

"Then she was fantasizing—"

"Come on. I thought you were more of a man, admit it. Why would she fantasize? Huh, prick?"

And I blew. I said:

"Because she'd been running away from a shitty childhood with an alcoholic father and an alcoholic mother. You got drunk so much she never knew who you were. Or who she was. Why was your precious 18-year-old daughter in New York, anyway, you self-important old sot? Couldn't've been much fun watching Dad stagger around. She had more of a family here in this shithouse than she had with you—"

And he took a swing. Hit me in the sternum and knocked me, quite ignominiously, off the bar stool. Berry, thank God, came down from the stage, tits flying, and tied Watson up in a clinch.

Whereupon he started to cry on her neck. I took a walk outside and left it to the woman.

But I was pissed. They seek me out, the angry and the unstable. Maybe some pastoral odor comes off me still. I don't know. Meanwhile, it has become obvious that Cherry's diary is hot stuff. And everyone, certainly Colavecchia and Daniels, is disposed to believe her version, not mine. Not Mike the Prick's. Did Cherry want to hurt me? I never saw that in her. Not once. But look how things have turned out.

Mike. They've turned out this way because you live in the House of Lies. He's right—brothels are more honest. Here everything has distortion built into it. Young children who pretend to be femmes fatales. Nudity that is a costume, damn it. Promises sold for a dollar. Colored lights and blaring music. And the stinking haze of alcohol. You wonder there are misconceptions? You wonder that fantasies bloat and take precedence over the real?

Unholy corruption—well put.

And an unholy corruption that—without drugs and electronic poker—is losing money. Think I'll replace Salome (her silicone job went sour, the incision got infected—she says), replace her with Tanya. Tanya and her mailing list. I'll have to pay extra, but it'll pick Monday night up.

One funny incident. Bert got stuck in a men's room stall. He came out sideways because of his turtle's carapace—and the chest part jammed against the door's lock mechanism. So he was wedged in the stall. I had to climb over from the sink and push, while two customers yanked on his arm.

I'm sorry Bubbles is dead. I'm sorry I couldn't save her life. I'm sorry.

MOND—

TUESDAY, JULY 19TH

A day gone by. I'm no longer hysterical. I can hold a pencil in my hand.

I'm making my last entry in this journal. Tonight I'll go to Ethel's place and hide it somewhere in the garage.

I'm not sure whether what I've written here is incriminating. But that's not strange: I have trouble thinking clearly about most things now. I expect Colavecchia and Daniels to search my apartment before very long.

If you find my journal—Daniels, you cocksucker, and Colavecchia, you asshole—if you find my journal and are intelligent enough to read it—THIS IS WHAT HAPPENED, THIS IS ALL I KNOW.

We were outside for at least twenty minutes, Joe and I, playing chess on the fender of a Yellow Cab. I was 4:20 a.m. (TT) and 4:10 real time when I closed the bar. I thought no one but Tanya was inside when I left to finish the game. I checked the men's room, as I have been taught to do. I checked behind the bar. I opened the kitchen door and had a look. Then I went outside—because you could go stark mad waiting for Tanya to get ready.

But it's *not* impossible—Joe will tell you this—it's *not* impossible that someone came out after I left. We were intent on the game. The cab fender was about two-and-one-half car lengths up (east on Northern Boulevard). Right under the street lamp. We play there so we have light to see by.

Someone could've come out. Someone *must've* come out—if, as it seems, the rear door was locked from inside.

Because I didn't do it.

And then I beat Joe and we gossiped for five or six minutes. He said, "Well, *I* don't haveta wait here all night. That porcelain doll doesn't have *me* wrapped around her little finger. What's she do at night, put her body in Saran Wrap and refrigerate it?"

He said that.

And I said, "Women," and I walked to the door and pulled on the handle because I was gonna shout inside to Tanya. *But the door was locked.*

I knew right away things were off-kilter. Why would Tanya lock the door? I yelled to Joe, who had already reached the corner, "It's locked. I didn't lock it and it's locked."

"So unlock it, dumbo," he said. But he started walking back toward me.

I unlocked the door—my keys were buried under a bag of salted peanuts in my pocket. I know I hadn't touched them for hours. *I* didn't lock the door.

And I went in.

Jesus, didn't you look at me afterward? Didn't you see I'd been crying? I was HORRIFIED by what I saw. I will carry that horror to my grave.

Tanya lay naked on the stage. Hips twisted, arms above her head. And her long neck was broken. Broken. Broken so absolutely that the back of her head had gone flat against her spine—and her Adam's apple pushed out as if a baby's fist were poking through her throat. All her fake fingernails were torn backward. Tanya had struggled. And her G-string was jammed in her mouth. And her teeth were long—long—like Rita's.

I turned away then.

I know nothing more than that.

.   .   .

They say Tanya had been dead for twenty minutes or so. That may be true. I know, if it weren't for Joe Solomon, I'd be under arrest now. On my way to life imprisonment.

I didn't kill Tanya. I didn't.

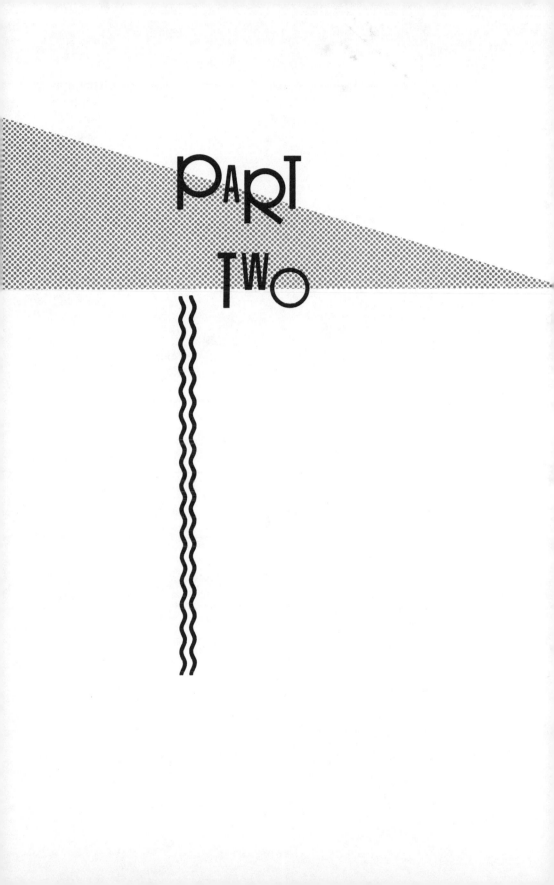

PART

TWO

Rereading my journal now, almost two months after Tanya Suslov's murder, I am overwhelmed, poleaxed by the dread of it all—again. Though hellish events have transpired since then, Tanya's death cauterized my heart. God knows, I will never be the same. I stepped from young manhood and its hope, its resilience, its pleasant uncertainty, to a kind of frantic, quick middle age. I knew my own mortality. The bones had stopped growing, the reflexes would lose some bounce each day. And I was on the way to becoming a bitter cynic.

I have been at deathbeds: I am not squeamish. Highway 83 ran just north of the Lekachman church. Six or seven times a month troopers would call me out to an accident (Schantz blessed no one after 8 p.m.). Once, a man's entire right arm came off in my hand, as we tried to extricate his body from a burning car. I vomited. But I didn't nurse on it. If anything, I relished the macabre. It didn't take the gleam off my boy's soul.

But Tanya had been so *exquisite.* She represented something, I guess. Maybe I thought that she—of anyone in our generation—should have been exempt. Not from death—but from mutilation. Tanya without her beauty was *nothing at all.* To see her head torn back—looking like one of the terrified animals that shriek as they stare upward in Picasso's *Guernica*—to see that was to see her pathetic, small inner workings. The nakedness *under* her bare skin (that skin turning gray before my eyes). The flimsiness of this contraption we live in—and the flimsiness of the things we live in it for.

And, of course, my priesthood was forfeited. If not at once, then soon, inevitably. That much I knew even as I turned away from her corpse and into Joe's embrace. I suppose by now everyone in the English-speaking world is aware of what happened at The Car. NUDE TOPLESS BAR MURDER the *New York Post* front page crooned. There are certain stories that lend themselves readily to elaboration—every aspect of the topless business was examined: on Donahue and Oprah and ten different in-depth special TV reports. And I was at the cross hair of everyone's high-powered aim. An "enigmatic figure," Jimmy Breslin wrote. I couldn't have said it better myself.

I will be going away next week. But, while I am still in New York, I hope to complete my journal—writing, this time, with knowledge of what came next, day after merciless day. I kept a few notes, and, Lord knows, there are newspaper clippings enough to remind me. But it will be hard to recapture the immediacy and the astonishment—and harder yet to tell what I found out about my brother.

But I will try.

TUESDAY, JULY 19TH and WEDNESDAY, JULY 20TH

The police closed us down for two days—The Car was a crime scene, of course. I could understand that. But, it soon got pretty obvious, the police also had a grudge against Mike Wilson. Daniels and Colavecchia were professionally embarrassed—naturally they had to reopen their investigation of Bubbles's death—and this they held against me for some reason. (I *told* them Bubbles had been murdered. I knew she hadn't committed suicide. What more did they want from me?) Daniels and Colavecchia now had a supervisor—that must've galled them—a black named Cribbs. They also had to deal with the narc people, with an IRS man, with health and building inspectors—and, endlessly, the media. Everyone wanted a piece of me. I schooled myself to think three full beats before I answered any question. Before asking if I could go to the john.

So they searched and searched The Car. One reefer stub would've finished us, one bottle of Nyquil—I knew that. But by some miracle they found nothing. I sat alone at the bar making myself "available." They checked the basement, they rummaged through every case of liquor and every carton of potato chips. They removed every bottle from the bar. They drained the sinks and opened each toilet tank. And as I sat there, every once in a while, despite myself, I'd glance at the chalk silhouette of Tanya's body on the stage. Tanya's head just overlapped the place where Bubbles had shook her last spasm out. I told Ethel that: she said, "I think we'll need a new carpet, I'll get right on it."

Despite her callous approach, I was grateful to Ethel. Ethel was the one person who didn't think I had killed Tanya. (Everyone else presumed it'd just be a matter of time before I gave myself up.) Ethel, as I did, suspected Leonard—or Linese and Leonard, or the Gaucho, Linese and Leonard. (Leonard, in fact, seemed to have an alibi.) Ethel retained Morton Weintraub, who had been associated with Roy Cohn, to defend The Car and get it reopened. I refused representation, fool that I am—I thought it would be taken as a sign of guilt. Part of me, I know, was entertaining a death wish. Because, you see, I had bad dreams and was no longer sure of my own innocence.

They questioned me for hours at a time. Much of this was purely informational: who were my regular customers, what was my routine for closing The Car at night, which girls knew Rita and Tanya and Bubbles? And, every now and then, almost jocularly, Daniels or Colavecchia would ask, "Is that when you did it? Were you angry because she wouldn't fuck you? D'you hate women that much?" And I would count my three full beats and say, "Now that you've had your fun, let's move on."

I know now—I suspected then—that Joe was the hole in their circumstantial case. After all, he was an ex-cop, an experienced witness, and not someone any prosecutor would want to go one-on-one against. Yet Joe, too, had not ruled me out. Yes, he thought, someone could've exited from The Car after I did. But it wasn't that—it was my *chess game,* of all things, which confused him. Could someone like this—someone who had just committed a heinous murder—could such a person come out and play a concentrated, winning game of chess? As I had done. It didn't seem possible to Joe. (I had been playing chess for my life, I realize that in retrospect.)

At my invitation (before they could get a warrant, that is) Daniels and Colavecchia and Cribbs searched my apartment. Berry—she was sporting about it—verified that all the clothing and makeup articles belonged to her. Despite the embarrassment this caused, I was glad—having a lover made me seem, oh, more normal. And Berry was both loyal and hard to faze. When Daniels asked her,

"How can you be sure Mike wasn't two-timing you with Cherry and Tanya?" she said,

"Because Tanya was a lesbian and Cherry was a foolish child."

"Yet one was seen naked in his apartment. The other he made a special effort t'drive home. Don't you think those two facts might be related?" And Berry—she told me later—said,

"What about the guy who shot Mike's tires out? How come you don't think *that's* related?"

Which effectively shut him up. The tire assassin was a strong, if enigmatic, advocate of my innocence. Daniels and Colavecchia had dismissed the whole thing as an unconnected incident. But, by now, the media had learned about it, and there were questions at a press conference Wednesday morning. Cribbs, who spoke for the homicide department, was not well informed about the tire shooting and, so I was told, got pissed at Daniels and Colavecchia, who had left him hanging. Truth of the matter is—they were baffled. I was afraid they'd arrest me just to prove their competence. And competently send me away for 25-years-to-life.

In fact, though, I preferred the homicide crew to what awaited me, cunning and impatient, whenever I left The Car. Photographers spent the night on my fire escape. They followed me when I drove. A TV newswoman pretended to be my waitress at the Greek's until Spiro caught on and threw her out. A 20 foot square police line, box-shaped, was set up outside The Car. I wore a baseball cap, the bill jammed down, whenever I had to go out. I never said anything more than "No comment." Yet, by some miracle, neither the police nor the press had as yet discovered that I was a priest.

By Wednesday, though, I had already decided to resign.

By Wednesday, too, the *New York Post* had come out with a WHO-DUNIT headline. Diagrams of The Car appeared on page 5. Looking at it, even I was inclined to suppose myself guilty.

The rear door had been locked from the inside. (Joe Solomon ascertained that much immediately after he checked Tanya's pulse.) The basement is below-grade and windowless. Indeed, The Car has no windows at all—other than the train-like, tiny portals that face Northern Boulevard. My own testimony was damaging. If, indeed, the front door had been locked, then the unknown killer must have stepped out and turned his key while we were playing chess. One would presume he possessed commando skills of the highest order. Not to mention a key.

Yet there were, the police knew, many keys: Pearl, Ethel and Jako had copies. Bert had lost one set already (thank God—that was an element in my favor). Freddy and Leonard had left our employ without returning their sets. Keys enough were around. But, despite Joe's appreciation of my skill at chess, I was still the morning line favorite.

Daniels came up with the most imaginative angle. (I always thought Daniels was a bit unhinged. He resigned from the police force earlier this month for "personal reasons": a breakdown, I'd guess.) Once I asked him,

"How can I be implicated in these murders? You know I was in Nebraska when Rita died."

"Oh, yes," said Daniels. "That's clever. Where's your brother, Mike?"

"Tony? You think I know where Tony is?"

"Sure. It took two people t'kill Tanya. I think your brother did it, and you let him out the back door. Then you locked it behind him and went out, all neat, t'play chess with Joe."

"That's baroque," I said, "and what was our motive?"

"You don't like women. And you—you—you've got a homosexual fixation on your brother. The mustache—the mustache is what gave it away. Tony brought you up. You identify with him as an authority figure. When he started murdering women, you became his accomplice."

Like I said, they were baffled.

Meanwhile we were at a stalemate. Cribbs and his men had gotten hopelessly embroiled in detail work. More than a hundred women were interrogated. Lars-Erik and Norm came forward. Pearl and Leonard and Jako and Freddy and even Linese gave evidence. (The Gaucho was in Columbia.) Bert confused everyone by saying HE had been the last to leave. (Not true—just loyalty on Bert's part.) And, because it would've blown my own cover, I didn't tell the police about Augustus Manning.

The forensic experts concluded that Tanya had been killed by someone of "considerable strength."

Not a major insight. I had strength enough, everyone knew that.

THURSDAY, JULY 21ST

Thursday was, to say the least, unforgettable. It began with hideous dreams. I was among a race of people whose necks had been broken—whose heads hung down their backs, inverted. Each like the hood of a parka. They spoke to me upside-down and said, "We are the new ones. You have made us." And there was Jesus, nailed chest forward against the cross—His thorned head, too, thrown back. He said to me: "Because of you, men and woman no longer look at each other when they make love."

And I said, "Lord, I didn't do it."

And He said, "Answer me this. Should a man see a woman naked first—before he has known her soul?"

I said, "No." And then, "No" again. And then "No!"

And Jesus said, "Right this wrong. Lest forever you, too, see only behind you and have no hope of eternal life."

I woke at eight a.m. afraid to sleep again. And began writing my last sermon.

The phone rang nine or ten times an hour—requests for interviews and exclusive stories. Crank messages. I didn't answer. Then Costanza called—drunk, stoned or just inconsolable, some state that rendered her almost incoherent. But Costanza's bitterness toward me lost nothing in translation. I had meant to attend Tanya's funeral on Friday. But I dropped that idea after hearing Costanza's recorded message. She wanted a dramatic mano-a-mano. I wouldn't oblige her.

Just after ten a.m., to my bewilderment, Ethel called. She was all action. Weintraub had put pressure on the police department—as of noon The Car could recommence its normal commerce in nudity. Pearl was there. A carpet guy was there, and Ethel had hired a Pinkerton man for the front door. When would Mr. Mike arrive?

"Ethel. I mean . . . Tanya isn't even buried yet."

"I know," she said. "I know how you feel. But you've gotta overcome that. She died at The Car—but it isn't as if you or I killed her. Right? Leonard or the Gaucho must've ordered it. Maybe that dicksucker, Linese, I don't discount him. They wanna bankrupt us. They want us not t'reopen. You're letting them win, Mike. You're letting the murderers win."

"Ethel. There are people with TV cameras outside my apartment. Someone from the diocese is gonna recognize me."

Ethel was silent for a moment. Then, with her terrific resilience (when it came to other people's setbacks), she said, "Don't you think it's already too late?"

"Ethel," I said. Then it was my turn to be silent.

"I'm sorry," she said, "I've fucked your life up, haven't I?"

"Royally. Completely." There was anger in my voice: I left it there.

"I'll make it up t'you. Somehow, someday, I'll make it up to you, Mike. Right now we're in a war we didn't choose, and we're losing. Tony wouldn't've given up. He would've fought."

"We can't start at noon. I have no dancers. I'm not even sure I can get anyone. After all, two women have already died on that stage."

"People need money, Mike. Double the nut you're paying."

"Five o'clock. We can't start at noon. I'll put together a five-to-twelve shift."

"You're the boss," Ethel said.

I went up to the roof and, like Spider Man, I jumped across a narrow but (yaaagh!) five-story-tall airshaft and out through an apartment build-ing on the block behind mine. By cab to The Car—where I began phoning dancers: who were, on the whole, not afraid. Rather, the TV cameras outside on Northern Boulevard made them leery. (Most danc-ers hide their source of income from Mom and Dad or the grandmother who brought them up.) Also, they thought The Car would be like a stag party at Frank E. Campbell's—not well attended. I doubled the nut and offered my services as an escort. One girl actually said, "With you? No thanks, the subway is safer."

Finally I got the Silicone Sisters, who would've danced topless at the Jonestown massacre and who had hated Tanya anyway. I got Chinga. I got Glenda (on promise of reinstatement). And, of course, I got Berry. I wish, in retrospect, that I hadn't. But I did.

The pessimists were wrong (and Ethel, with her entrepreneur's sense, was spot on). At 5 p.m., the front door caved in. Men (and *women*) ploughed through, trampling Bert. Ethel's Pinkerton guy, hired to give the impression of safety, became like the doorman at Limelight. At one point he was actually accepting $5 and $10 bills to let customers in. But there was no room: I had to keep Pearl until 2 a.m. working with Connie. Men were lined three and four deep against the wall. Drinks got passed from hand to hand—the barmaids couldn't move.

I had done what Ethel wanted. Sales were up. We had just pulled in a miraculous draught of suckers. All it had taken was two murders. And my vocation.

Around 11 p.m., as I was humping beer cases from the basement with Jako (we actually ran out of beer), Bert yelled at me, "There's a girl here wantsta audition."

"It's too crowded," I said. "Tell her tomorrow afternoon." He left, I went back down, came up, and Bert said,

"She insists."

"Insist back."

"Says she's come all the way from Nebraska."

It was Kay.

She looked good—good. Kay was wearing jeans and a blouse. Her blond hair had been drawn back under a baseball cap (she felt uncomfortable as a female there). Unfortunately Kay also had a silk warm-up jacket on. It said UNIVERSITY OF NEBRASKA across the back.

"You look great," I said. I plunged my wrists into the ice sink behind the bar. I thought I was going to pass out.

"You look awful," she said. "I hate the mustache."

"It's my disguise," I said.

"Where's the linguini and the veal piccata? Don't you think I deserve an explanation?"

"You deserve more than that," I said. Kay turned away, toward the stage. Her eyes had begun to glisten.

"They aren't even pretty," she said. "I thought they'd be prettier than that."

"They're just human."

"Oh, and you're doing missionary work with the humans."

"Nothing so noble as that," I said.

But I couldn't hear my own voice. The pulse in my throat was too loud. Talk about women's intuition (helped along by the NEBRASKA jacket). At just that instant Berry and Kay locked glances. Berry, on stage, wasn't dancing. Her hands were on her hips—all provocation. And Kay had caught on. She, too, put hands on hips. Then, suddenly, Berry cupped her bare breasts in her hands, lifted them and—to challenge, to trump Kay, so to speak—ran her tongue over both nipples. Then Berry danced away.

Kay pushed through the crowd, out of The Car and, I thought, out of my life as well. When I reached the sidewalk she was gone.

Berry began to drink—she didn't like liquor, but it gave her sure access to her emotions. She sat with a good-looking off-duty cop, and hung her tits over his arm to irritate me. Then she sat with, of all people, Manning and ran a forefinger up his thigh. Manning was so discomfited he almost blew vodka through his nose. Berry was looking terrific: high emotion or spite can do that to a woman. And it didn't hurt that she was scarfing up more than $100 an hour.

Berry passed me on the way up for her 1 a.m. gig. I touched her shoulder, reaching through a three-man conversation to do so. And she said,

"Fuck off."

"Berry—"

"Fuck off." The three men were silent. Nothing is more engrossing than someone else's intimate hassle.

"Listen—"

"You brought your grain-fed porker in here t'inspect me, dintcha? With her oh so superior attitude. How's she make a living—counting 3×5 cards in a little box?"

"I didn't even know she was in New York—and you better cut down on the booze."

"I'm drinking to your health. That it should end. Skoal." Berry pushed through the trio of men, giving each an incidental free feel. Then she poked my vest pocket. "You better not be thinking of ditching me, that's all. I don't ditch. Hey, how is it t'have sex with a corncob up your ass?"

And, ladies and gentlemen—up she went, all smiles, to dance. I was mortified. And worried out of my cruet. The three men couldn't help

staring at me. Finally one, a big, fat, chirpy guy, said—with great respect—

"Excuse me, sir. Are you actually going t'bed with that beautiful
creature? No offense meant. I just wanna live my life vicariously
through you."

"Pearl—" I called out. "A round of drinks for these three guys. On
me."

It was a schizophrenic night. The crowd experienced gigantic mood
swings. And I—I alternated, from guilt about Tanya and Bubbles, to
delight at all the money we were raking in. From fear of discovery, to
relief. From annoyance with Bert—in that mob his turtleshell rendered
him absolutely immobile—to manic amusement. To astonishment
when, passing Pearl behind the bar, I felt a gun inside her short waitress
jacket. I said,

"Have you got a license for that?"

"Yes, I do," Pearl said, "and I'll pierce your ears at fifty feet, mess with
me. I'm not gonna be the third murder here, Mike. Understand?" I
understood. Pearl, too, suspected me.

But, most of all, I pinged from Kay to Berry, and pong, back to Kay
again. Disloyalties in love are more than just immoral. They impair joy.
Self-disgust is externalized—and lodges conveniently in the wronged
one. Steeped in Berry, I had begun disqualifying Kay. I had a stake in
her faults, for they seemed to excuse me. Now, having seen Kay again,
I was reminded—not only of her charm and goodness (and, yes,
beauty)—but of Lekachman and the slow, inexorable progress of the
church year. Advent and Easter and Trinity Sunday and Kay.

I wanted her back, but my rights, I knew, had been suspended. And
by then I was scared of Berry.

FRIDAY, JULY 22ND

Ethel rang up to tell me that Kay had just called her. It was 9 a.m. Kay
was staying at the Travelers Motel near LaGuardia. (She had asked Ethel
if Tony really owned The Smoking Car—as though, maybe, I had faked
my brother's disappearance as an excuse to leave Nebraska and follow
the skin trade.)

"I told Kay you did it all for me and the kids."

"Thanks—"

'It didn't seem t'impress her."

"Kay has a strong sense of what's right and what's wrong. After the last month I find that refreshing."

"She loves you a lot."

"That's what I'm afraid of. She likes t'deny herself pleasure because it feels good."

"D'you still want her?"

"Yes. But—"

"—you're having an affair with Berry." Ethel laughed. "Trust me—don't worry about Berry. She's a topless dancer. Get out t'the airport and bring Kay here. If she sees these kids, she'll understand."

Kay kept me waiting in the motel lobby for about 45 minutes. I was sleepless and miserable. I didn't look forward to being cross-examined. I'm not a fool: I knew it was time to come clean and throw myself on the court's mercy. I prayed: well, some finger exercises of prayer, anyhow. I wasn't ready to capitulate—but I sent out scouts to test the enemy's (God's) strength. He was there, as usual, in force.

Kay came down all blond and tall. With eye makeup and lipstick and heels. I-can-be-as-pretty-as-that-other-one, she was saying. Kay even had her contact lenses in—a sore point with me: when we first dated, Kay always wore contacts. After our engagement she put her glasses on (and I forgot to shave). It was the principle of the thing. Now Kay had The Law and The Prophets written all over her. She sat in the lobby, where a raised voice would be unacceptable, and waited for me to state my case.

"You ran out on me last night," I said.

"I was scared. I didn't recognize you."

"How did you know about The Car?"

"It's a national story. 'Mike Wilson, manager of'—I read that in an Associated Press piece. It's a common name, but it fit with someone who once mentioned four tits on the telephone."

"Do people know in Lekachman?"

"Some may guess."

"I'm glad you've come."

"Why?"

"Because, first, I love you. Because, second, you bring certain benchmarks of conduct and resolve that I need—if I'm gonna get through this catastrophic period. Because, third, I hope you'll forgive me someday for what I've done—and we can start on our life again."

"But you're seeing another woman, aren't you?"

"Yes . . . I have been."

"Past tense?"

"Yes."

"Does *she* know it's past tense?"

"Not yet."

"The tawny one with the long leg muscles and tits smaller than mine?"

"Bernadette, Berry, her name is. It was a special circumstance, Kay. I've known her since my childhood. She lived next door to Amanda. She knew all about me and I wanted t'keep her quiet."

"Oh. Your affair was an act of statesmanship, I see."

"No, I don't mean that. I just fell. But only with her—no matter what you hear people say. And with her it was like a return to second childhood. It was a revenge on my past. It was . . . something."

"It was a damn good screw—I'm certain of that. I don't think your friend leads with her intellect."

"Actually she's pretty bright at—"

"Oh, shut up, you stupid man."

"Yes."

"How can you be a priest and run a topless bar, Michael?"

"You can't."

"So?"

"I'm resigning from the priesthood."

"No—oh, no."

"On Sunday. Bishop Plunk has asked me t'concelebrate with him and give a sermon. I'm gonna confess and step down."

"No." She started to cry.

"Listen, it's nothing more than a formality. I'm finished anyhow. I'll be lucky if the news doesn't break before Sunday. It's a miracle it hasn't already. I just want t'go out with some dignity. Not with my hands on the hood and my legs spread, so t'speak."

"It's terrible. It's just such a terrible loss."

"Shit, who needs another priest? I went into the church because of my sexual guilt. I'll leave the church because of my sexual guilt. I'm not giving up my faith. And anyhow—don't tell me you wanted t'be a priest's wife."

"I wanted t'be your wife."

"Well, you still can be."

"No, I can't. You're just getting your track shoes on. You're too fast for me. Mike the priest, him I could've kept up with—he might even've owed me something. But, out there," she pointed to a plane taking off, "out there you'll run me 'til I drop. And then go on. You're a powerful man. And dreadfully, dreadfully good-looking. Though the mustache is gross."

"You think too much, Kay. I'm gonna go easy for a long time. Right now I want life in the exact change lane."

"Who killed those women?"

"I don't know. But everyone thinks it was me. Can I take you to Ethel's? I better reserve a room here tonight—my pad is staked out."

"I don't think I like Ethel."

"She's using me, I know. But I allowed myself t'be used. Lets us use her now. Come." She broke into tears. "What now?"

"Just show me the New York skyline, then I'll go home."

"You'll see it, but you'll stay," I said.

By noon there was line outside The Car. We had been featured on "Good Morning America" (Pearl made a guest appearance). Tanya's funeral, moreover, was well-covered by all the networks. On ABC, Costanza said, "I know who did it and he's gonna kill again at The Car." Guess who? That kind of prime-time advertising you can't buy.

About half my dancers volunteered for duty. Fear, they may still have had, but a topless dancer's first reflex is toward your billfold. And The Car was mobbed. Odalisque, who's maybe 50 years old (and a friend of Pearl's) made $350. At those wages death is a decent risk. Moreover, I was getting calls—even out of *Cleveland*—from high school girls who wanted to dance at The Car. We were the epiphenomenon of the year.

But Berry didn't call. I left messages. I even considered driving to her parents' home—but I thought better of it. I wanted to explain, cajole, somehow ease my guilt—and I wanted to squirm out of the relationship. But Berry, I knew, was strong and—yes, Kay—bright. And her love was involved with pride.

Bert saw to it, as much as he could, that no one got near me: reporter, or well-wisher, or hit man (people wanted *autographs*). That meant being near Bert, constantly whacking my knuckles on his iron shell. But it was also calming: Bert's myopia was an image for his attitude about life, i.e., Just watch what's in front of you, otherwise you might trip over it.

And I needed a grace period. I pulled out half my mustache in fidgets of anxiety. I wanted Kay, but I resented her moral superiority. I wanted Berry, but reason told me that no permanent relationship could thrive there. I was apprehensive about Sunday—Plunk would not be pleased. Most of all, I was pissed at God. My resignation (inevitable as it might be) was part spite. If I can't have what I want (the life of a promiscuous male), then (capital Y) You (God) can't have me either. Amen.

And—I know it was partly self-dramatization—I began to take blame for the murders. Suppose some avatar of myself, some externalization of my lust and anger, was stalking The Car. Such things are not unheard of. A priest in a topless bar—those are deadly extremes of the spirit. Even if I hadn't literally put my fingers around Tanya's neck, perhaps I had set a demonic notion free on Northern Boulevard.

I was trapped in The Car from noon to four a.m. (We got a summons for blocking sidewalk traffic.) Jane Healy of *National Enquirer* sent a note asking me out for lunch. I declined. I wondered how much money Tanya would've made working the crowd: it was, after all, another tribute to her drawing power. We couldn't chill beer fast enough. Lazarus, in disgust, absconded for two days. He was sick of getting stepped on.

Willow didn't help (yes, I had invited her back). During her 9 p.m. set, Willow began to stagger, then wobble, then gag. Then she collapsed. There was absolute silence—silence *heard* over the music. The two other dancers panicked. I fought my way forward and—"Hi, there"—up popped Willow, big joke.

I yelled at her. And, during her ten p.m. set, Willow staggered backward, hand to heart, as if she'd been *shot.* When she took the hand away, red liquid—from a theatrical blood bag—ran down into her navel.

At about midnight (TT) Joe Solomon led me aside. I had just spoken with Ethel—Kay and she had gone to see *Cats.* Kay was jet-lagged and would spend time with me tomorrow morning. I was optimistic. Ethel seemed upbeat. So what Joe said took me off guard. He said:

"Let's go outside t'the backyard. In case there's a trial we shouldn't be seen together."

"In case there's a trial?" I said, outside, sitting on an old soda cooler.

"I'm your entire defense," he said. "We don't want the jury thinking there's collusion between us. So I'm gonna come less often t'the Car. I wanted you t'know—I'm not avoiding you. I'm doing it for your sake."

"Thanks. Everyone thinks I did it. Pearl thinks I did it."

I know he wanted to say "Did you?" But Joe held back. Instead he said, "I know you're a priest."

"Pearl told you?"

"Not really. I've been around a while. Tony mentioned his brother the seminarian."

"So. I'm a priest. Does that raise your opinion of me? Or lower it?"

"Well. It makes me think that you've been under terrific pressure—"

"I'm not celibate. Episcopal priests aren't Catholic priests."

"Sure. But there's still a certain amount of repression."

"Joe. Joe. Don't go Freudian on me. Please. It's beneath you. If you think I did it, tell me."

"I don't think you did it. I'll say that in court."

"Thank you. I mean that. And I didn't do it."

"Let me go in first, so no one thinks we've been together."

At 3 a.m. I jumped into the Lincoln, which Bert had revved up for me on a side street. Three media cars tried to follow, but they were over-scrupulous about the law. I lost them by running six red lights in a row on Northern Boulevard at about 60 mph. It's in the genes. When I reached Queens Plaza, I made a U-turn and headed back to LaGuardia along 35th Avenue. By chance I turned left at 103rd Street—which put me a half-block behind Rabies.

There, parked in front of a hydrant, stood a red Cadillac. Linese sat at the wheel. He wasn't alone. He was talking to Joe Solomon.

SATURDAY, JULY 23RD

Wendy Wilson, age 5, greeted me at the door—nude. When it came to feminine blandishments I was getting no relief whatsoever. I averted my eyes and said,

"Hadn't you better get dressed, Amy? It's almost 10 a.m."

"Mommy said you liked women with no clothes on."

"Did she now?" Ethel appeared then and gave Amy a nice twist of the ear.

"I was joking—like Roseanne Barr, to whom I can relate. I didn't think Amy would strip for you."

"I'll give her a Saturday night booking."

"Not my child."

"I wish you'd been a little more protective of your brother-in-law. Of me."

"Whaddya mean? I hoofed all over New York with Kay yesterday." Ethel lowered her voice. "She's in the pool. And she's got some body on her. You have a good eye—and, believe me, a good eye is required with that one. The way she dresses, so ultra secretarial, you'd need a Mars probe t'see if she has tits at all."

"Kay is reserved. She can be . . . strict. She isn't a pragmatist like you or me—"

"She's perfect for you. You need a bit of a ball and chain."

"On Sunday—if the world hasn't zeroed in on me before then—I'm resigning from the priesthood."

"Shit."

"I don't hold you responsible, Ethel. Probably what I did, running The Car, was at least more dramatic, classier than, say, having a lukewarm affair with some lonely housewife in Nebraska. Which I would've had, I'm sure, somewhere down the line. At least I just hurt myself this way. I won't be compromising an entire congregation."

"Mike. Anything I have, you know, money, whatever—it's yours. You—" it seemed she got shy "—you could stay here. If that apartment's too dull. I was thinking anyhow maybe t'build another room out over the porch. For you."

"I'm fine."

"I just want you t'know you're welcome. Those kids think of you as their father."

"They're good kids," I said. "How is, ah, Kay's mood?"

"She's coming around. Listen, she loves you, she'll forgive you. But just lay off Berry from here on in."

"I'm finished with Berry."

"She ain't finished with you, but . . . Go ahead, go on out t'the pool. Kay's waiting."

And, of course, Mr. Tact, I went and did the wrong thing right off. Instant trauma. Kay was standing poolside, back to me, head down, toweling off—in a black one-piece suit that was certainly scandalous in, oh, 1918. I came up, all sincere like we were taught in seminary, and touched her ever so gently on the shoulder.

Kay, however, stood bolt upright, saw me, covered her body, SCREAMED and dove into the pool, towel and all.

Glub.

She came up, snot in her nostrils, nearsighted without corrective lenses, and yelled,

"You bastard."

"That," I said, "was a rather extreme reaction."

"You were looking at me, you were judging my body."

"Kay, you're wearing a nun's bathing suit. Where did you get it, from Frederick's of the Vatican? I couldn't see *anything.*"

"Don't get cute and easy with me." Kay had come to the side near

where I was kneeling down. She was clothed by water. "I'm not compet-
ing with those low-lifes who dance for you. I won't compete on their
grounds."

"You compete just fine—"

"No, I don't." Time to switch the tone.

"I hear you and Ethel had a nice time in New York."

"Oh, yes—Ethel is peachy, she's afraid of losing her meal ticket."

"Try t'be kind. The kids are great, aren't they? She can't be all bad—
that's what I tell myself. With kids like that."

"You know what I saw in New York?"

"What?"

"A woman hit by a car. A lot of men with sores on their legs.
TRANSVESTITES. Two cab drivers fighting—"

"I thought *Cats* was a musical—"

"Ha-ha. And when I saw all that, I thought. *He* lives here. *He* was born
here. He's comfortable with all this misery. Who are you, Mike?"

"Why don't you climb out of the pool and talk?"

"Who are you, Mike?" she said again. And I, well, I like a dashing
gesture (though I did take my wallet out first)—what I did was splash,
clothes and shoes on, into the pool, beside Kay. And put an arm around
her: figuring all that wet inconvenience deserved an embrace. But I was
wrong—Kay detached my arm from her shoulder with an athletic shrug.
My left shoe came off and sank.

"Who am I?" I asked. "I'm a guy with very good intentions. And bad
judgment, I guess. I guess there's a lot of anger inside me. And lust, of
course. And I guess I'm insecure. Otherwise I wouldn't be fucking up
the best part of my life because I feel unworthy of it. I don't like myself.
And I'm playing hard-to-get with God. When I should be running to
Him." She stared at me. "Jesus, Kay—give me a break. I don't know who
I am. This last month has turned me inside-out." She still stared. "Say
something."

"You've hurt me terribly," she said.

And then Kay kicked off, back-stroking across the pool. I put my head
down on the blue tile edge. When I looked up Ethel was standing above
me. She was nude under her housedress, I saw that.

"Hmm," said Ethel. "I have some clothes of Tony's you can put on."

They fit me perfectly.

Meanwhile, The Car was turning into an upscale disco with nudity.
The sort of place you went slumming in. Mercedes and Cadillacs pulled
up outside. We were getting—a sure sign of acceptance—well-dressed

female customers. People started ordering liqueurs I'd never heard of. We took out the ravioli buffet and fit in two extra tables. Between Thursday and Saturday I sold more than half a month's liquor supply. I went to three dancers a shift every day. Little Norm said to me, "Linese is thinking of having someone killed at Rabies—just so he can compete."

Mike Wilson was the cynosure of all thrill-hungry eyes. A middle-aged woman, well-preserved by science and very drunk, said, with her hand on my shoulder, "You can come home and kill me any time." Not tonight. And the watcher of watchers was Pearl—we were not getting along well. I resented her suspicion. Pearl, apparently, thought I'd garrote her with my shoelaces some night. And there were moments when I wanted to.

Colavecchia and Daniels and Cribbs came by—just to remind me that I was, oh, one tongue slip away from a Riker's Island holding pen. I tried not to take it personally: I knew they were embarrassed by the case. But they certainly were unpleasant.

"Making a big profit, huh?" said Daniels. "Isn't an ill-wind that doesn't blow some good. Nice new suit you got."

"It's not new. It's my brother's. Why don't you find him?"

"We don't think he wants t'be found," said Cribbs.

"The Gaucho's back in town," said Colavecchia. "How d'you feel about that?"

"I don't know—I've only met the man two or three times. Why don't you question him?"

"We're trying, believe me," said Daniels. "How d'you feel about lesbians, Mike?"

"Tout à son gout," I said.

"That means everyone to his taste," said Cribbs. Daniels was not mollified.

"Don't leave town," he said.

Around 1 a.m., on that last night of my priesthood, a dancer named Didi yanked me toward the kitchen. I didn't know her well—pretty, short, from Commack, Long Island, wanted to own a limousine service. A Jewish American Princess in exile. But now Didi was agitated: her oviducts had really gotten in an uproar.

"Mike," she said, "I can't go up."

"Why not?"

"My boyfriend just came in. He's by the cigarette machine. Oh, God, if Raul sees me. Oh, God. He doesn't know I do topless." By the cigarette machine was a Sylvester Stallone, with tattoos that said DEATH and POLLUTE. "Shit, shit, he's coming this way. What do I do?"

What Didi did was wave to Raul. The best defense is a good offense. For her—not for me. "Raul," she said, "Raul. Hi, over here." Raul, who had the distracted look of those-who-are-about-to-urinate, probably wouldn't have noticed Didi, if she'd've shut up. Instead he went absolutely red. His nostrils opened. His fists clenched. He elbowed through six people as if they were nothing more than low cloud cover.

"What're you doing here?" he said.

"Same as you are, sightseeing. I want you t'meet Mike, he owns The Car. I met him this morning while I was shopping t'buy a vibro-massage for your mother—and he said, you know, come see the joint, since, you know, it's so *notorious* these days. So I thought I'd peek in."

Didi had pulled it off. She had managed to distract Raul from her to ME. (Luckily for Didi, she had a black sheath dress on—not a G-string and a net bra or something.) Raul looked at me. Then he looked at his fist. His fist flexed itself like a pedigreed animal. Then Raul simply lifted me by the chest hair and draped me back over the bar. It was what you might call a powerful sensation.

"You hitting on my chick?" he asked.

"No," I said. My arms were pinned under me and I had no footing. He was obscenely strong.

"You don't invite no lady to this pusball joint. Never. This pusball joint is for hookers and sluts. Right?"

"Oh, so right." He hoicked me up higher by my hair.

"You apologize t'this lady and say you never wanna see her again."

"Would you let go—"

"Say."

"I apologize, Didi, it was wrong of me t'ask you here. And, let's not meet again." Raul let me down, agh, slowly. Then he took Didi by the arm and jerked her toward the door. But she forgot her purse, and came back. As Didi passed me, me with both palms on my aching, hand-depilated chest, she said, "Do I still have a Thursday booking?" They're another species, I thought, dancers. They're wired for a different kind of current.

And so, on that last night of my priesthood, I went into our kitchen and pressed my chest against the refrigerator. The incident had been so quick and trivial—I mean, compared to the deaths of Rita and Tanya and Bubbles—and yet it was so painful, so humiliating, that tears of frustration, just two of them, condensed under my eyes. I wanted to hurt someone. I wanted to be in power. I wanted to knock some dick loose, as Tony used to say.

Instead I took Tony's jacket off. It was too warm against my sore chest. I put on a light cardigan sweater, one that I kept in the kitchen for when our A/C got too strong.

And found a small sack of cocaine in the pocket.

I threw it from the rooftop before I hurdled (yaagh!) across that five-story-tall airshaft on my way home. (There were still three or four photographers staking out my apartment. TOPLESS MURDERER GOES TO BED.) I might've stayed away another night, but Tony's clothes had begun to make me feel eerie. Jako, for one, was totally spooked by my outfit. "Don't come no nearah," he said. "Some of you's dead and some of you's alive—and I don't keer which is which."

I tiptoed down from the fifth floor to the second and spotted Kay on the landing there. She was sitting cross-legged outside my door, reading *Howard's End* in the dim light. She wore blue jeans and sneakers. Her hair was down, contact lenses in. I had the visual drop on her (she expected me to come from below) and, for a moment, I took advantage of that. I watched Kay scrape inside her ear. And turn a page. She was, as always, as vulnerable as she was strong. And sexy here: defenses down, engaged. I was moved.

"Kay. Don't jump, it's me."

"Oh—" She closed the book, but not without marking her place.

"I came over the rooftops, like a cat burglar."

"Oh." Kay stood. "Michael, I was bitchy today. I was unforgiving and cruel. I was what my father taught me never t'be—uncivil."

"I understand—"

"It's seeing you when we're around Ethel—the anger I feel toward her, but I'm too polite t'express it. Then that anger gets lumped on top of what I already feel toward you—the hurt part. So you get a double dose."

"I deserve—"

"And even if our relationship is over—"

"Is it over?"

"Don't interrupt me. I said *if,* isn't that enough? Even if, I still cherish you as a friend and you're in trouble. I wanted t'be with you on this night—before you—"

"Resign."

"Yes."

"That was kind of you. I'm glad you came. Shall we go out and get coffee?"

"Over the roof?"

"No. Well, you could go down the stairs, and I could meet you—"

"Don't you have coffee in there?"

"Of course. I wasn't sure if it was—well—*proper*."

"Oh, bullshit," she said, using the word self-consciously. "Let's not make Kay out t'be a total prude. I've had coffee in a man's room before."

"Whose room?"

"Oh, Professor Higgets."

"He's ninety."

"Open the door."

So I did. And I flicked the lights on. And I said, "I haven't had time to straighten up." And—

Saw Berry lying nude on my living-room couch.

"Straighten up isn't the word," said Kay.

Berry came awake and said, "Hi." Then she saw Kay and sat upright. Berry jerked a pillow over her vitals. "What is this, Mike, a free show?"

"Well," said Kay. "If you'd *ever* wear clothes these things wouldn't happen."

"Wait—" I said. And BOTH of them, in simultaneous pique, said,

"What's the meaning of this—" Kay said "Michael" and Berry said "Mike," but they were p.o.'d at the same guy.

"Uh," I said.

"I thought," said Kay, "that you'd broken with her."

"I have. Only. I haven't been able t'tell her, Berry, about it. The phone—"

"Don't believe him," said Berry. "I mean, you're not sucker enough t'believe him, are you?"

"Maybe I do and maybe I don't. It's none of your business."

"Listen," said Berry. "I know him—since he was 9 years old, I know him. You know some priest out in Nebraska who blesses old ladies. I know *him*. People like you cock and bulled Mike into this guilt trip about serving God. He's a man, not a faggot priest. Whyncha just go home and leave us New Yorkers in peace?"

"Lay off, Berry," I said.

"No," said Kay, "I think she's probably right."

"She is NOT right. This has been a terrible misunderstanding. We're all embarrassed and—"

"You feel something for her," said Kay. "She's at home here, I can tell that. I shouldn't have come. I apologize. To both of you. Goodbye."

And Kay left.

"Berry," I said.

"Let it go, Mike. Come into my arms and be my king."

Berry got up then. She was nude and I was clothed—there is always something unsettling about that contrast. It's what makes *Dejeuner sur l'herbe* seem obscene. The clothed ones are taking advantage. And then, on top of that, Berry stumbled. Her nudity, for one instant, wasn't graceful. The awe I had felt for her body slipped away. And then, for a moment, I saw her eyelids flicker uncontrollably. A spasm of flickering. And the anger in me took over. I announced what my secret self had known for weeks—but had hidden, because I still wanted to fuck Berry, still wanted her to ornament my self-esteem. Now that I was through with Berry—now that I had chosen Kay and safety—I said,

"What're you on? Crack? Heroin?"

" 'Scuse?" Berry put one hand over her nipples in mock befuddlement. But it didn't work. I was clothed and she was nude: for a good reason police interrogations proceed that way in savage lands. Somehow the naked feel guilty—not innocent as you might think. And, to underline the authority of my clothing—it is a cruelty I will never forgive myself for—I took her by the bare, sweet shoulders and shook her brutally.

"What is it? What're you on?"

"You hurt me," she said.

"You do drugs, don't you? You even sell them. You took the coke I had under the sink and you switched it for some kind of French laxative, didn't you? Right?" She didn't answer. "No one else had access to it but you. You're on something, right?"

"I have a little problem with heroin. Yes."

"Heroin. My God."

"It's not the end of the world." Berry had picked up a sheet and draped her nakedness with it. This gave her some courage. "I don't skin pop. It's not needles and things. And AIDS. I just snort a little."

"Please leave."

"Oh. Oh, yes. I'm beyond the pale now. What a wonderful excuse t'leave and go back to Miss Nebraska."

"Please leave."

"Mike. I'll detox. I've done it before on methadone. I'll do it again. I'll do you proud. But I can't handle it without you. I can't give you up and give up dope at the same time. Be there for me."

"Be there for you? I don't even trust your kisses now. I don't even know if you're in love or in a trance. And—" It came to me then. "You . . . you made me go up against Leonard because you wanted his drug franchise at The Car. You're not afraid of him. You're so desperate you're not even afraid of Leonard. And if you're not afraid of Leonard you're too scary for me."

"Give me another chance. Forgive me."

"I don't have to," I said. "I'm not a priest any more."

I went into my bedroom then. I pulled Berry's drawer out, brought it back, and dumped her belongings on the living-room floor. Nothing further was said. I returned to my bedroom and shut the door behind me. Five or six minutes later I heard the front door slam.

God forgive me, I didn't see her again after that.

SUNDAY, JULY 24TH

I made my way out to St. Lebbeus in Bayside early—it was a four p.m. service. Afterward, Plunk was scheduled to bless St. Lebbeus's new, remote-control-operated bell tower. I wanted time to rehearse my sermon. I speak without notes and need to have all the topic headings memorized. I felt good—though not happy—about my decision to resign. After Saturday night's head-on collision (with strong elements of Restoration farce) between Berry and Kay, I didn't feel, uh, hallowed, shall we say. Anyhow, I thought, what choice do I have? Muammar Qaddafi had prospects for advancement in the Episcopal Church compared to me.

At about three-thirty, I left my air-conditioned car and walked four blocks to the church. The heat had congealed into a communal mustard plaster. I shone with sweat. There were thunder clouds stacked on the horizon like huge, psychotic Michelin Tire men. The St. Lebbeus people were edgy: they had a refreshment tent set up outside that was just itching to become a hot-air balloon with the right updraft. Keep it short, I told myself. Bad enough to offload your shame on these good folks, don't make them miss their macaroni salad, too.

Plunk was already in the little vesting alcove—quite stuck, head half in, head half out of his chasuble. (He had left his glasses on. They got hooked on the collar material.) Plunk was grateful when I rescued him—and I felt like a heel for involving his diocese.

At which moment Augustus Manning came in.

"You're late as usual, Gus," Plunk said. "There was no one t'help me, until Mike came. I would've suffocated in my own chasuble."

Manning said, "Ah." Then he stared at me, stared back at Plunk, took one step sideward, dropped his valise, which hit Plunk's crosier, which fell, whacking Plunk across the back of his neck.

"You are the *clumsiest* man, Gus," said Plunk.

"Ah," said Manning.

"Are you having a stroke or something?" said Plunk. "Or is it just your normal befuddlement?"

"The heat," said Manning. I knew, by this time, that he would offer no threat. Manning was plainly terrorized by my presence.

"Yes, the heat," said Plunk. "I, of course, will haveta endure the heat, mummified in purple. Go, sit with the congregation, Gus. Michael and I and Mr. Bennett will manage. Just get me a copy of the bell-tower program."

"Yes," said Manning. He looked once at me and backed out.

"Between you and me," Plunk said, "Manning dropped the chalice once—just after preparing the sacrament. Suffered some kind of psychosomatic paralysis in his left arm. For years."

"I may have startled him."

"Oh, yes. I'm sure. Seeing a priest in church. Very unexpected, that. No, ever since the accident there's been something wrong with him." Plunk picked up his crosier and took a few practice three-wood swings with it. "Well, make your sermon short and make it interesting."

"It'll be interesting," I told him.

I saw Kay—left side of the nave, ten rows back—when I climbed the pulpit stairs to begin my sermon. I was grateful that she had come. Especially after her heart-to-heart talk with Berry. Manning had his hands clasped between his thighs—groin-level prayer, I thought. I opened the Bible in front of me, though I knew my text by rote. There was a stomach-grumble of thunder to the west. I inhaled. And noted, with resignation, that some parish historian was videotaping the entire service.

"Matthew 5, verses 27 and 28. 'Ye have heard that it was said by them of old—Thou shalt not commit adultery. But I say unto you, That whosoever looketh on a woman to lust after her hath committed adultery with her already in his heart.' " I paused. I stared down at Manning. He had begun to sit forward: a kinetic something had engaged his body. "Jesus was a tough prosecutor. He made no legalistic distinction between the thought and the act. If you look at a woman with lust in your heart, Jesus said, it is as if you had taken carnal advantage of her.

"We live in an age of technicalities. A child may be aborted before a certain month, not after. Men plead insanity to escape murder charges. Pornography is free speech and not a rape of our sensibilities.

"Have you read the headlines this past week—or have you modestly averted your eyes? I refer to the sensational murders that took place in a topless bar twenty minutes from here called The Smoking Car. Two young women were brutally killed. The murderer is unknown and still at large.

"Me, I'm surprised that more such crimes don't take place. In fact, those murders are just an image, an emblem, an *acting-out*, of many inner murders. Murders of the spirit that occur every day in places like The Smoking Car.

"A case can be made for nudity as art. A case can be made for dancing as art. But, let's face it, they're shoddy cases, pretty much. Between the topless dancer and her admirer there exists a sexual charge that both insults and cheapens the human soul. IT IS NOT HARMLESS, no matter what apologists may tell you. It grinds the affections and stupefies those who seek beauty. It is not something Christians should countenance. It is certainly not something priests should countenance.

"I know," I said, "because, for the last month, I have managed The Smoking Car."

A low, droning "Ehhhhh?" noise came from the congregation. Kay put a handkerchief to her mouth. I looked down at Manning, but his seat was empty. I thought of Hamlet's guilty uncle racing from the play. And, for the first time then, I suspected him. But I went on.

"You don't understand what I'm saying—you weren't prepared for this, and I'm sorry t'trouble you on such a festive day." Thunder rolled, but I had their attention. "Let me repeat, make it clear. Day by day and night by night, I ran a topless bar. I, a priest of God so ordained.

"I took over The Smoking Car for reasons that I thought were extenuating. Good reasons. Charitable reasons. But you cannot employ sin in the service of good. And no one, believe me, should tempt the devil. I have sinned. I have alienated people I love. I have brought suspicion of murder on myself. And, most of all, I have embarrassed my priesthood.

"Which I now resign."

Carefully—but gracefully, thank God—I lifted my vestments off. I laid them across the lectern. I was down to my clerical blacks. I popped the collar.

"You see a man devastated. But he is still a Christian man. I have resigned my priesthood, I have not renounced my faith. The greatest sin of all is despair. Because it is *always* in God's power to forgive. And those who despair deny His power, deny His very essence. I—in such a precarious state of soul as I am—cannot afford t'commit that last sin.

"And so I will now descend and sit among you. And, when the sacraments are prepared by this kind and holy bishop, I will approach the table, hoping—as we all do—that I will not be turned away."

Plunk didn't turn me away. He did, however, say, as he administered the chalice, "I hope you choke on it."

I understood his feelings. What baffled me was the reception I got while exiting St. Lebbeus afterward. A significant ad hoc committee had formed—at least twelve parishioners and most of them women—*supporting* my right to manage a topless bar and celebrate the mass.

"We're with you 150%," said one middle-aged lady. "These aren't the dark ages. You have a right t'take your ministry wherever God calls."

No way I could explain that God hadn't called. *Ethel* had called. I began doubting my ability to communicate in English. Somehow they were mad at that "conservative old chauvinist" Bishop Plunk. The whole issue was neatly inverted. I was challenging the Plunk status quo. A young priest with unorthodox ideas (but plenty of passion) was being persecuted by the Episcopal auto-da-fé.

At which point the new bell began ringing. People cheered. Then it was noted by all that the ringing had become rather inane—rather like the first bars of "La Cucaracha." Over and over and OVER again. The mechanism had gone haywire and could not be unplugged. The insistent repetition of "La Cucaracha" is, believe me, exquisitely maddening. I felt sorry for those people—I had ruined their celebration. In fact, one old man pointed at the bell tower, then said to me, "You did this. You brought this down on us."

I went over to Plunk. I said, "I'll call you."

And Plunk said, "Oh, please do that. Please." And turned his back on me.

Then thunder crashed, and I got out of there.

Kay caught up to me as I ran for the Lincoln. Her face was flushed. When Kay's really emotional a hectic blush rises up/along her throat. It's attractive.

"That—that took guts," she said.

"Thank you for coming."

"What did that group of people say? Were they very cruel?"

"Actually," I said, "I think they wanted me t'run for the state assembly—but listen. This storm is passing. I'm no longer an active priest, so I can do unseemly things. Bert'll run The Car tonight. You wanna see New Yawk? Lemme take you to a quiet place by the ocean. It's called Coney Island."

So we did. Some off-color places wear their sleaze as if it were a fine veneer. Coney Island is one of those places. Kay was both fascinated and afraid. As for me, I was into frightening myself—to numb the fear of being the non-Rev. Mike Wilson. There is at Coney Island a cylindrical machine called the Hell Hole—it whirls so forcefully that a kind of centrifugal glue sticks your body to the wall. THEN, the floor drops twenty feet. And you are hung there, saved only by the substitution of one physical law for another. As the law of Jesus, *agape,* perfect love, obviates the law of man. But you must spin—ah, spin hard—to keep Jesus's law in effect. Or the downward weight will prevail.

As you might guess I was looking for significance that night.

Kay and I did well. I love showing her things. And she has—great quality—a genuine interest in whatever event or artifact you might bring to her attention. Kay has never developed an ironic stance—critical, but not ironic. There is no cynicism in her. (New York *babies* cry cynically: "You think you could bring a bottle, it's too much trouble, huh?") She swept me up. And, sure, we were both a little frenzied in our pleasure, trying to avoid The Subject. But—after a beer or three—I began to feel hopeful again. We were having fun together, is what I mean.

We got Monday's *Post* at 2 a.m. PRIEST RAN TOPLESS MURDER BAR, it said. "Defrocks Self in Emotional Ceremony." There was a picture of me, vestment neck pulled up, looking like a Ku Klux Klansman.

"I better get you to Ethel's," I said. "Before the vultures gather."

"Not Ethel. Not tonight. Somehow I don't see me being civil to Ethel right now. I'm afraid I'd tell her just what I think of her."

"A motel?"

"No."

"My place must be under surveillance." I thought a moment. "Unless you're game for a little adventure."

"A *little* adventure would be an improvement."

· · ·

So I rang each doorbell in the apartment building behind mine, and, as always, some sap let us in. We sneaked up five stories to the roof, across the heat-squishing asphalt, to the parapet.

"You jump over that?" Kay said.

"It's only like three, four feet across."

"But it's many, many, many feet down."

"Watch." I got up on the ledge and jumped across. Then I jumped back. "Don't look down is the trick. You ran track in high school. Here, look, I'll draw a distance of five feet from . . . say this piece of pipe t'that stick." I did. "Okay, jump." Kay did. "So what's the difference?"

"My imminent death."

"It's in the mind."

"You want me t'jump across that canyon?"

"Yes."

"Why?"

"Because it's the only way we can have coffee and a decent night's sleep. Here, I'll go first—give me your purse—and I'll be ready t'catch you."

I stood on the far side, hands out, waiting. Kay considered. She put her hair back in a knot as though she might be more aerodynamically efficient that way. Then she looked at me and said, "I've followed you t'New York, I can go another four feet." And jumped.

And almost missed. Kay had taken off on her right leg—but, for some reason, the left leg had reservations. Her leap was ultimately hesitant— and I had to grab Kay by the blouse front to keep her from dropping backward, down. We fell to the rooftop, in an embrace of relief.

"I thought," Kay said, "you wanted me t'die. I thought you were going t'let me fall."

"I didn't," I said. "I can't afford another death."

"Is that why?"

"Also I love you."

And we kissed fiercely. We wolfed each other down.

It was hot in the apartment: still, I shouldn't have taken my shirt off. But I was impatient as usual and, because of that, I overbid a weak hand. Kay sat on the far side of my kitchen table, against the wall—in a position the 82nd Airborne couldn't have taken by frontal assault. We were both a little bemused, even shaken, by what had happened on the roof. Both of us probably overvalued it. Both of us were still defensive.

We held hands across the table. For a while she and I talked about my now limitless (or empty) future, then Kay said,

"What'd you tell your girlfriend about me?"

"Tell? Nothing. It's none of her business. And she's not my girlfriend."

"Did you tell her we'd been having sexual problems? That I wasn't good in bed?"

"No. Hell, no."

"The infidelity maybe I can understand. And bear. But not the humiliation. I'm a private person, Michael. I was brought up that way. *Never* do I want my personal life discussed."

"Hey, I wouldn't do that." Then, because Kay had irritated me with her moral hard-lining, I said, "I know you well enough by now."

"Do you? Do you really? And is that a—a burden t'you? Old uptight Kay?"

"No, it isn't a burden. And you're not uptight, you're morally correct. I respect that. And I hope for your forgiveness."

"May I ask—have you broken with what's her name?"

"Yes," I said. "I threw her out last night, after you left. But—"

"But what?"

"But she may not have broken with me."

"She loves you. Poor Michael. Everyone loves him. Everyone needs his pastoral care."

"I'm not a priest anymore. I'm just a guy."

"Just an attractive bachelor with a lot of money in New York. Hard times."

"What're you getting at, Kay?"

"Well—the bonds are broken. Lord God almighty you're free at last. One can hardly expect you t'settle down now. This is your big opportunity t'sow some more wild oats—"

"Kay, go easy."

"No. No. Listen t'what I'm saying. It makes perfect sense. This just *isn't* the moment for you t'settle down—certainly not with me."

"Kay—"

"Let me *finish*. It makes perfect sense. After all, I knew you back when. When the touch of your hand conferred a blessing. When you had God's franchise. Maybe you still do. Maybe not. But I certainly can't just drop my respect for—my awe of—your office. And you don't want that. You want t'start new. You don't want someone who, every day, reminds you of what you were."

"I want you—"

"Yes, I'm sure. But not just me. You've felt all that power you have over women—"

"Stop it. Power over women? In the last month I'll tell you what I've felt. I've felt fear. And bodily pain. And shame. And my own deceitfulness. And in the midst of that, three women have died. My brother is probably dead. I'm one piece of evidence away from a murder trial— and the superstitious part of me says I'm guilty. That's what I've felt this month. And it hasn't been pleasant. I've learned, Kay. I've learned a lot."

"I hope," she said. Then, standing: "Show me your bathroom."

As Kay moved by me, I reached for her long waist. Two considerations motivated me. One: I wanted the comfort of her touch. Two: I couldn't remember whether or not Berry had left her spare diaphragm in the medicine cabinet. So I put my head into the crook of Kay's neck, swung her as if in a pre-rehearsed routine, and brought us down together on the living-room couch.

It was a miscalculation. First of all, we were *hot*—and my naked chest was both threatening and sweaty: mammalian. Second, Kay had last seen that same couch occupied by a naked and bitchy rival. Third, you just don't go spontaneous on Kay. She has to think things out.

"Not now, Michael. Let me up."

I didn't. I kissed her. I said, "Kay, Kay."

"Let me up." And she pushed at me.

"How very forgiving," I said.

"Forgiving doesn't mean I haveta cough up my self-respect. Forgiving doesn't mean I haveta be another trophy on your apartment wall—"

"Oh, forget it." I let her up. "Forget it."

"How do I know that woman doesn't have syphilis or AIDS—?"

"Please. I really wasn't trying t'crowbar you into bed. I'm not that desperate."

"Goodbye, Michael."

"Come on. I didn't mean desperate that way—"

"Goodbye, Michael." And Kay was at the door. "I don't think I'm the right woman for you just now. Maybe some other time."

"When I grow up?"

"Yes!" she said. "Yes, dammit, when you grow up."

I fell asleep on the couch. Kay was still far from me. Moreover, I had forfeited the protection of my church—all its institutional resources: advice and work and community and, yes, medical benefits. Naturally I had disagreeable dreams. First, Jesus asked me to take up my cross and follow Him—but the stupid thing was too heavy. It was made of rusty steel girders riveted in place. Then I began—I don't know—receding from everyone and every place. Things got smaller: I was at the wrong end of the telescope. Or I got small. Then I felt pain across the middle of my forehead and I was blind. "The yolks of my eyes have broken," I thought.

Then Jako's call woke me up.

I heard his voice on the Phone-Mate speaker. It was full of grief.

"Mr. Mike," he said. "Please be there, Mr. Mike. Ohhh."

"Jako," I said. "What's wrong?"

"I can't move, Mr. Mike. I got the phone in my hand and that's all I can do."

"Did you fall? Are you sick?"

"Mr. Mike, it's no fair—"

"What Jako? What's up?"

"There is a dead person in here with me, Mr. Mike. She looked at me."

"She? A dancer? Who?"

"Your own Miss Tulip."

"Berry . . . Jako. Just stay where you are and don't touch anything."

"Oh, don't you worry 'bout that," he said.

MONDAY, JULY 25TH

Someone had decapitated Berry.

Her head was on the bar, jammed upright, eyes open: looking more puzzled than afraid. And her nude body, stringed with blood, sat three stools away, leaning forward over the bar—the way confirmed drinkers sit. I didn't begrudge Jako his nervous collapse. It was *horrid*: the feeling of detachment in it. The head staring out. The nude, headless body hunched. There was dreamy terror in that composition. As if the killer were bored with it all. Murder is one thing—but murder without passion is abominable. And everywhere I stepped, Berry's clotting blood sucked at my sneaker soles.

She had been executed on the stage. I found an axe propped against the cigarette machine. The blade was glossy, as women's fingernails are, with blood. It gleamed with blood. And there was a seashore smell, of salt and brackish tides.

. . .

I called Ethel first. I wanted to have Weintraub with me. Then I rang the homicide department. While we were waiting Jako and I sat by the phone holding hands. Most of all, I didn't want to think of that warm, brown otter-child who had shared my bed. Berry, that child, bore no resemblance to what lay on the bar, what slumped over it. Most of all—I am ashamed to say—I was too afraid for myself to care about her.

"I read by the paper," Jako said in a small voice, "how that you're a reverend."

"I resigned yesterday."

"Still you could bless her, isn't that so?"

"I am. Inside I'm blessing her."

"She was a nice girl. But she messed with drugs too much."

"I didn't know," I said. "I didn't know."

Then the door opened and half the entire world came in.

We all went down to the precinct house in Long Island City—so that Mike Wilson could experience the outward and visible signs of incarceration and be intimidated. Let me tell you, the insincere green of those walls is enough to stagger anyone's resolve. Weintraub, throughout, was conducting a real estate deal with the Helmsley people on his cellular phone. I think he presumed I was guilty. At one point, while waiting for his opposite number in the Helmsley organization, Weintraub leaned over and murmured, "There any insanity in your family?" He was planning a plea bargain already. Instead of life imprisonment at hard labor, I'd get life imprisonment weaving baskets. Yet I couldn't complain about Ethel. Weintraub was expensive and he got respect. His time must've cost Ethel thousands—or the virtue of two of her female children.

My mind, needless to say, was on high simmer. Colavecchia and Daniels asked questions about Berry. But, in fact, they told *me* more about her than I told them. Berry was a known drug dealer, with one arrest for heroin possession three years before. (She got probation.) This news was stunning enough. But then there was the question of her love for me.

How much, I wondered, had been real—how much a junkie's riff? Part of me, the coward part, was trying to rationalize guilt. The truth was, Tanya's death had affected me more. By this time certainly my surprise mechanism was worn through. I allow myself that. But, yes, to some God-forsaken degree, I felt relief that Berry had been killed. And every-

one around me, I thought, sensed it—this guy has just seen a decapitated corpse and he's remarkably unemotional. The decapitated corpse
of his girlfriend no less. Daniels and Colavecchia and Cribbs took it all
in. That really worried me: suddenly they were being so *nice*. Maybe
it was Weintraub. Maybe (I favored this theory) Colavecchia and the
others thought they had me cornered.

Because, of course, I could provide no decent alibi. Berry had been
killed some time between 5 a.m. and 8 a.m., when I was asleep on the
couch. Or so I said. No one had seen me enter or leave (one of the
"photographers" was a cop) until 8:24, after Jako's call. I told them
about my secret approach from the rear apartment roof. This seemed
to embarrass them (the cops on stakeout had missed that). But it also
gave me the M.O. of an Iraqi terrorist. Hell, I would've arrested me.

At a point, just before we reached the precinct house, I said,

"Guys, just once, I'm innocent. I didn't do it."

"It's a formality, Mike," said Daniels. "We just wanna get your testimony down."

"You're really a Catholic priest?" said Colavecchia.

"Episcopal. I was until yesterday."

"Well, whatever. You're a fuckin' New York celebrity. Like Bernie
Goetz or Robert Chambers."

And so I was. The entire block had been cordoned off. Several hundred media people—even media people from small FM stations—were
backed against blue police sawhorses. Not to mention that unaffiliated
tribe who follow the lurid as an avocation.

"One word to a newsman," said Weintraub, "and I double my re-
tainer."

The *New York Post* late edition said—what did you expect?—HEAD-
LESS, TOPLESS. MURDERER STRIKES AGAIN.

Weintraub was firm. "These are the ground rules," he told Colavecchia and Daniels and Cribbs. "My client is appalled at the murder
of this young girl. He'd like t'help your investigation. *However*—the
moment I feel you're treating him not as a friendly witness but as a
suspect, that moment I order him t'shut up. I'll rule on the questions,
Mike. Don't answer quickly, I may wanna object."

At that moment a sergeant entered. He took Daniels aside. Then
Daniels and Colavecchia and Cribbs all left for a conference. Weintraub
called the Helmsley people. I stared out the window until a cameraman
spotted me: then I ducked back. Daniels and Colavecchia returned.
They looked sour.

The questioning went on for at least three hours. It began, as most slow intimidations do, with trivial data. This time the murderer had exited out the rear door—there was a slight, but noticeable trail of blood. It ran from the door, down a narrow alley, and ended at the sidestreet curb—where, presumably, the perp had gotten into his car. Oddly, there were also bloody cat paw-prints. This, I felt, was a bit of evidence against me. For all his Lizzie Borden whacking, the murderer somehow hadn't scared the cat. Yes, I was on good terms with Lazarus. Yes, said Weintraub, and so was Jako: Jako might've let the cat out. But, said Daniels, Jako came in the front door. But, said Weintraub, he was in shock and barely able to function for over thirty minutes. He could've put Lazarus out during that time and forgotten about it. Daniels let the matter drop. He went into another office, made a phone call and came back in.

"Do you know a woman named Kay—or Katherine—Lyons?"

"Sure. She's my fiancée, or was. She just flew in from Nebraska t'visit. I'd really rather not involve her in this."

"Sorry. It's germane. When'd you see her last?"

"Yesterday. We went to Coney Island—t'relax after my resignation."

"Did she come t'your apartment?" I hesitated. "Well?"

"For a time, yes."

"For how long?"

"Coffee, that's all. Time enough for coffee and cake."

"Did you make love t'her?"

"This conversation is just about over," said Weintraub. "Don't answer. Where's this leading, Daniels? You obviously have information I don't have—tell me now or we'll just wait for discovery. And you'll lose my client's valuable help."

"Okay," said Colavecchia. "Kay Lyons says she spent the entire night with Mike. Mike, however, says she just had coffee. Coffee gives him time t'wash the dishes, climb over the roof, and commit murder. So who's telling the truth?"

And Weintraub, with brilliant spontaneity, said, "All right, my client has been lying. We'll concede that. He was trying t'protect his fiancée's reputation. I advised him against it—but with all the allegations of sexual misconduct, you know—" Weintraub turned to me. "Tell them the truth, Mike. Kay spent the entire night with you, didn't she?"

"Yes." I said. "She did."

They certainly didn't want to believe me. It exonerated their best suspect. And Kay—obviously—had a stake in her fiancé's release. Cynicism was in order. How had Kay entered and exited my apartment without being seen? She really unnerved them then. She took Cribbs up to my building roof. There Kay pointed out our secret route. When he was still skeptical, before he could stop her, Kay jumped the four foot airshaft.

Over and back.

An expression of love, I think.

TUESDAY, JULY 26TH and WEDNESDAY, JULY 27TH

I had attained, if not fame, then a fine grade of notoriety. It was awful: like those dreams where you find yourself naked and mute on the Seventh Avenue subway. Bag packers in the supermarket stared at me—and forgot to wrap my ice cream in plastic. The pharmacist would say, come back in fifteen minutes—and, when I did (I got a valium prescription), every employee was loitering three feet from the prescription counter. My block was virtually impassable. Those who might have been undecided on the subject of my guilt or innocence were ready to hang me because of the double-parked press cars. Like a Euripidean chorus, the Jewish ladies would yell "Bum and murderer" as I walked down the street.

I thought of moving to Ethel's house—but she didn't want her children exposed to the media rush. Weintraub backed her: he felt it was important for me to stay away from Kay. I considered a motel: but I didn't really want to be alone. So, instead, I spent some nights on the Starship Enterprise.

Which is also Bert's two-bedroom—one-mess—apartment. I opened his front door and this life-sized Klingon warrior shot a phaser gun at me. Flash, flash, flash. You walk carefully, and *single file*, through Bert's apartment. There is a path six inches wide between this display of Trek-shit and that display of Trek-shit. Fanzines. Plastic Scotties and plastic Sulus. (Bert's shower stall looks like a beam-me-up transporter.) Autographed photos. Studio posters. Wind-up tribbles. Remote control Federation starships. The chairs we sat in were "authentic replicas" (?) of furniture found on the Enterprise's bridge. It was absurd. It was claustrophobic-making. It was appraised at $260,000. "And going up as we sit here," Bert said.

· · ·

So that's what I did for two days: watched Bert's collection appreciate, while, on TV, my character did the opposite. The parish chronicler had sold his video of my resignation to one of the networks. Over and over again I relived my defrocking. Then there was the TV psychiatrist who spoke (very judiciously) about repression in the church—and the violent reactions it could foment. He mentioned Rasputin. Everything I might have done was "alleged," of course. And alleged and alleged again.

In another sense, though, my prospects *were* appreciating. Weintraub reported a newspaper offer of $125,000 for my exclusive "life" story. "Don't bite," he said. "That just sets your bottom figure." Meanwhile he was maneuvering to have The Car reopened. The blood had been cleared up, new flooring put in, but Jako had suddenly lost all his hair—every follicle dead from shock. "And," said Weintraub, "be good t'your girlfriend. She has you by the short ones."

"I'm innocent, Mr. Weintraub," I said.

"Sure. But innocence is a lousy defense. You don't wanna go t'trial—even though I'll get you off. You don't want two years of me."

"Bert," I said, hanging up. "You ever been married?"

"Neh." He was cataloguing his collection on a PC. "Where would I fit her? A wife."

"Well, have you had girlfriends?"

"I had a mother. Enough. Man should learn from his mother—one woman is enough."

"The dancers don't arouse you?"

"Fortunately I can't see so well."

"If you could—see them, I mean."

"I'm a collector, Mike. Finding one of my *tsatskes* is a turn-on. It completes a piece of my existence. Now, for you, women are a collector's item. Each of them completes—nu?—a piece of your existence. This one brings out the big romantic in you. That one makes your petzel stand up in a different direction. Another maybe is spiritual. Men like you borrow a personality in bed. My father was a big womanizer. 'Today,' he would say, 'I found out I was a singer.' This girl told him he could sing. 'Today—I understood what it is t'be tender.' Some other chippy said he had a big heart. To this day my mother hates him. He was like a jigsaw put together by women."

"It's an interesting idea," I said.

"But that's the good part I told you."

"What's the bad part?"

"The bad part is—most of these women are lying. My father couldn't sing a note—the cat would run if he opened his mouth."

"Maybe I should start collecting."

"Don't be snide. You see this mess? Better a mess in the living room than a junkhouse in the heart."

"Are women the same? Do they derive their personalities from men?"

"Women come finished from the womb," Bert said. "It's the difference between egg and sperm. The egg is *there.* It's the little sperm that needs a road map. So they show us: 'Yoo-hoo, over here.' It reduces to biology."

"I'll get another beer," I said.

The *New York Post* headline on July 29th was: PRIEST HAD HISTORY OF SEX HIJINX.

The Ottomanellis, in their grief, had made a statement to the press. "Even as a teenager," said Mr. Ottomanelli, "Mike Wilson was a pervert. He got a sixteen-year-old girl pregnant." (Amanda was sixteen and *so was I*—but he made it sound like Mike Wilson had gone poaching at a Brownie Scout convention.) He blamed Berry's drug trouble on me. He blamed her topless career on me. He said the police were covering up. And he announced a $5,000,000 lawsuit against the Episcopal Church for—I don't know—failure to inspire morality or something.

Worse, though, Mrs. Ottomanelli told Daniels that Berry had gotten a phone call at 4:30 a.m. It had woken the whole house. Berry dressed. Berry said that a nightshift worker had been taken ill. That she'd been called in to replace him by her "boss" at the "restaurant." Me, it was generally presumed. They didn't mention the six ounces of cocaine and the two dozen bags of heroin found in Berry's bedroom closet at home.

"Who did it, Bert?" I asked. We were watching the episode where Spock falls in love.

"If *you* didn't?"

"I like that. You think you're watching TV with a murderer?"

"It wouldn't surprise me. After Auschwitz who can be surprised? I feel safe. I'm not your type."

"Who did it?"

"Me maybe."

"Seriously."

"Why not?"

"But you weren't even there when Bubbles died."

"We don't know Bubbles was murdered. Tanya and Berry—you can be sure they didn't commit suicide. Neh. Mike, I was there, I had access, why not me?"

And, for a half-moment, it seemed plausible. The domineering mother, like in *Psycho.* The repressed sex life. The strength, Lord knows. And all the goddam LUNATIC JUNK in that apartment. Bert was *crazy.* He could've done it.

The two of us, sitting in this kackamamie room, building cases against each other.

Then Weintraub called. He felt that the Ottomanelli press conference had done damage. Cribbs might have me arrested just to save face. But the $125,000 deal had gone up to $175,000. And there was a message from Rev. Augustus Manning.

I called. Manning was oblique. Said he had something important to tell me. We agreed to meet in Bowne Park at 11 a.m.

And so I spent the night building an indictment against Manning for the murders of Rita and Bubbles and Tanya and Berry. I forged keys to The Car for him. To him I attributed astonishing physical strength. And the motive, of course was easily come by: we were all repressed, we priests, weren't we?

And, in a sense, from Berry's murder to the end, I never entirely ruled myself out.

THURSDAY, JULY 28TH

I watched Manning for a few moments from my Lincoln. He was seated on a bench near the duck pond in Bowne Park. Feeding squirrels. Manning had shorts on. And, under his KISS-FM T-shirt, he sported paps. They were almost feminine. He wasn't fat particularly—he just had the slackest skin I have ever seen on a human being. His cheeks hung to jowls. And under each eye there was a big purse of flesh.

"Sit," he said. I sat. He gave off a sour odor: it reminded me of a Paris pissoir. Sleep, I guessed, had been snubbing him. He handed me a bag of peanuts.

"Is this an official meeting?" I asked.

"No," he said. "I'm acting on my own. But I think I can help you."

"How so?"

"The diocese, indeed the national church, has taken a terrific drubbing because of your antics."

"I'm sorry for that."

"There are . . ." he touched me on the shoulder, "there are people in the Diocese of Queens, important people, who feel you shouldn't have stepped down."

I stared at him.

"I happen to be one of those people."

"Excuse me. Did you just say—I *shouldn't* have resigned?"

"First of all—if I may make an important theological point—you cannot resign from the priesthood. A priest is ordained forever according to the Order of Melchizedek. You are still a priest."

"Yes. But I will not function as a priest. I can't consecrate a chalice in my present state of alienation. I'm not fit."

"Who says? My word, we ordain lesbians in this church with great pomp and honor. You didn't commit adultery—neither you nor the young lady were married. You were helping your sister-in-law and her four small children. And surely—surely—you're not saying you murdered those women."

"No. I didn't."

"Then I see it essentially as a First Amendment issue—and I'll back you on that. So will many others. This is, after all, an activist church."

"Come again?"

"There are people in Queens Diocese who think we should take the high ground. It never pays t'get defensive. Look what happened t'Reagan with Irangate. He should've said 'Of course we did it. By our interpretation, the Constitution grants a president the authority to act at his discretion in foreign policy matters of great import. Others disagree. Fair enough: let's bring it before the Supreme Court. Meanwhile, we apologize for nothing.' End of Irangate. Can you see what I'm getting at?"

"Frankly, no."

"All right. There are important people, myself included, who feel that your case should be handled as a civil rights issue."

"My First Amendment right to earn a living from nudity?"

"I repeat—what've you done wrong? You were indiscreet, but passionate. You did a favor for your sister-in-law. In the process you hoped t'bring some Christian love to a tawdry and jaded enterprise. Do I haveta remind you what Jesus said about His mission? It was to save sinners—not those who are already blessed by grace."

"But I hid my identity. I didn't preach—"

"You were biding your time for the auspicious moment. Then, well, these terrible murders took place. It got too late. Listen, you could be a tremendous asset to your church. You're handsome. You're smart.

You're certainly glib as hell. Your resignation speech was excellent theater. There are churches across the river in New York Diocese— down in the Village, say—who would kill t'have you as their rector. You've had national publicity. You could do more for the Episcopal Church on the Oprah Winfrey show than a hundred monks praying. Stop thinking about yourself for a moment and think about feeding your flock."

As if to illustrate, Manning offered a peanut to the squirrel beside him. It was another hot day. I stared at a naked infant girl playing with her bare-shinned mother in the shallow water. But, to tell truth, I was numb with fear. The devil was sitting on a park bench. It had to be him. Who else would be so persuasive? Manning had almost convinced the ratio-nal me. And the world of Christ was stood on its head.

"The Oprah Winfrey show—"

"A syndicated column. You could be a bishop some day. And a good one."

"Well," I said thoughtfully. "The good thing is—what adds credibil-ity—the good thing is . . . *you've* been at The Car all along. I can say I was working there under your pastoral supervision—"

"No," said Manning, "you can't tell them that."

"Sure I can. What about *your* civil rights?"

"Don't play games, Mike. I'm not stupid."

"Games? If it's all right for Mike Wilson t'be in a topless bar—why not you?"

"Because I don't have any official position at The Car. I don't have the compelling reasons for being there that you have. I was—"

"Just committing a sin."

"I'm 56 years old and I don't intend t'let myself be judged by a child." I stood up.

"I don't judge."

"Wait—"

"Manning—whether liberation theology allows for it or not—sin still exists in the world. Things *can* be wrong. Me, I'm all wrong. My soul is an open sore right now. I've given in to lust and to greed and to anger—I'm so sick I almost find you plausible. But one thing I don't want t'do is—is take this disease I've contracted and spread it. I can't perform the eucharist. I can't even get on with the business of repenting yet—so steeped am I in guilt and fear. I'm a very unhappy man. And an evil man. But I still know the difference, thank God, between a sin and a civil right. Here."

I was positioned to his left. When I handed back the bag of peanuts

Manning seemed stricken. He jerked his hips around on the park bench. He might've been wearing an invisible straitjacket. Then he reached across with his right hand and took the peanuts. I stared at him. Manning took his left forearm and, with his right hand, he raised it.

"Doesn't work any more," he said.

That was my day for clandestine meetings. At about three p.m. Kay and I managed a motor rendezvous in the IHOP parking lot on Northern Blvd. Kay got into my car. Then she sat, her back against the passenger door, her dress above bare knee. She looked, I must say, pretty and oh so satisfied with herself. I put my hand on her calf.

"You shouldn't," Kay said. "It might constitute tampering with a witness." She thought that was very amusing.

"You're committing perjury," I said.

"Uh-huh."

"It doesn't bother you?"

"Oh, it does. It wouldn't be worthwhile otherwise. If it didn't bother me, I mean."

"Are you so sure I'm innocent?"

"No. I think you could've done it—you have enough anger in you. It scares me."

"Then why?"

"The pleasure it gives me of once—just once—making you beholden t'me. You don't know how my love has floundered in insecurity. In fact, you don't know *me*. I'm not this person—I'm much freer, more open, when I'm not with you. With you I feel, One slip and he's gone, Kay. Play it close t'the vest. And, inevitably, I assert at the wrong time and defer at the wrong time."

"I've never noticed that."

"Oh, come on—don't be polite just because I hold your life in my hands. Face it: our relationship was a mass of sterile matter. We might as well have been married fifteen years."

"I love you."

"I don't doubt it. You love kittens, too. And right now—boy oh boy, d'you crave stability. And here I am. Stable as a doorstop."

"Do you love me? Talk about anger—I think I hear some inner rage there."

"Oh, I'm furious with you. Furious. The sordidness of it all. This scene. My aunt in Lekachman just wrote saying, in so many words, don't bother coming home. Decent people, you know, decent people can smell out an evil situation. Even at 2,000 miles."

"Look, Kay. Just hours ago I turned down an unofficial offer from the diocese—they wanted t'give me my priesthood back. They wanted t'turn me into a First Amendment martyr."

"Only in New York."

"And I said no. I do not make excuses for my behavior. I ask forgiveness."

"Did you love her?"

"Berry?"

"Who else? She was buried today. Someone at the graveside said you deserved t'be made a eunuch. Did you love her?"

"No—"

"Then why did you—"

"*To get laid,* of course. What else? Listen, Kay, my feelings for Berry are so confused now that I really can't answer you. She was a heroin addict and I didn't guess it until last Saturday night. God knows, she functioned better than I did. She was also a child of my childhood. We understood each other. She knew my brother. There was no one here— no one but Berry—that I could be open with. And, yes, she was sexy. And, yes, I loved the love for me that I saw in her eyes. I can't separate myself from her—I can't say Berry was just a slut, let's forget her and start again. Good God, I was being a slut, too. What right have I t'judge her?"

"This is not the time t'be Christian. I need reassurance. Want a cigarette?" She pulled out a pack of Marlboros.

"A cigarette? You don't smoke."

"See, that's what I mean. I've smoked since I was fourteen, but never around you. When you came over t'my place I used to dash around and collect the ashtrays. But you never noticed. I was a librarian and you were a priest—guess who got the most attention?"

"So competitive."

"Say you love me again."

"Say *you* love me first."

"I can't. It would impair my credibility as a witness. By the way, I told Detective Cribbs we did it three times on Saturday night. Uh . . . people can do it three times in one night, can't they?"

"I can."

"Oh, of course—with Berry you were Superman."

"You asked me a question, fer God's sake." I inhaled, held. "I love you," I said.

"Good. Because Ethel told me t'tell you she's gonna reopen The Car tomorrow. Weintraub got or threatened t'get an injunction against the police department."

"Tomorrow? It's wrong. It's impossible. I'll talk her out of it in the morning."

"You don't have a chance."

"Watch me," I said.

FRIDAY, JULY 29TH

I beamed down from Bert's place on Friday morning. Ethel was hard at work. She had Weintraub on one phone and our exterminator on another. Pearl sat beside Ethel, holding a yellow legal pad. When I slid the aluminum door aside and entered the glassed-in sun-porch-cum-TV-den, Pearl turned away from me. Something about her reaction brought back a story about the old cancer-ridden Sigmund Freud. Some ditzy female poet—her name escapes me—thought it would be nice to get analyzed by Freud himself before The Great Man kicked off. So she bugged him and bugged him. Freud agreed reluctantly. But the sessions didn't go well. One day, the poetess is rambling on about her self-perceptions, and she feels—thump, thump, thump—a fist pounding on the couch. It's Freud, And he's furious. He says, "I know why this is not working, I know—YOU THINK I'M TOO OLD TO FALL IN LOVE WITH." Poor Freud. But that was just the same anger I was feeling from Pearl. Sexual anger. She thought I was the murderer. And *she was insulted that I hadn't made an attempt on her life.* At that instant, I realized that she, Pearl, had come a bit unstuck. It makes a difference—when first you realize that someone whom you've known is, well, crazy. It clears things up. And yet, through all the long time of their friendship, it hadn't bothered Ethel.

"Give me a minute, Mike, honey." Ethel said. "I'll be with you. Go out and see your girlfriend."

I did. But I was pissed off: here I am, I thought, vocationless, under suspicion of murder, unable to sleep in my own apartment—and Ethel's treating me like the Japanese houseboy. Disgust claimed my attention and it was a half second or so before I saw Kay. Then watched her. She was surrounded by little girls at the poolside. The youngest, Ellen, was in Kay's arms—getting, yes, gobbled up. Kay was kisses and little bites and hickey-sucks all over Ellen. Ellen giggled and squirmed. And Kay pursued her with ravenous, foolish, warm affection. It was another Kay I hadn't been informed of.

"Hello," I said. The children stared up at me (as sometimes they do to this day, hoping I'll perform the big trick and turn into Tony). "Child-eating can get you into trouble."

"They're delicious," she said. "Especially now when I'm so sick of grown-ups."

"Reporters been out there all this time?"

"All this time. Did you see *Newsday*? They went and fished out my college yearbook photo—I look awful and it's on the cover, 'Mystery woman,' it says."

"Show business."

"I had an argument with Ethel last night—I told her what I thought. That she was using you. We're not on good terms this morning. It's time t'quit, Mike. A little longer and people might think you enjoyed this line of work."

"You're right," I said. "I'll give her an ultimatum."

Ethel listened. She has a doctorate in manipulation. Ethel knows this much: that when someone is *really* annoyed—and you can't work the usual snow job—you listen carefully. You take the person's complaint very *seriously*. Then you ignore everything he or she says.

"Right," Ethel told me, "I feel the same way you do. Give me until September 1st—then you're out of here."

"Ethel—"

"Mike, look at it this way. The police won't let you leave the city anyhow. And, well—don't get me wrong, please—but it's costing me a fortune t'have Weintraub defend you. Believe it or not, worse, the Ottomanellis may sue The Car—lack of safety precautions. Like that woman who sued the motel when she was raped. We've had one, two . . . seven down days this month. I hadda borrow on my savings t'meet the payroll. Give me a month—"

"August 15th and I'm gone," I said. "But today is impossible. There are no girls—"

"I've taken the liberty of making a few phone calls." She handed me a list. "That's your schedule through Sunday night."

"Girls—I mean—they *want* to dance . . . ?"

"Well, a large percentage are Brazilian girls who would dance nude for Jack the Ripper, but . . . the rest will come around. The place is gonna be packed today, Mike."

"Jesus, Ethel—you feel *good* about profiting from this? Why don't we open a waxworks?"

"A waxworks? D'you know someone who could do that?"

"Ethel. I was being sarcastic."

"I know. I know." But did she? I was never sure. "Believe me I can tell when someone's being sarcastic. I lived with your brother for eight years."

"Where is Tony, Ethel?" She turned to me. "Were there other girls besides Rita?"

"Don't do this to me, Mike. My womanhood is pretty shaky right now. A thing your young friend doesn't want to understand."

" 'Young friend'? Kay?" She nodded. "You had an argument?" She nodded. "Kay is a strong woman."

"Oh-oh," said Ethel. "You picked one there."

"I love her," I said. "And she wants me out of here. Now I've already lost my profession and my right t'privacy—help me to keep Kay at least."

"Ha," said Ethel. "Don't worry about losing that one—you could get rid of lung cancer easier."

"No. You don't understand Kay. She's highly principled. She'll leave me, even if it hurts her."

"No, Mike. She won't. No woman could resist a chance t'reform—ta-dah—the topless priest. Passionate young man gone wrong. Passionate, *handsome*, dark, driven, young man."

"Okay, *you* tell Kay I'm working 'til August 15th. I haven't got the courage."

"She's wrong," Ethel said, "that mustache looks good on you."

It was Mardi Gras on Northern Boulevard all afternoon and all night. We had lured the freaks out. When I got to The Car at noon, there was a double line of customers waiting to get in. It ran past Big Marty's store and right around the corner. Like a damn movie premiere. Not just the raincoat crowd—there were couples, college kids. We had become part of the New York experience.

And, behind a police line, looking tough as shower clogs, was a task force from Females Against Smut—one of whom clipped me above the left ear with a raw egg. I swear a network cameraman said, "I'm focused . . . Now!" just before she threw it. Anyhow, Kay told me later, I looked like John Kennedy on the Zapruder film. Blam from behind. Someone had spray-painted EXPLOITS WOMEN across our facade. (Some exploitation, at $1500 a week tax free.) I turned when the egg hit me—to the TV world I must've resembled Mussolini just before they strung him up by his heels. And the antismut crowd let out with, "Woman killer! Woman killer!" In the midst of all this confusion Linese and his idiot manager Dutch were handing out flyers for Rabies. We had killed his box office—along with four women.

"Fuckin' vulture," Linese yelled at me. "Fuckin' vultures, you and Ethel. Why doncha shut that fuckin' morgue down—it's a disgrace t'the Boulevard. Why'n'cha sacrifice fuckin' virgins on the stage in there, you sicko prick."

"Only people who die in your joint," I said, "are customers. Of boredom."

"You've had it, Mike. You're gonna do time for this."

I took three, four steps toward Linese, but Dutch intervened. And Bert pushed out the front door to second me. It was a standoff. Linese got back into his red Cadillac. I watched him pull away. And then something registered. It was a red Cadillac, but it was a different red Cadillac.

The gross on Friday was almost $15,000. You had to adjust for the increased overhead, though. For instance: every match pad, ashtray or coaster that said THE SMOKING CAR on it disappeared—mementos of the lurid. Bert even caught some momser (as he called him) chipping pieces off the bar—as if it were the Berlin Wall or something. He had planned to set the wood in Lucite and resell it as bracelets and earrings. I maintained a nice level of paranoia all night. To me it felt like a costume ball—everyone was in disguise. I knew there were at least two or three plainclothesmen. Not to mention the reporters and free-lance magazine writers. It was hard to say where the audience ended and the show began.

We weren't short on attractive dancers. Six auditioned that night—including two 18-year-old hardbodies, who had flown to The Car from *San Diego:* Elizabeth and Lenore. I hired them on the spot. Then Ugly George pushed past Bert with his video camera and silver suit and phony sound dish. He offered to shoot a regular cable TV show at The Car. He'd do us that big favor. This man has made himself into an anti-celebrity by convincing otherwise normal women—housewives and secretaries—to undress on the street or in dimly-lit hallways. Bert threw him out. George seemed to relish that. Better than being ignored, I guess. It was, as I said, a freak show.

But I felt safe there. And, by midnight, rather than run the gauntlet outside (or lead the media to Bert's apartment), I decided to camp out at The Car. One of my dancers had left a bedspread—she thought we allowed floor shows. I sent Jako out to buy milk and cereal for breakfast. I suppose part of me wanted to experience The Car alone—to challenge it. To debate with the ghosts. Connie disapproved: she thought I was being morbid. And it worried Bert. But I was adamant—and I locked the door after them.

There was really no other place to sleep—so, after praying for a long moment, I spread my sheet out on the stage. Pearl's sweater, balled up, served as a pillow. I had a long chug of Wild Turkey and curled up where three women had died. Someone kicked the front door for about five minutes, then gave up. I tried to find a comfortable position. Finally I stretched out flat on my back. With the lights off, in silence, it had a spook house touch.

A creaky spook house. I thought I heard doors open. I thought I heard a muffled footstep. I felt vulnerable—like something set out as bait. But, for fifteen minutes or so, I reasoned anxiety down. Then I *heard* a quiet metal crash, and I rolled off the stage onto my stockinged feet. I took the Wild Turkey bottle by its neck and waited.

"Shit," a voice said without much inflection.

Someone was in the women's room. I flipped a light on—then I went to the door and kicked it open. A girl sat there: she was ringing—as a gong will, when it is struck. Ringing: she was all shivers. She held a straw in her hand, and her thin body, in shorts and T-shirt, seemed to contract around that straw. Even after my brusque entry, the straw took all her attention.

"Oh," she said. "Is everyone gone?"

"Who're you?" I said.

"I, you know, I came to audition. And I stayed in here. You told me to."

"No, I didn't."

"Huh? You said—you know—t'hide in the john 'til after everyone was gone. Hide there. Then you'd audition me."

"I've never seen you before," I said.

"No? Well, okay, maybe—I'm a little high. Huh . . . But, wait, I remember that mustache."

"Where'd you see this mustache?"

"Uh—he picked me up on Queens Boulevard."

"In a car?"

"No—a *bicycle*. What else, a car."

"And you let strange men in cars pick you up?"

"I was—you know. Turning tricks."

"What kind of car was this?"

"A car. I don't follow what *kind* of cars."

"And he looked like me?"

"Yeah. Afterward, he tipped me fifty dollars t'come in here."

"What's that, heroin?"

"My last," she said. "Or I'd give you some. I really would. But I can't cop until noon tomorrow."

"You haveta go home," I told her.

"I don't have a home," she said. "My parents, you know, gave up on me."

"You can't stay here."

"I'll go down on you," she said. "I'm good at that."

"No, thank you. I have trouble enough. I'll let you out."

"Please," she said. "Let me sleep here. I got raped last night, sleeping in the park. I won't bother you."

And I thought, It's too late now, anyway. They're outside still. If they see her leaving at 5:30 a.m., it'll be in the afternoon edition. (She didn't look 18.) Maybe by the time Jako and Bert arrive, when the beer distributors get here, her exit will pass unnoticed. I'll let her dance one or two sets, then she'll leave. I was very tired.

"Come," I said. "I have a sheet out on the stage. You can sleep there."

"I'm cold," she said.

"Well, come then."

She was a coltish thing—long legs, not shapely, but firm and resilient. High, soft breasts that lumped themselves together. And a charming, sleepy smile—the smile of a person who was resigned to everything. Except a day without her drug. She pressed herself against me like plastic explosive: she fitted into every bend and crevice of my body—I was the mold and she the statue. It wasn't sexual. It was like a child sucking its thumb. A kind of female nest-making.

And I was superstitious about her. I thought, as her body laminated itself to mine, that maybe she was bringing a message from Tony. Or maybe her warmth was a gift from him. Alive, dead. But that was over-wishful. This is not such an extraordinary mustache. I see them all the time. She sighed and said, "Whatever you want," in her sleep. Around 7 a.m., Lazarus climbed on top of us.

The girl was gone when I woke up. She had taken all the loose change from our two cash registers. I never saw her again.

SATURDAY, JULY 30TH

Joe Solomon came into the kitchen at 11 a.m., while I was shaving with a travel razor Jako had bought me. I wasn't up to par. In my last year at seminary I had developed a duodenal ulcer. Now I felt that dull drill-bit just under my sternum again—screwing pain in. My stool was black. And my breath, I'm sure, stank like Beelzebub himself. Jako wasn't much better off. He talked to himself all the time now, not just half the time. And, for some reason, he would count his fingers every five minutes or so. Sometimes he missed one—and you had to point it out, otherwise he got panicky.

"Long time, no see," I said to Joe. "We're under siege here. People fight their way in and throw money at us."

"There's a line outside already."

"Anything new?"

"Well, the governor has proposed a state income tax law requiring every topless bar t'file something he calls a "gratuity estimate" for each dancer it employs. Sort of a 1099, I guess. Based on a percentage of sales—some formula. They call it The Smoking Car law."

"Fame."

"That's quite a girl you have."

"Kay? My alibi?"

"She's got the homicide crew totally off balance. They don't believe a word she's told them, and yet they say 'Yes, ma'am' whenever she opens her mouth. In fact, the reason I'm here—it's a flag of truce kinda. They'd like your help."

"What they'd like, they'd like me t'confess."

"Yes. That would be the ideal, but—"

"Fuck 'em," I said.

"Now don't be too hard on the guys. This is not your average sensational case. They're under pressure. They can see promotions passing them by."

"So?"

"They want you t'know that—if you've been shielding someone—they can be very reasonable about immunity and state's evidence. And I believe them."

"Who would I be shielding? Do they really think I'd protect someone who might kill again?"

"Suppose the someone were dead."

"Dead?"

"A man named Augustus Manning committed suicide early yesterday morning." I cut myself with the razor. "You knew him?"

"Yes. He was a priest."

"So it seems. He left a cryptic note mentioning The Car. And you."

"I knew him as a customer. Hardly more than that."

"Yet you didn't mention him t'Colavecchia or Daniels. They'd like t'know why. You should have."

"Joe, from the day I left Nebraska I haven't done one blessed thing right. Except my resignation."

"Were you protecting him?"

"Of course I was protecting him—from the humiliation I've just gone through as a priest. Not because he was a murderer."

"They think he did it, Mike."

"It can't be."

"The man was a manic-depressive apparently. He had beaten his wife on numerous occasions before they separated in 1972. He has the right profile."

"Joe, Manning was the man in the floppy hat. He used to sit by the buffet table, way in the back. Remember?"

"Him? That was Manning? Well, he was big enough. And—"

"And he was another repressed priest."

"You said it, I didn't."

"Thing you guys should realize by now—the Episcopal Church doesn't repress its priests *enough*."

"You could get that idea."

"Joe—" I turned to him. There was shaving cream on my face. I looked silly, and it caught him off guard. "I saw you with Linese a coupla nights ago."

"Oh," he said. I noted a sharp reaction, but the nature of it escaped me. Shame at being found disloyal maybe—maybe something more portentous than that.

"Yes?"

"It's nothing. I consult on security matters." Joe took out a card. It said, "THE WISDOM OF SOLOMON, Residential-Commercial Security Consultants. Ex-NYPD." And his phone number. "Linese owns a lot of buildings."

"Oh."

"Linese is a scumbag—but his buildings're legitimate."

"Forget it, Joe. Y'know what they say about paranoids."

"Sure."

"But—" I couldn't help saying it: I *was* paranoid. "If it comes t'trial—don't change your testimony, Joe. Linese would love t'see me do hard time."

"Mike—" he said.

I turned back to the sink. I didn't trust Joe. After a moment he left.

By midnight I was so sick of topless—the whole mincing, perverse charade—that I almost closed The Car down, Ethel or no. I loathed all that high-camp *teasing*. Wet tongue over lower lip. Butt cheeks half-inched apart. Dance steps that pantomimed some excerpt from the *Kama Sutra*. This, I thought, is what children do when they play grown-ups. This is, yes, childish.

And, much more than I would admit, Manning's suicide troubled me. I had been savage toward him. Out of malice. After all, only Manning in all this sordid environment had been morally inferior to me. And so I sicced myself on him—the wounded straggler. The priest who had not been scrupulous enough to resign. Inexcusable as sins of lust may be, dry sins of gratuitous cruelty are far worse. God—if I may speak for Him—can have compassion on the hot sinner. Murderous Moses. St. Paul, an accomplice in the death of St. Stephen. There is energy in such sins that can be turned to a torrid rush of blessedness. But grace could never transform what I had done to Augustus Manning. It was just cheap.

But why had he patronized The Car? Not for the sexuality of it: the man had no real sexuality in him. For two reasons, I thought. One: to participate in the routine humiliation of women. Topless has always been about that: profitable humiliation. And Manning's other reason—well, I suspect he wanted to get caught. Problem was: nobody, not even his church, cared much one way or another. Until the deaths.

Just after two a.m. I came down with a galactic case of the runs and befouled my own underwear.

"Bert," I said. "I've had a little accident. I think I'll go back t'your place for a while and take a shower."

"No problem," said Bert. "Happens t'me all the time."

I tried not to speculate on that. I asked Lars-Erik to bring his Plymouth around—I'd dive from The Car into Lars-Erik's before the media could react. And then take a cab back.

The crowd was absolutely pulsing. Sure, the music supplied certain erotic rhythms—but this was different. A Brazilian girl of torrential beauty, Dolores, was dancing with Cleopatra and Shane. Dolores had taken an ice cube and, with it, had given her body a sheen. The disco lights reflected from her. Her breasts were gala-round, high, so buoyant—the glare lent them exquisite definition. And she was dancing at just the right speed. Many women dance fast, so that their nakedness will be blurred: it is the smallest modesty. Other women dance too slowly—the eye, bored, slips away. But Dolores moved to the exact beat of an orgasm—and, along with that, she had grace and imagination. I saw men with their mouths open: as if, like cats, they had a Jacobson's gland—that smeller of sexual traits—just behind their upper lips. They were *inhaling* Dolores. And she, in response to their response, in a sea of dollar bills, had performed mass hypnosis. She had entranced the room. No man there would go home innocent of her.

And I knew she was only 18. 18 and a virgin: shy. It frightened me, her power. I ran for the front door.

But I stopped dead in front of Bert's apartment. Something wasn't kosher: the Klingon had begun firing his phaser. I could see a flashing light along the threshold crack. The Klingon was wired to Bert's door. He began firing when it opened, and you could only turn the damn machinery off by pressing a button behind his left knee. Someone was in Bert's apartment.

I should've gone away then—called 911. Six days a week I'm not a particularly brave or reckless man. But the intruder, whoever he might happen to be, had caught me at the wrong moment. I was, shall we say, *hyper*. I had been ducking confrontations for half a month. I was weary and afraid, and I was in the mood to make someone pay for it. More than all that, probably, I needed to take a shower.

Carefully, quarter inch by quarter inch, I inserted my key. Then I hurled the door open. There, by the on-off lighting of phaser blasts, I saw Leonard. A disgruntled Leonard. He was bent forward, back to me, shoveling through a pile of Trek-abilia. He was dredging the room for something. Leonard didn't even turn around when he heard the door hinges crack. He just said,

"This place is a dump. We'll never find it in here." The "we" should've alerted me. "T'hell with it—I'm gonna put a decent light on." He turned then and saw me.

"Leonard, you fuck," I said.

"You?" He stood up: all six foot five inches of him.

"What're you doing here?"

"I'm working for the census bureau. Hey, you gonna call the cops?

I don't think you wanna see fuzz any more'n I do. So long, schmuck."

And, with indignation, as if angry that I had interrupted him, Leonard went for the open door.

But I closed it. Leonard stared at me—on-off, on-off went the phaser light. And then he pursed his lips and blew on me—like maybe I was thistledown, inconsequential. And he grabbed the doorknob.

I had never hit a man with all my strength—let alone in the face. I think most males fantasize about that sort of blow. The side of Leonard's face was exposed to me, bent just a bit forward as he leaned for the doorknob. I let go a right-hand punch that had everything behind it: leverage, 180 pounds, the full torque of my body and a lot of self-disgust.

Leonard's left eyebrow split open and he fell forward on both knees. My hand screamed. I stood back as Leonard, more from reflex than intention, tottered up. He came at me arms out—for Leonard, contact with his prey was essential. Blood ran down into his mouth.

"That's the end of you, priest-fuck," he said.

"Did you kill them, Leonard?" I said.

"That's the end of you."

He bulled toward me—but, instead of fear, I felt a mean sort of clarity. I wanted there to be blood *all over* his face. I wanted it—and I didn't care if Leonard killed me in the transaction. My body was electric. I jabbed him three times: nose, nose, nose. On my third jab the bridge snapped and Leonard began to howl,

"I'll KILL you!"

But one eye was puffed shut, and the pain was starting to uncoordinate him. By then, also, Leonard knew that he had engaged another sort of being. I was a mongoose, a ferret: I hope never again to encounter that vicious me again. It is enough, once, to have known true animal exhilaration—when all the restraints of sense and a civil nature are gone. I could've killed Leonard in that flashing room.

One. One. One. I jabbed him, and his head whip-lashed back. Leonard covered his face with both arms and shuffled ahead, hoping to pin me against something. But I stepped aside, and he staggered knee-deep through Bert's mania. Leonard fell. For a moment I thought he might give up—and it disappointed me—so I stood back, took his measure, and kicked Leonard as hard as I could in the ribs.

It was a shitty thing to do. And it was almost fatal: Leonard got part of my leg, but I twisted free. He stumbled to his feet—he was swaying, he seemed a dancer. And then pain from my kick came through the switchboard of his nervous system. He roared and went silent—breathless. Diaphragm frozen. And I hit him full in the mouth with my right.

At just arm's length. I snapped off the punch, I gave it twisting English, I was analytical about it. And bridgework—bridgework that I didn't know Leonard had—came out like a fighter's mouthpiece.

"No more," he said.

But I hit him—on the ear, in the throat, behind the neck—until he fell. My teeth were chattering. I was up on my toes. I wanted to hurt him more.

"Enough. Please," he said. He lay crouched, his lacerated face was falling apart in his hands.

"What were you looking for, Leonard?"

"Berry's bag. My coke. She stole it from me."

"Did you kill her?"

"Nohhhhhh. Nohhhhh," he said.

"Who killed her? And Rita and Tanya and Bubbles?"

"I dunno—uh. Uh."

And a light went on.

The Gaucho was standing just inside Bert's door. He had a gun in his hand. It frisked me. The barrel snout went from my groin, across my stomach and heart, to my skull.

"Hey, Mike. What's this bad behavior, huh? You kicked shit outa my man here."

"Put the gun down and I'll kick shit out of you, too."

"We never got off on the right foot. I give you money. I promise you help. I'm a gentleman ten times over. And still you got this big boner for me. What's the problem, amigo? I do my thing, you do your thing. Why can't you show respect?"

"Show respect? Like blowing my car to bits while I was in it?"

"That, for me—believe what I say—for me that was a practical joke. You should laugh at a practical joke."

"I don't laugh."

"Mike, listen. This is big business I'm in. I got people on the payroll, I got mouths t'feed. Get up, Leonard, you big faggot." Leonard started to rise. His face was huge, fat and red—except where the bridgework had been. That part of his face had collapsed. "We're gonna go now. Gotta get my man here fixed up."

"You had them killed, didn't you?"

"Mike, man, I'm not like that. You got me wrong. I don't kill women and I don't kill priests. Lucky for you. Even the cops don't think I did it."

"It had t'be you. Who else? For God's sake, who else?"

"What about you, Mike? Look what you did here. Look what you did t'Leonard. You're a very angry man. You'd kill your own mother, I think."

SUNDAY, JULY 31ST

And how, you might ask, was my spiritual life in those days? Furtive is a good word. Deceitful is even better. My prayers—I continued to pray almost out of spite—were rather petulant in fact. Part of me was punishing God. Part of me was frightened almost to inertia. You understand that a priestly vocation brings with it habits, good and bad, that are comfortable. I had lost those bearings. I missed, most of all, the repressive standards, the Thou-shalt-nots. A vista of freedom—the kind that any Christian layman knows—opened in front of me. It was nauseating. Too damn *possible*. I developed a spiritual agoraphobia. I think that's why I came to make my home, perversely, in The Car. I didn't join the devil. I claimed sanctuary with him, so to speak.

Most of the time, mind you, certainly from Berry's murder forward, I expected to die momentarily. My bones felt fragile. My stomach ate itself. I knew, of course, that I wasn't *that* bad—I wasn't Dr. Mengele or Stalin, whoever. But my sinfulness was dramatic enough: it seemed to be pointing out, emphasizing, some natural law. My lost vocation and my troubled sexuality and the murders and The Car seemed all one continuous phenomenon. And, to some degree, in retrospect, you could say they were.

I suppose—I had long supposed—that my sexuality and my spirituality were conjoined. That I prayed from the groin, so to speak. This is true, in a fashion, of all people. Biological life-energy foments even the so-called higher self. But, with me, that paradox was accelerated. After all, I had been driven to the priesthood, rightly or wrongly, by an act of sexual excess. But sublimation is a tricky business. And lust, like water in a leaky basement, will find its way through, never mind how well patched the surface may be. There were transformations taking place. No matter how decent my intentions might once have been, the mixture of holy and profane had become volatile. It excited all the molecules around me.

I was subject to unsavory dreams. Most often, in some guise, I found myself confronted by the Saviour's nakedness—the sensuality one resists in some of the lusher old paintings of the Crucifixion. Jesus The Man: before Whom, most often, we avert our eyes. These were intertwined with dream memories of my own father's nakedness—I had seen him stripped once and the child-me was fascinated by his genital size. Most of all, I guess, I wanted to denude myself—of the lies and justifications and the endless, repetitive layers of motive and counter-motive. I wanted to be, well, made bare. Instead, I dreamed that the Virgin Mary was on stage auditioning for me. It was too horrid. I awoke. And awoke. And awoke.

Plunk was celebrating on July 31st at a church in Rego Park—I had ascertained that much even before Joe told me about Manning's suicide. By then, I presume, deprived of any Christian environment, I was trying to endow Plunk with the authority and personhood of THE CHURCH. It was an honor, I'm sure, that he would far rather have been spared. But I had no confessor. And I wanted my perilous spiritual condition to be lifted from the abstract and made real. I wanted it on the record, one might say.

Plunk, I must admit, wasn't pleased to see me at the altar rail. He recoiled—I had jarred him out of a mellow meditational haze and that's always annoying. Plunk probably saw or smelled my confusion at once. He didn't want to mess with it on a hot Sunday morning. But afterward, out of professional civility or something, he gave me an audience.

"Get in my car. You've got ten minutes. You're not gonna screw up my golf game, too."

Plunk had a BMW, and he was an appalling driver. Worse, he had Grand Prix pretensions. He triple-shifted, got himself in the wrong gears with great flair, and even went through a red light. In retrospect, I suppose, he might've been apprehensive about what I was going to lay on him. I said,

"I apologize for the trouble I've caused you. I lied. I used the pulpit you so kindly afforded me t'work out my own personal drama. I embarrassed—"

"Oh, shut up," Plunk said. "First of all you—you could never embarrass me. Nor am I even surprised. A priest in a topless bar—you're nothing more than the absurd but logical result of my church's outreach to permissiveness and extremism. In fact, I've been expecting someone like you for some time." He downshifted. "What will you do now?"

"Do?"

"Will you continue working in the fleshpots?"

"Yes. For a while. My thinking is—I hope it isn't just a rationalization—I think the thing hasta be finished. I have t'get to the end of it."

"Maybe."

"It's been hell. I'm not enjoying myself. But I'm hoping t'find a meaning somewhere. Perhaps when the murderer is caught—"

"You aren't that murderer, I take it."

"No. Except as we all are."

"What happened to your knuckles?"

"I beat someone up last night."

"Oh. The seminaries really turn them out these days." He accelerated to 50 mph in a school zone.

"I wanted t'talk about Augustus Manning."

"Don't," he said. "You know nothing about Gus on the one hand. On the other you know more than I care t'hear. I can do this much for you at least—I can absolve you of all blame in that matter. Gus was looking t'find an occasion for death. A moment. You needn't flatter yourself. You were the setting, not the cause."

"Good. I'm glad of that."

"I understand that Gus approached you. I understand that he felt your case was a political opportunity. That you still had a place in the clergy here. I don't share that view—I want you t'know that. I think we're all lucky t'be well shet of you, as my West Virginia relatives would say."

"Thanks. I didn't wanna be St. Joan fighting for Episcopal nudity."

"We are a troubled church." He sighed. "I think—I hope—you're under the Diocese of Omaha still. Let Bishop Watts cope with it. That'll ruin his lunch."

"Okay."

"Look—I have no measure of your sincerity—"

"I'm not fully repentant yet, if that's what you mean. I'm feeling sorry for myself—"

"Yes, well. What I mean t'say is—I mean t'say that it's possible, not likely but possible, that you will be a better man for this. A better Christian. But it will take enormous alertness on your part. You must never drop your guard again. You've pushed it to the edge. God can and will forgive anything—but there comes a time when the soul itself closes off. Keep open. Keep open, that is, unless you're an utter con man and wasting my afternoon."

"I'm shaky. I don't know how much strength I have. My faith is in jeopardy. I can feel it."

"Take notes," he said. "Just in case the Lord, Whose wisdom is beyond me, provides some useful occupation for you."

"I'm writing it out."

"Well, what else can I do for you?"

"I—" I thought for a moment. "Would it be presumptuous if I asked for your blessing?"

"It certainly would be. In a year maybe. Come by in a year."

"I will."

"I'm gonna have a wicked slice off the tee all day, I know it. I'll forget t'keep my head down."

"I'm sorry," I said.

"I'm responsible for my own golf swing, thank you. Don't take too many burdens on yourself."

"Pray for me," I said.

"That's what I do for a living," Plunk said. "And a lot of thanks I get."

We continued to pull them in—even on a Sunday night. Average-looking dancers were taking down $350 a gig. Connie pleaded with me for just one set—she was working behind the bar—and made $125 in a half hour. We had installed a red velvet rope outside: and there were lines from 7 p.m. to at least 2 or 3 a.m. I couldn't keep my shelves stocked. For the first time in Smoking Car history—as a favor to Norm, who had invited three movie producers over—we had to reserve a table.

I had borrowed a king-size sleeping bag from Bert. My apartment was still being staked out. And, after my experience with Leonard and the Gaucho, I knew that Bert's address was in the public domain as well. I felt badly about that (Leonard had bled on some valuable first-edition Trek fanzines). And, anyhow, I belonged at The Car. I was waiting the demon out.

Weintraub came by, poked a finger at my sternum, told me to "shad-dap" and left. Carol Carter of ABC News gave me a copy of her book, *Witness to New York*: "For Mike, with love. I hope we work together some day." Lars-Erik did an oil portrait of me: it sold for $600. Around midnight Colavecchia and Daniels stopped off.

"Went t'see Leonard," said Daniels. He looked at my fists. "Leonard tells us you're the one who turned him into street pizza. What a mess. Leonard says you're definitely a homicidal type."

"He was trespassing."

"Aren't you supposta forgive trespassers?"

"I sinned, I'm sorry. When're you guys gonna produce the murderer?"

"When you confess."

"Confession isn't required in the Episcopal church."

"Mike," said Colavecchia. "you can tell Weintraub—we'll probably arrest you Wednesday or Thursday. We've broken your girlfriend's flimsy alibi. We've got someone who says Kay Lyons was someplace else. We might arrest Ms. Lyons, too—if you make things difficult."

"Do your worst," I said. I felt they were bluffing, but I was uneasy, nonetheless. Kay was vulnerable: guilty, in fact. She had committed perjury. These men, I knew, didn't have much sense of humor left.

"Your other girlfriend—Ottomanelli, remember her? The Gaucho says, for a line of coke she used t'let him fuck her up the ass. For a priest you have nice friends."

"Mike," said Colavecchia, "you do drugs?"

"No," I said.

"Maybe you better start."

At 4:30 a.m., I let Bert and Connie out. Then I checked the kitchen, each men's room stall and the damned women's room. Empty. I spread Bert's sleeping bag on the stage. Then I went behind the bar and made myself a stiff Tom Collins. I was so tired I had pins and needles in my feet. Probably I was forgetting to breathe. I sat for about ten minutes on a bar stool, letting the alcohol take effect.

Someone began knocking on the front door.

I ignored it: we were often subjected to harassment of one kind or another.

Then a female voice called out. It was Kay.

"Good morning," she said when I let her in. "I brought you some sustenance." Kay had bagels and cream cheese and, though it was moonlit outside, she wore a light plastic raincoat. I brought her some white wine. We sat together at a table near the stage. Kay seemed, not nervous, but *nerved*—small talk and superfluous gestures. I guessed that the past week had gotten to her. It had gotten to me.

"Kay," I said, after a moment, "Colavecchia and Daniels were in tonight. They're gonna maybe arrest me sometime this week."

"They can't—"

"Wait. That's the *good* news. They said—I don't believe them—but they said *you* might be arrested, too. Apparently they've got a witness. Someone who says you weren't at my apartment the night Berry died."

"Who?" Kay asked: panic tightened her pupils.

"I don't know."

"One of the kids? But they're too young."

"Kay—I'm sick about this. I do so regret getting you involved in it." But she was distant: thoughtful. "Are you all right?"

"Well," she said after a moment. "If they're gonna arrest me, there's no time t'waste. Is there?"

"How d'you mean?"

"Oh," said Kay with a coy hand-flip. "It's time I gave you a present."

Kay got up and, as if in a trance, walked over to the jukebox. She had heels on: that surprised me. I noticed it because her gait seemed self-conscious. She was sending different call letters out. Then Kay pressed several buttons on the machine and turned to me.

"Make the disco lights go on," she said.

"I just turned them off," I said. "I'm tired of loud music and glare."

"Make the lights go on," she said.

I went behind the bar and flicked the main switch. Tina Turner was singing—she wanted to be my private dancer. It's a song that can make drunken topless girls cry. Then I looked up.

Kay was on stage. She waited for a certain musical rhythm, as a surfer might wait for a wave. Her head was down: her hands were buried in her long blond hair. She had taken off the raincoat—she wore a T-shirt and a black Apache dancer's skirt. Her skin was very white. I wanted to stop her. It wasn't necessary, it was the thing I needed least just then. Or so I thought. But you do not reject such gifts of love.

Kay.

She didn't move badly. But she wasn't *there* yet. She was dancing inside herself. Her eyes did not engage mine. Yet she, we both understood it, Kay was auditioning for me. And part of me, the auctioneer, judged her as flesh. Kay's legs were wonderful, a bit heavy in the thigh, where heaviness is prized, and very long. There was a lovely definition line from sternum to navel. And, as she lifted the T-shirt off, I saw the upthrust of her breasts.

You must understand, to appreciate her courage, that we did not really know each other naked. Our love-making, such as it was, had been done in dark or narrow places. I had never seen her upright and nude. I didn't know the special slung sweetness of her breasts: the perfect U's they made. She had an outrageous red silk burlesque bra on. Her nipples—so pink they were white—crushed themselves like children's noses against a store window. I wanted her.

But still, even after the Apache skirt dropped, she hadn't acknowledged me, her audience. Kay wasn't ready to get *that* naked yet. She wore a high-cut black G-string, with gold lettering on it. And there was a birthmark—in the shape of an hourglass—above her left buttock. I stepped forward. I was at the foot of the stage. Kay danced, as if trying to drive her inner self out. But she was still hidden—in the flailing hair, in the down-lidded eyes. In a modesty that foiled exposure.

Then her hands went to the bra-snap: it is, in any woman, a beautiful moment. Hands up and behind: as bound captives are led away. Hands up and behind: doing a little, girlish, intimate mechanical act. And the bra came away. For a second, bashful, her breasts nestled behind her arm. Then, with a gasp, Kay let them fall. They were very large: they were *important*. But they were still a child's breasts: innocent and surprised to be so full.

And Kay danced for me.

I had to help her now. The music would end soon, and in the bareness of silence, she would be just a small public spectacle. So I did what men do. I took out a $100 bill and touched her thigh with it.

The contact startled her. Kay was pulled from the cloister of her self-absorption. She looked down at me. She smiled. Perhaps she had expected something like this. Kay bent to accept the bill. She made a kissing face, the sort, no doubt, that she had seen other girls make. But Kay miscalculated. In looking at me she also caught herself in the mirror. And she was not prepared to accept that—the bald, gawked-at evidence of her shame. Kay's knees gave. She collapsed sidewards, awkwardly, on one thigh—as the woman in *Christina's World* sits, twisted, away.

"I'm so embarrassed," she said. "I'm so embarrassed."

I intended only to comfort her. To praise her bravery and tell about her loveliness. I leaped up on the stage. But, when once my hands had felt her overheated skin, had slid beneath her breasts, a firestorm swept us. We broke through. We came together like magnetic poles attracted. We were matter and antimatter. We were its synthesis.

I mean, we made ferocious love in silence under the hectic disco lights.

For maybe an hour we lay on the stage—half in, half out of Bert's sleeping bag. Kay was experiencing herself in another mode: I let her alone to do that. She touched my body with curiosity and a fresh sort of proprietorship. I enjoyed the fondling. My arm went back, lazy, unsupervised. My hand touched her G-string. I held it up between us—it was inside-out, registering the suddenness of my assault on her body.

"Pretty sexy," I said.

"I was terrified."

"Where'd you buy the equipment?"

"I didn't. The girls were playing with it in the garage. There's a whole drawer full of dancer stuff in an old bureau. That's how I got the idea. I mean, can you imagine me, Kay, shopping for G-strings in a store?"

"The kids were playing with it?"

"Well, it was a little big for them. For me, too. I had t'make some tucks in the G-string." Kay took it from my hand. She turned the G-string right-side-out. My breath came fast, then didn't come at all. I sat up.

There were words in gold lettering on the G-string. BOSS LADY, they said.

MONDAY, AUGUST 1ST

I put off writing about this day for more than a week. Then I sat at my desk, Scripto pencil in hand, and sketched complex geometrical designs. My mind would not engage the subject. I was blocked. Margie Strang, my therapist, says that isn't unusual. I've experienced a traumatic shock—psychic and physical: it's hardly a revelation that the mind has cunning defenses. In a certain part of my brain the power went off—it would not allow the software of remembrance to be processed.

What you will read here was not written by me. I am not that rational and detached. This section of my story was transcribed (and edited in places) by Margie Strang from tapes I made while under hypnosis. The original dictation is both disjointed and repetitious. Marge has given it structure (also, I hope, some of the original dramatic intensity). I know what happened, of course, in general terms: I wasn't driven mad or autistic by that terrible Monday. But I am shaky still—and not willing to jeopardize the frail equilibrium.

That is: I have not read what you are about to read now.

It was a long day.

You must realize that I didn't, properly speaking, suspect anything then—on that Monday morning after Kay left The Car—but my subconscious mind must've been knitting and unraveling all night. My subconscious mind was way ahead of me. I suppose it already knew about Tony. Certainly I woke with feelings both of loss and fright. Or, perhaps, I never truly woke. Because that long day had a fantastic quality to it. And, Lord knows, the peculiar sense of trappedness—touched by dread and fatalism—that our nightmares enforce.

Yet, probably, I would never have guessed the truth if it hadn't been for the cat.

. . .

I called Ethel from The Car every half hour until about noon. And each time I got little Wendy, who said, "My doll has AIDS," and hung up. At noon my mood changed. I wasn't sure, after all, that I wanted to interrogate Ethel. Yet. Ethel demagnetized my compass: I wasn't confident of my judgment around her. And maybe I felt it was a mistake to put Ethel on her guard. Instead, I decided to approach Pearl—albeit circumspectly. But Pearl had a dental appointment and didn't get to The Car until way past three. As things turned out that appointment almost cost me my life.

Her face was swollen. Pearl looked like someone chewing tobacco. Also her lower lip had gone blubbery from Novocaine. The Car was packed. In Pearl's absence most of the bartending had fallen to me. (Bert breaks things: he doesn't *see* glass well.) I was pressured even with Raven and one Silicone Sister covering our table customers. Pearl saw my agitation, interpreted it as annoyance with her, and avoided me. But then Pearl had been avoiding me for a week. When Connie came in—to dance the 5 to midnight—I put her behind the bar. Then I went over to Pearl. I said:

"I'd like t'have a word with you."

"I'm busy," she said.

"Connie will handle business for a while—come into the kitchen."

"With you? Oh, no—you got somethin' t'say, you say it here in front of witnesses."

"Pearl," I said, irked. "D'you think I'm the killer, for God's sake?"

"I think what I think," she said.

"Jesus, of all people, you know why I came here. Why I've stayed here."

"Why?"

"To help Ethel and the kids out financially, of course."

"Oh, Daddy Warbucks, thanks so much. You think I believe that? Ethel is loaded and you know she's loaded. You're not so dumb as all that."

"I'll leave tomorrow. If you think Ethel doesn't need me, please tell me so. Because I'll be outa here before you can say 'fuck this.' And what d'you mean, she's loaded?"

"Ka-mon, ka-mon, ka-mon." Pearl lit a cigarette. "Shit and shinola, where d'you think Tony got the cash t'buy this place? You're his brother f'Chrissake. You weren't exactly, you know, descended from great wealth, the two of you. Right?"

"So where did he get the money?"

"She didn't tell you?"

"No, she didn't."

"Then maybe, I don't know . . . maybe I should keep my trap shut."

"Pearl. Please. If you know something that might help me—t'make a decision, t'protect myself—then say so. I'm sick of being in the dark. I'm sick of surprises."

"I can't believe you don't know. Ethel talks about it all the time. She's proud of it."

"Something illegal?"

"No. No. No. Not illegal."

"Then where did my brother get his money?"

"From Ethel. Her father owned two big liquor stores. I think he sold for a million five. And you can bet—with the house, with the place in Pennsylvania, with whatever else she does—you can bet she's worth twice that now."

"But there are debts—"

"That's what she says. All I know is, Tony and her, they were gonna expand this place next year. They were gonna shut down for three months, put new lighting in, two stages—the whole shooting match. If she's gonna shut down for three months, why's Ethel need you so desperately? For your looks?"

I stared at Pearl. Under those circumstances, if she were right, my devotion to The Car did seem perverse. But there was one more question I had to ask her. Even though, by then, I could guess the answer.

"Was Ethel ever a topless dancer?"

"Is the fuckin' Pope Catholic? Of course she was. That's how she met your brother. He was the night manager at Pemberton's out on the Island. You didn't know that?"

"I didn't." I picked up my jacket. "But there's something I do know—on the best authority."

"What?"

"I know there's always something wrong with a topless dancer."

I hit the door like a fullback breaking into the secondary. I intended to have it out with Ethel that afternoon, then. But I was unused to heat and light, and the sun blinded me for a moment. I swayed. A reporter from the Jackson Heights *Free Press* came up to me with a small tape machine. I brushed him aside, turned right, saw Lazarus asleep in the dry-cleaning store window, smiled at that, walked to the corner planning my showdown with Ethel—

And almost collapsed.

I held to a parking meter. I was faint. The *Free Press* man rushed up to me—my moment of vertigo had shocked everyone on the sidewalk—but I shook him off. I stood upright. I read the sky. At that moment I knew what had happened to Tanya and the others. Not in detail, but in principle. I knew and I was aghast. Because, just in the dimmest way, I understood the vicious, twisted force that had snapped Tanya's neck. There was only one thing left to do.

I ran at Lazarus.

He was asleep, as I said, in the dry-cleaning store window. I yelled. Lazarus woke. Then, while both my palms slammed the plate glass, I began to leap and kick. I went berserk. The *Free Press* man backed away. And Lazarus, ears down, slouched low, began running. He ran to the rear of that long, dusty room. He ran under the roller-coasterish, rusted, huge mechanical clothing rack that dominated it. Lazarus disappeared.

I waited a moment. People had begun to gather: they weren't sure what attention I required. I stood back from the plate glass. I stuck my sore hands under my armpits. Then I started walking back to The Car. I knew, pretty much, what I would find there.

The basement trap door was up. And Lazarus, all indignation and loose fur, was sitting on the bar.

I could hardly manage the Lincoln. Each time another tumbler clicked into place—which was every other block or so—I tended to hit the brake. I was saying, Stop! to myself, I guess. Don't go any further—there are mysteries that should remain sealed. The Lincoln jerked to a half-halt, then accelerated, then halted, all the way to Ethel's.

Some facts I was certain of. Other facts were based on hypothesis, but had a grim plausibility to them. I was sure, for one, that Lazarus could travel from Big Marty's Dry Cleaning to The Car—through the party wall in the basement. If *he* could, perhaps a man—or yes, a woman—could also. Much of that wall was covered by our beer cooler. But I didn't investigate—the police, after all, had scoured The Car on at least three occasions. They had found nothing. The connecting passage was well disguised.

I knew, further, that there was a back door to Big Marty's. It opened onto a side street (60th) off Northern Boulevard. Having snapped Tanya's neck, the killer could've retreated through our basement, crossed over, gone up through Big Marty's, and then exited out onto 60th—while Joe and I were waiting for Tanya to appear. And Tanya didn't scream, *because she recognized her killer*. Because that killer's appearance in The Car, even after hours, was unremarkable.

Everyone suspected me. Pearl, Joe, even Kay at moments. Everyone, that is, except Ethel—she had dismissed the question of my guilt out of hand. I had been grateful to her: Ethel's loyalty, in large part, had convinced me to overlook some of her more shameless manipulations. But what if Ethel *knew* I was innocent? What if, worse, her loyalty were a front? After all, Pearl suspected me, and Ethel had done nothing to dissuade her. And the thought hit me: suppose Ethel is protecting some-one else. Suppose she's trying to frame me.

So—by the time I reached Ethel's—I had thoroughly demoralized myself. Such subtle maneuvering (and the suavity to put it over) is symptomatic of a disturbed, yet powerful, mind. Maybe, I thought, this is not the time to confront Ethel. She was cleverer than I. She might turn against me. For one, she could probably break Kay's alibi. Good God, perhaps it was *Ethel* who had contacted Colavecchia and Daniels.

Whatever else, I certainly couldn't challenge Ethel in front of Kay and the kids—that would've been both cruel and dangerous. The fact was: I didn't have evidence enough to accuse her at all. I planned to take Ethel for a ride—on the pretext of discussing Weintraub and my possi-ble arrest. I would study her reaction when I brought up the police and Kay's alibi. I would draw Ethel out.

But Ethel wasn't at home.

Wendy, naked again, answered the door. She had her terminally ill doll under one arm.

"Hi, Daddy," she said.

"Where's your mother?"

"Oh, she went t'the country," Wendy said.

There was a baby-sitter: a girl of about fifteen with glasses and skin like peeled rubber cement, who lived down the block. Yes, she told me, Mrs. Wilson had gone to her country house for a day or so. No, there wasn't a telephone. Yes, she knew the address. But, now that I men-tioned it, gosh, she couldn't find the piece of paper Ethel had written it down on. My nieces were unhelpful—Amy said the summer place was in California. Wendy thought maybe Virginia sounded good. I called Pearl at The Car.

"Ethel has gone t'the country house," I said. "I haveta speak with her about my case. D'you know where the house is?"

"If Ethel needs a break, maybe you should leave her alone."

"Please, Pearl. Let me be the judge of that. Do you have the address?"

"Of course. I've been there several times. But you could never find it. It's way out in the boonies—past New Milford. Why'n'cha let it go 'til she gets back?"

"Because I can't let it go. My fuckin' life is at stake. Give me the address. I'll be responsible."

I waited while Pearl found her purse. I sketched an enormous dragon of geometry in the time it took. Pearl brought her address book back. She began thumbing slowly through it. I could've shrieked.

"Hope I don't get in trouble for this," she said.

"You won't, you won't. I take full responsibility."

"16 East Copper Lake Drive. It's a dirt road. I think there's a mailbox with Wilson on it. It's in Cahoga, Pennsylvania. C-A-H-O-G-A," she said over the music blare. "You'll haveta ask instructions."

"I will. Tell Bert t'run things. Tell him I'll meet him at The Car late tonight—to pick up the take."

"Is that all?"

"Yes. No. You just told me Tony and Ethel were gonna expand The Car. How?"

"Inta the old dry-cleaning store, of course. Where else? Through the roof?"

"Who owns the dry-cleaning store?"

"Ethel. She bought it last year. I told you, she's loaded."

I functioned, after that, like someone obeying vague post-hypnotic suggestions. I bought gas. I bought a Rand McNally road map (it showed Cahoga near the northwest corner of a state forest preserve). I got on the Deegan, then I headed west, across the George Washington Bridge, toward Route 80 and the Delaware Water Gap. But it was rush hour, a tractor trailer had stalled atop the Alexander Hamilton ramp, and it took me 75 minutes just to reach the G.W. By that time I could barely sit—I rose up/over the steering wheel like some jock bringing a loser home. I was frantic.

But at least I didn't have to worry about Kay. She had gone shopping in Manhattan, the baby-sitter said.

Music seemed absurd under the circumstances. Talk shows were inane. Anyhow—there is nothing more conducive to morbid thought than a car ride—I pestered my reasoning, I came to intemperate conclusions. I thought these were excessive, the result of a heated sensibility, but they were not excessive. They were, if anything, underdrawn.

For a while I pretended the trip might turn out to be a positive development. I'd be alone with Ethel in an isolated setting. I wouldn't have to consider Kay and the children. And, given Pearl's insights, I could demand an audit of all accounts. I now knew that Ethel had had access to Big Marty's. Colavecchia and Daniels were unaware of that. It was obstruction of justice on her part. We all had cause enough to be angry with Ethel. But, no, I wasn't yet ready to accuse her of murder. My mind could not sustain that premise. She was a nursing mother, for God's sake.

Still, as Route 80 was pulled beneath me, I recognized that Ethel had had not only access but opportunity as well. She was at The Car on the night Bubbles died. She had inspected the women's locker room. Ethel could easily have placed strychnine where Bubbles—an inveterate pill eater—might have found it. Or laced her drink. And as for Berry—Berry told Mr. and Mrs. Ottomanelli that her boss had called at 4:30 a.m. Ostensibly she meant me. But Ethel was Berry's ultimate employer. If Ethel had called . . . well, if she had exercised her authority or adduced some persuasive reason, Berry would certainly have come down to The Car. In fact, I realized, only Ethel (or I) could've drawn Berry from bed at that hour. And I hadn't called Berry.

These were mere exercises in abstract logic, provocative as they may have been. It was in the area of motive that a blackness—it was almost a fainting spell—hooded me. We were talking about the three women with whom I had been most associated—at least in Pearl's mind. And Pearl was Ethel's eye at The Car. As the miles clicked off, I came to understand (just in a prefigurative way) that Bubbles and Tanya and Berry had been killed because of me. I had been blaming myself all along—the-Priest-whose-sins-are-visited-on-everyone—but that blame had been a kind of self-indulgent melodrama. Now I thought—My God, I did. It's coming true. I am the motive behind those deaths.

For just then, while crossing the Delaware, I fingered my mustache. And, dully, knew. I was Tony for Ethel. I was Tony for her children. I remembered how Ethel, standing at poolside, had flashed her private parts. There was a hideous sexuality at play—Tony, in my person, had been unfaithful to Ethel with Bubbles and Tanya and, oh, poor, decapitated Berry. Berry, who had presumed to wear a G-string that said BOSS LADY in the boss lady's bar.

I am my brother's keeper, I thought. I've kept Tony alive. But only in Ethel's mind. For, by that time, if not long before, I had conceded the fact: my brother was dead.

. . .

Predictably, as darkness came down, I got lost over and over again. My concentration was permeable, frail. Part of me, I guess, hoped never to reach a destination. I was somewhat familiar with Route 209 north of Stroudsburg. As a teenager, I had gone white-water rafting on the Delaware several times. It's a lamentable highway. The speed-limit varies and, because it is often both curved and populous, good time cannot be made. In my impatience, I decided to drive the hypotenuse of a highway right triangle. I turned off 209, onto Route 739, heading to Lord's Valley and Route 84. It was a miscalculation.

Deer threw themselves at me. I killed, I think, a possum. The pavement was narrow and banked for self-destruction. Then I caught up to a lazy, obstreperous thunderstorm. Rain turned my windshield to melting glycerin. Hail fell. It's a sign, I said aloud. A sign to slow down. And, finally, I had to pull over. I put my seat belt on then: I had been driving without it. A challenge to all the forces aimed my way.

Cahoga wasn't, strictly speaking, a place. It was more idea than location—a general theory that included whole square miles of isolated barn and lakeside cabin. There was a sign that said WELCOME TO CAHOGA on *both* sides. As though Cahoga existed only in the thickness of the sign's metal. But Cahoga was everywhere, too: Cahoga Lake and East Cahoga Road and Cahoga Real Estate and Cahoga Plumbing Supply—but no Cahoga people. House lights shone—high on hills, behind barking dogs. At last, by pure chance, I hit West Copper Lake Drive. And rode for 20 minutes in the wrong direction on it.

By that time, I now realize, I had half circled Copper Lake. I didn't know it, but West Copper Lake Drive was about to become East Copper Lake Drive very near Ethel's house. Instead, uncertain and impulsive, I made a tight U-turn, then headed *back* the way I had come. As a result I circumscribed the lake, just about. And when West Copper became East, it was at number 348. I still had almost ten miles to cover.

And, of course, I passed right by 16 East. The mailbox had an I and an L and parts of an S and an N painted on it. Not much else. There was no number at all. So, when I came to 14 East, I had to make yet another U-turn on Copper Lake Drive. Ethel's house was at the end of a long, pot-holed dirt lane. There were no lights on. I had missed her: if, in fact, she had been there that day at all.

My hips were locked in the sharp residue of tension. I could scarcely stand upright. The night was soft, moist: it smelled of the earth they keep baitworms in. I could hear a laryngitic frog—presumably Copper Lake lay just behind Ethel's place. I felt foolish: her absence seemed to refute my case. There was—at the far corner of the headlight beam—a swing set, a red slide and a sandbox. These homely items had a stabilizing effect on me. I thought that I'd been wrong: and I was glad of it.

Still, I went up to the house. It was a glorified A-frame, done in ersatz Swiss Chalet. A wide redwood sun deck circled the place—one corner held an unfilled jacuzzi. Ethel fed birds, I saw: that by itself seemed to exonerate her. There was a rocking horse on the deck. And a hammock on a metal frame: Tony had read *Sports Illustrated* in it, I was sure. I knocked on the glass front door. It didn't concern the frog: he continued to quack. I wiped my face. Then I walked back to my car.

Reluctant to start driving back at once, I sat on the ticking, warm car hood. It was breezy: pine branches shushed me. The headlights picked out a half cord of wood. Split logs lay on either side of a big stump. And I saw, then, on my mind's screen, Tony chopping. Ethel chopping. With, yes, an axe. Hairs on the back of my neck rose. I slid off the hood. There, to my right, lay a balled-up piece of pink Kleenex tissue. I bent down. It was dry. The driveway held puddles, grass had wet my sneakers. But the Kleenex was dry. Someone had been there since the thunderstorm. I had just missed Ethel.

I picked up a stone. Without announcing an intention to myself, I walked quickly back to the sun deck and up its short staircase. Yes, I had a sense of foreboding. Most of all, though, I had simply come too far that day—too far to leave without doing *something*. I took the stone and, in two precise chops, I shattered the window nearest the front door lock. I reached in behind the knob. I stopped.

A smell like the stench of Satan's feces came from inside Ethel's house.

I backed to the porch rail. It was Rita all over again. The stink of death, the stink of human corruption. In that huge, gamy odor I could smell a perverse sensuality: as if, even at the end, those who had died were marking their territory the way male animals do. With a heady musk that rushed from that broken window out, onto breezes, and across all Pennsylvania.

I staggered to the Lincoln. I had the BOSTON SUCKS T-shirt in my trunk. Over this I poured a can of St. Pauli Girl. Then I tied the whole sopping muck across my nose—I applied it like a poultice—and went back to the house.

There was a short entryway behind the door—coat racks and a closet, an umbrella stand. Immediately after that I came to the big A-frame room. Moonlight shone down through banked windows in the

cathedral ceiling. It picked out an ominous shadow. I stayed at the
doorway, gagging even through the beer. I had come quickly to the
smell's lair. It was here. My hand felt a light switch.

Tony was black.

He sat nude on a barstool, staring up. His rotten flesh was dark
purplish gray. In places it shone with the juice of decomposition. In
places Tony was already mummified. His lips had drawn back to express a stupid Peter Sellers grin. But the eyes were gone.

A young girl stood on the bar in front of him. A rope was slung under
her armpits: Ethel had hoisted the body from a bedroom loft railing
above. Her name, we were told later, was Leslie Torres: a 17-year-old
Hispanic hitchhiking from Scranton to New York. What she was doing
here with Tony and Rita—when Ethel interrupted them—I haven't the
heart to speculate about. She, Leslie, wore only a pink G-string. Her flesh
was the color of Tony's. And it was fragile. My movement there disturbed its equilibrium. With a sloshing sound, Leslie fell. The rope had
parted her decaying joints. She collapsed across Tony's knees, then
slumped onto the floor. A large rodent ran from behind the bar with
something between its teeth.

In my will I've asked to be cremated.

Tony was my brother, but I couldn't bless him. I flipped the ceiling
light off, and I ran. I ran out of the house, down the steps, past my car,
almost to Copper Lake Drive. I would've screamed, but I was afraid to
let corruption enter my mouth. Finally, I threw the BOSTON SUCKS
T-shirt into the underbrush and hunkered down. I was not particularly
sane at that moment. I gagged a couple of times—but I had eaten little
and could only hawk mucus up. It was the damned *tableau* that horrified me—not murder itself, nor decomposition—but the scurrilous
theatricality of it all. Ethel's passion, which I might have sympathized
with in some degree, was absorbed and negated by her gross exhibi-
tionism. To kill in anger is one thing. To humiliate the dead is perverse
beyond perversity.

I went to the Lincoln. My hands weren't shaking. The engine started
easily. I fastened my seatbelt. I spread the map out. It was nearing
midnight. These things I accomplished with stunning calm. I knew, for
instance, that it wasn't time yet to call the police. They would only
detain me: I had to get home. I backed my Lincoln down/along the dirt
lane. Everything had become clear in my mind. All my reflexes were on

call. I came to Copper Lake Drive. I listened for traffic. Then, with a graceful twist of the wheel, I backed out.

Into a three-foot ditch.

It broke then, my scrupulous calm. I yelled. I hit the car's ceiling with my sore fists. I even tried to pray—but my mind was quicksilver, here and there, around and behind. I had a fierce urge to urinate—but, when I zipped down, my groin was in such spasm, it was so *hard*, that the release burned and sputtered. I held to the car fender and teased composure back into my nerves. I was close to prostration. And my left rear wheel was hopelessly involved with the ditch.

If I live to be 100—if I experience war and famine and pestilence—still I will not endure three hours more dismaying than the next three hours were. It was Monday night, and these were weekend homes. On either side of me, for several miles, I had seen no glimmer of habitation. I was isolated and without recourse. Ethel had no telephone and, in any case, I would never have reentered that house. So I chose to wait, engine running on a quarter tank of gas, lights beamed toward the road. But only one car came—a Jaguar convertible—and that roared past before I could flag it down. After a while I just stood, arms crossed, in the middle of Copper Lake Drive. I was prepared to throw myself in front of any vehicle that might drive by.

Tony was dead. Neither he nor I had had much luck with our sexuality. Somehow that unhappy word, *fornication*, settled in my mind. I had run away from fornication to the priesthood. And, in time, fornication had driven me, panting, away from holy orders again. Tony had found sex to be lethal. We got away with very little, we Wilsons. In the 17th century, I knew, each orgasm was imagined to be a little death: men shortened their life spans, used up vital essence, whenever seed spilled out. Death into life, life into death. A paradox to construct the universe on. And here, now, fifty yards away, the ripe scent of my poor, lecherous brother crept out over the woods.

And, of course, I knew it wasn't over. Kay had yet to die: there would be symmetry in that. Ethel, if anyone, had a symmetrical mind. I couldn't—*couldn't, couldn't*—remember whether I had told the babysitter where I was going. If I had, and if the babysitter had relayed that information to Ethel, then Ethel would realize her secret was out. (Perhaps, in fact, Ethel had wanted me to discover Tony and Rita—who could appreciate better than I the symbolic weight of that tableau?) But the babysitter was stupid, I thought, and negligent. On that negligence Kay's life depended.

Finally, as if it were the figment of my longing, a tow truck came. But the driver was out on call and late for an accident in Cahoga. No matter how I cajoled him (I said that my wife was giving birth in New York and offered a $50 bonus tip) the man was adamant. I would have to wait my turn. He radioed into the night, but the only other truck was thirty miles west on Route 84. He left. And didn't return until 47 minutes later.

I got back on the road just after 3 a.m. From Stroudsburg to New York, with one stop for gas, I drove 85–90 mph. No patrol car pulled me over. I thought that strange, but fitting. This was, after all, a family affair. I would see to its conclusion personally: I owed my four nieces that much at least. Never once—though she had killed my brother—was I angry at Ethel. Her actions had certified her madness. And who can find fault with the mad?

It was 4:38 when I hit the George Washington Bridge, 4:47 when I crossed the Triboro. I had no clear strategy in mind. It was too early, anyhow, to wake the household up. I thought maybe I would offer Ethel a ride in the morning—then confront her, comfort her, absolve her before I drove to the precinct house. Something of that sort. Most of all, I didn't want my nieces to see their mother cuffed and taken away. Nor did I want them to know who had killed their father.

I parked outside Bert's. Tiredness hung from my face like a caul. I smelled of putrefaction. There was an all-night bodega on the corner. I bought a Coke and leaned back against the wall to suck some caffeine up. A man said, "You using the phone?" And—because his voice was gruff and dismissive—I said, "Yes." I made a call—that call—out of spite. I rang up my own Phone-Mate. Ethel often left messages on it.

There were three audition requests, a quote for our new bar stools and—I dropped my Coke can when I heard it—Kay's blithe voice: "Where've you been all night? For some reason Ethel wants the three of us t'meet at The Car after hours. So I'll see you around 4:30 ayem. Maybe I should dance for Ethel—what do you think?" And I thought, you're dancing for Ethel already, oh Jesus, Saviour of us all.

I got to The Car in six minutes. Northern Blvd. was still. I double-parked and went quickly to the door. It was locked. I inserted my key, then stopped. I had remembered Ethel's strength, remembered her yanking Pearl out of the water with one arm. Reinforced by fear and the special manic power of her delusions, Ethel would be formidable. I went back to my car and got a tire iron out of the trunk. I could, at least, fend Ethel off with it—even if I were unable, as I would be, to strike a woman down. Then I turned the key and stepped in.

Silence. But several work lights had been turned on. I knew that the performance, if there were any, would be on stage. I raised my tire iron. Then I sidled around the partition. I was right.

Kay hung upside-down, nude, from the trapeze.

I rushed to the kitchen and got Jako's linoleum knife from his kit. Then, holding Kay's waist with one arm, I sliced the trapeze ropes. We fell together. Kay was unconscious, profoundly sedated, but alive. From that position, hung upside-down at the knees, her face and throat were engorged with blood. There were superficial cuts, X-shaped, above each nipple. Lengths of blond hair had been sheared off and strewn around. I spoke to her. She didn't acknowledge sound. I slapped her, in my panic, roughly. She swallowed and that commonplace reflex encouraged me. I let Kay's head rest upright against the mirror. Then, disengaging myself gently, I went to the pay phone.

And heard someone walking down below.

Perhaps I should just have stayed where I was, called 911, and let the police supervise Ethel's capture. But I wanted her taken at the scene. That would be conclusive proof. And, yes, I was curious to see how Ethel had pulled it off. Curious, even more, to meet her face to face. Would Ethel be the same bluff, sardonic person I had known at poolside? Or would her eyes now be wild—in a kind of werewolf metamorphosis? Would she stink of feral acts? I had to know if—if I should have *guessed* it long before. If I had been derelict: allowing my instinct as a brother-in-law to jam my radar. And three young women to die.

I took my tire iron. Then, after listening for a full minute, I heaved the trap door up by its metal ring. There was a light on down below. But no one had been startled by my entrance. Cautiously, crabwise, I went down the wooden staircase. My heart was playing a snare drum solo. I waited. Among and between all those stacked cartons there were a half dozen nooks where a person might conceal himself. I flushed each one out: nothing but shadows. And then I saw what I had expected to see. Though I would never have found it on my own.

The entire beer cooler had been moved sideways. It ran on four oiled tracks. Beside the cooler was a two foot wide doorway—and I knew why Ethel always reminded me not to stack cases there. (The passage had been built and camouflaged by Prohibition Era bootleggers. Tony and Ethel must've come across it by chance.) The party wall, however, had shifted slightly with time. There was just leeway enough, behind the beer cooler, for a small cat to insinuate itself through to Big Marty's—even when the metal chamber had been shoved back into place.

I peered into the adjoining basement. No light shone there. But, with illumination from my side of the sliding door, I could see that it was unoccupied. Just to my left, against the wall, was a wooden staircase made—I would imagine—by the same carpenter who had fashioned ours. Ethel was up that staircase. I figured she wouldn't leave The Car until Kay had died. It made sense for me to lie in ambush just this side of the cooler. But I was concerned that Kay might go into shock before then.

So I crossed the threshold and, holding my breath, I climbed the staircase.

I came out at the rear of Big Marty's—just under the mechanical rack, which at that point had risen, in its roller-coaster way, to a height almost ten feet overhead. By dim streetlight from the store front, I saw skeletal coat hangers dangle. Nothing moved. I thought perhaps, hoped perhaps, that Ethel had gone already—yet it didn't make sense: Ethel would never have left the sliding passage open. She was somewhere in the store.

I moved forward: the light, after all, was in that direction. The mechanical rack, having traveled for fifteen yards at a ten-foot elevation, came down in a gentle slope until it was at eye level. I stood near the store counter. Ethel, I thought, would be crouched on the other side. But she wasn't. Ethel was behind me—she had stepped from a small, curtained dressing room—and, as I turned to oppose her, she struck me with some sort of steel reinforcing rod. Above my left ear.

I went down. I never lost consciousness, but—for a moment—there was no essential communication to my extremities. My left ear had become a loud, cavernous place. Blood splashed into my palm. The best I could do was crouch head down, in anticipation of successive blows. But Ethel didn't strike. She was behind me, over me. She attached something to my foot. Then, quite gently, Ethel drew me upright in a powerful Heimlich grasp.

"Tony, baby," she said. And she wet the nape of my neck with her tongue.

I didn't even fight it. Given my dazed state, her hug was invincible. Ethel lifted me, then set me down again. Her right hand, reaching from behind, found my genitals and held them. She pinched me there: she wanted to arouse me. Her teeth bit my earlobe. Her legs had come around my thighs—it was as though she were the male, I the submissive female. She ground herself into my body.

"Tony, Baby," she said.

"Ethel. I'm not Tony. I'm Mike. You killed Tony, don't kill me, too."

"Aaaaaah-no," she groaned. It might have been a cry of recognition and despair. It might have been a cry of orgasm. Then Ethel set me free. She backed away toward a small control panel beneath the rack. I tried to walk off—I had some vague idea that I could exit through the store-front door and out onto Northern Boulevard—but I was brought up short. I stumbled. I was on a leash. Something had arrested my left foot. I bent to look. A thick wire cable ran from my ankle to the mechanical rack.

"Tony, baby," Ethel said. And she clicked the control-panel switch.

A mechanism whined. Hangers began jangling. With a jerk the clothes rack took off toward the rear of Big Marty's. I was dragged on my behind for ten feet, scouring the floor, shoving old cardboard boxes aside. The rack moved inexorably. And then it began its long slope up. My entire body hung from that one ankle. Skin was sliced through. I hung four feet off the ground, flailing, bending my body upward, double, trying to disengage my foot. I screamed. I know how foxes feel, caught by one paw in a trap. I screamed like a girl.

And, yard by yard, Ethel followed me. She had another length of wire cable in her hand. With it she flayed my chest and head. Each blow cut. And, at each blow, Ethel elaborated on her anger toward men.

"You had to do it." She cut me. "You *had* to do it." Cut again. "Couldn't"—cut—"keep it in your pants, could you?" Ethel cut and I screamed. "I'M SICK AND TIRED OF YOUR PATHETIC COCK." She cut me there. "After all I did for you," cut. "After the money you pissed away on your dancing whores," cut, cut, cut. "And gave me clap," cut. "And shamed me"—cut—"in everyone's eyes," cut and cut. "And took my womanhood away. You lousy *pimp*."

"Please," I screamed. She thought I was Tony. I would be Tony for her. I begged Ethel in my brother's voice. "I'm sorry," I said. "Please let me go, I'm sorry."

The rack began its slope down again. My head smashed into the floor. And on the way down Ethel's cable whip caught me across the nose bridge. I felt intolerable pressure in the left eye socket. Something there, some soft component, gave way. I was sightless in that eye, bumping and flailing through the metal rack's half circle. I knew my Achilles tendon was almost cut through—and, as the rack sloped up again, it broke. My ankle was a floppy thing, loose. Another round trip and it might amputate itself.

Then Ethel stopped the machine. I hung, swaying. She had a gun in her hand. She held it against my temple.

"I'm doing this because I love you," she said. "I'm doing this because you can't help yourself." She kissed me. "You're a beautiful thing, but you're a slut. I won't be humiliated again, Tony. I won't. I'm your wife and the mother of your children. And I *made* you, Tony."

"I'm—I'm Mike," I said. "I'm not Tony."

"Does it matter?" Ethel said. And she put the gun into my open mouth.

I have not really been alive since that time—so apparent was my death to me then.

But Ethel heard a noise. A noise of flapping, enormous footsteps. And, *chest first*, Bert ran through the dry-cleaning store window. (He had come to deliver the night's take to my bed in The Car.) Glass rained down behind him like fangs closing. Bert staggered through. He knocked the counter over. Bert might not have seen Ethel even then, but she fired at him twice and got his attention. Both slugs ricocheted off his metal chest. For a moment they wrestled, belly to belly, trying to use the leverage of their weight. Then Bert and gravity rode her down. They shared the gun: it was gripped between their hands—her right, his left. Gradually Bert inched the barrel back, away from him. Ethel was losing her grip.

But, just before she did, Ethel surprised Bert. Instead of resisting him she went with his strength. Ethel turned the gun barrel away from Bert's head towards her own. Bert let her: he took the guilt on himself, he exonerated me. Ethel fired and blew her forehead away.

EPILOGUE

It is sometime in November now, the 17th or 18th, you lose track of time on the road. I write this in a motel room just outside Tucson, Arizona. All six of us are painfully sunburned from a day in the desert, and the smell of Vick's is like tear gas around me. We have been heading west, as Americans often do when they need to heal.

Amy has lapses—now and then I can see Ethel's fury in her eyes. But probably I'm over-sensitive to such things. They're children. The younger two don't really know what happened. And, yes, we've hidden it. That's one reason we're on the road. The girls understand that Mommy and Daddy were killed in an accident together. "Together" is important right now. And, fortunately, I had become for them a useful, if not wholly convincing, imitation of their father anyhow. (This meant, however, keeping the mustache—which Kay loathes—at least for a while.)

Kay agreed to marry me in spite of that: in spite of the harem I bring with me now wherever I go. Indeed, I could never have adopted my four nieces, if Kay had not given her support. She must love children—she's two months married and two months pregnant. We follow the get-it-over-with-now-and-hand-the-clothes-down school of family planning. And I couldn't expect Kay to mother Ethel's children without giving her offspring of her own. People will think I've converted to Catholicism.

Kay says—passing me with a child under her arm—that she married me because I'm a cripple now. That she was waiting for something to slow me down. She exaggerates. I walk pretty good, limp or no: the reconstructive surgery on my ankle was done by a top pro-football orthopedist. And there is even hope—guarded hope—that I may see out of my left eye again. Healing time is needed, clots have to dissolve, before anyone will propose an operation. But, Kay says, I look handsome wearing my black eye-patch. Who needs to see in three dimensions anyhow?

I'm not angry at Ethel: and I consider that a great gift of grace. Anger is a distraction I can do without. We've learned since that Ethel had spent much of her mid-teen years in a mental hospital. (Her father, evidently, raped her repeatedly throughout her early girlhood.) Ten days before her death, Ethel went to Weintraub and made a new will. She left me everything "in hope that he will take care of my children who, as I do, love him deeply." I have not speculated on the nature of her love. As I have not speculated on her need to kill me. Ethel was mad. And is, right now, in heaven.

We hope to make a home in California. We sold The Car and Ethel's house for nearly $500,000 between the two. (As yet no one will buy the Cahoga place.) And I've received an obscene amount for my story. Kay and I intend to write the screenplay together. Marriage we may survive, artistic collaboration will likely destroy us. The profits from *Topless*, as I call it, go into a trust fund for the children.

I would like to be a writer—though I'm not sure how much talent I possess. Next time I write there won't be such a sensational true story to tell—and that will be my test. People distrust fiction these days. Storytellers aren't held in high regard. People care only about what really happened, because their imaginations have lost muscle tone. If *Topless* had been a novel, probably no movie company would've bought it.

And someday—when I am a grown-up, when I have finished doing what children do—someday I may present myself to the church again. That's a long time off. I am not repentant in all ways yet—though I repent my unrepentance absolutely. But I have seen things, felt things, that deepen my faith in God and His Son. When those things are finally clear in my mind, I may be able usefully to communicate them. For we are both of the spirit and of the body. That paradox animates the mystery of our nature. As it animates the mystery of Christ's great Incarnation. It is the reason why we are sinful. And the reason why we are interesting.

Some day, as a priest of God perhaps, I'd like to talk about all that.

ABOUT THE AUTHOR

D. KEITH MANO is the author of seven previous novels. He has written more than eight hundred articles, stories, columns, and essays for such periodicals as *The New York Times, Sports Illustrated, People,* and *Esquire*. He is a contributing editor for both *Playboy* and *National Review*. He has written episodes of *St. Elsewhere* and a play, *Resistance,* for his Broadway actress wife, Laurie Kennedy. Mr. Mano has two children, Roderick and Christopher. He lives in New York City.